Masque of Passion

There was a new woman stirring in Lisa. David had raised her curiosity and he appealed to her sense of rebellion. She had been in a cage and he had part-opened the door.

He grabbed hold of her hair, then took her hand and guided it to where he wanted it most. She closed her fingers around his erection. Lisa needed to feel him inside her; wanted him to share in her intense pleasure. There was no turning back.

Masque of Passion

TESNI MORGAN

BLACK
lace

Black Lace novels are sexual fantasies.
In real life, make sure you practise safe sex.

First published in 1998 by
Black Lace
332 Ladbroke Grove
London W10 5AH

Typeset by SetSystems Ltd, Saffron Walden, Essex
Printed and bound by Mackays of Chatham PLC

ISBN 0 352 33259 X

Prelude

The rhythm of a tango echoed from the petal-shaped horn of an old-fashioned gramophone. The tempo was measured; the sound bitter-sweet with an underlying melancholy. Violins, an accordion, a hint of guitar, a piano and the whisper of a snare drum. The compelling beat grew soft, then louder: romantic, aggressive and passionate.

The woman thrilled as she moved to her partner's lead. He was compelling, too. He guided her feet and bent her body to his will, like a sapling before a strong breeze.

They were alone in the sombre ballroom, the atmosphere one of decadent luxury. The drapes were crimson and black and light filtered down from an art deco lamp, a sunburst in orange, gold and lemon.

Their images were reflected over and over in huge, gilt-framed mirrors – a timeless, ageless couple dancing.

The light glinted on the purple satin and sequinned evening gown with narrow shoulder straps and a cleavage that plunged to her waist. Her skin shone with a pallid lustre. The satin clung to the curves and hollows of her body, outlining breasts, belly and hips. It was slit to the thigh on each side. Every time she moved the

1

skirt opened, revealing long, lovely legs covered in polished black silk, the stockings upheld by garters just above the knee.

Sometimes there was a flash of the russet wedge that furred her pubis; sometimes the white flesh of her buttocks was laid bare momentarily; sometimes the deep amber crease between them.

She could smell her own arousal. Essences crept from the secret garden of her sex, mingling with Phul-Na-Na perfume, her partner's pungent hair pomade and the musky, masculine odour of his sweat. It was a combination that made her ache with lust, and her nipples pressed against the slippery satin while her clitoris swelled with need between the plump labial lips. Desire crept over her skin like an irritation then retreated into her depths and became a molten ember waiting to erupt into flame at his touch and his rhythm.

In keeping with the role she was playing, her auburn hair had been set in Marcel waves and tight curls. Her make-up was heavy, with a scarlet Cupid's bow mouth, bright spots of rouge on either cheek and a thick layer of mascara spiking her lashes. Drop earrings swung as she danced. A bronze snake wrapped its coils round her upper arm, its eyes two glittering rubies.

Her partner was as agile and sinister as a panther in a black pinstripe, double-breasted suit. A wide-brimmed fedora was canted low over his eyes, and his patent leather dancing shoes were part covered by white spats. He looked like a gangster in an early Hollywood silent movie, exuding animal magnetism.

That's what we are tonight, the woman thought. Stars in a picture show.

The music stopped. He held her pressed to his chest, one arm clamped round her lower back, his big hand spread wide over the dimple at the base of her spine. She tipped her face up to his and his steel-grey eyes bored into hers. He smiled faintly, and his other hand tightened round her fingers as he held her right arm crooked and pulled in against him. She could feel his erection rising, nudging her belly through the cloth of his trousers and the satin of her dress. Hot, damp and demanding.

A servant stepped from the gloom, wound the gramophone, turned the record over and replaced the tone-arm, then vanished into the shadows. The woman shivered as the music began again and her partner's leg passed between hers, his feet placed precisely, her own following through the intricacy of the sweeping steps. Dip, sway, kick, slide, back to position. Their bodies assumed new shapes, arrangements and designs, with him leading and giving subtle indications.

She kept her knees slightly relaxed – flexible yet firm. She felt his smooth-shaven cheek against hers, her breasts brushing his chest, his hard phallus and his complete control of her, both now and for all time.

He bent her backward over his arm, then pulled her abruptly upright again, while holding her even tighter. The music swelled and her heart pounded in unison. She could feel her juices wetting her inner thighs, but did not falter. He spun her round. She did a graceful twirl, skirt flying open, and was once more in his arms, his feet forming a neat, delicate pattern around hers.

She indulged in a reverie, though remained alert. He was her master, this ruthless man. His present costume as a member of Chicago gangland suited his personality. Too handsome; too filled with that dangerous charisma which few could resist.

She was aware that he was conscious of her desire. Without breaking the dance, he lowered his head and fastened his lips around her right nipple, sucking it hard, the frisson between his tongue and the thin fabric firing electric shocks from that sensitive tip to her love-hungry bud. He left her quivering breast and his mouth captured hers, his fleshy tongue diving greedily between her lips and tangling with her own.

She almost collapsed with the force of lust spiralling

through her body, but a jerk of his arm reminded her. The pattern of the dance must continue. Step, flex, bend – one, two, three.

She knew he was tango mad. Born too late by seven decades, he had missed out on its heyday, but was determined on a revival: not the tepid, sanitised, strictly ballroom parody, but the genuine, disreputable article created in the brothels of Buenos Aires.

The relentless beat – the music that spoke of dark, obsessive passions – excited and inspired him. Cruelty and pride, love and hatred, sacrifice and jealousy – each emotion was conveyed by tango. And she had become as infatuated with it as she was with him. And with the games he played and the parts he acted out – the bizarre rituals for which the correct clothing must be worn.

She trembled, the heat of their bodies interacting between them.

He guided her across the shining tiled floor with catlike steps, not stopping till her back ground against a pink-veined marble pillar. It cooled her burning flesh. His hands pushed aside her bodice and cupped her breasts, thumb pads rolling over her nipples that rose stiffly to the touch.

His mouth hovered over hers, tongue tip tracing her lips from corner to centre. She moaned, avidly opening in welcome. He plunged his tongue inside, exploring every part of the dark, warm cave, and her tongue was a barb, returning each caress. His spittle was sweet, and she surrendered to those fierce, penetrating kisses. She could almost taste his blood and hear it singing in his veins.

He kissed her as if he was sucking out her soul, and his hands mauled her while his nails dug into her skin, leaving a trail of pain. Her hunger was rising like a madness in her, blinding her to all save him.

Her fumbling fingers found the waistband of his trousers and tore at the fly buttons. She reached into the opening, encountering silk boxer shorts, and went fur-

4

ther to touch the wiry hair that coated his lower belly. She closed one fist round the thick shaft of his penis, rubbing gently over the velvety skin, while her other palm nestled his balls, feeling the swell and tension of them.

He groaned and opened her sexual secrets with his fingers, holding the petals apart and massaging the soft wet core of her, then finding that engorged nub of flesh wherein lay the source of her satisfaction. She whimpered and lifted her pubis to that magical caress, rocking to and fro, her mouth contorted like a mask in a Greek tragedy.

He stroked her as the tango beat pulsed and she reached a crescendo that ended in a blur as she spilled over into orgasm – immersed, lost and dislocated in a welter of ecstasy.

He lifted her effortlessly and her legs folded round his waist as he impaled her on his phallus. She clung to him, her arms linked behind his head as he raised her up and down on his mighty weapon till he shuddered and bucked and came.

The tango, too, reached its climax, the final notes an accompaniment to her sharp pleasure cries.

Chapter One

'*A*nd now, ladies and gentlemen, we come to Lot 112: a miscellaneous collection of glass and china.'

The auctioneer spoke jovially, surveying the audience from his place at the rostrum. 'What am I bid? Shall we start at twenty pounds? Twenty pounds, anyone, for this useful lot? I'm sure you'll find bargains in the box ... great-granny's brandy decanter, I shouldn't wonder, with a drop left in the bottom. No? Well, then, who'll give me fifteen?'

One of his assistants, a dour-looking person in flat cap and brown overalls, tilted the wooden crate on the table. Glass flashed and china gleamed beneath a coating of dust.

That's a reasonable price, thought Lisa Sherwin, standing at the back of the furniture repository-cum-warehouse where Messrs Deacon, James and Balfour held frequent sales. She waved her folded catalogue where Lot 112 was already ticked.

'Ah, I have a bid from that beautiful young lady over there,' crowed the auctioneer, a stout, sandy-haired, middle-aged man who was none other than Mr Balfour himself. 'Any advance on her offer? May I say eighteen?'

He leered at her and she bristled at his patronising

manner. There were disadvantages in being 23 and presentable, even in this day and age of equal rights. Some men never had and never would recognise it. Balfour was one of them. He reminded her of the older tutors at college, still stuck somewhere in the last century.

The crowd shuffled their feet and shifted in their seats, not particularly interested. They were eager to move on to the more important lots of the day – a pair of chairs, reputedly by Chippendale, and a painting called *Lady and Dog*, believed to be the work of a Gainsborough pupil. These were out of Lisa's league as yet – but one day, she promised herself optimistically – but this was only the beginning.

She thought Lot 112 a foregone conclusion, experiencing that thrill which was like no other on earth. Her fingers tingled in anticipation of taking it to her flat and examining her treasures. Maybe there would be nothing of worth – just a load of junk. Maybe she would come across a real find, overlooked by other punters at the pre-sale viewing.

It was the uncertainty that was so thrilling. Excitement made her heart thump. It was far more stirring than anything else she knew – even sex. But then, sex with her fiancé, Paul, had slipped into dull routine. Not that it had ever been brilliant, but of late it had become positively stressful – for her at any rate. He seemed oblivious, grunting and bucking his way to orgasm while she faked it.

She was waiting for the auctioneer to bang his gavel on the rostrum and take her name when she became aware of a movement to her left. A man stood there, leaning an elbow nonchalantly on a bow-fronted rosewood chest of drawers labelled Lot 130.

He nodded almost imperceptibly to Balfour, who now said, 'Eighteen I'm bid. Twenty anywhere?'

Damn! Lisa thought, doing quickfire sums in her head. There were porcelain figurines which she had hoped to purchase. But another glance at the rather arrogant, swarthy, dark-haired man decided her. She would not be defeated.

Again her crumpled catalogue lifted.

The dark man smiled across at her with a flash of even, white teeth. He was tall, she noticed, wearing a pair of battered 501s and a soiled T-shirt. Broad shouldered, whiplash lean, very casual and confident. And those jeans were a tad too tight, emphasising the bulge behind the faded fly fastening. Lisa could feel herself blushing. She assumed her most icy mein and dragged her eyes away.

Sweat trickled between her breasts, dampening the cream lace brassiere that cradled her full breasts under a loose cotton shirt. It was hot in the saleroom with the noonday sun pouring through the high windows, and she wished she had worn shorts rather than trousers. Her tension mounting, she stiffened her spine and nodded vigorously at Balfour.

He smirked beneath his scrubby moustache and said, 'Any advance on twenty?'

One or two people began to fidget, wondering if they were missing out on something. A plump lady in a flowered hat signalled. A wiry dealer behind her winked at Balfour. The bidding went higher, encouraged by the dark-haired man.

In a ferment of anxiety, Lisa kept up with it, accepting the challenge which this raffishly handsome stranger was issuing to her, and her alone. She was convinced that he did not care about the rest. Why was he doing this? Was it simply to drive home the lesson that novices like her should not tangle with the big boys?

She pushed back a lock of curling brown hair that clung to her sticky forehead, and concentrated. The bidding had reached £30 more than she had intended to pay. The flower-hatted lady shook her head. The ferret-faced man behind her dropped out. Now there was only Lisa and the annoying, impossible-to-ignore stranger.

Their eyes met and she was riveted. His features were striking, with high cheekbones and a slightly bent nose which looked as if it had been broken in a scrap. But it was his eyes which distinguished him – the extraordinary power and persuasiveness of his piercing green eyes.

'Have you all done, then?' Balfour asked, his voice breaking the spell.

'Thirty-two,' said the dark man, and his lips lifted in a teasing smile as he glanced at her.

'Bastard!' Lisa muttered under her breath. She felt as if she had been running a marathon. Her pulse was jumping all over the place and her shirt was wet at the armpits and cleaving to her back.

There was a pause, a waiting, breathless stillness, and then, 'Thirty-five,' she pronounced clearly.

'Thirty-five it is. Everyone finished?' Balfour waited a moment, then brought down his gavel. 'Sold for thirty-five pounds to Miss . . .?'

'Sherwin,' Lisa said quickly, flushed with triumph, rage and worry.

'Thank you, Miss Sherwin,' Balfour said crisply, entering her name in a ledger. 'Pay before you leave, please, and collect your goods.' He turned his attention to the crowd, saying, 'Let's press on. There are many items to get through this afternoon.'

They shuffled and coughed, examined their catalogues and settled down again as two auctioneers' helpers carried in a threadbare chaise-longue and placed it on the platform near the rostrum.

Lisa, feeling curiously deflated and somehow cheated as she had overspent and would have to forego the figurines, walked across to the clerk near the door and drew out her cheque book. As she wrote the amount, she prayed there would be enough in her account to cover it. The rent was almost due for the showroom below her apartment and with any luck this would be

9

paid in promptly and restore the balance of her overdraft.

'You gave over the odds for it,' murmured a low, husky voice in her ear. It sent a tingle along her arms, down her spine and into her epicentre.

She started and looked round. Her adversary was grinning at her. She glared up at him. He was so tall that the top of her head did not quite reach the pit of his throat. She wished she was wearing high heels instead of flat toe-post sandals.

'No thanks to you,' she snapped, briskly returning cheque book and catalogue to her shoulder bag. 'Why did you continue bidding if you didn't think it worth it?'

'I wanted to see if you had the balls to go on,' he replied laconically and, to her horror, she found that she was achingly conscious of his muscular body so close to her own.

His white T-shirt contrasted almost shockingly with his deeply tanned face and bare, darkly furred arms. His hair curled at the nape of his neck and flopped over his brow, and she caught a whiff of Calvin Klein's Eternity, overlaid with a woody aroma which could have been that of shower gel.

Just for an instant she was tormented by a vision of him naked, with water cascading over him, gleaming on his iron-hard body and tight flanks, trickling into the forbidden area of his genitals and streaming down those long, strong legs.

She fought for control, her mouth suddenly dry and her sexual juices wetting the cotton gusset of her panties. All the frustration she suffered because of Paul seemed to rise up in a great, unfulfilled torrent of longing.

'Miss Sherwin? Are you OK?' the stranger asked, and one of his copper-hued hands grasped her elbow. His fingers seemed to sear her skin. She dragged her arm away.

10

'Perfectly. It's just the heat,' she faltered.

'I know. Terrible to be indoors on such a lovely day. What say we find a quiet pub by the river and have lunch?' he suggested, no way deterred.

'I can't,' she said at once, though there was no real reason why she should not accept his invitation, apart from the obvious one that he was just too confident of his ability to charm her. 'I'm meeting my fiancé,' she added, retreating into safety by letting him know she was already committed.

'I see,' he answered, still smiling, his bright emerald eyes seeming to bore into hers and read all her secrets. 'Another time, maybe. My name's David, by the way. David Maccabene. Here's my card. Could I give you a ring later?'

'I don't think so,' Lisa declared, taking the card but not offering her telephone number. She panicked as she struggled to lift Lot 112. She wanted to escape this disturbing man.

'Here, let me help you. Where's your car, Miss Sherwin?' he asked, taking the crate from her effortlessly.

Outside, the heat hit them as if they had opened an oven door. Sunshine slicing across the car park formed blinding white patches and deep purple shadows. Lisa went to where her elderly Ford van waited, unlocked the rear doors and David stowed Lot 112 inside.

'Thank you,' she said stiffly, longing for him to go but wanting him to stay, tossed in a maelstrom of emotion.

'That's OK. Any time. Will you be at the auction next week?' he questioned, resting his lanky limbs against the hot metal of her car. His legs were crossed and his pelvis thrust upward, prominently displaying his full crotch.

'I don't know,' she said, suspicious of his motives and doubting that he was sincere.

'Not a regular dealer? Just buying for yourself?'

He asked too many questions and Lisa bristled as she

11

went round to the driver's side and let herself in. The leather seat scalded her thighs through her thin trousers.

'I'm not dealing . . . not yet,' she ventured, closing the door and winding down the window.

'Don't get into it, Miss Sherwin. It's a tough old business,' he warned, the light slanting across his eyes and running over his nose and finely moulded lips.

'You're a professional?' she asked, making conversation as she wondered how it would be to lick his mouth with her tongue and taste the sweat forming on his upper lip.

'I turn a coin here and there,' he returned casually. 'I'm glad you didn't stay to bid for the so-called "Gainsborough school" portrait. It's a fake.' Then his face became serious and he added, 'Promise to get in touch with me if you ever consider spending a hefty wad on something like that. Will you, Miss Sherwin?'

'I have no intention of going for expensive items,' she answered frigidly, trying to quell the tumult of her senses. She wished he would stop leaning in the window and looking at her so intently. He breathed sexuality from his very pores and it was totally unnerving. 'Goodbye, Mr Maccabene.'

'Goodbye, Miss Sherwin,' he said with mock formality, and bowed from the waist, then saluted, as she started the engine and slipped the van into gear.

She moved off, so agitated that she almost forgot to buckle her seatbelt, thinking of nothing but putting as much distance between herself and that infuriating man as she possibly could.

As Lisa drove towards West Deverel, she allowed the peace of the area to enfold her, thoughts of David Maccabene retreating. It was good to be living in the old market town again, with its broad central street, timbered cottages, eighteenth-century houses and squat, square-towered Norman church. It had been the centre of the Somerset wool trade up until the last century.

12

Though she had completed her three-year stint at Warwick University, leaving with an honours degree in history and art, she had never really settled there, popping home whenever she could get away.

Now the road unwound like a grey ribbon in front of her, and familiar landmarks came into view. The Fleece and Firkin inn at Little Deverel, the lane leading to Highfell Woods and the standing stones on Starhill, the trout farm, the lake where as a child she had gone fishing with her father.

She reached the market square and her destination: the showroom and apartment above it which she now owned. There was a lane to one side of the building and she parked her van, opened the back and started to heave at the crate.

At once the closely clipped fair head of her tenant, Martin Troon, popped round the side door of the shop. 'Need a hand?' he asked.

'Thanks,' she replied gratefully.

'You look knackered. Leave it for a moment,' he ordered, turning and shouting into the depths. 'Phil! Put the kettle on.'

'Will it suit me?' his partner, Phil Stevens, answered from within.

Martin lifted his eyes heavenward. 'He says that every time. Honestly, darling, sometimes I think he'd bore a glass eyeball to sleep.'

'But you love him,' Lisa said with a grin, having listened for hours while they complained about each other after a falling out.

Martin shrugged his tanned shoulders under his skimpy black vest. 'I'm a glutton for punishment.'

She shoved the box back inside the van and locked the doors, then followed Martin into the showroom. Pot-pourri spilling from sacks on each side of the floor perfumed the air – rose petals, lavender, sandalwood and citrus, an endless variety of scented powdery leaves, stems and blossoms. Shelves above held an amazing display of knick-knacks. Martin was the one with taste while Phil was his business partner and accountant, as well as being his lover.

The shop, aptly named Charisma, was already renowned for incense, fragrant candles, myths and magic figures complete with crystals, ceramic fairies in woodland settings, pottery, dried flowers, gift cards, wrapping paper, Celtic jewellery, Victorian reproduction dolls and the biggest selection of teddy bears that side of the border.

'Meet Mr Humphrey,' Martin said, lifting a large red Steiff bear from among his furry companions. 'He's one of a limited edition. Comes with his own papers and all.'

'How much?' Lisa asked, reaching out to touch the bright fur and gaze into Mr Humphrey's friendly eyes.

'Three hundred and fifty to you,' Martin answered with alacrity.

'You know I can't afford it,' she reminded him. 'Poverty struck, that's me.'

'How did you get on at the auction?' he asked, replacing Mr Humphrey before putting up the CLOSED sign and leading her into the storeroom.

It was all white paint and sparkle, with a sink, microwave oven, kettle and coffee maker. The back door stood wide open, leading to the parking space beyond, protected by high stone walls and a steel gate.

'I did OK,' Lisa replied, sinking into a wicker basket chair, aware that her feet were aching.

'Did you get what you wanted?' Martin said, hazel eyes sharp in his thin, clever face.

He perched on a packing case, long-legged and elegant in form-hugging jeans. The light glinted on the three gold hoops in his left ear and another piercing his eyebrow.

'Yes, but I had to pay more than I intended.'

'How so?'

'Someone was bidding against me.'

14

'The bitch. Was it anyone you knew?'

'No – a pushy, insistent dealer,' she answered angrily.

His brows shot up. He was just too intuitive for comfort. 'A man?' he questioned. 'It must have been to rattle your cage like this.'

'Yes.'

'Good-looking?'

'Oh, yes . . . and he knows it.'

'Ooh, sounds delicious. Tell all,' Martin insisted, with a wriggle of his lean hips.

'I don't want to talk about him. He's a shark,' she said stiffly.

'I'm sure you're dying to. He's got to you, hasn't he? Come on, you can't fool me.'

'Really, Martin . . . I'm not interested. I've enough on my hands with Paul.'

'He's such a stuffy old thing,' Martin declared, dismissing him with a shudder. 'You can't possibly marry him, much as I want to be a bridesmaid and wear daffodil-yellow taffeta.'

'That would never be allowed, and you know it,' Lisa replied, smiling widely. 'I doubt I'll be permitted to add you to the guest list.' Then her expression darkened as she muttered, 'His mother wouldn't like it. Anyone would think it was her wedding. She's a right pain in the arse.'

'And Paul's so homophobic that it makes me wonder if he's not a closet gay,' Martin opined. 'You know what they say about those that shout the loudest. Is he getting better in the sack?'

Lisa pulled a wry face. 'Not much. He won't admit there's anything wrong.'

'That's men all over. I've had to train Phil and he's just about learning what to do. Isn't that so, Philip, you old trout?' Martin addressed his partner, who was setting out mugs and taking milk from the fridge.

'Whatever you say,' Phil agreed, winking at Lisa. He was a muscular man with a short haircut and military moustache, and wore a spotless white shirt and chinos. 'Who am I to argue with your queenly highness?'

'Absolutely,' Martin proclaimed.

'I couldn't afford to buy more stuff at the auction. I hope I'll have enough to fill a market stall,' Lisa broke in, changing the subject.

Martin cast her a shrewd, understanding glance, and asked, 'Is there anything we can do to help?'

'You do!' she cried impulsively. 'You help me all the time, just by being there.'

This was true: she felt at ease with them. There was no pressure, no male ego trying to put her down. Martin in particular understood the feelings of women, almost like the sister she had never had, yet he was protective too, dropping his effete pose and becoming aggressively macho if the need arose.

'You've been great to us, too,' he said, leaning over to pat her hand. 'The rent on the shop is so reasonable. It's given us a real start and you've helped Charisma take off over the past eight months.'

'Why can't I make relationships work?' Lisa suddenly asked.

'You just haven't met the right man yet,' Martin told her. 'Paul's wrong for you and caught you when you were vulnerable, after your dad died.'

'You're probably right,' Lisa agreed. 'When my father died I didn't know where to turn – and he was there, offering to take charge of me.'

'But he wasn't your first lover, surely?' Martin enquired, his eyes wide with disbelief.

Lisa could feel a blush heating her face as she admitted, 'I bedded two students – '

'At the same time, darling? How bold,' Martin interjected.

'No . . . not together . . . separate affairs, brief and not entirely trouble free. I lost my virginity to Ivan. It wasn't that I was terribly keen, but I wanted to get it over and done with. Then there was Harry. Ah, the handsome,

16

charming, entirely unfaithful, womanising Harry. That ended when I arrived home unexpectedly one day and found him in bed with my houseshare girlfriend. End of romantic illusions.'

'Men are scum, ruled by their dicks,' Martin declared in heartfelt tones. 'So you've settled for dull Paul. You'd rather be safe than sorry.'

'That's right. Now I can't very well get out of it.'

'You can, you know. You can do anything you like.'

Lisa sighed and shook her head, thrown by her meeting with David Maccabene and alarmed by her body's flagrant sexual response to him. That's all it was, she was sure – nothing but sex.

She waved away a salad-filled baguette that Phil offered, and went on, 'I hope the market thing works, but I need to get a job as well. This place needs a fortune spent on it. The roof, for example. Dad was so generous, opening up the showroom as a gallery to promote the work of struggling artists. I couldn't afford to do that. If I can make a success of buying and selling antiques, it may avert disaster.'

'Let's drink to that, sweetie. Have another cuppa,' Martin insisted. 'Then Phil and me will help you get that box upstairs. I'm dying to see what's in it.'

After they had lugged Lisa's purchase through the front door, up the stairs and into her living quarters, it was two o'clock and time for Martin and Phil to open for business.

'Phew!' Lisa exclaimed when she was by herself. Leaving Lot 112 unpacked on the living-room carpet, she entered the pine-fitted kitchen and opened a can of Coke.

She was grateful that Martin and Phil had been there with tea and sympathy. She regarded them as her closest friends, despite the fact that Paul made no attempt to hide his dislike of them.

'He's so macho . . .' she sang quietly as she wandered out to the roof garden beyond the lounge.

This had been constructed over the downstairs extension and Frank Sherwin, Lisa's father, had turned it into a delightful spot in which to sunbathe, or wine and dine cronies on warm summer evenings. Flowers tumbled from hanging baskets and rioted in terracotta pots. The murmur of a trickle fountain soothed the ear, and he had made an area into a Zen garden for meditation, complete with rocks and gravel and bonsai trees.

It was easy to maintain and Lisa enjoyed keeping it as he would have wished. Apart from this, the apartment itself was decorated with flair and exuberance: antiques mixed with modern pieces in harmonious profusion. It was her home and she didn't want to leave it, but Paul had other plans.

'Sell up, darling,' he had declared, once she had accepted his engagement ring – a small, conventional diamond cluster.

'But I like it here!' she had started to protest.

He had closed her mouth with kisses and snuggled her down on the couch, his hands taking possession of her breasts. 'You can't go on living alone,' he had said decisively, unfastening her bra. 'We'll have the best house on the estate. Nothing shoddy … a Georgian reproduction facade, double garage, patio, swimming pool and the garden landscaped. You'll love Kingsmead. It's going to be the best.'

Paul had inherited Everard Homes Ltd from his father. He was ambitious and had had the money to buy land during the recession – a large amount of land on which he and several other builders were constructing a model village, with a green around a duck pond, shops, a cinema, schools, a golf course and a sports centre. Lisa had seen the plans and could not fault them – if one liked living in such a well-heeled, close-knit, utterly safe community surrounded by woods and with security guards on call.

'It reminds me of the Stepford Wives,' she had said when he took her round proudly. He had been mortally

18

offended, glowering darkly during the drive back to West Deverel.

She had not agreed to move, despite his continual harping on about it. And lately she had been vague about the date of their wedding.

Now she sat on the edge of the little fish-pond and watched the meaderings of the fat golden carp as they lazed beneath the lilypads. The garden was a sun trap and she dabbled her fingers in the cool water, her eyes alighting on the hose.

She was uncomfortably hot and her clothes were sticking to her. This was a secluded spot. There were no houses overlooking it as the building backed on to a park. Lisa unbuttoned her shirt and took it off, then unhooked her bra and released her breasts. She sighed and closed her eyes in relief, placing her palms beneath the undercurves of the full globes, lifting them and allowing her thumbs to brush over the prominent nipples.

Instantly aroused, they rose into hard peaks. Hurriedly, she untied the drawstring of her baggy trousers and kicked them off. Beneath, she wore a brief pair of cotton panties. Without further hesitation, she turned on the hose and stood beneath the sprinkler. The water was tepid, heated in the plastic pipe by the sun all morning. She moved the jets over her body, the spray seeking out every inch of her and lingering between her legs where her panties clung, soaking wet. It was exquisite.

Thoroughly drenched, her skin glistening with myriad droplets, she switched the hose off and moved to the padded lounger, water running from her in rivulets. After spreading a beach towel across it, she lay down, relishing the build up of sensation between her legs. Soon she would release it. Like a cat luxuriating on an old garden wall, she stretched languidly, drying out in the sunshine and enjoying the feel of her fingers plucking at her tingling nipples.

Images filled the screen of her brain – Ivan, with his long, thin, pale-skinned cock, and Harry, with his circumcised, thick and upward curving member, the helm bare and shiny. It had always sprung to attention for her but, alas, not only for her, sharing its largesse with other girls.

Sex with these lovers had been a novelty at first, but a grain of discontent had soured it for her. They sometimes took the trouble to satisfy her, though more often than not were intent only in releasing the seed from their testicles.

Then there was Paul, and here the memories were shot through with frustration and anger. She had tried to tell him what she needed to bring her to orgasm, but he was convinced that all proper women came when their men did. He was determined on simultaneous orgasm. They had tried it every which way – with him on top, sideways, backward – while he strove to make her climax. It had become almost a point of honour with him.

Once he had rejected her attempts to explain her desires, she had capitulated, her confidence draining away as he hinted that he did not go along with 'all that messing about'. He thought fellatio and cunnilingus were activities for perverts.

She could still hear him saying, 'My cock is all you need. Come on, let's try again. Now, if you lie this way and I put it in and drive deep, that should do the trick.'

It didn't, but she pretended it did, just to shut him up. It seemed that he had no idea about the clitoris, and wouldn't have a clue what to do with it even if he was enlightened. So she suffered his love-making and, eventually, gave up hope. She started to resent him, avoiding caresses which would stoke her fires but not satisfy them. Masturbation was easier and absolutely fulfilling. No letdown; just a sweeping pathway to bliss.

And she must do it – now!

Aware of little but the compelling force driving her

actions, she trailed her fingers over her mound, tracing round the rim of her labial lips through her panties. Every hair covering her pubis seemed to be ultra-sensitive, responding to her light touch.

The triangle of damp material was drawn tight into her crease and as she ventured a finger between her legs, she could feel her nub swelling and smell the oceanic fragrance of her juices. She closed her eyes, still seeing the red penumbra of the sun through the lids. Its fiery warmth caressed her breasts, her nude body and her pudenda. It was like a highly skilled lover who would know exactly how to bring her to ecstasy.

Unbidden but vivid, a picture of David Maccabene formed in her mind. Her clitoris quivered and her finger pressed against the delicate little bud. She allowed her imagination full rein as she pushed her panties down, freed her legs from them and splayed her thighs so the sun and her finger could heat her tiny, rampant organ.

She indulged in one of her favourite fantasies, where she occupied an examination couch in a doctor's surgery. This time the medical man was played by David.

'So, you've never climaxed before?' he said, in a sexy accent.

'Never.' Lisa nodded, waves of heat laving her. There was a heaviness in her loins as if all her blood was settling there.

Though it was her own fingers playing with her bud, she loved to act out scenarios of her own creation. Today, David was her co-star, and she aroused herself even more by pretending that they were being watched and he was a doctor complete with white jacket and stethoscope, explaining about the female genitalia to a group of medical students.

'Her breasts are extremely sensitive,' she imagined him saying, and touched her nipple as if it was him performing this act of homage. 'This must be remembered if one wishes to successfully arouse a woman and make her wet. If she doesn't lubricate, then you've lost

21

her. She won't be excited enough to permit penetration and if it is forced on her while she's dry, then she will experience discomfort and even pain.'

'Are you a gynaecologist?' Lisa enquired of him in her fantasy sketch. 'You must be. You're so right, and know so much about it.'

'I specialise in female arousal,' he answered, and she felt fingers parting her secret lips, dipping into the honeydew and spreading it over her hungry bud as he continued to address his students. 'The most important part of a woman's sex is her clitoris, designed exclusively for pleasure. It has no other function. It's like a miniature penis, with a little hood, but it doesn't eject fluid.'

As Lisa listened to these imaginary words, her fingertips worked on her bud, inflaming it with little slaps and squeezes, circling it, arousing it to frenzy, then stopping and keeping herself in suspense, her finger hovering over the engorged head while the spasms faded. Retreating from the orgasmic edge for a moment, she concentrated on the image of David, then returned to press down on it again.

The phantom students were in a highly excited state. Lisa could see them in her mind's eye. The women were lifting their skirts and fingering their own pink clefts while the men unzipped their trousers and released their cocks, rubbing them energetically.

Lisa moaned, in two worlds – the garden and the mysterious place which she shared with the imaginary Doctor David Maccabene. He had straddled the couch and was lifting his penis from his pants. He plunged it into her. It was long and thick, the glans fiery red. Was it possible that she could take all of it? No problem. She was so wet, swollen and expanded that he sank it easily into her sheath, prodding deep inside her.

Lisa panted at the thought and once more located the fleshy pearl crowning her cleft, continuing the magical, slow, slippery massage. Her head fell back, fingers fluttering over her clitoris, then grinding it harder.

'I can't wait any longer!' she cried aloud, and released the pressure in one short, savage burst, coming against her finger. A rush of ecstasy swept over her.

'Good God! What on earth are you doing out here naked? Cover yourself at once!'

An outraged male voice ripped through the wonderful aftermath of orgasm, shattering it completely. She opened her eyes and jerked into a sitting position, surreptitiously wiping her wet fingers on her discarded panties.

'What does it look as if I'm doing?' she answered sharply, consumed with guilt. 'Sunbathing, of course.'

He strolled over to her, a big-built man in a cream poplin shirt and lightweight grey trousers, his jacket slung over one shoulder and his tie loosened. He was fair haired and blue eyed, a football player and sports enthusiast. Bored to death, Lisa had sat through many a match and replay on the television and even endured live performances, shivering in the cold while being deafened by the war whoops and chants of the fans.

Strong and muscular, Paul's physique was such that Lisa feared it would run to fat if he did not keep up the exercise, and too many visits to the pub with his mates to celebrate yet another victory or mourn a defeat would later produce a beer belly. Yet without him she would be alone – and this scared her.

'Well, OK, but do you have to do it naked? Can't you wear a bikini or something? Someone might see you,' he growled, standing spread-legged in front of her. In spite of his so-called indignation, she could see that he was aroused, his penis tenting the front of his trousers.

'Oh, yes. Who? A passing seagull, perhaps?' she answered sarcastically, then added, 'Please move. You're blocking out the sun.'

'You want to be careful. What about skin cancer?' he

warned, but his eyes were glued to her bare breasts, tanned to a golden brown by frequent indulgence in the garden.

'I use masses of screening oil, and it's my body, anyway,' she retorted, sad because he no longer turned her on.

Once she had thrilled at the sight of him. Where does love go? she wondered bleakly. Is it always like this: a slow disintegration as the couple get to know one another? Now she got more of a thrill out of dreaming about a man she had just met – one, moreover, who had succeeded in ruffling her feathers.

Paul refused her request to move and leant a little closer. There was a bright, lustful gleam in his eyes and his full, rather loose lips were parted. 'Were you playing with yourself?' he asked in a breathy voice.

Lisa blushed under her tan. 'No,' she lied. This was too precious a secret for her to share with someone so insensitive.

'I think you were,' he chided, half scolding, half tormenting. 'You had a hand between your legs. You were frigging yourself, weren't you? I can smell it. What a disgustingly pervy thing to do!'

'Don't you ever wank?' she returned, amazed at her daring. Something had happened to her that afternoon: something significant.

'I might have done when I was a teenager,' he replied, and one of his broad fingers flicked her nipples. 'But I don't need to, do I? I've got you.'

'Do you want a drink?' she said, to put him off track. He could rarely refuse such an offer.

'Great. A cold lager. I've had one hell of a day. The bloody plumbers didn't turn up, then when they finally arrived they'd forgotten half the heating equipment.'

Lisa pulled on her pants and bra, and as they walked inside through the French windows, she prepared herself to listen to a litany of his troubles. He had not even asked her how she had fared at the sale. After pouring him a glass of beer and an orange juice for herself, she carried the drinks into the lounge where he was already ensconced on the chesterfield.

She could be patient with him now, soothed and made happy by the deep, powerful feeling of her climax, echoes of which still tingled throughout her being.

He took a long pull at his glass, then held out an arm, indicating that she should sit beside him. She obeyed, more out of habit than desire, though wanting the feel of a cock inside her to rub against her slippery vaginal walls and add to her sense of orgasmic well-being.

'I hope you weren't playing with yourself,' he said, one of his hands clasping her breast, finding the swollen nipple under the lace and tweaking it. 'You don't have to do that. You've got me. Look, my cock's all ready for you.' He unzipped his trousers.

His penis shot out, a serpent uncoiling to full size. Considering his bulky frame, it wasn't all that impressive. Knowing her part, Lisa dutifully took it in her hand, running her fingers up and down the shaft and lingering on the glans where a drop of dew had already escaped from the slit.

Still lost in a cloudy haze of satisfaction, she bent over him and opened her mouth, hovering over his phallus. She felt his instant withdrawal, then he grabbed her by the hair and lifted her head. His wet lips crushed hers, and his tongue forced its way into her mouth.

Despite the knowledge that she was wasting her time, her sex responded, clitoris throbbing again. Paul moved his cock in her hand and his pelvis arched. Then he said breathily, 'I want to fuck you. Let's go to bed.'

'Why can't we do it here?' she murmured.

'Bed is best, and afterwards I can watch the match on the portable telly.'

A quick fuck and then telly. His needs were simple, and Lisa was ashamed of the resentment that welled up. It was not all his fault. She had known their tastes were widely different when she started to go out with him.

Not for him intellectual movies by directors with statements to make. He called them 'head films' and preferred action. He liked middle-of-the-road pop music; she was a theatre-goer and opera buff. He read nothing but newspapers, particularly the sporting pages, and she was into novels by female authors who had a lot to say about the male/female paradox. She liked Scrabble. He enjoyed playing poker for money with his mates. He was subject to road rage; she was an ice-cool driver.

A friend had described him as 'a man's man'. Lisa sometimes wondered if she would have found his company more stimulating had this been so in a literal sense. Martin's suggestion that Paul might be hiding in the closet amused her, and she wondered if there was a grain of truth in it. All this male bonding at the rugby club was highly suspect.

She could not push this from her mind as they went to bed and followed the usual routine of love-making. First he kissed her, open mouthed, beer tainting his breath, then fondled her breasts. By this time, his organ was ready and he mounted her, crushing her into the mattress. He never took his weight on elbows and knees. No, she had to be flattened beneath his bulk – a position in which it was impossible for her to take an active part in the proceedings.

She lay there while he thrust his penis into her body, muttering, 'You're all juicy, love. Excite you, do I? That's my girl.'

She did not reply, though tempted to deflate him by explaining that her own touch had made her lubricious and her own finger had brought her a thunderous orgasm. Her thoughts wandered as he groaned and pumped. She made a shopping list in her head and took it to the supermarket. By the time I've reached the

26

frozen peas he'll have finished, with a bit of luck, she said to herself.

I can't marry him, she decided in a sudden burst of clarity. Spend the rest of my life taking part in this charade? It's impossible!

Yet her body responded to the powerfully thrusting member buried in her depths. She needed more than her own fingers sometimes, and was desperate to embrace a man who would involve her in powerful, even devious, experiences of the flesh. She yearned to feel a tongue on her clitoris, a mouth on her nipples or a penis inserted at just the right moment, when she was boiling over and ready, lava hot.

Her passion flamed again and she ground her pubis against the base of Paul's phallus but could not achieve the right pressure on her clitoris. As she struggled to do so, he came in a great heaving movement, collapsing on her and crushing her flat.

Her desire died abruptly. Disappointment flooded her. She wanted to scream, 'Get off me, you selfish pig!' but did not quite dare, even now.

I'm a coward, she mourned as Paul shifted over, sighed and lay flat on his back with an arm flung over his eyes. I'm too insecure to blow him out.

Soon he was snoring, while she lay there, restless and aching for another orgasm. One was rarely enough for her and had Paul not interrupted her so rudely, she would have pleasured herself again as she worshipped the sun.

Raising up on one elbow she stared down at the sleeping man. Her heart contracted and she felt an unwilling tenderness. He looked boyish, the harsh lines soothed away. Despite the fact that he was a successful businessman he was still immature. That was the trouble. It was like going to bed with a fumbling schoolboy.

'Paul,' she whispered, lipping round his ear and

sticking her tongue inside it. 'Paul, wake up. I want to talk to you.'

He squinted up at her, disgruntled at being disturbed. 'What's the matter?' he grunted.

'The wedding,' she began, wondering how to break the news that she wanted to call it off or at least postpone it till they had seen a sex therapist – if he would ever consent to such an invasion of his privacy.

'Everything's arranged,' he said and yawned widely, then rolled over on his side, away from her. 'Go to sleep. I'm bushed.'

'But, Paul ... I don't want ... I can't ...' she faltered, and then lost her nerve. Could she burn her boats? He was the last remaining link with her girlhood and her father.

He stretched out an arm and took her hand, saying sleepily, 'It'll be great, love. A big affair ... good publicity for the firm, too ... us moving into Kingsmead. I've booked the church for the middle of August, and the Bear Hotel for the reception. Mother will do all the arranging. She's good at that sort of thing.'

Don't I know it, she thought impatiently. Mother this, Mother that. I almost hate the woman.

Oh, God, she sighed to herself. I can't do it to him. Poor sod – he can't help being a typical male. Maybe if I marry him, things will get better. But as she got up to make herself a coffee, she heard a voice inside her head saying, 'Who are you kidding?'

It sounded very like David Maccabene.

Chapter Two

'Where the hell have you been?' demanded Lady Fiona Cardwell as she dismounted from her chestnut mare in the stable yard. 'You're an unreliable bugger, David.'

He gave an unrepentant grin, heaved his broad shoulders from a convenient hitching post against which he had been lounging, and strolled over to her. 'I thought you liked being buggered,' he said, bending his head to kiss her full on the mouth.

'I do. That's the trouble,' she drawled, removing her hard hat and giving her shoulder-length bob a shake.

David could feel himself hardening. He wanted to take her into the stable, lie down with her in the straw and fuck her. She had that effect on him, with her straight, light-brown hair, grey-blue eyes and flawless complexion. Her body was a tantalising cross between that of leggy teenager and model-material siren, built in that fine-boned way typical of aristocratic English-women.

But he knew that while she had gone through the motions – educated at Roedean and then united with an earl in what had been considered the marriage of the year – she had the morals of an alleycat and was blessed with an insatiable libido that had found its match in him.

'Don't fret about what I may or may not have been doing, Fiona,' he advised levelly, as a groom took her mare.

'I may as well save my breath. You're quite determined to go your own way,' she answered, with angry eyes and sulky mouth.

'That's true,' he agreed, and linked his arm with hers as they wandered towards the imposing Palladian frontage, a double flight of stone steps and magnificent, domed entrance of Newstead Manor. 'I'm here now and we're still friends, aren't we?' he added, bending to kiss her cheek, smooth as silk under his lips.

'Are we?' she responded, pulling away and flicking him with her crop, the blow hard enough to sting. 'Then why didn't you come to luncheon, as we had arranged?'

'Completely slipped my mind,' he confessed with a shrug. 'Got caught up in an auction. Stayed on to see fools lose their money on a Gainsborough that wasn't. You know how it is.'

She gave him a searching look, saying, 'I know all too well, darling. You simply can't resist anything that involves buying and selling and pretty women. Was there a pretty woman, you conniving bastard?'

He grimaced and gave her a lopsided smile. 'You know me too well. I can't put one over on you.'

'I don't advise that you try,' she said coolly, as they strolled through a hall as big as a ballroom and into the library where a footman had already brought in a tray of coffee. 'We're too involved. I could ruin you if I set my mind to it. You'd never deal again, my friend. No one would touch you with a bargepole.'

'Is that a threat?' he asked, cocking an eyebrow at her while admiring her style.

'Of course not,' she purred, settling herself on one of a pair of gold and green upholstered couches either side of the Italianate marble fireplace. Her jodhpurs were so exceedingly tight that David could see the division of her cleft and the round curve of her sex lips. His penis thickened and he itched to rub her clitoris through the stretch fabric.

'A teensy word of warning, that's all,' she continued, taking up the coffee pot and asking, 'Milk and sugar?'

'Black,' he replied, watching her slim hands as she poured the rich, dark liquid into tiny, gilt-edged cups. Such elegant hands, and so skilled at masturbating him. 'You know my preferences by now.'

'Just checking,' she said. 'You could have reverted to plebian habits since last we met.'

'Snob,' he teased, his eyes feasting on her as she sat there like an evil little fairy.

'Peasant,' she returned, sweetly.

'And aren't you glad of it? Like a man that's different to Nigel and his ilk, don't you, Lady Fiona?'

'The proverbial bit of rough?' she asked, and slipped her arms from her hacking jacket. Her nipples were like twin studs pressing against the cream silk of her shirt. He wanted to bite them.

'Hardly,' he demurred, and smiled at her outward calm that concealed a furnace. 'I went to public school and uni.'

'But you have the instincts of a market trader ... a dealer ... a con man,' she continued, and lay back on the couch, watching him with heavy-lidded eyes as her hands rose to undo the pearl buttons and open the front of her shirt, baring her small, pert breasts to his gaze. 'Was Fletcher Robillard at the auction?' she asked, fondling her rosebud nipples. 'Have you seen him lately?'

David experienced a spasm of irritation, and shot back, 'D'you want to spoil my day?'

'Haven't you and he patched up your differences yet? A pity, for he's drop-dead gorgeous, darling. I'd like to get to know him better.'

Some of David's good humour drained away. Fiona

31

knew how to needle him by mentioning his chief adversary – that crafty individual who usually managed to acquire the pieces David had set his heart on.

'No, he wasn't there. Nothing of value to tempt him . . . and neither was Tanith, more's the pity,' he replied, deliberately throwing in the name of Fletcher's partner, a woman whom he knew Fiona regarded as a rival. She was equally glamorous and twice as immoral, if that were possible.

'Good,' Fiona said vehemently. 'She's a tramp. A piece of shit.'

David chuckled and said, 'Bloody hell, Fiona, that's a bit strong. Sounds to me as if you don't like her.'

'Too right! But you do, I take it. Just because she has big tits. I'll bet they're implants. Are they, David? Have you squeezed them?'

He knew where this sparring would lead – straight up to the master bedchamber which she occasionally shared with her husband, Lord Cardwell. Not often, as Nigel showed a predilection for his own sex. This left her free to follow her fancies, and these were legion. Her appetite amazed even David – men, women, it was all the same to her, providing they were good looking, witty and a cut above the average.

As he sat scrutinising Fiona and allowing the hunger for release to build up in his loins, he thought about Lisa Sherwin. He was baffled by her refusal to lunch with him and determined to pursue her. Beautiful she undoubtedly was, but he had sensed vulnerability under the facade and glimpsed unhappiness in her eyes.

He respected women for their intellect as well as their bodies, and could generally see through their pretences, in much the same way as he could spot a fraud a mile off in his line of business. He followed his hunches, and had come to the conclusion that Lisa Sherwin had not yet reached her full sexual potential. He intended to do something about that.

But there was Fiona, who imagined herself in love

with him, or so she maintained. David had already experienced embarrassing examples of her jealous temper and learned to his cost that she was not entirely trustworthy if crossed. More than one rival had felt the blast of her fury. She loved madly for a short while, then turned her fickle attention to someone new.

Just for now, he was the star in her firmament. It seemed that his casual approach made him all the more desirable in her eyes, but he refused to change the habit of a lifetime just to please her. Yet he accepted that he had to be careful how he handled her. Their relationship was not entirely based on bed-shaking lust.

He had met her through mutual friends and, although they were copulating within half an hour, there was more to it. Once the first flush of passion was over, Fiona had explained that money ran through her fingers like water. Nigel was generous but she needed more. He was away a great deal and the attics of Newstead Manor were stuffed to the gunnels with relics of bygone days – most desirable relics which would net a fortune in the right places.

She had told David that she needed his expertise to dispose of some of these forgotten family treasures. A bargain had been struck and it had proved a generous source of income for both of them – a seemingly bottomless pit of useful revenue.

Remembering how much was at stake, David now moved from the Louis-Quatorze chair on which he had been seated and dropped down beside Fiona. She wafted expensive French perfume, her own ambrosial juices, leather and horse sweat. It was a heady combination, hinting at the kind of privileged background he had always hankered after.

She placed a hand on his knee, and her almond-shaped nails fastened there possessively. 'Why don't I divorce Nigel and marry you?' she said in a sultry whisper.

'Leave all this?' he asked, making a sweeping gesture

that encompassed the gracious, book-lined room, the deep carpets and heavy brocade portières, and the many fine portraits, statues and trappings acquired down three centuries of wealth.

'Why not?' she murmured, and her hand drifted higher till it rested on the fullness at his crotch.

'Because, Lady Fiona, you'd be bored within a week,' he said, feeling his penis swell. 'You need this kind of lifestyle. It's food and drink to you.'

'Well, maybe not quite yet,' she agreed. 'I suppose Nigel and I must at least produce a couple of sprogs to carry on the line. Then I'd get a much better settlement.'

'Sensible girl,' he commented, while she dragged a tormenting finger up his fly. 'Can you get Nigel to cooperate?'

'No problem,' she answered with a lascivious smile. 'He swings both ways, my dear. He'll fuck me often enough to do the job, when I give the go-ahead. What an awful thought – motherhood! Not my kind of thing at all. But duty must be done. I say, wouldn't it be tremendous fun if I had your baby, not his? He'd never know. How do you fancy having your son occupy the great, crested Cardwell cradle? It's Regency, you know, the genuine article, and he'd be the next earl.'

'You can't be serious, Fiona!' David exclaimed, even his deep-rooted cynicism taking a knock.

She gave a tinkling laugh, her eyes filled with malicious mischief, and cried, 'I'd love to pull a flanker on the dowager. She's an awful old bag.'

David could feel the length of her thigh pressing into his, her body hot from a brisk gallop on the moors and the lust engendered by the chafing of the saddle on her delta. She was definitely unstable. His child an earl? He had to admit the idea was intriguing.

Now she was rubbing herself against him and he could no longer restrain his basic urge. His cock grew larger, his jeans causing uncomfortable pressure as it reared up, slanting across his belly. His balls ached. He had been on the edge of arousal ever since meeting Lisa. His predator's instincts needed to capture and possess her, and he had gone to Fiona not to apologise for breaking their date but in the sure knowledge that she would relieve his frustration.

The afternoon sunlight slanted through the tall, narrow windows, glancing off Carara pillars, cedar-wood architraves and the busts of former Cardwells depicted as Roman emperors crowned with laurel wreaths. Fiona unbuttoned his jeans and lifted out his stiff penis, playing with it as if it were a toy especially invented for her delectation and delight.

He allowed her the freedom to explore him, supine on the couch, his dark curly head resting on the deeply cushioned back and his long legs spread to give her free access to his genitals. She took the tip of his cock in her mouth and sucked it, using her tongue as if she were tasting a particularly luscious lollipop.

David could feel his scrotum tightening and the rushing sensation starting in the base of his spine. Orgasm was very close. In a second he would come into her throat. And why not? he thought, while thought was still possible. She likes to control me. She sucks and slurps so excitingly, like a greedy little animal. I hope to God the butler doesn't enter in the middle of it. There's no way I could stop. He'd just have to watch me spurting, my spunk dribbling down her ladyship's chin.

It was coming, that terrible, wonderful release. He could feel it racing down his spine, into his groin. His balls were hard and his penis even bigger as the tip pumped against the roof of her mouth. A shattering climax swept over him, drawing a shuddering gasp from his lips as Fiona milked him dry.

She let his cock slip free, limp now but still swollen. She had swallowed most of his semen and wiped the residue from her mouth on the back of her hand.

'My turn,' she whispered, but stopped him as he

tugged at the zip of her riding breeches. 'Not here. I've a better plan.'

Knowing her quixotic nature, David pondered on what this might be. Fiona liked novel venues for her sexual activities – the more unusual the better. She took his hand in hers and rushed him across to the door, up the central staircase, along corridors and then climbed a further set of stairs leading ever upward. He knew the way as he'd been there several times. It led to the attics.

The house was quiet, sunk in late-afternoon somnolence, and the staff were gainfully occupied far below. The vast attics were under the eaves of the great house, above the servants' sleeping quarters. The light was dim there, penetrating cobwebbed dormer windows and falling on the lumber of generations and items that were no longer needed but too valuable to throw away or donate to the church fête.

The door snapped shut behind them. 'Woohoo ... watch out for ghosts!' David teased in a hollow, funereal voice. 'I'm the spirit of bad Lord Balfrey Cardwell, serial killer of 1680, come back to suck your blood and crush your bones, after I've had my wicked way.'

'Shut up, David!' Fiona said, and gave a shriek as he clasped her from behind, pulling her lithe body tightly against his. He could feel himself hardening again, his prick swelling in his jeans.

He cupped her breast in one hand, and walked the other down over her ribs, finding the seam of her breeches that disappeared between her thighs. She was damp and hot there, and his finger pressed the material closer, stroking her clitoris through it.

She gyrated her hips, wriggling her bottom against his crotch, then freed herself, weaving among furniture shrouded in dustsheets. There was an old spinning wheel, a large rocking horse, a doll's house, rolled up Persian rugs standing on end, several tiled wash-stands, Chinese vases, brass ornaments from days when the male Cardwells had served in the Raj, and innumerable objects all guaranteed to raise the blood pressure of experienced antique dealers.

It was an Aladdin's Cave and a rare opportunity granted to few, and David knew he had been lucky. So far, no one had the slightest suspicion of his complicity with Fiona. Nigel had never bothered to take an inventory, and the contents of the attics had been forgotten about. It was Fiona, rooting through the place with above-average curiosity and avarice, who had discovered them.

'Look what I found the other day,' she said, pausing by a trunk, half hidden under a tapestry. It had brass corners and oiled cane banding – a valuable piece of old-world luggage in itself. She threw back the lid. The smell of mothballs arose chokingly. A ray of sunlight flashed on tarnished tinsel drapes, velvet cloaks and ruffles, paste gems and feathers.

'Isn't this fabulous?' she carolled, snatching up an armful. 'I reckon some of these are getting on for a hundred years old.'

'It looks like it,' he said thoughtfully, holding up a tailed evening coat with satin lapels. He put it on, posing in front of a fly-speckled pier-glass on a mahogany stand. 'We could make money out of these, Fiona.' He pounced on a flat, round object, gave it a tap and it sprung up into a silk opera hat. 'Marvellous invention, this,' he went on, placing it on his head at a rakish angle. 'Suits me, don't you think? I look a proper Stagedoor Johnny.'

'Except for the jeans,' she said, eyeing him up and down. 'We're not selling them, so keep your greedy hands off. I want to play dressing up.'

She disappeared behind a screen and presently emerged wearing a cerise-pink satin corset, her breasts rising over the lacy edging, her nipples red as raspberries. Her pubis and tight, neat buttocks were framed by long suspenders clipped to the tops of white silk stockings, while her feet were encased in high-heeled mules with diamanté buckles.

Close-fitting white kid gloves covered her arms to above the elbows and a black feather boa was slung around her shoulders. A cartwheel hat, lavishly loaded with plumes and silk roses, topped her hair which she had swept up and fastened with tortoiseshell combs.

'What do you think?' she exclaimed, posing wantonly with one leg raised to further expose her fair bush and the pinkish brown line of her labia, glistening with silvery moisture.

'Very fetching,' David said, his heart beating fast. His cock was fully erect again.

She paced towards him, swinging her hips invitingly, and said fiercely, 'Let's pretend I'm a whore.' She suddenly grabbed him by the arm, stronger than she looked.

'What d'you charge?' he asked, playing along with her.

She studied him, her legs widespread and the full glory of her fascinating fork unashamedly displayed. 'Get your kit off, Maccabene,' she ordered. 'We'll discuss the price later.'

He eased out of the tail-coat and pulled his T-shirt over his head, the air playing on his skin. She touched one of the wine-brown discs that crowned his pectorals. The nub hardened under her caress and his cock twitched. She brushed her hand lightly across the dark hair of his chest, and down the thin line that scrawled past his navel and beyond.

'How many prostitutes have you had?' she asked, and disappeared from his view, passing behind him.

'I've lost count,' he lied. In reality, he had never found it necessary to pay for sex.

'And did you have them naked, or did you keep your clothes on?'

'That depended on circumstances – whether it was an

all-night session or a quick screw up against a wall or in the back of a car.'

'Did they enjoy you?'

'They did it for the money. That's the way of the whore. They have something to sell and the punter pays.'

'Like you, David. You sell to the public, just like a whore. Isn't that so?'

'Perhaps,' he agreed, wondering what she was up to now.

He shivered as he felt her fingertips tracing the path of his spine. The hairs on his arms lifted and his balls hardened. He heard her sharp intake of breath, and then she said, 'Drop your jeans.'

Smiling briefly, he unbuckled his belt and kicked off his sneakers. He wore no socks or underwear and the denim slithered down below his hips. He eased the tightness over his calves and tossed the jeans aside. There was a heady excitement in the idea of fornicating amid this treasure trove – as there was the first time they had done so. He wanted to congratulate Fiona on her inventiveness. She really was a remarkable woman. Amoral and mad, of course, but that was part of her charm.

Naked, he stood, his penis ramrod stiff and upward curving, as he contemplated her next move. When several seconds had passed, he could wait no longer, and called over his shoulder. 'Well, whore, where do we go from here?'

He felt her close behind him, and started as something penetrated the tight-muscled cheeks of his arse, probing intimately. He had hardly accepted this invasion before it was withdrawn. There was the swish of leather and he jerked forward involuntarily, driven by searing pain as it contacted his bare flesh.

'I'll teach you to use a crop on me!' he shouted angrily, and dropping all pretence, swung round. 'Want it rough, do you? Two can play at that game.'

Before Fiona could protest, he dragged her to where an iron bedstead stood in a corner and sank down on the sagging mattress. As she threshed and cursed, he bent her over his knee, her nude backside raised high, and brought his open palm down across her shapely butt with shattering force.

Fiona yelped, but he held her wrists tightly in one hand and aimed another smack at her bottom, then another. He was warming to his task, his engorged cock prodding into her side as she lay across his lap. And though tears ran down Fiona's face and she yelled loudly at every slap, he knew that she was wildly excited.

'Don't, David! That's enough,' she sobbed at last, lying limp, her nether cheeks fiery red and the imprints of his fingers clearly outlined on the flesh.

Making no attempt at gentleness, he pulled her up and over on to the mattress. Sprawled on her back, she watched him with wide, tear-washed eyes. He moved up to stretch beside her and his mouth sought her nipples above the corset's edge, chewing, teasing, rousing, tormenting and sucking them till they swelled and reddened.

She tugged at his hair, giving melodious moans as his hands moved down the cerise satin. His lips found the flatness of her bare belly, the hip bones rising in sharp peaks either side. He tongued her navel, then parted her love lips, his fingers moving as if he was touching silk. He wet them with her juices, then massaged her kernel. She clawed at him as though he were spanking her still as he brought her to pleasure's crisis point.

He held off for a second, while she screamed in protest, her hips pumping upward in pursuit of that tantalising touch. Now he was above her, crouching like a great cat. He parted the opening of her sex with two fingers, drinking in the sight of her glowing, luminous flesh, the sheen of her honeydew and the brown hair curling round his fingers.

He brought his mouth down to her cleft, inhaling the pungent odour of her arousal, like vanilla and sea-washed shells. His tongue stabbed her clitoris, agile and sharp, and coiled round the little organ, flicking over the head and dragging piteous moans from her throat. His mouth grew more avid, sucking at her swollen lower lips, dipping into her vulva and then going back to her clit. He found himself seeking ways of giving her absolutely undiscovered pleasure.

She was quivering, and held his head fast between her thighs, muttering, 'Don't stop, David. Oh, God, yes, that's right. Do it like that . . . suck me, darling. Make me come. Ah . . . ah . . .'

Never releasing her from the spell of his mouth, he reached up with both hands and his fingers fastened on the crests of her nipples. At once, he felt her shudder and knew that she had reached that pre-orgasmic plateau from which there was only one escape – complete surrender to bliss.

He was floating in a dark world of desire, aware only of Fiona's hard nub under his tongue and the smell of her in his nostrils. She stiffened and gasped, her hips rising involuntarily from the mattress, and then she cried out as the climax vibrated through her.

She clung to him, sobbing, and while she still convulsed, he thrust his phallus into her pulsating vagina. She kicked her legs up round his sweating back and locked her arms in a stranglehold as he plunged in and out of her, his pleasure intensified by the spasms that clenched round his penis, drawing it deeper and deeper into her body as if she would absorb him completely. He was inspired by her hunger and carried away by her lust and came in a hard, furious burst.

Later, as the attic darkened and they dozed on the faded patchwork quilt, she stirred in the circle of his arms, moved up to kiss his mouth and said, 'Let's do it again.'

* * *

41

'You won't have time; not with the wedding so soon,' Paul said decisively to Lisa over breakfast the next morning. The sunny kitchen was redolent with the aroma of freshly roasted coffeebeans.

'But, Paul, I want to do it. There's enough stuff here to fill a stall twice over, and I bought a box of china at the sale yesterday. You didn't ask me how I got on,' Lisa said, spreading lime marmalade on wholemeal toast, then resting her elbows on the kitchen table as she transferred a slice to her mouth.

'Sorry, I forgot,' he grunted, laying aside the newspaper. 'Anyway, as I've already said, I think it's a daft idea. You'll tire yourself out, and won't make much money. I'd have thought you had enough to do.'

'Like what? Rush round the shops looking for a bridal gown?'

'Most women find this exciting,' he replied, a scowl settling on his craggily handsome features.

She tried again. 'I want to have a go, Paul. Don't you understand? The weekly flea market at the Corn Exchange is famous. I was lucky to get a pitch. And you know I enjoy going to auctions, looking for bargains.'

He sighed heavily, pushed back his chair and got up, big and burly and domineering. 'Have it your way,' he conceded reluctantly, 'but don't blame me if it goes wrong.'

'I won't. Don't worry,' she returned sharply, thinking, Over my dead body. You'll be the last to know if I fail. 'You're not working, are you? It's Saturday,' she continued, hitching her bare feet on the rung of her stool, her short dressing gown opening over her brown legs.

'Sorry, love. Got to see a man this morning. There's a deal going down concerning power-showers.'

'You see?' she said reproachfully. 'You're always making deals and haggling. Why can't you understand that I want to do exactly the same?'

'This is business. Our future depends on it,' he explained, looking down at her as if she was an

42

unreasonable child. 'You don't need to bother about an income.'

'But I want to,' she argued, then suddenly realised that it was hopeless. She backtracked before it escalated into a full-scale row. 'What about this afternoon, then? I thought we might go to the lake and have a picnic.'

'No can do. Meeting some of the chaps at the gym. But I'll take you out tonight,' he added magnanimously. 'And tomorrow we're expected at the barbecue. Mother wants to check over the guest list with us. So far, you don't seem to be inviting many people to the church or reception.'

'I don't know many people. One or two from university, perhaps. You won't let me ask Martin and Phil.'

'I've told you before, they wouldn't fit in,' he replied firmly. 'Mother would find it awkward.'

Squashing the irritation caused by the mere mention of his mother, Lisa gripped the sleeve of his bathrobe.

'OK, though I can't understand your attitude towards them. Paul . . . we need to talk,' she began, and plucking up her courage, plunged on. 'Things aren't quite right between us.'

His brows drew down in a frown. 'What? We're OK, aren't we?' he asked.

'Yes, we are. Well, no . . . not exactly. It's sex.'

'Sex? You get enough, don't you? We have sex every night. What more do you want?'

Oh, dear, Lisa thought, her spirits plummeting. Now I've got to explode the hoary old myth that men know all about sex, and if any hint is made that they don't then their masculinity must be in doubt.

'It's not quantity I'm talking about, but quality,' she struggled on. It was like pushing a boulder up a steep hill.

He ruffled a hand through his hair till it stood up in spikes. He looked bewildered. 'We've been through this before. I thought we had it sorted.'

'We could be more adventurous,' she suggested tentatively. 'Sex is like any other activity. We have to learn. Jesus Christ, you wouldn't go out in a car without having driving lessons, would you? It's the same principle.'

'None of the women I had before you ever complained,' he said huffily.

'Could it be that is the reason why the affairs didn't last?' Lisa ventured, marvelling at her nerve.

'Not at all,' Paul replied, his face darkening with anger. 'It's you. You're strange . . . not quite normal.'

This was the cruellest thing he could have said, and she had feared to open the subject again because he had done it before. Now she took it with a calm that astonished her. She had been reading up on the male ego – a delicate thing, apparently.

'On the contrary. I'm very normal,' she said, and her voice was cold. 'Why don't we learn a bit more about it together? I've a book I bought lately, a lovers' guide, and it's really detailed. It could give us lots of ideas.'

'I don't need one. I know what to do,' her fiancé said stubbornly.

Lisa suddenly lost her temper, a hot surge of indignation making her want to slap the smug expression from his face. 'That's not true!' she cried, leaping up. 'I need more foreplay! You want to start shagging as soon as we get our clothes off. You touch my tits a few times which gets me going and then, when I'm just warming up, you're in and away, going at it like a steam train. Then you roll over and sleep, leaving me wondering what to do with the rest of the night.'

Oh, hell, she thought, as soon as the words were out. Now I've done it.

He stalked towards the bathroom, saying over his shoulder, 'If you don't like it, then I won't do it any more.'

'Don't be ridiculous!' she shouted, running after him. 'We're supposed to be getting married, taking vows and being with each other till death us do part. At least take

44

a look at ways to improve our sex life. It's very important.'

He stopped at the door and turned to look down at her, genuinely confused. 'All right, if it'll make you happy,' he conceded grudgingly. 'But I'm not trying any of that kinky stuff.'

Her heart soared and she stood on tiptoe to kiss him. 'That's all I want, Paul . . . for us to try. Let's start now.'

She dropped her robe and skipped into the shower. He followed slowly, obviously not quite sure. She spun the taps and stood under the warm jets, her face lifted to the exquisite warmth. He stood beside her awkwardly. She dashed the water from her eyes, reached for the chestnut-scented gel and, ignoring his reticence, poured a fragrant puddle into her palm and began to rub it all over him. By the time she reached his genitals he was already hard, despite his reservations.

She soaped him generously, lifting his balls then working up the length of his shaft to the clubbed head. 'You see,' she crooned, delighted with its response. Her breasts were aching and her clitoris was rising from its shrouding cowl. 'This is fun, isn't it?'

'I'll be late for my appointment,' he grumbled, though his penis jerked in her hand.

'Damn your appointment,' she declared, but when he tried to lift her on to his cock and penetrate her, she held back. 'Do the same for me first. Lather your hands and wash between my legs. Go on, I dare you.'

He did as she asked, but she had the feeling it was only because she had suggested it. She stood close to him under the jets, working her pubis against his fingers, feeling the sensation growing more acute. Would he carry on till she came? She hoped and prayed for it, but was so tensed up that she got stuck, wanting to come but unable to scale the heights. She knew that if she had been there alone, she would have achieved the acme of bliss in a few seconds, using her finger or the bar of soap.

She could feel Paul's impatience and knew that all he really wanted was to possess her swiftly and get on with his day. Her loins were heavy with need; her clit an aching, unfulfilled nub of erectile tissue.

Why should I satisfy him? she thought rebelliously. God knows, I've tried my hardest to explain. She retreated to the other side of the shower, leaving him angry and puzzled.

'Aren't we going to –' he began.

'No,' she said crisply, washing away the gel and stepping out. She grabbed a fluffy white towel and wrapped it round herself like a protective cloak. 'You haven't been listening to a word I've said. Just go, quickly, so I can pleasure myself in peace.'

He looked so shocked that she almost laughed.

She paced into the bedroom, leaving him standing in the shower, his penis deflated, limp and pathetic.

He trailed after her and dressed, while she towelled her hair and watched him. The silence was like a third person in the room. When he was ready, he picked up his briefcase and stared at her. His eyes were like those of a whipped dog. Lisa's conscience pricked, but she resolutely conquered her guilt.

'I'll pick you up later, then,' he said, uncertain for once in his life.

'OK,' she answered offhandedly.

'And . . . Lisa?'

'Yes?'

'Go ahead with the market thing, if you like.'

'I was going to. I'm seeing about it this morning.'

Thinks I need his permission, does he? He's got another thing coming, she thought savagely.

Yet inside she wanted to cry. We'll have to work it out or separate, she decided miserably. And I don't really want to break it off. In many ways, I like the guy. He's strong, dependable and loyal, and if I play to his rules, I shall want for nothing – except freedom. Can I really give up my independence? More important still, can I carry on coping with this raging desire to learn about all those wonderful, exciting ways of making love which I'm sure are out there somewhere?

'Valerie Garston speaking,' said the blonde-haired woman into the porcelain and brass mouthpiece of a reproduction turn-of-the-century phone. She was sitting at her dressing table, attending to her make-up.

'It's me, Mother,' Paul announced.

Always glad of contact with her son, Valerie's voice brightened as she said, 'How are you this morning? Everything all right?'

'I suppose so,' he replied. There was interference on the line and she guessed he was using his car phone.

She waited, instinctively knowing there was more to come. 'You sound a touch gloomy,' she prompted.

'It's Lisa.'

It would be, Valerie thought, fighting off an ignoble feeling of jealousy. 'Lisa? Isn't she well?'

'Yes, just being difficult. She's rabbiting on about this crazy idea of running a market stall ... just won't budge. She can be bloody obstinate at times.'

'I thought we'd talked her out of it,' Valerie rejoined, dipping her free hand in a jar of moisturising lotion and applying it liberally to her face.

'Seems not. She's been buying bric-a-brac at auction sales and intends to open at the flea market next Wednesday.'

'Well, dear, we'll have to go along with it, won't we? She'll soon tire of the work. It's hard. I know. As a Woodlander, I've organised White Elephant stalls at charity events. I'd hate to do it for a living.'

Lisa's mad, Valerie concluded. How could she possibly want more than she already had? She was engaged to Paul, soon to be his wife! Valerie did not approve of her, having hoped for a meek, compliant daughter-in-law who would walk in her shadow. She had dreamed of proposing her for membership to The Woodlanders, the female branch of that exclusive and influential band of businessmen who called themselves The Foresters and practically ran West Deverel between them. Somehow, she could not see Lisa fitting in.

'I've told her that, *and* reminded her that she'll have enough on her plate getting ready for the wedding, but she won't listen,' he complained, almost whining – a sound that was music to Valerie's ears.

'Be patient, Paul,' she advised, being sweetly reasonable. 'Bridal nerves, I expect. After all, it's a big step for someone like her – she'll have to change her lifestyle. Don't worry. I'll guide her.'

'Will you have time to talk to her at the barbecue?' he asked anxiously.

'I'll make time. Rest assured. This is only a blip. Natasha and I will take her in hand. A shopping spree, I think. Get the wedding gown sorted, and other things, too. She does dress in a rather weird way, darling. Very much like a student. Always looks as if her things come from second-hand shops – all those gypsyish skirts and scarves and sandals.'

'I'll have to go. Thanks, Mother. See you tomorrow about six, OK?'

'Fine, darling. Goodbye.'

Valerie replaced the rose-patterned receiver in its cradle and studied her reflection critically. A tiny spasm of annoyance rippled the calm waters of her serenity. She regretted that it was necessary for Paul to marry at all. She was fond of her daughter, Natasha, but he was her lodestar, her first-born, her clever son who never failed to make her proud.

When he had told her he wanted to marry Lisa, she had bitten on the bullet. He must have whatever he desired, though she had already selected a girl whom she considered much more suitable. However, he had found an unexpected ally in Mike, her second husband.

'She's OK,' he had said after they had been introduced to Lisa. 'A bright girl, Val. You've known her for yonks,

48

haven't you? Wasn't she at school with Paul and Natasha?'

'She was, but they lost touch later,' Valerie had replied slowly, wondering if his interest had anything to do with Lisa's looks. There was no doubt that she was beautiful – not conventionally, perhaps, but striking none the less. 'Her father was eccentric. He refused to join The Foresters.'

'More fool him,' Mike had said with a shrug. 'No wonder he left her so poorly provided for.'

'How do you know that?' she had questioned sharply.

He had merely smiled, tapped the side of his nose, and replied, 'Ways and means, Val. There's not much happens around here without me getting to hear of it.'

Mike. Valerie's eyes slitted and her lips parted as she thought about him. Five years her junior, she had married him eighteen months after her husband died. John Everard had been steady and unexciting, but he was the father of her two children and she had taken a step up the social ladder by capturing the man who had employed her own father as a bricklayer.

Valerie was proud of her achievements when she recalled those early days. John had left her a rich widow. Paul carried on the business, and Mike had wooed her with a relentless determination that had aroused the dormant sexuality within her.

She had discovered him to be a man of strong passions, in the workplace and out, and had thought herself transported to paradise the first time they made love, pre-empting the civil ceremony at the registry office.

Fired by memory, she opened her burgundy satin negligée and lifted her big, luscious breasts in both hands, weighing them as she weighed Mike's balls sometimes. She loved to feel them moving in the wrinkled sac.

'Not bad for a woman in her late forties,' she murmured, looking at herself from all angles. Swimming

49

and working out pays off, she thought, but I need to keep it up. Mike has a roving eye. Then she reminded herself that he couldn't do without her because his firm had amalgamated with hers. Besides, I've made myself indispensible, she told herself, entertaining other Foresters and hob-nobbing with their wives.

Yet there was another side to Valerie; a secret, lascivious side she shared with no one.

I'm wicked, she thought, thrilling with a delicious sense of shame as she rose from the brocade-covered stool and unfastened her robe, letting it slither to the deep pile, damask rose carpet.

Her body shone forth, smooth skinned and lightly tanned. Her breasts fascinated her, the nipples like large brown eyes returning her stare in the mirror. She feathered her fingers over them and they crimped into pleasant stiffness, ever darker and tighter. Her labia became swollen and wet with desire.

She opened her legs, taking up a widespread stance. Her eyes were drawn to her fork, covered in a crisp bush many shades darker than her hair. The vertical line slicing across her mons stretched open to reveal the pink petals of her labia, crowned by the glistening jewel of her clitoris.

Valerie ran her hands down her body, past her waist and across her rounded belly till her fingers made contact with her delta. She gasped, wanting more. She needed to see that place where Mike took his pleasure. She tilted the floor-standing cheval glass and, turning, bent and twisted round, looking at the image of her straight thighs and the generous globes of her buttocks.

She found the view enchanting: the downy purse of her pudenda with its two halves and the fascinating bud of her anus above it. She watched as her hand appeared between the hillocks and began to stroke the mouth of her sex. Slippery liquid formed, coating her labial wings. She inserted a finger into her vulva, aware of the ridged, velvety lining, and imagined how Mike must feel when his penis rubbed against it. Her finger was not thick enough: she missed his large, thick cock, and added a second finger to the first.

This was better, affording greater stimulation of her vaginal walls, but as when with a man, she knew she would never climax that way. She needed to massage her clitoris.

Her movements hurried and driven by excitement, she took lace-frilled pillows from the brass bedstead and heaped them on the floor. Then she lay down, her shoulders propped by the cushions, and watched in the mirror as, with legs spread and knees raised, she abandoned herself to sensation.

With her left hand she held apart her labia. Roused even more by the fragrance of her own juice, she spread it up her cleft to the throbbing nub. Skilled at this game, she permitted her middle digit to subject this miniature organ to hard friction. Her nipples ached and she used one hand to pinch and fondle them, now toying gently with her swollen clit to allow the fiery, near-orgasm feelings to die back a little.

With delicate strokes, she played around the head rising proudly from its cowl. She circled and teased it, her touch light as a breeze. The waves rose in her lower back, flooding into her womb, receding, mounting ... and carrying her ever closer to bliss.

Her heart was thumping, the need taking over. She massaged her clit firmly, out of control now and possessed by lust. Her hips lifted from the carpet, pubis raised for ever greater contact with her finger. A tingle started in her toes, rising up her legs into her thighs and gathering in her pleasure bud till she convulsed, swept away in a mighty orgasm that left her panting and shaking.

She collapsed, her legs slack. Her finger rested on her spasming nub, contractions spilling through her vagina. With her eyes closed and her head to one side, she rested, at peace.

51

After a short while she got up, dressed herself in white panties and bra, put on a flowered silk shirt and expensively tailored trousers, took a last glance at herself in the mirror and went off to the hairdressers before dropping in at a coffee morning held in aid of repairs to the church, organised by the mayoress.

Chapter Three

Mike Garston picked up the spatula and flipped over the steaks sizzling above the glowing charcoal. He could feel the sweat dampening his neatly styled greying hair. He was a big, ruggedly handsome bull of a man with a thick neck, blue eyes which crinkled at the corners and a strong, self-willed mouth, deeply indented by lines on either side.

Behind him, he could hear his guests chattering. He smiled sardonically as he noted that the voices were getting higher and more uncontrolled under the influence of a generous supply of supermarket plonk.

He was familiar with fine wines, but never wasted them when he could get away with something inferior. He had concluded that the present company would be unlikely to distinguish between a ten-year-old Bonnes-Mares and an Australian burgundy laid down last season.

And neither would Valerie, he reflected, staring across the patio to where she held court near the trestle tables ladened with an outdoor feast. His cock twitched in his baggy Bermuda shorts as he saw the ample curves of her breasts straining against the bodice of her navy-blue linen dress. She had proved to be surprisingly highly sexed, something he had not expected in John Everard's widow.

All in all, the marriage had proved beneficial, and he had attained his ambition to join his building firm with Everard Homes Ltd. He and Paul were a force to be reckoned with, sweeping away or swallowing up any lesser enterprises that stood in their way.

Taking Valerie as his wife had been a small price to pay. Even as he deliberately roused his lust by dwelling on that lush, overblown body, pampered skin and the hungry cavity between her legs, he despised her. She was common, vulgar, overdressed and snobbish; very much at home at the ridiculously shallow coffee mornings she enjoyed with the wives of local dignitaries, most of whom belonged to The Foresters.

He lifted the succulent steaks on to a grid to keep warm and opened a pack of beefburgers. His secretary and aide, Maggie Turner, dithered at his side, saying, 'Shall I pop the meat into baps, sir?'

'Yes, and tell the masses it's feeding time at the zoo,' he replied caustically, his deep voice bearing traces of a Home Counties accent. 'Ask 'em who wants onions or tomato ketchup or whatever.'

'Yes, Mr Garston,' she murmured, a meek creature who he cruelly likened to a marshmallow. She was utterly devoted to him and gratefully accepted any crumbs of attention he cared to cast her way.

He watched her, as a cat watches a mouse, irritated by her lack of social graces but aroused by the way her bottom wobbled under an extremely brief denim skirt and her breasts bounced in their 40D cup brassiere – a pink one which showed through her white blouse.

As she leant forward from the waist to address a seated guest, Mike caught a glimpse of matching pink cotton panties caught between her crease. They would be damp, he knew, her juices flowing merely because she breathed the same air as himself.

He wanted to finger her, feel her pressing her pubis

against him, then turn her round, urge her to her knees and allow her to give him head. Then he would dismiss her. He did this sometimes in the office during a lull, when he was bored. It gave him dark, sadistic pleasure to leave her frustrated, and when she rushed out after he had pumped his seed into her eager mouth, he imagined her going into the women's toilet and rubbing her clit to bring herself off.

And these people milling around the terrace near the azure swimming pool? What were their turn-ons? he wondered, as he played the generous host and fostered his image of a genial, big-hearted man.

He knew he was popular, opening his wallet for good causes and playing Santa Claus in the children's ward of the hospital at Christmas. He was also an enthusiastic member of the Deverel Thespians, a versatile group of local amateurs who combined both straight plays and light opera in their repertoire. His fruity baritone and dashing performance as the Pirate King in *The Pirates of Penzance* had earned him acclaim in the *West Deverel Gazette*.

Oh, yes, *everyone* admired Mike Garston, he thought with a smile. He was such a great fellow; salt of the earth.

The sun was still hot, though the trees threw long shadows over the terrace and pool. A few teenagers splashed in the water, the giggling girls flaunting their burgeoning breasts and the boys horsing around and showing off, driven by an influx of testosterone. The air quivered with primitive sexual awakening.

Their elders sat on white wrought-iron chairs under striped umbrellas or crowded round the bar where a waiter poured drinks. They were getting noisy now, any pretence of gentility dropping away as alcohol coursed through their blood. The women shrieked with laughter and flirted while the men entered into heated discussions concerning politics, business or football teams.

Bossa nova drifted on the warm breeze, and couples started to dance to the sensual beat.

The house, a trendy, converted farm dwelling, stood rock-solid beyond the patio. Shrubs grew in ornamental troughs and stone urns and variegated ivy clung to old walls. The lawn was velvet smooth, all carefully maintained by a gardener.

The sickle moon that had hung, phantomlike, in the sky all day, glowed luminously as the sun sank. It was going to be a gorgeous, romantic, perfumed evening, and Mike wondered dourly whether to get drunk. This way he would deaden his feelings, and stem the raging desire engendered by the sight of Lisa coming towards him on Paul's arm. They had only just arrived, and he admitted to himself that he had been waiting impatiently for this moment.

He adopted a paternal grin and clapped Paul round the shoulders. Then he pecked Lisa on the cheek, his cock stirring in his shorts at the smell of her. The scent of her hair and body reminded him of honeysuckle and jasmine and adolescent love-making in a cornfield. It was a disturbing combination.

'Glad you could make it!' he boomed. 'Have a steak ... have a beer ... I shouldn't try the wine, Lisa, my dear. I'll fix you a Margarita. Take over, Paul, there's a good chap. Plenty more steak in the fridge. Oh, look, here's your mother. She'll lend a hand.'

He succeeded in inveigling Lisa into a quieter part of the garden after arming himself with two tall glasses of the tequila cocktail. His blood was racing, thrumming in his groin, and his penis was impossible to control.

'How are you?' he asked, urging her to join him on a bench. 'I suppose Val is giving you no peace. She's tremendously excited about the wedding.'

'I know,' Lisa replied, and Mike caught a hint of reluctance in her voice. 'But I'm rather busy with other matters.'

'Yes?' he encouraged, crossing his legs in order to

trap that rampant serpent. He was proud of his stalwart thighs, tanned, muscular and upholding his torso like solid tree trunks.

'Do you remember when I spoke about selling antiques?' she went on, relaxing, her bare arm almost touching his. The bushy fair hair covering his skin rose at this near contact.

'I do indeed. I thought it extremely enterprising,' he told her, easing a little closer till his thigh lay alongside hers.

She wore a flimsy, semi-transparent skirt of floaty Indian cotton. He could see the coppery sheen of her sun-browned legs and make out the dark triangle at their apex. The snake in his crotch pressed against his imprisoning thighs, a tear forming at its single eye.

Her hair was spangled by wildfires of gold, falling around her heart-shaped face in ringlets and twists, and the deep oval neckline of her cropped top gave him an uninterrupted view of the division between her breasts, high and firm and young. He could see she wore no brassiere, the brown nipples poking against the tight fabric.

Mike was in torment. He had to move carefully. Any additional friction on his cock would make it explode in ecstasy. Yet he desperately wanted to move and longed to take Lisa in his arms. He wanted to whisk her away to somewhere private and sheath his aching weapon in her flesh. He envied Paul, with a blistering envy that robbed him of reason. He now despised that mother's boy – that conceited nincompoop who had captured this stunning, intelligent, sensitive beauty.

Now she was smiling at him, her eyes as bright as diamonds as she said, 'I'm glad someone approves. I was beginning to think that maybe Paul was right, and I'd be wasting my time.'

'No way,' Mike said firmly, daring to take her hand in his. 'You can trust me to help you. After all, aren't I your stepfather-to-be, who will lead you to the altar on the great day?'

She laughed and did not withdraw her fingers, saying, 'Thanks, Mike. I appreciate that. I miss Dad very much.'

'Of course you do, and I'm sorry it happened. That drunken driver didn't get a heavy enough sentence. Call on me any time you need advice. I'll be only too happy to help. Meanwhile, go along with Val's plans. It'll be great when you're a member of the family.'

Great indeed, he was thinking, his mind alive with schemes. Great to have her under his control; leaning on him, maybe. He would stir it subtly and, after a disagreement with Paul, she would come to him and he would comfort her. He would become her ally and then woo her till she was willing to accept him as her lover.

'Mike! Where are you?' Valerie's loud voice broke into his reverie.

'Coming!' he shouted back, and drew Lisa up with him. 'Don't forget,' he whispered. 'Any time you need me, I'll be there.'

He lost her in the crowd after that, but as soon as he could get away from Valerie, he dragged Maggie into the summerhouse and demanded harshly, 'Suck my cock!'

It was odd to be up so early – literally at the crack of dawn. Lisa loaded up the final box and closed the van's rear door. No doubt I'll wake at the very last moment and have to scramble to get there in a few weeks, she thought, but this is the first time and I've got a colossal attack of stage fright.

The town was quiet. There was no one about except the postman, but when Lisa reached the Corn Exchange as the church clock struck seven everything changed. It bustled with activity.

'Mind you get there when the doors open,' the organiser had advised, his eyes twinkling under grey brows as thick as couch-grass. 'Your dad was always an early bird. He never missed when there was something he was going for. That's how he got your mother. The prettiest woman I've ever seen. You're the spitting image of her.'

Nice to have another ally, Lisa concluded, thinking of Mike while she found a parking space. She was careful not to make the fatal error of leaving her van where someone else had a prior claim. She did not want to make enemies so soon.

Before unloading, she walked into the old building, the lower portion of which was given over to town events such as the flea market, the annual flower show and rummage sales. She had been allotted Stall 16, towards the back. The prime positions nearest the doors were already taken.

Trying to act as if this was an everyday occurrence, she busied herself. She draped a chenille cloth over her table, then hefted in the first of several cardboard boxes. At once, she was aware of interested eyes focusing in her direction. Leaving the box half hidden under the cloth's bobble-fringed edge, she fetched the rest.

The eyes were more intent now and, as she started to unpack, so other stall holders gathered. It was disconcerting. They left their half-finished tables and sidled forward – two or three at first, then more than a dozen – before clustering round like wasps at a jam pot.

'You're new here, aren't you?' enquired a wizened, brassy-haired woman, picking up a lace-edged tablecloth and holding it to the light. 'I specialise in linen, but it must be perfect, you understand. No tears, no wear, no darns.'

'There's nothing wrong with that,' Lisa exclaimed, remembering seeing it spread on her paternal grandmother's table when she was taken to her house on festive occasions. Rumour had it that the lace had been made by a French ancestor, noted for her fine work.

'Oh, I dunno,' the women observed dubiously. 'See

where it's been folded? It's paper thin there. What d'you want for it?'

'Twenty-five pounds,' Lisa announced boldly, remembering reading somewhere that it was unwise to ask too little.

The woman looked as outraged as if she had said £500. 'Couldn't possibly give you that, deary,' she remarked, pulling down the corners of her mouth. 'I've got to make a profit. How about ten?'

Lisa was in a quandary, and it was hard to think clearly with the others poking about in her precious boxes. She had hoped to get it all set out attractively before she started selling. £10? It was tempting. That would pay for the stall, but –

'It's worth far more than that,' said a modulated voice from the next table. Lisa looked across and saw a woman smiling at her. A slim, well-dressed, middle-aged lady with beautiful skin and pale gold hair. 'The lace is exquisite.'

'Well, that's all I'm prepared to offer,' the linen dealer declared and took herself off.

'Don't let things go too cheaply,' Lisa's neighbour advised, leaving the canvas folding chair on which she had been sitting behind her neatly presented goods.

Lisa noticed that the other dealers had melted away like snow in sunlight when this woman spoke, so that at last she was left in peace to arrange her items to her own satisfaction.

'I've never done this before,' she explained. 'But I hope to become a regular.'

'I'm an old hand at it. Antiques are my hobby; you could say one of my passions. I'm in the fortunate position of not having to make money by dealing, but I come here every week. You have some nice pieces.' She held out her hand. 'My name's Daphne Nightingale.'

Lisa took it, her own hand feeling uncouth in contrast to the delicate bones and cool, soft skin belonging to her new friend. 'I'm Lisa Sherwin.' Her face grew pink with pleasure. 'You really think I have something of value to sell?'

Daphne nodded, her blue eyes, hedged with brown lashes, sweeping across the contents of Lisa's table. 'Yes, indeed,' she assured her. 'You have that rare thing called taste, my dear. One is born with it. So many of these self-styled experts know next to nothing about antiques. They're only interested in making a quick profit. I'd like to advise you on pricing, if I may.'

'Oh, please!' Lisa cried eagerly. 'I haven't a clue, really. I've visited markets like this one and have a vague idea, but I'd welcome your help.'

'Good. Now why don't you leave your labels and I'll put a price on these things. Perhaps you wouldn't mind popping across to the canteen. I'd love a cup of tea. No sugar, thank you,' Daphne said with a smile, taking up her biro. 'Don't worry. I'll keep the wolves at bay. The general public won't be officially allowed in till nine-thirty, so we've got plenty of time.'

She paused by the side of the table where Lisa had placed a carved umbrella stand. It had seemed an ideal receptacle for a lace-trimmed parasol, a pair of golf clubs, a croquet mallet, a walking cane with an ornate handle, two riding crops and a long-handled carriage whip.

Daphne touched the latter and half drew it out of the stand, a musing, far-away expression appearing on her finely drawn features. 'Where did these come from?' she asked, letting the whip slide to rest and picking out a crop. She swished it experimentally, and nodded as if satisfied that it was still pliable.

'I don't know . . . here and there . . . From the estates of deceased relatives, I expect. Most of this stuff belonged to my father,' Lisa answered, puzzled by the question. To her these objects seemed of little value, though they were undoubtedly old.

Daphne returned from the distant mental regions where she had been wandering, saying with a smile,

'We won't let these go for a song. Someone will pay handsomely to own them. Off you go now. Fetch that tea.'

'Right,' Lisa replied, gathering up her purse, not to be confused with the bumbag she wore round her waist wherein lay a float of small change.

She glanced back to see Daphne examining and labelling and was relieved to have found such a friend. There was something trustworthy about her, which she decided was probably a rare quality when it came to trading.

The freckle-faced girl running the refreshments bar was kindly and efficient, chatting lightly as she served tea, coffee and homemade cakes. She was plump and vivacious, and a mini skirt stretched around her wide hips while her large breasts were emphasised by a skimpy top. She smiled a lot, exchanging repartee with the customers.

'You're new, aren't you?' She addressed Lisa pleasantly.

'That's right.'

'Hope you do OK.'

'Thanks.'

Lisa balanced two cups and a packet of shortcake biscuits on a plastic tray and headed back to Daphne.

The time passed remarkably quickly as Lisa arranged and rearranged her stall, amazed by the high prices Daphne had put on some of the items. Daphne returned to her own table and, shortly after nine, the public started to trickle in. Martin dropped by to wish her well. Later, Mike visited briefly on a similar mission.

Lisa did not have a moment to spare as people stopped, picked things up, haggled, purchased or walked on, and her bumbag was soon comfortingly heavy. She began to get an idea of what the punters were seeking. This was an antiques market, not a jumble sale, and those who only wanted to pay car-boot prices soon lost interest and drifted away. The genuine *aficion-*

ados sought objects to beautify their homes or, if they hunted for particular bygones, to add to their collections.

There was a slight lull after an hour. Lisa leant on the stall, aware that her back and legs were aching, but filled with a surge of confidence. The table was looking decidedly depleted. There were pound coins weighing down her bag, and a crisp bundle of fivers, tenners and even a twenty.

I could go home now if I wanted, she thought. I've already made a handsome profit, but then, I didn't have to buy much. Most of this stuff was gathered by my hoarder father. All I had to do was root through the loft. If I decide to go on with this, I'll stash the money and spend it at auctions, she told herself.

'Having a good time?' asked David Maccabene, swimming into her field of vision.

She swallowed, her heart racing, then managed to say, 'It's great. I'm enjoying it.'

'I hope the dealers didn't rook you,' he went on, casting an eye over the table.

'They tried, but the lady next door came to my rescue,' she admitted, chiding herself for the feeling of nervous excitement that swept through her like a tornado.

He was too attractive for his own good – or hers. She resented the barrier of the table between them, wanting to press close to him. While appearing disinterested, she glanced at his handsome face, long legs and agile body. He wore a different pair of jeans, equally tight but newer, the demin dark blue, not faded. A shirt with a granddad-style neck unbuttoned over a coppery chest, the sleeves rolled up above his elbows, showing sinewy, hairy arms. She wondered how he would react if she were to lean over and unzip his denims. Would his cock spring free, pulsing with desire?

Why did he have to appear? she wondered, sighing aloud. I was getting on fine and was even forgetting my frustrations, but now they've come back with a vengeance.

'I like the spelter warriors,' he said, picking one up and examining it. 'The Victorians knew a thing or two about detail, didn't they? What a fine guy! Just look at his armour, and that lion's mane hanging from his helmet. He's a barbarian, I guess, and the other is a Christian knight.'

'They're two hundred pounds for the pair,' she said unnecessarily, for he had already glanced at the price tags. 'And I won't separate them. It detracts from the value.'

'Nothing off for a friend who hopes to become something more?' he suggested with a look in his eyes that made her nipples peak under her T-shirt. He was staring at them speculatively, and a hot blush suffused her face.

'Daphne priced the warriors,' she began, fighting the impulse to make him a present of them – a curious aberration for the hard-headed dealer she hoped to become.

'She is rarely wrong. A most knowledgeable lady.' He nodded, an impudent grin spreading over his features as if he read her like a book.

'You kn-know her?' Lisa stammered, making conversation in order to control herself, refusing to admit that she was gravid with lust.

'I have that pleasure,' he answered, and called across the gap between the stalls. 'Good morning, Mrs Nightingale!'

'Good morning, Mr Maccabene,' she replied levelly. 'Don't beat her down. The price is a fair one. They are a splendid pair of figures, and undamaged. Spelter is in demand these days, but you are already aware of this.'

'I am, but I want these for myself,' he said, exerting his considerable charm. 'I shan't be selling them on.'

Daphne watched the interplay between him and Lisa with cool detachment, then returned to serving a young man who was seeking Goss China as a birthday present for his mother.

'I'll take them,' David said suddenly, turning back to Lisa.

She was dumbstruck. He wasn't haggling!

'You will?' she exclaimed.

'Is that so strange? I'm a collector too, you know. Oh, yes, I do actually live in a house, not a saleroom. I like to be surrounded with pleasing things ... beautiful things ... like you, Miss Sherwin. Can I add you to my collection?'

'I'm not part of the deal,' she answered frostily, but her pulse hammered as he leant closer, regarding her with his tigerish eyes.

'Was I suggesting that you were?' His tone was reproachful. 'Heaven forefend, Miss Sherwin! What about dinner tonight?'

'I've already told you. I'm engaged.'

'Give him the elbow. You know you want to.'

'Do I? You take a lot for granted.'

Her hormones were in a frenzy, every instinct urging her to lie down on the boards in front of the stall and have him make frenzied, noisy, uninhibited love to her. Her vagina ached with longing and her clitoris quivered, rebels both refusing to listen to the cool voice of reason.

David took a roll of banknotes from a back pocket and peeled off several, handing them to her. 'Check it. I think there's two hundred quid there,' he said.

She reeled from the brush of his fingers against hers as he passed over the money. He kept a momentary hold of her hand and tickled the palm with his middle digit. It was an intimate touch, suggestive of him frigging her clitoris.

Heat swamped Lisa. She felt like blancmange inside, and was filled with lubricious, lecherous longing to have him do just that. I wish I had an assistant, she thought in a rush of panic. A sensible, reliable person

65

who would count the notes and tell him if he was cheating me. I can't see straight, let alone check money. I hope he takes the warriors away right now, and never comes back.

'Do you want them wrapped? Shall I find a box?' she asked, her voice unsteady as she fumbled about under the stall.

'Don't worry about it. Is the cash OK?' His eyes were bright with laughter and knowledge and desire. 'What are you looking for?'

'Newspaper ... Something to put them in ...' she stuttered.

And he was there, dropping on his heels beside her, half hidden by the cloth. Oh, God, I'm trapped here with him! she thought, alarmed and excited.

His fingers were on hers again, prising the wad of notes away as he said, 'Stash this before you do anything else. You don't want to lose it. There are villains about.'

He unzipped her bumbag and tucked the money inside, then his hand lingered on the curve of her waist where the strap lay. His face moved closer; smiling green eyes and firm lips. She watched, mesmerised. His touch moved from her waist to the tip of her breast, softly caressing the sensitive little crest.

He paused, smiled, and said, 'Are you going to cry "sexual harrassment", Miss Sherwin?'

She could not speak. Kneeling in front of him, almost between his thighs, speech was an impossibility. All around was the clamour of the market. She could see the feet of passing people, but it was as if she and David were alone on a mountain top. She remembered her fantasy in which he had featured as a doctor and her belly clenched. Her panties were wet around the gusset. She was glad she had worn a skirt or that wetness might have seeped into the crotch of her jeans.

His mouth advanced, so close now that she could see the darkness of his stubble and smell his hair. She raised her hand, almost yielding to the desire to bury it in

66

those sepia curls. He did not touch her again, and her nipple felt bereft. Now he simply squatted there, waiting for her to make the next move. Her face was lifted to his, a tingling sensation rushing through her core and adding to the moisture between her secret lips.

He was going to kiss her, she knew it.

'David? Are you there?' cried a cultured, bossy, female voice.

'Yes, Fiona, I'm here,' he answered without moving, winking conspiratorially at Lisa.

'Come out,' the voice said imperiously.

'In a moment. Miss Sherwin and I are just concluding a deal,' he replied in an untroubled way, never taking his eyes from Lisa as he whispered, 'I'll pick you up at seven.'

'Do you know where I live?' she asked, too stunned to argue.

'Oh, yes. I made it my business to find out.'

With that, he stretched his long limbs and rose to his full, impressive height. Lisa took longer, reluctant to face whoever it was who had called him.

When she finally crawled out from under the table, it was to find herself staring into a pair of angry blue-grey eyes set in a perfectly formed female face. She immediately felt scruffy, sluttish and of little account before this woman's casual elegance.

She registered a designer dress in a natural shade of raw silk, pale stockings and burnt umber shoes of superb Italian craftsmanship, a string of amber beads and a wedding band worn behind a sparkling sapphire and diamond engagement ring.

Relief mingled with alarm. The woman was married. Hard on this followed the thought that that wouldn't stop a man like David.

'The figures?' she blurted out.

'They'll be OK just as they are,' David assured her, and the amusement in his eyes was hard to bear. 'Meet Lady Fiona Cardwell. Fiona, this is Lisa Sherwin.'

Fiona nodded, ice cool, then slipped her arm through his possessively and drawled, 'Darling, have you finished? I insist that you take me to lunch. I'm sure there's nothing here to interest you.' Her eyes cut to Lisa.

David ignored her. He was staring across the room towards the entrance, his head up like a warhorse scenting battle. There was a hard edge to his voice as he said, 'Look what the cat's dragged in.'

Lisa followed his gaze and saw a tall, lean man walking past the stalls, accompanied by a woman. He paused here and there, then moved on. People engaged him in talk. He seemed well known, if not exactly popular. His head rose above the crowd. He was almost as tall as David and very nearly as good looking. His black hair was swept back from a high forehead and tied at the nape of his neck. His face was hawklike, with an aquiline nose, narrow lips and the fierce, concentrated gaze of a raptor.

'How wonderful! I didn't expect to see him here!' Fiona exclaimed, and lost some of her cool.

'Or her. What a magnificent piece of arse,' David retorted.

'Who cares about Tanith? Fletcher's the one to die for,' Fiona snapped back at him tartly.

Lisa was conscious of dark undertones in their exchange. What was going on here? She had thought herself attending a simple, straightforward venue where the driving force was trading, but now it had suddenly become a seething morass of sexual tension.

Fletcher and his companion strolled towards them at a leisurely pace. His broad-shouldered body and rangy limbs were clothed in a black polo-necked sweater and black chinos. His aura was one of sinister sensuality, and Lisa's skin prickled.

The woman drew all eyes. It was not entirely the flaming red hair forming an undeserved halo round her head, or even her blazing blue eyes and creamy skin. It had more to do with her commanding bearing. The upper half of her superb breasts swelled over the scooped neckline of her tightly laced black PVC bodice. Her shapely thighs were bare beneath the fringed hem of a pair of demin cut-offs, so short and tight that her female parts were likely to be exposed every time she bent over.

Fiona's upper lip curled as she said, 'Hello, Tanith.'

The redhead nodded, and they both bristled. Had they been cats, they would have stalked round each other with tails fluffed out to twice the size. 'Hi, there, Fiona. Doing a spot of dealing? I shouldn't have thought that was quite your style,' Tanith said silkily, and her eyes switched to David.

'Just nosing about,' Fiona replied, her arm tightening round his.

'See anything you fancy?' Tanith enquired, looking him over as if he was a stallion at stud, her gaze lingering on his groin area.

'Maybe,' Fiona answered, as she made an assessment of Fletcher's obvious attributes. He moved with the agility and smoothness of a dancer, muscles rippling under the form-hugging Armani sweater.

He smiled sardonically as he took her hand and kissed it. 'Lady Fiona. It's been a while,' he purred, his deep voice like a spine-tingling caress.

David withdrew his arm from hers and turned back to Lisa. The spelter warriors still stood on the table and Fletcher picked one up. 'They're sold,' David said crisply.

'A pity,' Fletcher sighed, and looked directly at Lisa, adding, 'I've not seen you here before.'

'My first attempt,' she answered, flustered in the presence of these vastly different yet equally attractive men.

'I see,' he said and held out his hand. 'Welcome to the fray. My name's Fletcher Robillard.'

'Lisa Sherwin,' she replied, and placed her hand in his, her nerves jumping at the cool, firm grip that had a hint of steel.

He released her and began to examine the contents of the umbrella stand. The clubs were scrutinised, as was the croquet mallet, and then he pulled out the whip. He stood back and lifted his arm and the long leather thong whistled through the air.

The crowd started, exclaimed and tittered nervously, and Lisa quivered, the fine down on her limbs standing on end. Fletcher smiled thinly, his eyes as cold as the Arctic Sea. Next he chose one of the crops, examining its silver-mounted stock and the tiny wedge of red leather at its tip. One eyebrow shot up quizzically.

'Who owned this?' he asked.

'Not me,' Lisa replied hurriedly. 'I don't ride ... Well, I had lessons when I was a little girl, but had to give up. Too expensive, you know. I wouldn't have whipped horses, anyway. I think it's cruel.'

'I wasn't talking about whipping horses,' he said. His handsome face turned to hers, the hard line of his lips curving slightly as he held the crop in his right hand and lightly tapped the thong against his left palm.

'I found the stand in my loft,' Lisa struggled on. 'The whips and things were lying about in boxes. I thought it would be useful for holding them.'

'You have an eye for arrangement,' he went on, and though he had not moved, it was as if he had come suffocatingly close. 'I shall buy the stand and its contents, if the price is right.'

'They are all marked,' she said, nervously aware of undercurrents beneath the surface of this apparently normal conversation. She had the sudden, uneasy feeling that Fletcher was playing a mysterious game.

He drew out the Malacca cane and balanced its weight in one hand, then examined the tags and played with the crops again. Lisa's mind was clouded by images of debauchery, his very presence conjuring scenes where perhaps one man, or even two, and a woman as well, introduced her to the refined arts of erotic passion.

Fletcher was the kind of man who would be anathema to Paul. It was satisfying to think how annoyed her fiancé would be at her associating with him.

'Don't try to knock the price down,' Daphne said, keeping her eyes on Fletcher. 'It's reasonable. The whip alone would fetch that in some quarters.'

'And what would you know about whips, Mrs Nightingale?' he asked sarcastically.

Daphne's eyes crinkled with amusement; wise eyes in which lay a wealth of experience. 'Don't underestimate me, Mr Robillard,' she advised. 'Certain devious delights concerning the paradox of pain and pleasure were not invented by your generation. They have been practised for centuries, probably since man came down from the trees and stood upright. That's one of the troubles with the young. They always think nothing of significance happened before they were born.'

'I yield to your superior years,' he answered, with an ironic bow, then turned his attention to Lisa. 'The price is steep, Miss Sherwin. Supposing I offer you a round sum for the whole lot, stand and all? Will you drop a little?'

Lisa's eyes sought Daphne, who smiled and nodded, calling across, 'Providing your offer is realistic, Mr Robillard.'

It was a substantial sum, and Lisa was dizzy, doing rapid calculations. Nevertheless, she did not let him have it all his own way, and his lips tightened as they bargained. She felt she had done the right thing. He would have despised her had she proved too malleable.

As it was, she tingled with an excitement which was not entirely due to the thrill of haggling, but had more to do with this lean-hipped, grey-eyed individual who moved in closer. He loomed over her, and her breath shortened. He smelled of some divine, expensive aftershave, and she could feel him hardening as he pressed against her side, the thick shaft of his cock stirring promisingly.

71

And why shouldn't he be aroused? she thought, filled with buoyant, new-found confidence. I'm attractive, aren't I? David certainly seems to find me sexy. She wanted to curl her fingers round Fletcher's prick and rub it through the black trousers.

This was so delirious a thought that she nearly lost her power to bargain. She took a step away from the temptation of him and fought for control over her wayward flesh. In a few moments, they reached a mutually satisfactory agreement and Fletcher paid her in cash, just as David had done.

Tanith and Fiona were sparring for David's attention, but Lisa noticed that he was watching her keenly, trying to hear what she and Fletcher were saying. She smiled to herself, and her spirits rose even higher.

Then Tanith moved over to look at Fletcher's purchase and her crimson lips smiled at Lisa without malice. Though it seemed she and he had some sort of under-standing, she lacked the jealous spite that oozed from Fiona.

'What do you do?' she asked chattily as she perched on a corner of the table, bracing one leg on the floor and swinging the other in its laced, high-wedged espadrille.

'I was at college, but now I'm back in my home town,' Lisa informed her. 'I'm interested in antiques and thought I'd have a go. I've studied history and antiqui-ties, and need to find a job.'

'How would you like to work for Fletcher and myself? We're partners and run several shops. We need an assistant right now. The girl we had before has left to have a baby.'

Lisa looked at her, surprised and questioning. There was a note in Tanith's voice and a look in her eyes that made her hesitate. The offer was a tempting one and, on the surface, seemed ideal. This stunning man and bril-liantly seductive woman wanted her to work for them. She would see them almost every day, become their colleague and friend. The prospect was blinding.

'I'll have to give it serious thought,' she hedged. Events were moving too fast.

'Here's our phone number,' Tanith said, holding out a card.

The market closed at four o'clock and, by the time Lisa had stashed what remained in the van and driven home, she knew she would have to hurry if she was to be ready by seven.

She felt guilty and rebellious and was bubbling over with excitement. She had proved to herself that she could do it. The day's adventure had been profitable and fun. She had met new people and expanded her horizons. Paul wouldn't like it at all.

But he was not seeing her that night. He was engrossed in weighty Forester matters, secrets to which she, as a mere female, was not privy. She thought it all rather ridiculous but Paul took it extremely seriously. It was part and parcel of business, so he maintained.

She went round the flat, throwing open every window. She was preoccupied, at one moment tingling with anticipation at the thought of her date with David, and in the next riven with guilt and apprehension. Was she making the most awful mistake of her life? How was she going to explain it to Paul?

Then the new woman who was beginning to stir in her depths took control, reminding her that Paul spent time having dinner with business associates and there was no harm in her doing the same. Yet she knew and gloried in the fact that this was completely different. David raised her sexual curiosity and appealed to her sense of rebellion. She had been in a cage and he had part-opened the door. The rest was down to her.

Immersing herself in the bath, she lay back and made plans. She would take the job with Fletcher and Tanith and prove herself highly efficient – maybe even end up in partnership with them. As she visualised this dazzling prospect, she relished the caress of the warm, scented water, parting her thighs so that wavelets washed over her lower lips, exploring her cleft like tiny, insidious fingers.

Fletcher. David. Tanith of the big breasts and seductive eyes.

She had entered the market that morning hoping for distraction and the chance to be independent. She had left it on a high-flying surge of hope. Her body began to heat at the memory. She ran her soapy hands over her breasts and the nipples swelled provocatively. She lingered on them, pinching the crimped buds.

Keeping one hand stretched across her chest, the heel of her palm rubbing her left nipple and the tips of her fingers on the right one, she allowed her other hand to drift downward. Her skin felt smooth, its tan contrasting pleasingly with the white suds. The brown wedge of pubic hair was wet and curling. Parting the wings of her labia, she slid a finger between. Triple sensations now; nipples and clitoris throbbing in unison. It was unbearably sweet.

Soft, lapping, invisible tongues caressed her, the deep, rippling arousal spreading through her loins and belly. She relaxed and closed her eyes, the pulse within her rising like the tide. She knew it would not last long. The need was too urgent, the hunger too intense. Her senses swam and she was suddenly engulfed in a whirling rush of oblivion.

She gave a shuddering sigh and was brought back to reality. Time was running on. She washed quickly, then left the tub and stood dripping on the bath mat while she filled the basin and shampooed her hair.

What to wear? David, though casual, would know all the smart places to eat. Draped in a towel and with another wound turbanwise round her head, she went through the wardrobe with growing dismay. The white dress with the lace yoke? Too girlish. The trouser-suit? Too formal. Nothing pleased her, though she had felt happy enough in these things before.

At the very back, she found a River Island dress of two summers ago. Made of black cotton, it was cool and not too formal. England sweltered under a heatwave and it would have been more sensible to have gone nude, were this possible. This almost diaphanous, flowing, button-through dress was the next best thing, with shoe-string ties and a heart-shaped neckline. After moisturising her body and applying perfumed spray, she slipped into a black underwired bra and a pair of tanga briefs, then put on the dress.

I look positively virginal, she decided, standing in front of the mirror. What a lie. I'm still glowing after bringing myself to orgasm. I can smell my own secretions, even though I washed well. The odour of sex is so strong. Will David be aware of it?

She applied make-up sparingly and swept her hair back, securing it with a velvet scrunchie. Just time to swallow a glass of orange juice and listen to the music that had obsessed her ever since seeing a ballet production of *Dracula*.

The music coiled through the lounge, darkly sinister and oddly sad. I wonder if David likes classical music? she wondered. As for Fletcher, he was a completely new and intriguing acquaintance, and one who she determined to know better.

She curled her bare toes in the carpet and thought about him. He reminded her of the ballet's hero/villain – the lost and damned vampire who women found irresistible.

The orchestral music, now loud and threatening, now soft and seductive, rang through the flat, and Lisa became absorbed in it, then came to herself, realising that someone was pressing the doorbell.

She turned down the volume and opened the door. David was propping himself against the lintel. He smiled at her, saying, 'Lovely music. Who wrote it?'

'A new British composer. It's the score for the ballet *Dracula*.'

'It reminds me of Prokofiev, with hints of Bartok,' he responded.

She was astonished, delighted and unable to believe that she had at last found a fellow music lover.

'That's true. It's a stunning work. They took the horror story to the stage and made it sensuous, thrilling, frightening –'

'And erotic?' he put in, watching her intently from under the black bar of his brows.

She flushed and nodded. 'Oh, yes, very erotic.'

'Where is it being danced? Maybe we could go together,' he suggested, still standing on the doorstep.

Lisa wanted to throw her arms round him and kiss him. 'It's not being done again till next year,' she said. 'But they're performing *Romeo and Juliet* soon. The nearest venue will be up north somewhere.'

'I'll find out where and get tickets. Will you come with me?'

'I'd love to, but . . .' The enthusiasm in her voice died as she remembered Paul.

'Your fiancé wouldn't approve?'

'That's right. Look, come in. I shan't be a minute,' she said, and bent to retrieve her sandals from under the couch.

'Nice flat,' he commented, a swashbuckler with tousled, curly hair, but a cultured rogue who appreciated ballet.

'Yes,' she answered, picking up her handbag.

They had never been so alone before and the intimacy of the situation bore down on her like a tidal wave. The bedroom was so close. A few steps and they would be in it; on her bed, tearing off their clothes, uniting their flesh.

'Are you ready?' he said, his voice jerking her back to reality.

He drove her to an old pub called The Dove, and they ate in an alcove off the main bar, a room with oaken tables and benches, uneven floors and low, beamed ceilings, and a large inglenook fireplace where logs would blaze in winter. 'It's been an inn since fourteen-something,' he informed her, lighting up a cheroot and observing her through the blue haze.

A waiter had cleared the table and now served coffee.

'The meal was wonderful,' she said, the taste of salad niçoise lingering in her memory, along with fresh crusty rolls and a sinfully fattening gateau.

He looked pleased, saying, 'The Dove's in all the good food guides. I thought you'd like it.'

'Did you? But you hardly know me,' Lisa said, losing her shyness now she felt comfortable with him.

She felt his leg against hers on the bench and became aware of a heaviness in her groin and desire coiled like a tense spring in her womb.

He turned to look at her. Lifting one finger, he brushed it gently across her lips. 'You've a smidgin of chocolate there,' he murmured, and transferred his finger to his mouth, sucking in the trace. 'And another bit, over there.'

This time she captured his finger between her lips, rimming his nail with the tip of her tongue. The pad of his thumb rested on her lush, red, lower lip. She fluttered her tongue over it as she moved her hips a little. He shifted closer still, pressing his leg against hers.

He withdrew his hand, and said, 'Shall we go?'

When he rose, she could see the thick line of his cock lying inside his close-fitting jeans. A tiny quiver of triumph shot through her.

Outside, the sky was flushed with crimson in the west, and the moon was rising in a golden haze, attended by a retinue of stars.

'Would you like to see my house?' he asked, as he started up his Range Rover.

'All right,' she agreed, wishing she had refused that last glass of wine.

She was all too aware of him in the driver's seat, his

strong hands resting on the wheel and his strong face planed by the strange light when the world hung between sunset and darkness. His thumb in her mouth had merely been the forerunner to something larger and firmer. It was his penis that she desperately wanted to suck.

He lived two miles from The Dove, wheeling into an untidy yard surrounded by the dark bulk of out-buildings. He walked round to help her down, his fingers closing over hers and not letting go. He led her towards a long, low, barnlike structure, took out a key and opened an oak door, black with age.

Wall lights sprang into being, and she was in a beamed and panelled hall, with a twisting staircase rising to a gallery, and a huge room to one side into which he conducted her. It smelled of old wood and beeswax, a place which robbed her of speech. It was furnished in a variety of styles, but the whole came together in a way that was both calming and stimulating. There was so much to see and so many rare and lovely objects to admire, from the ancient Bokhara rugs on the floor and the Persian prayer mats on the walls to the hunting scenes and landscapes, pottery and glass, weapons and helmets and the full regalia of a samurai warrior.

'Coffee?' he asked, bringing her down to earth.

'Please,' she replied, sober all of a sudden and feeling humble in the face of so much experience. He knew antiques inside out.

The kitchen, with a farmhouse feel but blessed by modern technology, was situated off the main room. She left him to it and wandered round, gazing at everything in stunned awe. She was pleased when she found the spelter warriors standing in the window embrasure. He had really meant it when he said he wanted them for himself.

'Aren't you afraid you'll be burgled?' she asked, as he returned bearing a tray.

'I've got a full security system. It costs to have installed but it's worth it, one hundred per cent.'

They sat on a divan, heaped with bolster-shaped cushions covered in rich fabric of ecclesiastical hues. The Turkish coffee was thick, strong and sweet. David poured from a curiously turned pot which looked like a small minaret.

'You've travelled?' she asked.

'I wish,' he replied, with his lopsided grin. 'Despite all you see, I'm not rich.'

'Unlike Lady Fiona,' she said slowly, wondering why she had found it necessary to mention that woman's name.

His smile broadened. 'Very unlike.'

'You know her well?'

He put down his cup and drew her into his arms, saying, 'What you really want to ask is, Am I fucking her? The answer is yes ... but not right now. I'm here with you and it's you I want. Forget Lady Fiona.'

'You're frank, I'll grant you that,' she muttered, weakening at the feel of his lips on the sensitive lobes of her ears and the tender nape of her neck.

'I'll never be anything else but that with you, Lisa,' he promised. 'There will be no deception between us.'

This was it: she was actually about to be unfaithful to Paul. Somehow the idea did not seem appalling. Her betrayal was fully justified by his wilful neglect of her needs.

David's lips moved to her mouth, his tongue-tip exploring the curves of her closed lips until she could wait no longer and opened them, soft and wet and yielding under his seductive touch. His kiss was utterly fulfilling; long, deep and inspired. He took his time, slowly relishing every inch of the delicate lining of her mouth. And while he kissed her, his hand cupped her breast, tracing the shape of the nipple through the cotton.

She shuddered, lost in a world of sensation, his

attention to her mouth and breasts making the deep heartland of her womanhood ready to receive him. Now, still holding her, he released her lips and lay back, snapping open his waist-button and sliding down his zip. He took her hand and guided it to where he wanted it most, and she closed her fingers round his cock. It was in proportion to the rest of him – big enough to fill her to the utmost or maybe even too big for her to take without discomfort. She was ready to try.

She started to stroke it, while his eyes caressed her face and his hands touched her mouth, then her breasts, baring them to his gaze by pushing aside her dress and bra. She lowered her head and eased his foreskin back over the glans, wetting it with her saliva and licking at the salty libation that glistened on the tip. She wanted more and more of him, needing to feel him in her moist female depths.

His eyes were unfocused now, and his cock rose harder and higher against her parted lips. She could feel the veins on the underside of his shaft pulsing and could tell by the jerky rhythm of his hips that he was almost there.

He suddenly clamped a hand in her hair, holding her still, and whispered, 'Not yet. I want to watch you come first.'

He slipped her buttons undone and took off her dress, then unhooked her bra and eased away the tiny panties, while she lifted her pelvis to aid him. Now she was naked, the admiration in his eyes making her proud of her body.

'God, you're beautiful,' he murmured.

His fingers caressed the slope of her breasts. He lingered at the nipples, then sucked them, each in turn. It was a glorious feeling, an answering pulse throbbing in her clitoris. He laved her nipples with his wet tongue, then licked his way down to her belly, circled the navel and travelled to her pubic floss.

His fingers toyed with the tight curls, exploring all

her secret folds, then he opened her like a flower and found the hard nub wherein lay the seat of her pleasure. She kept her hand on his member, rubbing it gently and imitating his strokes on her clitoris. She wanted him to share her intense pleasure. His wet tongue fondled her bud. He sucked it into his mouth, then licked and fluttered and fondled till hot waves of feeling rose within her, rose and retreated, then rose again, each one higher than the last.

The foaming waves crested, broke and carried her upward, higher and higher, and she cried out in her extremity, coming against his tongue. He kept it there, gently soothing, bringing her down, down, down, then thrust his cock into her convulsing core as he joined her in an orgy of ecstatic bliss.

Chapter Four

*A*nother Wednesday. Another market successfully concluded, but no sign of David since that fateful night a week ago. Just a note pushed through Lisa's front door, saying, 'Gone to France buying. See you soon.'

There had been Paul, of course, but Lisa had put off his sexual advances with the excuse that it was the wrong time of the month. This was sufficient. Like most men of his type, he was almost superstitiously afraid of the mysterious female cycle.

'He lives in the Dark Ages,' she said to Martin, in whom she had confided about David. 'It was a perfect excuse because he never comes near me then. My God, if I ever had a baby he'd make me give birth in a hut well away from the tribe and stay there for weeks, then he'd burn it to the ground.'

'Unclean! Unclean!' Martin chorused, grinning puckishly.

'I can't imagine David behaving like that. But then I'm trying to forget him. He might at least have had the decency to phone. I'm a fool. What did I expect?'

'You shouldn't have expected anything,' Martin said sagely, flicking round the showroom with a feather duster. 'Then you wouldn't have been disappointed.'

'That's all very well, but it means I can't rely on anyone,' she moaned, as she helped him rearrange shelves.

'An unrealistic attitude,' he went on, looking under a teddy bear's frock and remarking, 'I'm glad to see she's wearing bloomers.'

'Frilly ones, too,' Lisa said, smiling. He always cheered her up and made her laugh.

'So I should think. Can't have her upsetting the others, though I suspect most of them are gay. Look at this one in the sailor suit. He's as camp as Christmas,' he went on, treating the toys as if they were alive.

'I hate being let down. I feel such a fool. He had sex with me, then buggered off. And then there's that bitchy Fiona. Has she gone with him? It hurts, Martin. It really does.'

'Impossible to avoid, I'm afraid, girl,' he replied, then pounced on his tortoiseshell cat, sunning itself in the window. 'Come out of there, Alfie! That tapestry cushion is for sale, not for you to park your butt on!' He scooped Alfie up in his arms, scolding affectionately, and the thought struck Lisa that he'd make a wonderful parent.

'Caring, loving, wanting – all part of being human,' he continued, scratching Alfie in that ticklish, feline place just under the chin. 'You can't go through life avoiding disappointment. I should know, dear. I've been there and –'

'It makes me afraid to even try,' she broke in.

'I know, but until you make room in your heart for good times, you may not recognise them if they up and hit you on the nose. When you're feeling shitty because someone's let you down, make an extra effort to pamper yourself. As Oscar Wilde said, "To love oneself is the beginning of a lifelong romance."'

'I didn't know you were a philosopher,' she returned. 'Where did you pick that up?'

'In a treatment centre ... too much booze,' he

answered, his light tone concealing a wealth of painful experience.

She hugged him impulsively, Alfie and all. He really was a very cuddly sort of person. She said, 'I'm sorry. I really didn't know. I've noticed that you never drink, but I thought it was to do with weight gain or spoiling your complexion or something.'

'That too. It doesn't do 'em any favours.'

'I'm sorry,' she repeated, feeling inadequate.

'That's OK. I don't hide it, but it's not the sort of thing you shout from the rooftops. Nothing's ever wasted, though. It put me in touch with myself.'

Lisa smiled, beginning to feel better.

'Anyway,' he continued, 'shafting David wasn't a waste of time, was it? You got off on it, didn't you?'

'Oh, yes,' she sighed, awash with memories.

'That's OK, then. Hang on to it. And you must have enjoyed getting revenge on Paul. Ooh, I'll bet you flexed your claws. Are you going to tell him?'

'Not yet,' she said, slowly stirring her tea. They had retired to the storeroom, Alfie stalking off huffily with his tail in the air.

'Will you?' Martin asked.

'I'll see what happens.'

She was determined to be cautious. No diving in at the deep end. There was too much at stake. Not only her peace of mind but her business venture. The stall was taking off. It was imperative that she visit another auction very soon.

Martin lit a cigarette and asked, eyes gleaming with mischief, 'Tell me all about David. I want every single detail. What did he do? What's his place like? And has he got a whopper?'

Lisa blushed. 'Well, yes, as a matter of fact, he has.'

'Is he cut or au naturel? Did he use a condom? Did he make you come? You know you can tell me.'

It was like talking to a close and very special girlfriend. 'He hasn't been circumcised. Yes, we were careful, though he said he'd been tested and was in the clear. I haven't, but I suppose I should, though I can't imagine Paul plays away, can you?'

Martin screwed up his eyes thoughtfully. 'I don't know. You never can tell. Men are such immediate creatures. They get a hard-on and have to put it somewhere. They don't think.'

'Don't you trust Phil?'

'As far as I can throw him,' Marin declared, and lifted the teapot. It was shaped like a little house. 'Another?' he said, and poured when she nodded. 'But, my darling, I've told him in no uncertain terms that if I find out he's been cottaging I'll chop his bollocks off.'

'And you would.'

'Too right I would.'

That flash of anger reminded her that he was a force to be reckoned with. She wouldn't like to cross him, and imagined that Phil felt the same. The wrath of Martin was probably enough to keep him on the straight and narrow.

'I'm invited out to tea tomorrow,' Lisa said, changing the subject.

'Where? Can I come?' Martin loved meeting new people and playing to the gallery.

'Not this time. Later, perhaps. Remember me mentioning a woman called Daphne Nightingale?'

'Yes. What a great name. Shall I change mine to Martina Nightingale? Wonderful for my drag act.'

'Shut up and listen. She lives off the Mall, in Cranshaw House.'

'Nice district. Very upswept. But you'd better let me meet her sometime to get a suss on her. I worry about you, Lisa.'

'I know you do, Martin. Thank you.'

'I'll send Arnaldo with the car,' Daphne had said.

Lisa wondered about this as she got ready. She had seen a man helping unload at the start of the market

85

and then pack up at close of trading, the goods being transported in a white Mercedes R reg. He was a background figure and Daphne had not introduced them.

The day had been a classic summer one, cloudless and bright, and Lisa had lazed on the roof garden, almost making herself late. It had been a last-minute scramble to be dressed by 4.30. She pulled on a thin, fitted shirt and a long skirt, was sparing with make-up, and let her hair fall loosely round her glowing, sun-kissed face.

She was just putting on her sandals when the bell rang. 'OK. I'm coming!' she shouted, and ran down the stairs.

She flung open the door and stopped short. A man was framed there. He removed his peaked cap and said in an accented voice, 'Miss Sherwin?'

'Yes,' she answered, confused as he was not quite what she had expected. He was as formal as an under-taker in his black suit and the person she had seen with Daphne had worn jeans.

'I'm Arnaldo Fabroni. Mrs Nightingale sent me,' he said, stepping to one side. His eyes lingered on the swell of her breasts, then he looked past her into the hallway.

Her heart beat faster, affected by his appraising look. It made her sharply aware of her nipples chafing against her cream bra, visible through the thin shirt.

Now she could see his features more clearly, and he was handsome in a distinctly foreign way: stocky but broad shouldered, with olive skin, lustrous brown eyes and wavy dark hair. He was older than Lisa had expected – forty-something.

His suit was smartly tailored, the single-breasted jacket covering a high-buttoned waistcoat. Wide shouldered, his body tapered to a narrow waist, and slim-fitting trousers enclosed his lean hips and under-scored the not inconsiderable bulge behind the front closure. His white shirt emphasised his swarthy complexion, fastened at the neck by a plain black tie. It was only then that Lisa realised this was a uniform.

He smiled at her suddenly, and her shyness vanished. He had a charming smile that lit up his eyes and transformed his whole face, dispelling the Mediterranean melancholy that possessed it in repose.

Unaccustomed to being chauffeur driven and feeling as if she was taking part in a 1930s movie, Lisa walked out and closed the door behind her. She returned the driver's smile and accompanied him to the waiting car. This was another surprise: a gleaming maroon vintage Bentley with classic lines.

Arnaldo opened the passenger door and stood back so that she could enter. Lisa caught sight of Martin and Phil peering nosily out of their shop window, and Martin grinned, nodded and gave her the thumbs up sign.

With the luxurious feel of genuine leather squidging beneath her bottom, Lisa made sure her skirt covered her legs and watched Arnaldo surreptitiously as he slid into the driver's seat. His shoulders rippled under the smooth fabric of his jacket, his hair brushed the collar and his hands controlled the wheel. The car purred into motion, gliding along, the interior smelling of sandalwood freshener mingled with top-quality calfskin.

I could get used to this, Lisa decided. Having him driving me, waiting on me . . . servicing me? Yes, the idea appealed, and she fantasised about living in a stately home somewhere and ringing for him when she felt horny. Nothing binding, and with herself in charge. He would do as she ordered.

'Arnaldo,' she would say. 'I want a massage. Use that perfumed oil the sheik has just sent me from Arabia.'

And, lying on a padded couch in her superbly furnished bedroom, she would wait in delicious anticipation for the feel of his hands working over her body.

'Is this right, madame?' he would say, not uniformed

now, but naked save for a very small towel round his hips.

Then he would lean over her, his oiled palms soothing away every tiny ache, and the towel would open and she would see his erection on a level with her face. She would only have to part her lips and stretch out her tongue to touch the tip and taste the salt of the pearly droplet standing at the slit, then ease a little closer and suck the bulging head into the warm, wet cavity of her mouth.

His hand would trail along the insides of her thighs, and she would part them laxly. His fingers would brush through her pubic floss, opening the gates of her secret garden and coaxing her clitoris from its hood. Then very gently, he would finger stroke her. Heat poured through her loins in a molten flood and she gave a mewling sound.

'Are you all right, Miss Sherwin?' Arnaldo asked, and she snapped out of her dream, seeing his eyes watching her in the rear mirror. They were alert and bright and lustful.

Colour flushed her cheeks and she clasped her handbag on her lap, covering herself as if the impossible could happen and he might see the agitation in her genitals.

'Oh, yes . . . perfectly,' she replied frostily.

He smiled again, a knowing smile which made her all the more hot and chaotic inside, then he said, 'We are almost there.'

So was I, she thought rapidly. How little you know, or perhaps you *do*, sexy and beautiful Arnaldo.

What use was her recent shower now? Wetness matted the hair around her sex, and sweat pooled between her breasts in their lacy, underwired baskets. Her clitoris throbbed between her swollen labial lips, and she was sure she could smell the scent of her arousal rising above that of talc, shower gel and even the pungent fragrance of Samsara.

Such a strong, feral odour. Nothing could disguise it. It was cunningly designed by nature to lure the male, encourage his erection and ensure that he impregnated the female. It's all a trap, she thought bitterly.

The Mall was a level shaded walk, and a tree-lined avenue led from it, with detached Edwardian mansions set back from the road. They had iron railings enclosing large gardens and rear entrances to what had once been coach houses, now converted to garages or even annexes, though some remained as stables, the occupants well able to afford horses.

Lisa knew the area well and had often strolled there, mulling over what she would do if she won the lottery. Buy one of those, certainly. It would be top of her list of priorities.

Quiet, peaceful, secluded and cocooned by wealth and privilege, Cranshaw House dozed in the late afternoon heat. The Bentley rolled through the sensor-controlled gates and came to rest at the front steps, gravel crunching under the tyres. Lisa had barely reached for the door handle when, with a click of his heels, Arnaldo was opening it for her.

He escorted her up the wide, shallow steps to the main door under a shell-shaped portico. It had solid brass fittings and art nouveau stained glass panels depicting peacocks with trailing, folded tails. A vestibule gave access to a spacious hall, dark and cool, with mosaic tiled floor, brown dados, William Morris wallpaper, picture rails, cornices and a lofty, ornately plastered ceiling.

The house had been built at a time when the British Empire looked fair set to last for ever. It was solid, overblown and impressive. Doors under carved architraves stood on either side of the hall, with passages disappearing into gloom at the back. A grand central staircase swept upward, the sunset glow pouring in through a full-length landing window, forming vibrant green, citrus-yellow and blood-red patterns on the woodwork.

Hunger possessed Lisa, an envious, craving, avaricious need to own this magnificent abode. And Arnaldo seemed a part of it, that cool, suave manservant who might have stepped right out of a Merchant Ivory film. The perfect gentleman's gentleman. Only in this case he belonged to a lady.

'This way, please,' he said, in his soft, mellifluent accent, and opened a double cedarwood door on the right.

'Ah, there you are, my dear,' Daphne said, rising from the depths of a wingchair facing tall French windows. These overlooked a spread of velvety green lawn, hedged by laurel and rhododendron bushes.

A sprinkler cast a misty spray over a life-sized stone nymph being embraced by a leering satyr. His hairy goat legs were pressed against her buttocks, his phallus buried deep between them. His hands clasped her breasts, the nipples poking through his fingers, and she wore an expression of extreme ecstasy – eyes rolled up, mouth open – like a saint being martyred.

'You like them?' Daphne murmured, standing close to Lisa, her skin breathing out the flowery scent of Chanel's Cristalle. 'Beautiful, aren't they? My husband brought them back from Italy. They once graced the garden of a Medici prince. He acquired Arnaldo, too. He's been with me for years, haven't you, *caro*?'

She smiled at him, and the look that passed between them was electrifying.

'They're lovely.' Lisa nodded, and a frisson of excitement, fear and anticipation clawed at her vitals. 'But not quite what I expected.'

Daphne looked at her intently, and said, 'Nothing is ever what one expects. Sit down, dear. Arnaldo shall bring in the tea things.'

Lisa perched on the edge of an ebonised chair with a

gilded leather back and glanced round the room, oddly nervous. 'It's all so perfect,' she breathed. 'You know so much about antiques. It makes me feel such an ignoramus.'

Daphne gave a tinkling laugh. 'It was my husband's doing, and he inherited the place anyway, lock, stock and barrel. It hadn't been changed since it was built and furnished in 1900. He had it rewired and the plumbing and central heating updated. He was American, you see, and couldn't bear the damp English climate.'

Lisa was conscious of a change in Daphne. They had only met twice before in the market atmosphere, and she seemed different here – relaxed, almost playful. She was very beautiful, despite her years, held herself proudly and had kept her figure. She was now wearing wide-legged trousers in oyster silk, with a jacket to match which had flowing sleeves and a low neckline edged with lace. Her hair, though highlighted, was abundant and coiled in a loose knot at the nape of her neck.

Her face, throat and slender hands were lightly tanned, and her eyes sparkled, holding a wealth of wordly wisdom. Long amber earrings dangled on each side of her face, accentuating its fine bone structure, and a rope of the same fossilised resin lay between her breasts.

'You've lived in America?' Lisa asked, as Arnaldo carried in a tray containing delicate china, a cake stand and a plate of cucumber sandwiches cut paper thin.

She tried to keep her voice steady, a bubble of excitement in her belly as he leant across to hand her a napkin. It was impossible to control the fiery spasm that darted through her loins as she caught his interested glance and inhaled his aftershave.

'Thank you, Arnaldo,' Daphne said, and reached for the Georgian silver teapot. He did not leave the room, but took up a stance near the window, stiff backed with arms folded over his chest.

Daphne handed a cup to Lisa and offered the cakes. 'No, thank you,' she said. 'I'm trying to cut down on sweet things.'

'Very wise,' Daphne agreed, selecting a sandwich and then glancing back at Lisa. 'I, too, avoid them, though it's hard. You have a lovely figure, my dear, rather like my own when I was young, and your eyes are such an unusual colour ... almost violet. My husband would have appreciated your beauty.'

'It's kind of you to say so, but I'm quite ordinary really. Is he still with you?' Lisa asked, sipping her tea self-consciously.

For some reason that she could not quite fathom, she was feeling distinctly uncomfortable. Daphne was regarding her in a speculative way, and she was all too aware of Arnaldo. She could feel his eyes boring into her back, a prickling sensation inching down her spine.

'He died some years ago,' Daphne answered, bone china cup held in her pink-lacquered fingers. 'He was much older then me. Twice my age when we married.'

'Really? I can't imagine having an old husband,' Lisa said, filled with curiosity about Daphne, the house and the mystery which she was becoming ever more convinced lay at the heart of it.

Daphne gave her a slow, considering stare, then lowered her voice and said confidingly, 'It was enlightening, to say the least.'

'How did you meet him?' Lisa felt it rude to ask such personal questions, but it seemed that Daphne was eager to talk.

'It was at the outbreak of the Second World War,' Daphne said, her eyes misting as she looked back over the decades. 'My parents, fearing for my safety, sent me to New York to stay with my godfather, Walter Nightingale. I never saw them again. Not long after I had gone, they were killed in an air raid.'

'How dreadful for you. Mine are both dead, so I understand how you felt,' Lisa said, leaning over impulsively and touching Daphne's slender hand where it lay in her silken lap.

She felt Daphne tremble, and then seize her in a surprisingly strong grip. 'I'm aware of this,' she said.

'You are?' Lisa was puzzled, part of her wanting to pull away, but another wishing to stay close to this interesting woman.

'Your history is not unknown to me. I am very careful in my choice of friends,' Daphne went on, with a peculiar intensity in her voice. 'I have few ... only Arnaldo. We live here alone, and I don't encourage callers. We like it that way, don't we, Arnaldo?'

'Yes, madame,' he replied.

Unable to resist, Lisa looked over her shoulder at him. He was still in the same position, awaiting his mistress's instructions. Lisa had a gut feeling that these concerned herself.

'He does everything for me ... and I mean *everything*,' Daphne said, and her grip on Lisa's hand became stronger. 'I feel drawn to you, and I hope you'll permit me to help you.'

'In what way?' A warning tocsin rang in Lisa's brain. There seemed to be a hidden agenda in every word Daphne uttered.

'To teach you about antiques and, perhaps, about life. There is no pressure, Lisa. Whatever happens is of your choosing.'

'What do you want of me in return?' Lisa stammered, disconcerted by Daphne's intent stare and the feel of Arnaldo so close to her.

'For you to use my knowledge in a way I no longer can. I had no child, Lisa, and I feel the lack now. There is much I can teach you, lessons I wish to impart to someone younger. Will you let me do this?'

Lisa lifted her shoulders in a confused shrug, saying, 'Yes ... I'd be glad to learn, especially about the trade. But I'm engaged and Paul doesn't like the idea of my working.'

'I saw your ring and guessed. Does Paul make you happy? Do you love him?'

'I'm not sure,' Lisa confessed, twisting the ring round and round on her finger. 'He represents security, and reminds me of the days when my father was alive.'

'That's no reason for marrying him. I don't think you're keen, are you? Is there someone else?' Daphne asked sharply.

Lisa was reluctant to mention David Maccabene; ashamed to admit they had had sex and now he had wafted off into the blue. Also, it seemed that Daphne and he were acquainted, and she had an uneasy feeling she would warn her against having anything to do with him.

'I'm sort of entangled in this marriage thing. Paul's mother has it arranged, a big do, with half the town invited . . . Well, the people she considers suitable. She's a snob of the first order,' Lisa said bitterly, voicing her resentment.

Daphne shook her head, the rays of the dying sun forming a nimbus round her. 'So far you haven't given me one valid reason for agreeing,' she said slowly. 'I know all about marrying in haste and repenting at leisure. Don't do it, my dear. Is he a skilled lover?'

'No!' Lisa shot out.

'Then call it off. My husband was, and this kept us together, although I can't say that I was happy with him. But he was inventive and sex was never boring. He controlled me . . . mastered me. Do you know what it's like to have a master?'

'No. I don't think I'd enjoy that. I want to be independent . . . of Paul . . . of all men,' Lisa almost shouted, horrified to feel hot tears scalding her eyes. 'I want to be like you! Free to do what I want when I feel like it. You have your own business and that's my ambition. Did you always deal in antiques?'

'Indeed, no. Walter was the collector. A rich man who could indulge his whims. That's how he came to marry me. I was one of them. Possibly the most important and certainly the most expensive whim he ever had,' Daphne replied drily, her coral lips curving in a pensive smile. Then she gestured to Arnaldo, commanding, 'More hot water, please.'

'Yes, madame,' he said, before bowing and leaving the room.

'You loved him?' Lisa asked. She leant forward, her skirt opening over her knees to reveal toast-brown legs and sandalled feet.

Daphne spread her hands in an expressive gesture. 'I asked you that just now, but what is love? An overworked, hackneyed word. Walter was a powerful man; a business tycoon who dominated me from the time I was thirteen. He was unmarried and had no children. I filled this gap, and he was so proud of me. I went to the best schools, met the best people, all descended from New York's exclusive four hundred, though everything had been shaken up by the war.'

'But?' Lisa put in. 'There has to be a "but" somewhere.'

'Yes, there was a big "but", I'm afraid. I resented him and all he represented. I longed to go home to England but was completely under his thumb. He was my legal guardian, you see. So I ran away.'

'Where?' Lisa was enthralled, losing her sense of unease and wanting to hear more.

Arnaldo returned with the hot-water jug. He placed it on the tray and retired to his place by the window, but not before subjecting Lisa to a searching stare that focused on the way her button-through skirt opened over her legs. One knee was thrown over the other, exposing the backs of her thighs and the strip of cream lycra that stretched over her secret lips.

'You want to know what happened to me?' Daphne asked.

'Oh, yes, please.'

'I had a talent for dancing and singing. One which he

had encouraged so that he might show me off to his friends. Many a night I had been made to perform when he was throwing a party. So now I decided to use this to earn a living. New York is a huge city, and one may lose oneself in it, particularly in those far-off days. So long ago. A different time. A different world.'

'How brave you were. I don't think I could have done that,' Lisa mused, as the sun slowly sank and the room grew dim.

'"Needs must when the devil drives",' Daphne quoted. 'And Walter was a devil, all right. I was sixteen and he wanted my virginity. I was determined that he shouldn't have it. Idealistic, I dreamed of falling in love, and giving myself to my beloved. And yet, Walter fascinated me. He appealed to all that was dark and perverse in my nature. I was afraid of this; afraid of what it might do to me if it was released.'

'So you left him?'

'I went into hiding, dyed my hair and changed my name. It took him eighteen months to find me.' Daphne's mouth hardened, and her eyes turned to flint. 'I thought I had found my Prince Charming, but he proved to be a pimp. Yes, that was the company I was forced to keep – a cabaret performer in dives on the seamy side of town. I sank so low after he abandoned me that I worked in strip joints. He had broken my heart. I no longer cared who used my body, just as long as they paid.'

Lisa sat frozen in the chair, too shocked to speak as she listened to this incredible confession.

'I ended up in a peep show,' Daphne continued. 'Nightly I'd gyrate my naked body in front of a large window in a boxlike compartment. Men watched me through the smeared, steamy glass, unable to touch me but wanking themselves off, each of them in his private world, separated from the others. They were sad little men, creeping through the squalid streets to find me and the six other girls, each of us working shifts. Failed

96

men, madmen, obsessives, who knows? I didn't care as long as I had my wages at the end of each session.'

'So you weren't exactly a prostitute?' Lisa asked at last, and a slow, heavy feeling permeated her loins as she imagined herself cavorting behind glass in front of several men; holding her breasts, rubbing her nipples and diving a hand down to fondle her pubic hair.

'Not precisely. No one touched me – only myself and sometimes one of the other girls if the management decided to hot it up with a lesbian scene. The cubicle was softly lit, and the music seductive. I couldn't see the faces of the watchers because the glass was a two-way mirror, but I knew they were there. They were anonymous, but I wasn't.'

'You weren't embarrassed?' Lisa whispered, the build-up of tension in her sex distressingly strong.

'Embarrassed? Oh, no. In the heart of the darkness that had corroded my soul, I revelled in my power. There might be five or six men out there, hands buried between their legs as they handled their balls and stroked their cocks to climax.'

It was so strange to hear such a ladylike person using crude language, adding to the eerie, other-worldly sensation that was crawling over Lisa.

The room was almost dark now, and Arnaldo switched on a table lamp with a bronze base and an opaque glass shade fringed with fine beads. Daphne's face was thrown into relief, and her complexion warmed and the lines smoothed away. She seemed little more than a girl as she sat there, lost in her recollections.

Lisa was with her every step of the way, her vivid imagination picturing the dungeonlike basement beneath a busy sidewalk where women catered for the lusts and dreams of clients.

'Not only women, of course,' Daphne continued, with that unnerving telepathic sense she appeared to possess. 'Good-looking men, too. Everyone was catered for; young, old, rich or not so rich. Every sly, devious, forbidden desire was brought to fulfilment. We lived in goldfish bowls for the entertainment of those woeful failures who would never know the bliss of sex with love . . . sex given openly and freely. They had to buy their satisfaction.'

'Do you hate men?' Lisa breathed, her nipples taut against her top, and the gusset of her panties drawn tight between her unfurled labial wings. The need for Arnaldo was rising to boiling point.

Daphne smiled serenely. 'I don't hate them. Not any more. I did once, but Walter cured me of that. He gave me back my soul.'

'But I thought you disliked him, too?'

'My dear, you are still young. One day you'll understand that there are many facets to liking, or loving, or even hating. Things are not all black and white. There are many shades of grey between, and many ways of enjoying sex.'

'But you didn't enjoy showing yourself to those men, did you?' *She did, and I could*, Lisa thought, and hot waves of shame and desire sent the blood racing to her face.

'Sometimes I did. I've told you, it empowered me. Haven't you ever wanted to masturbate with a crowd watching you?' Daphne's question made the heat leave Lisa's cheeks and swamp her delta, making her pleasure bud throb.

'I don't know . . .' she faltered, aware that she was lying.

'I'm sure you do,' Daphne said firmly, and advanced a hand to glide over Lisa's knee, so cool against the warm flesh. 'There were times when I would wallow in the slime, enjoying my cage in that hell of dubious desires. I'd squeeze and pinch my swollen nipples, then keeping one hand there, slide the other down and brush my fingers through my bush, separate my folds and frig myself. I'd lean forward, feeling the cold glass pressing against my breasts and letting the punters feast on the dark, aroused circles of my nipples ... So near, yet so far.'

'You tormented them?'

'Teased them a little ... made them ache with want. Their pricks leapt in their fists, smearing their hands with pre-come juice. Maybe they even spurted their milky-white tribute to me ... their untouchable goddess.'

'How did Walter find you? Was it there?' Lisa whispered, unable to stop lifting one hand to her breast and fondling the rock-hard nipple poking through both fragile brassiere and thin shirt.

'It was. Unbeknown to me, he was a voyeur, and if he couldn't organise a situation where he could indulge this passion, then he used peep shows. Fate ordained that he visited my goldfish bowl one night. Of course, I had no idea he was there, but he was able to view me ... my breasts, my wide-open slit ... He saw me, he recognised me, he wanted me.'

'I was called into the manager's office after the show, filled with dread, thinking that maybe I'd not been doing my job properly and was about to be dismissed. I had the rent to find on my miserable room in a tenement, I had food to buy ... I was so sick of being poor. And there was Walter, suave in top hat, tails, the lot. He had been to the opera.'

'Was he angry with you?' Lisa's heart was beating fast, her blood throbbing in her veins.

'No. More sorrowful than angry. He took me to supper and we talked. Or rather he talked while I stuffed myself with food ... I'd seen nothing like it for almost two years. I drank, too. He ordered champagne to celebrate. We went back to his house near Central Park. It felt like going home. There, in his bedroom, he put me across his knee and spanked me.'

'Like a naughty child?'

Daphne laughed and her long throat arched, earrings

99

swinging. 'Oh, no . . . nothing like a child! He punished me like a master chastising his slave. It was my first taste of domination, and I found it such a sweet release. The sharp, burning slaps eased my guilt and raised my libido. Walter was an expert in the fine art of pain and pleasure. He spanked my naked buttocks till they stung like fire, then anointed his hands with scented balm and soothed away the pain. His fingers slid between my crack, massaged my aroused pussy lips and found that little pearl of pleasure, playing with it till I came in so strong a surge that I lost consciousness for a moment. I'd never had so marvellous an orgasm.'

'Did he have sex with you?'

'Not right away. He used my breasts like a vagina, pressing them together to form a tunnel and working his enormous cock up and down between them till he ejaculated, spraying my face, my hair, even my eyes, with semen. Next day, he had me see his doctor, to make sure I'd not picked up a disease. Once I was pronounced clear, he went ahead with the wedding plans. I was just eighteen. Remind me to show you some photographs taken around that time. I think you'll find them stimulating.'

Daphne's cameo features were flushed about the cheekbones, her eyes shining like sapphires. She slipped undone the buttons of her silk jacket and her breasts rose towards Lisa, cradled in a black bra, the nipples exposed through slits. Brown and distended, they seemed to look at Lisa questioningly.

Lisa could not move, overwhelmed by what she had heard and what she was now seeing. As if on cue, Arnaldo moved over to stand behind his mistress. He slid his hands across her shoulders, caressing them through the silk, then, slowing, advanced towards the naked tips of her breasts. He seized one between his thumb and forefinger, and drew it further from the open-tipped brassiere. Daphne closed her eyes and leant her head back against him.

While he fondled Daphne's teats, his eyes met Lisa's, holding her fixed and when she looked away – unable to stop watching him arousing Daphne – he smiled widely over even, white teeth.

Daphne gave a long drawn sigh and opened her eyes. Arnaldo continued to fondle her breasts, cupping both in those strong hands, his thumbs revolving over the nipples.

'Do you want him to do this to you?' Daphne asked Lisa.

'I don't know . . . He's yours, isn't he?' she gasped.

Daphne chuckled, arching her spine so that Arnaldo could push the bra down from her breasts. They swelled over the edge, full and alabaster white. The nipples were engorged and suffused with blood, the brown tinged with scarlet.

'I told you, Lisa, I want you to share my experiences. What better way to begin than with him?'

'I couldn't!' Lisa protested, almost leaping to her feet, then sinking back on the chair as the glory of the proposition hit her.

'A massage, perhaps? He's a trained masseur.'

My daydream in the car! Lisa thought, panicking. What is she? Some kind of witch? She seems able to read my mind.

In a daze, she felt herself being raised from her chair, Daphne on one side, Arnaldo on the other, and taken from the room and up the staircase. Her footsteps were muffled by thick carpet and her eyes filled with the images of a long corridor, the shaded wall lamps interspersed with paintings in gilt frames. They were extraordinary pictures, classic in style, of couples straining in sexual congress. Some featured women and men, others men with men or women with women. All were beautiful, lewd and exciting.

'Walter's collection, but only part of it. There are others,' Daphne said, her jacket still unfastened and her breasts forced high by the tightness of the brassiere cutting like a band beneath them.

They paused before a door. Arnaldo turned the handle. Lisa was guided over the threshold into a room which took her breath away. The light was subdued and the windows draped in sumptuous brocade curtains, swagged and fringed and held back by cords ending in heavy tassels. The colours were rich and flamboyant, the bed a brass four-poster with blue enamelled plaques and a tester upheld by a crown. The towering edifice was draped in lace. The rugs were Persian and the ottoman and deeply cushioned settee were upholstered in bird-of-paradise fabric. The scene was reflected in mirrors with carved foliate surrounds.

'Here we can be private, darling,' Daphne said, and guided Lisa towards the bed. 'Are you prepared to allow us to pleasure you?'

This was such an unusual request that Lisa was bereft of words. Taking her silence as consent, Daphne signalled to Arnaldo, who unbuttoned Lisa's shirt and lifted it over Lisa's head. He stood back, considering Lisa's nipples that had stiffened against their covering. Reaching out, he pinched one, then pressed the palm of his hand against it, commencing a circular motion.

Lisa arched her spine and thrust her breasts high, the pleasure stabbing her womb. She wriggled her hips and moaned. Arnaldo moved to the other nipple, scratching it through the lace. Her free hand dipped down to seize the hem of her skirt and ruck it up about her waist. Then his fingers pressed into the cleft dividing Lisa's sex; her panties were already wet. Finding the ardent little button of flesh, he rubbed it skilfully.

Lisa gasped, and she rubbed her pubis against his tantalising, deliriously wicked caress. Her oceanic fragrance rose from the heat between her legs, and she could smell him, too – stronger, more potent – and was filled with a mad longing to lie down on the bed with him.

He withdrew his hand, and Lisa stood there with aching nipples and a pulsating bud.

'Will you play our little game?' Daphne asked.

Lisa nodded, willing to agree to anything if only someone would ease the fearful desire pounding through her. She needed caresses, kisses, a mouth on her clit, fingers or a cock in her vagina. Desire raged through her, rampant and wanton, making her burn with frustration. She clutched at her damp crotch, remembering the men watching the girl in the goldfish bowl, and her loins yearned. She wanted to expose herself; to rub her clitoris to orgasm in front of an audience.

Lisa could see Arnaldo's erection tenting his black trousers. This evidence of his arousal added fuel to her already raging fire. Standing before her, he unfastened her waistband and her skirt fell to her feet. Then, so close that the solid mass of his hidden cock brushed against her belly, he reached round and unhooked her bra. He slid it down her arms and dropped it to lie by her skirt.

She wanted to fold her arms round her breasts and put a hand over her mound, but did neither. She was in the grip of such fierce carnal heat that her nakedness did not matter. Now Arnaldo discarded his shirt, displaying a stunningly beautiful muscular torso. His unblemished skin was coppery brown, his arms darkly furred, and there was a scribble of hair on his chest, through which the wine-red discs of his small male nipples gleamed. The dark hair scrawled down in a thin line to his navel and as he loosened his belt and his trousers slid a little lower, it formed a wiry thicket over his belly.

Lisa was enthralled. Even David had not had the power to move her like this magnificent specimen. Arnaldo possessed film-star good looks. He was a typically handsome Italian male; aware of his manhood, delighting in it and in the promise of pleasure.

By now, Lisa had forgotten Daphne, who stood watching them, her tongue tip peeping out between her lips. Arnaldo slid his arms round Lisa and pulled her into his embrace, his chest hairs brushing her erect nipples. She sighed and melted, rubbing her groin against his hardness. She opened her lips to receive his kiss, feeling almost faint with emotion, her senses swimming as she breathed in his wonderful smell, a combination of classy perfume and his own personal body odour.

He urged her towards the bed. The edge of the mattress caught the backs of her knees and she sat down, watching him with wide eyes. He sat beside her, took off his shoes and socks and then eased his trousers over his lean flanks. His serpent reared its head, a massive thing rising from its hairy nest. He guided her hand to it, saying, 'Touch me, Miss Sherwin.'

She reached out tentatively and her hand closed round his member, barely able to circle it with thumb and first finger. It throbbed against her palm, the shaft satin-smooth, and she ran her fingers over the purple-red glans, using its crystal tears as a lubricant.

Arnaldo sucked in a sharp breath, then eased himself from her grasp, sliding his hands under her hips and pulling her forward so that her legs, bent at the knees, dangled over the side of the bed. He sank between them, gently removing the tiny briefs, raising them to his nose and sniffing appreciatively before casting them aside.

Somehow this action excited her more than all the others, his uninhibited enjoyment in the scent of her secretions signalling him out as a man who adored women and everything associated with them.

She relaxed, her arms flung above her head, surrendering herself to Arnaldo, confident that he would not disappoint her. His lips trailed all over her from nipples to her waist, then around her navel and, finally, kissed her delta. He ran his fingers round the rim of her labia and into the juice gathering at her vulva. She spread her thighs wider, and held her swollen sex apart.

His hair tickled her thighs as he lowered his head and found her nubbin with his tongue, forking against it, sucking it, toying with it. He slipped two fingers inside her, probing and stretching the plushy wall, while his tongue rotated on her clitoris, flicking it, feeding on it, drawing it out till it was gem-hard. She was getting closer and closer to annihilation.

She gripped his head, holding him to her as she blossomed within, the sweet heat beginning to build. It rose from the tips of her toes, up the backs of her legs and into her groin, and she suddenly convulsed in an orgasm that forced a scream from her.

Arnaldo positioned himself between her thighs and, as she still spasmed, guided his shaft smoothly into her. He kissed her as he penetrated her warmth, his lips and tongue tasting of her juices. She kicked her legs round his waist and clasped him close, pulling him harder into her, his virile member filling her to capacity and butting against her cervix.

He came quickly, while her internal muscles still contracted to echoes of fading orgasmic waves. She felt his cock grow even larger and twitch within her and then heard him cry out as he reached a shuddering climax.

Daphne lay face down on the padded bench, naked as the day she was born. Arnaldo had applied a generous coating of perfume oil and was now massaging every inch of her.

'What do you think of Miss Sherwin?' she asked him lazily.

'As you say, she is beautiful and ideally suitable for your purpose, madame,' he replied, working down each knobble of her spine.

'You did remember to set the camcorder, didn't you?,' she remarked. 'There it will be, frozen in time. We'll watch it later. I shall enjoy seeing Lisa orgasm again, and your bottom going up and down. You have a lovely tush, Arnaldo.'

'Thank you, madame.'

'Thank *you*, Arnaldo.'

By now, he had travelled down Daphne's spine to the dimple at the division of her bottom cheeks. He kneaded the svelte rump and the backs of her thighs, then up a little, slipping his fingers between and spreading the oil around her anus, easing into and around the tiny nether hole. Daphne drew in a breath, and pressed against that invasion of her most private place. Arnaldo's finger disappeared within to the first knuckle, then the second.

A deep, secret flame ingnited in Daphne's core, adding to the arousal she had experienced all the time Lisa was in the house. While Arnaldo drove her home, she had been sorting through her photographs, each one bringing back a memory of times past as she decided which to show to Lisa when she next visited.

Had she loved Walter? She certainly missed him when he died. No one had taken such good care of her, before or since. She had been his slave but the submission had been voluntary. He might have mastered her, yet she controlled him, playing on his appetites. And her imagination surpassed his when it came to sexual diversity.

And I'm still enjoying it, even now when most women think they are beyond it, she thought triumphantly. Thank you for that, Walter. You trained me how to make desire endure. The young act as if they invented sex. Little do they know or understand.

Arnaldo's knuckle brushed against her fair bush, and the warmth within her grew as his finger stroked her labial groove. She parted her legs and he massaged more oil into the swollen cleft. His touch on her clitoris caused a rainbow burst of colour in her head. He moved behind her and she felt his thighs against her buttocks and the hot, heavy head of his cock.

He slipped a hand under her and his fingers settled on her stiff little bud. As he increased the friction he mounted her and, his weapon well greased by the lotion, penetrated the forbidden world of her rectum.

Daphne moaned as she took the full force of it. She was no virgin there: Walter had made sure she was well stretched, often preferring this tight aperture to the more conventional avenue. Arnaldo drew her clitoris out between his fingers, pinching the head and bringing her to an explosive orgasm that left her shaking.

Then he concentrated on his own release, pumping into her frenziedly. Matching his urgency, she worked her hips up and down on his shaft, slamming against him and feeling it driving into her secret depths. With a barking cry, he erupted inside her in a great surge of release.

He lay across her in the afterglow, then stood up, rearranged his clothing and wrapped her in a bath towel. She smiled up at him sleepily, and clung to him with her arms about his shoulders as he carried her into the bedroom and over to the four-poster.

'Shall we have a drink, Arnaldo?' she purred, catlike in her satisfaction. 'Bring in a tray and come to bed, my darling. We'll watch the video of our dear young friend, Lisa.'

Chapter Five

One of Mike's favourite stomping grounds was The Fleece and Firkin, situated in the village of Little Deverel, far enough away from the town to prevent Valerie turning up unexpectedly.

'A meeting with members of the Thespians,' he announced over breakfast. 'There's the Christmas panto to organise. Can't get these things moving too early, especially with the wedding and then our holiday in Tenerife.'

'I'm glad you booked again,' Valerie said, topping up his coffee cup as they sat in their gleaming kitchen. 'I love the Canary Islands. It's so clean and civilised. Such a nice type of people go there, too.'

She was not yet dressed, wrapped in a loose negligée of hunter-green polyester which exactly matched the kettle, toaster and sandwich maker standing on the marble-effect top. Having read about how fashionable this colour was in a woman's magazine, she had spent a lot of Mike's money kitting out her kitchen in the same shade, her perfectly usable but unfashionable pots and pans ending up in a charity shop run by volunteers drawn from the ranks of Woodlanders.

Their splendid farmhouse conversion had only been

completed five years ago, but already she had a yen to move into Kingsmead. She fancied the upmarket traditional-style homes that Mike and Paul were building. As she often said, she went for things that *looked* antique, but did not want the genuine article.

Junk shops, car-boot and rummage sales left her cold. In her childhood they had been her hard-up, working-class mother's salvation, but now Valerie cringed at the thought of being seen there, afraid people might think she could not afford to buy new.

She had tried, mostly successfully, to push her humble beginnings behind her, avoiding her sisters and brothers. After shunting her parents into an old folks' home, she had been secretly relieved when they faded away within a short time of each other.

'So you won't be in till late?' she asked Mike, leaning back and stretching in voluptuous luxury.

She tensed her arms over the sides of her chair and hollowed her shoulders so the curves of her throat and breasts were emphasised, the deep 'V' of her cleavage framed in nylon lace.

''Fraid not,' he replied, sheafing through his mail but registering, a little wearily, the animal attraction which she exuded in warm, feral waves.

Valerie was as hungry for sex as a bitch on heat, and expected him to provide it. Which he did, of course, though often firing up his lust when they were in bed by recalling the firm body of Lisa Sherwin, or even the plump buttocks and loose breasts of Maggie, who responded more than adequately to desire but did not demand affection.

'What am I supposed to do with myself all evening?' Valerie asked, pouting, and gave a toss of her hair which had a slightly brassy tinge in the morning sunlight.

She never appeared without make-up and had dusted pressed powder over her face, but Mike noticed the fine lines at the outer corners of her eyes and the puffiness beneath them. He sighed, having wakened with a hard-on after dreaming about screwing Lisa. Now a residual erection was still there, brushing against his cotton boxer shorts and summer-weight grey trousers.

Valerie noticed it and a delighted smile lifted her carmined lips. 'Darling!' she exclaimed, easing her chair closer and reaching down to press the semi-stiff rod lying somewhere between his groin and lower belly. 'You are rude, but I like it. Didn't you have enough rumpty-tumpty last night?'

He arched his pelvis against her palm, grinning as he said, 'I could never have enough of you, Val.'

Oh, the old, worn cliché, he thought. And she believes it, or pretends she does, though she's never one to face the truth even when it stares her in the face.

She wormed her finger into the top of his trousers, undid the waist button and eased down the zip, lifting his cock out. She stared down with bright eyes and a lascivious smile as it grew, and watched the foreskin wrinkling back and the reddish helm burgeoning.

'I should be leaving,' he murmured, half heartedly. 'There are prospective customers coming to view the show-house.'

'It won't take a minute,' she whispered breathily and, leaning over, let a drop of saliva fall on his glans, then polished the shiny, sensitive tip.

Her robe fell open and her big breasts swung forward; generous breasts with saucer-shaped brown areolae from which the puckered nipples jutted, large as cobnuts. Mike could smell the heat of her arousal rising from between her ample thighs, and caught a hint of his own emission clinging there from last night's coupling. It was a heady brew and, combined with her experienced fondling of his member, made it impossible for him to go.

There was that familiar ache in his balls and the heavy pulse stirring his cock which he never could resist. Valerie was breathing quickly, bent over her task, intent and eager, determined to milk him dry. He knew what she was thinking: If I drain him of the last drop of spunk, he won't even look at any other woman today.

Though she never accused him, he was sure she was suspicious, and covered his tracks carefully. It suited him to remain married to her at the moment, especially with Lisa about to become his step daughter-in-law. Complicated, but he thought he had it right, and the title had a forbidden, incestuous ring that made his penis throb.

'Oh, Val, that's great,' he murmured, his hand buried in her hair. A quick glance down showed him the barest trace of root regrowth, but her strong, capable hands compensated for the blonde lie, borne out by the colour of her pubic bush.

Her driving compulsion to watch him ejaculate added to his excitement. He knew how much she enjoyed seeing him spurt. He could feel that rushing sensation gathering like a latent storm in his loins. Valerie rubbed him harder and faster, and ecstatic release overwhelmed him, powerful milky jets shooting over her hand.

'Lovely,' she sighed, and massaged some of it into her naked breasts. 'So warm . . . so creamy . . .'

Mike collapsed against her, his penis subsiding. They both jumped as his mobile bleeped. He pulled it from his jacket pocket and spoke brusquely, then folded it away and did up his fly.

'Got to go, love,' he said, standing over Val and squeezing one of her pebble-hard teats. 'See you later.'

Valerie watched him leave, then when she was sure she was alone, slumped low on her spine, opened her legs and dipped a finger into her vulva. Drawing the wet tip slowly and sensuously between her parted sex lips, she spread her juices over her clitoris. As she massaged herself she imagined it was a man's hand doing it to her.

Several faces floated in her mind's eye, belonging to

111

men she fancied. Her solicitor, always so smooth and suave; her tennis coach, half her age and rugged. She had often secretly dreamed of taking the latter's penis out of his pristine white shorts and sucking it. Her heated imagination supplied a wealth of masturbation fantasies.

Her desire increased, her bud throbbing with painful intensity. She pushed two fingers of one hand inside herself while keeping up the rhythmical strokes over her clitoris with the other. Her pubis thrust high to meet the pleasure.

'Oh . . . ooh . . .' she murmured, rocking her hips and concentrating on her love bud.

Eyes closed, she visualised it, inflamed and swollen – her precious centre of enjoyment. She could feel it thrumming under her fingers, demanding release. Sometimes she could delay the moment of crisis, playing with herself for an hour or more, but not this morning.

Last night Mike had crudely raked at her lust without satisfying it. He did not always bother to please her, and his penis was sometimes an instrument of frustration not delight. Now she rubbed furiously until the waves of passion rose to a crescendo. A ferocious orgasm struck like lightning, tossing her high then dropping her down, her whole body shaking.

After this, feeling totally relaxed, she cupped her tingling mound for a while, then gathered herself together, poured another cup of coffee and planned her campaign. She would shop, (shopping was an addiction with her), lunch with one of her women friends, and later call on Paul at what she liked to think of as his 'bachelor pad'. If he wasn't with that girl, of course.

The very thought of Lisa made her hackles rise.

The Fleece and Firkin was busy, but Mike had booked his usual table in a secluded corner. This part of the inn was at least five centuries old and, unlike his wife, Mike appreciated ancient timbers, carving and stone. He enjoyed the atmosphere of a genuine posting house where stagecoaches had once pulled into the courtyard to change horses and give their passengers a chance to answer the call of nature, partake of refreshments and sleep.

His enthusiasm was shared by his companion, Joyce Murray, wife of the brigadier. She was also a member of the town council planning committee, and the principal boy playing opposite Mike's villainous Abanazar in the forthcoming production of *Aladdin*.

'Where does Valerie think you are?' she asked, smiling across the table at Mike, the opened menu held in her hand.

'I was absolutely straightforward. I told her I'd be discussing the pantomime with members of the cast,' he replied, then dropped an eyelid in a wink, adding, 'What I didn't say was that there would be only one.'

Joyce looked at him through her smart, tinted, wire-framed spectacles. They gave her a vaguely mysterious air. Mike thought she had beautiful eyes, wide spaced and expressive. Apart from this feature, there was nothing particularly noteworthy about her offstage, but when she trod the boards a remarkable change of personality took place. It was as if her glasses were a mask and, on discarding them, another Joyce bloomed; confident, bold, even depraved if the role demanded it.

This had hit Mike like a mallet when they had first acted together in an ambitious staging of *Les Liaisons Dangereuses* by the Deverel Thespians. Mike had landed the plum part of the arrogant Vicomte de Valmont and Joyce was cast as his ruthless mistress, the Marquise de Merteuil, in this eighteenth-century tale of lust, seduction and revenge.

It was during this that they had yielded to the sexual attraction working like yeast between them. They welded themselves together at the genitals whenever they could: in deserted dressing rooms, at the rear of

113

the church hall used for rehearsals, in the back of his car, at her house when Raymond Murray was away. The fire had inevitably cooled after the first hectic frenzy of lust, but there remained a steady ember which flared up whenever the Deverel Thespians went into production.

As now.

A waiter hovered and Mike ordered. While they waited, he poured Joyce a glass of Chardonnay. They occupied an alcove designed for intimacy, although they could hear light conversation, the chink of cutlery, the clink of china and the undemanding strains of popular classics piped through concealed speakers.

Joyce was wearing a blue cotton dress with low-heeled white court shoes. She carried a matching hand-bag. Her naturally wavy fair hair was simply styled, and her outfit ladylike and discreet, but Mike's phallus stirred as he wondered if she wearing anything under it. He had discovered early on in their relationship that she often went without knickers, but he could never be quite sure until he had checked.

He slid along the banquette until he was seated beside her, then, under cover of the red and white check table cloth, he slipped a hand down across her knee, pushed up her skirt and skimmed over her thigh, finding that her filmy stockings were hold-ups with lacy tops. Her legs were placed neatly together, but as he approached the haven of her womanhood, so his fingers encountered no barrier. Neither silk nor cotton nor lycra stood between him and the object of his desire.

'You're not wearing panties,' he murmured into her ear.

Joyce did not move, her hands folded calmly on the table. Her eyes fixed on the panelled wall ahead of her, but Mike could see the little pulse fluttering in her throat where the collar of her dress was opened a modest three buttons.

Mike ran his finger up and down the tightly closed

cleft, no more than a line running vertically amidst the soft hairs of her mound. He pressed the fingerpad against the top of her slit. Joyce drew in a sharp breath, but gave no other sign of agitation.

He persisted, his finger penetrating deeper and forcing the tender clit head back against its stem, tracing it to its root. It swelled, and her labial lips swelled too, the secret door no longer so primly shut. Now her thighs had parted a smidgin.

Mike was positioned on the outside of the banquette so she was hidden from the rest of the room, his wide shoulders blocking her in. He lifted his other hand and touched the peak of one nipple, rubbing it through the blue cotton. He heard Joyce hiss, and felt her legs opening a little more. He kept up the steady movement of his fingertip on the fulcrum of her pleasure. Her nipple rose like a tiny nut under his hand. He palmed and circled it. Little beads of sweat formed on Joyce's upper lip and her glasses misted.

He was obsessed with the notion of making her climax before the waiter brought their order. His finger was dry on her clitoris, and he ventured lower to where her vulva kept guard over her portal. There he encountered a pool of honeydew. He smeared it up and over her sensitive, swollen gem. Almost at once he heard her breathing become ragged and felt her pelvis lift against his hand.

She flushed and panted and spasmed. He could feel her heart thudding as she tipped over into orgasm. He smiled and kissed her face, then her lips, feeling them soft and willing and wet under his, echoing the eagerness of her lower ones.

The waiter appeared, the food was served, and Mike admired the way in which Joyce behaved as if nothing had happened. She was so well brought up, a genuine middle-class lady – unlike Valerie whose aspirations to reach that exalted state would never be realised even if she lived to be 100. He was thankful for the tablecloth, which hid the massive bulge distending the front closure of his trousers.

'Why didn't you turn up at the barbecue?' he asked, handing Joyce a dish of succulent new potatoes tossed in butter and garnished with chopped herbs.

'We were away. Raymond wanted me to go with him when he attended some frightfully boring regimental reunion. I'd thought when he took early retirement that we'd be done with the army, but no such luck,' she replied, forking up a morsel of chicken pie for which the inn was renowned, the pastry being of melt-in-the mouth consistency.

'Have you been married long?' Mike realised that apart from her sexual preferences he knew little about her.

'I am his second wife. His children are older than me. Their mother died – of boredom, I suspect. The poor woman probably found it was her only means of escape.'

'Pretty drastic,' Mike demurred, refilling her glass.

'One gets that way living with Raymond. On, he's not such a bad old thing, and doesn't mind me working at all. He's generous and quite sweet and, frankly, I wasn't getting any younger.'

'And he likes acting, too.'

Joyce laughed. 'He can't wait to get into his dame gear for the panto and keeps asking me when Widow Twanky's costumes are arriving. Sometimes, I wonder about him. You see, our sex life isn't what you could call riveting. He's not that interested.'

'Just as well,' he whispered, and tangled a foot with hers under the table. 'Leaves all the more for me.'

When they had finished eating, the meal ending with a pineapple pudding served with clotted cream, Mike sat back and lit a cheroot while they drank coffee. It was then that he came to the crux of the meeting – the real reason why he had wined and dined Joyce and softened her up by lavishing pleasure on her.

'I'm rather worried about something, and would value your advice,' he began, reaching across the cloth and taking her hand, his thumb stroking the back of it.

She stared at him with those dark, partly screened eyes. 'Is it to do with the panto?'

'Oh, no. It concerns the girl my stepson is about to marry, Lisa Sherwin. She owns a building on the high street, a big old place with a shop. She lives in the flat above.'

'Is it listed?' Joyce asked, perking up.

'I believe so.'

'Then what's the trouble?'

'It needs extensive repairs. Other people may not be aware of it, but building is my profession and I can tell.'

Joyce frowned. 'Could it be a danger to the public?'

'It might be.'

'In that case, we'd better look into it. Has she carried out any unauthorised work? Possibly removed a feature without planning consent?'

Mike laughed softly, squeezing her fingers and saying, 'You make her sound like a criminal. Look here, I'll go over it, shall I? And report if anything is amiss. I may be mistaken.'

'Please do that, Mike, and let me know.'

He looked deeply into her eyes and said, 'What now?'

'It's a warm night,' she whispered, her lips curving seductively. 'Highfell Woods will be full of moonlight.'

'Let's go,' he growled. He snapped his fingers at the waiter and picked up the tab.

'He had sex with me,' Lisa said, legs folded under her as she curled on the couch in Martin and Phil's two-up, two-down cottage on the outskirts of West Deverel.

'Who did?' Martin asked, pausing in the doorway of the kitchen with an apron over his jeans. The most wonderful smell of roasting beef, potatoes and Yorkshire pudding wafted behind him.

'Arnaldo.'

'You lucky cow! That dark, yummy creature in the peaked cap?'

Even now she could not quite believe that weird evening of revelations. It was incredible.

Martin had asked Lisa to stay over on Saturday night and this was not the first time he had offered his hospitality. Phil's invitation was a foregone conclusion. He always fell in with Martin's ideas.

Paul had not liked it. Lisa got the feeling he was beginning to get the message.

'Oh, well, then,' he had said grumpily, 'if you're going to stay with those poofs, I may as well pop into Mother's after the match.'

'You do that,' she had agreed, with an irony lost on him. 'I'm sure she'll welcome you with open arms.'

'We can talk over the wedding,' he had said, brightening visibly. 'I've got to see the vicar. We must go along for regular instruction if he's to perform the ceremony. We should start now.'

'What a farce!' Lisa had cried. 'None of us ever go to church.'

'Don't be a pain, Lisa. We've already been through all this.'

It had degenerated into acrimony and Lisa had been glad to pack her overnight bag and turn up on Martin's doorstep. There was nothing Martin liked better than looking after friends, particularly when they were suffering some kind of trauma.

The cottage was quaint. It had been in need of decoration when he and Phil leased it, but they had worked on it in their spare time and it was almost finished. Centrally heated, courtesy of a wood-burning stove in the living room, the thick stone walls and little windows helped keep it cosy. It had a thatched roof, dormers and sloping ceilings in the bedrooms above. The stairs to these led from a door in the wall near the inglenook fireplace.

There were black beams in the lounge and a kitchen

built on at the back fitted with mod cons, and a further utility room housing the freezer, washing machine and tumble dryer. The decor was tasteful and in keeping with its antiquity, and the whole place was in immaculate order.

'You're much tidier than me,' Lisa remarked, sipping a glass of Bristol Cream and shifting Alfie, who had taken possession of her lap. He travelled everywhere with Martin, leaping into the car as soon as the door was opened.

'*I* am, you mean,' Martin returned, glancing at Phil. 'He's an untidy old bugger.'

'And you're a fussy queen – a proper nagbag,' Phil retorted good naturedly.

When they were seated at the kitchen table in front of a roast dinner complete with horseradish sauce and rich, dark gravy, Martin demanded, 'Come on, Lisa. Let's hear the gossip. Miss Nightingale? What's she really like?'

'Not what I expected, but then, as she said, nothing ever is.'

Lisa had not yet made up her mind about her, stunned by what she had seen and heard at Cranshaw House. After Arnaldo had made love to her, Daphne had helped her dress, gently and tenderly. A little later, Arnaldo had driven her home, once more the urbane chauffeur, said goodnight and left her.

She had slept little, tossing and turning and going over every moment of that strangely exciting visit. Is this what Daphne wanted of her from now on? It had obviously excited her. Far from being daunted, Lisa had found herself wanting to repeat the experience.

'Well, well,' Martin said when, between enjoying the superbly cooked meal, she had told them the whole story. 'She's a dark horse . . . or rather a dark mare. And Arnaldo is her gigolo . . .'

'I've always fancied being a gigolo,' Phil put in, lifting a glass of red wine to his lips and smiling at Martin over the rim. 'I knew a guy once who was a rich woman's plaything. He did really well out of her. She was always buying him presents – sportscars, gold watches, jewellery, silk shirts, Italian shoes, designer clothes. He shared them with his boyfriend.'

'You do realise he had to shaft her to get them?' Martin said frostily. 'I couldn't take on a woman. An elderly sugar-daddy, maybe.'

'I'm only joking,' Phil soothed. 'I'm happy with you, even if you are bossy. What's for pudding?'

Martin produced apple pie and custard, saying, 'Only plain fare, I fear. That's all I'm good at. Mother taught me how.' Having filled their dishes, he turned to Lisa, suddenly serious. 'Are you still friends with Mrs Nightingale?'

'Oh, yes. I like her very much and she's so wise. And Arnaldo is an ace lover.'

'You're getting quite experienced, aren't you?' Martin chortled. 'There's Paul, though we'll forget him, David Maccabene, and now this hunk. I'm jealous, I really am.'

'I don't want to think about it just now. Let's wash up and then see what's on the box.'

'Or how about a game of Scrabble?' said Phil.

'Both!' Martin insisted. 'It's lovely having you here, Lisa.'

'And it's lovely being here,' she replied sincerely.

When Lisa arrived back at the flat on Monday morning, a day later than she'd planned, she found an aggrieved message from Paul on the answerphone.

She listened to it, the good feeling she had acquired with Martin and Phil dissipating. Rewinding the tape and giving Paul a second hearing, she decided that it was high time she consolidated her position. If she was going to be independent, then she needed a more regular income than the market stall provided, so she took her courage in both hands and rang the number Tanith Marlow had given her.

120

'Hello?' Tanith said in dulcet tones.

'It's Lisa Sherwin. I met you at the market. Remember?'

'Sure I remember.' An unspoken question hung in the air.

'You asked me to call ... said you were looking for an assistant,' Lisa blundered on.

'Ah, yes ... When would you like to come and see us?'

'Today?' Lisa ventured.

'Make it around two-thirty. I'll look forward to that. Bye.'

It was one of those rare occasions when Lisa wished she had a better-looking vehicle. Much as she loved her old van, she longed to send it to that big scrapyard in the sky and buy something newer.

Fat chance of that, she reflected. I can barely pay the insurance on this, and I'm up to my eyes in bills. I'd like to be rich – not necessarily stinking rich, just comfortably off.

That's a lie, and you know it, she lectured herself.

I want to be not only stinking rich, but disgustingly, obscenely rich!

She studied the business card. The address was Hawkhurst Abbey, Dunscombe. The Deverel hills were honeycombed with villages and hamlets and she guessed it was one of those. Unfolding her road map, she examined various routes and located Dunscombe some five miles away. She ringed it with red Biro.

'Come on, Mavis,' she addressed the van. 'You can do it. I had thought of going to a car wash first and giving you a bit of a spruce up, but I don't think it'll make all that difference to your aged paintwork.'

It was a warm day, though the sun skulked behind a blanket of cloud. When she stopped for petrol, the garage attendant predicted rain. The road was unfamiliar, winding between hedges that bordered fields

121

where Jersey cows with swinging udders chewed the cud and gathered under the trees, and horses hung their big, noble heads over five-bar gates.

Crossroads. A signpost saying 'Dunscombe 1 mile', and she was soon driving down a narrow street with a few shops and a pub, then out again across a cobbled square, past a Norman church, and to the right where another, smaller sign said 'Hawkhurst Abbey'.

She swung into a leafy lane, drove half a mile and came to a dead end. Before her reared an enormous pair of ornamental iron gates supported by stone pillars topped by griffins on eternal sentry duty.

Help! Lisa thought. It looks spooky.

She climbed out and tried to open the gates. They were immovable. Then she saw the intercom and pressed the button.

'Yes?' a disembodied voice crackled.

'Lisa Sherwin to see Miss Marlow,' she replied firmly, refusing to let her frivolous mind conjure up the Adams Family.

The gates rolled on their hinges and Lisa drove between them.

A long, poplar-shaded drive faced her, and then the house, part manor, part ecclesiastical building. It was wholly awe-inspiring.

Valerie would absolutely hate it! Lisa thought, grinning to herself. Maybe I should suggest to Paul that we live somewhere like this after we're married, then she'd never visit us.

Married? Haven't I already decided that I'm not going to do it? she asked herself. Isn't this the reason I'm being so cold to him lately, apart from, being fed up to the back teeth with his selfish, clumsy love-making?

Jesus, you can't even call it that! she continued. Sticking his dick in me is more like it. Satisfying his lust. Though he's so snotty about trying anything new, he might as well buy a plastic doll with several orifices in which he can ram his organ. He doesn't want a real woman with feelings and desires of her own.

Lisa sat for a moment, staring through Mavis's midge-spattered windscreen at the house. It had all the rich stateliness of a Jacobean country seat, with wide mullioned windows, terraced balustrades and garden stairways. It should have been reassuringly pleasant, yet to one side stood a grey, forbidding pile, monastic in origin which overshadowed the later additions.

She got out at last, never taking her eyes from the formidable building, with its mystery and strange air of meloncholy, and a wildness that gave it an elusive, fascinating beauty. A fragrance pervaded her nostrils, made up of the leaf mould of hundreds of summers – the scent of decaying nature mixed with herbs from foreign lands.

The house seemed to be encircled by a triple ring of silence: the great walls, the still waters of the moat and the park with its mute army of trees.

The silence was suddenly broken. The front door opened wide and an exceedingly thin figure stood in its mausoleumlike entrance. The butler? Lisa wondered, as she advanced up the steps towards it. The androgynous creature was dressed entirely in black, its face covered by a white mask which was completely expressionless apart from the eyes glittering through slits and the narrow line of red lips.

'Miss Sherwin?' it said, and the voice did not give anything away. It could be male or female or a mixture of both.

'Yes,' Lisa answered, wanting to turn tail and flee.

'Miss Marlow is waiting for you. Please follow me,' said the creature.

She followed it through the door and past a carved screen into a magnificent panelled hall filled with paintings and heavy furniture, suits of armour, ancient weapons and pikes crossed with tattered banners. The fireplace was big enough to stand in and would have taken logs the size of a man.

Her footsteps echoed the servant's – she assumed that was what it was – and they paused at an oak door.

'Come,' said a voice in answer to the creature's gentle tap.

It stood back so that Lisa could walk through, its blank face disconcerting.

'Thank you, Lee. That will be all,' said the person who rose to greet her.

The red hair was recognisable, and the voice and the bright blue eyes, but apart from that Tanith Marlow was in disguise.

For an instant Lisa imagined that it was a slim young man wearing a dandyish outfit from an earlier era – the jazz age, perhaps. She wore a superbly tailored black evening suit and her hair was slicked back close to the skull, emphasising the high cheekboned face, slightly slanting eyes and wide, scarlet mouth.

'Sit down,' she ordered Lisa with a wave of her long, jade cigarette holder. 'We don't stand on ceremony. Mr Robillard is away, so you'll have to put up with me. May I offer you a drink?'

'Nothing alcoholic. I'm driving,' Lisa answered, sinking into the depths of a velvet-covered, deeply buttoned chesterfield.

'What a bore. Never mind, we'll go for coffee.'

Tanith walked across to the fireplace on her long, elegant, black-clad legs and tugged at the bell-pull. She glanced in one of the several ornate mirrors, touching a hand to her gelled hair and narrowing her eyes.

'You're trying on a costume . . . a fancy-dress party, perhaps?' Lisa suggested, unable to fathom why she should be wearing such clothes on a warm afternoon.

Tanith shook her head, coming to rest beside her. 'It amuses me to imagine what it must have been like as a young man in the roaring twenties. I'd have missed the Great War, and would be enjoying that hectic time of fast cars, all-night parties and sex-mad flappers. I adore the fashions worn then, don't you?'

'I do. The women's clothes were so glamorous. All those beads and fringes and things.'

'And do you like me dressed like this? Do I make a handsome man?' Tanith asked, shooting her a penetrating glance.

Lisa gulped, and was surprised to find her body responding. She felt her nipples rising and dampness dewing her panties.

'Very handsome,' she muttered.

'I think so, too,' Tanith said with satisfaction, running her hands down her sleek flanks. She then adopted a masculine pose, seated on the couch arm with one foot on the floor and the other swinging.

Lisa remembered her sitting like that in the flea market, and the glimpse of her sex with its coating of auburn fluff. It made Lisa clench her thighs tightly, bringing pressure to bear on her swelling nub.

At that moment Lee entered the room. 'Coffee,' she ordered, rising to place another cigarette in the elegant holder and reach towards the onyx table lighter.

'I hope you don't mind me asking, but is that a man or a woman?' Lisa ventured, when Lee had gone.

Tanith laughed, rocking back on the low heels of her lace-up, patent leather shoes. 'I'll show you in a moment,' she promised.

'I didn't know what to bring,' Lisa began, struggling to be sensible. 'I haven't worked for anyone before.'

'Don't worry about it. I'm sure you'll be fine,' Tanith said carelessly, and strolled over to stand by her. 'We're not slave drivers here . . . not in the accepted sense of the word. Come for a trial period.'

'You mean it?' Lisa cried, not quite knowing whether to be pleased or alarmed. This was a very strange household indeed.

'Of course.'

'Don't you want to discuss it with Mr Robillard?'

Tanith gazed at her through a blue smoke haze, then shrugged and said, 'I'll speak to him tonight, and you can come round tomorrow and have a chat with him. I'm sure he'll be as willing as I am to give you a chance.'

The smell of freshly roasted coffee announced the arrival of Lee. He was accompanied by another clone, wearing an identical mask. When the tray had been placed on the low table, Tanith said, 'Unfasten, Lee. Miss Sherwin is curious about you.'

Long, thin, pale hands gripped the zipper tag at the throat of his black, form-fitting catsuit. The zip ran all the way down, the stretchy material opening over a chest where the nipples were pierced by thick gold rings. There was another in the navel and, as a large penis unfurled, a further ring gleamed in the frenum.

Tanith took the cock in her hand and rubbed it up and down from base to tip, while Lee stood motionless, the white mask turned towards her. Now the phallus was huge, curving upward, and the tip was wet with juice.

She pulled the zip down across the crotch and up the other side, revealing the deep amber furrow of Lee's buttocks. Then she lifted his balls, holding them in her palm. They were too big to fit and sagged over the edge of her hand; luscious, sap-filled sacs ready to discharge their contents.

Still Lee made no movement or sound. Tanith beckoned Lisa, saying, 'Do you want to explore him?'

What on earth was going on? Lisa couldn't make any sense of the bizarre scene before her. But she advanced, almost against her will but ruled by curiosity and lust. Lee's hot length slipped into her hand, the skin as smooth as velvet and a pulse throbbing in the thick, corded veins. The tiny, single eye glistened with tears and, to her immense suprise, Lisa could not resist sticking out her tongue and licking a droplet into her mouth. It tasted fresh and salty, like sea-water. The gold ring was warm to her tongue, piercing the taut web of skin between the foreskin and the bulging glans.

She allowed his shaft to ride her hand, backward and forward, driven by her own volition, not his. Lee did not move a muscle.

Tanith stood in front of the other servant and said to Lisa, 'You think this is also a male?'

'I can't tell,' she murmured, absorbed in her own agonised heat demanding satisfaction, engendered by the feel of the pulsating, urgent need in Lee's cock.

Tanith seized the zipper hiding this one's body, and drew it downward with a metallic hiss. The gap widened, but no male organ sprang into view. The garment was designed like a quick-release stage costume. A couple of pulls on the zips and the lower portion fell away, leaving only a brief bodice in place. The sex was revealed: dusky-pink labia naked of hair, but also pierced. It was swollen and glistening, the thick love bud standing proud. A pale-skinned female stood there, as impassive as Lee.

Tanith picked up a short-handled whip from the couch and brought it down across the girl's rump. She bucked, but still did not speak. Lisa watched, her hands dropping from Lee's prick. Was she dreaming all of this? she wondered. Her life wasn't like this!

'Try her,' Tanith said serenely, and thrust the whip into Lisa's hand.

Then she pushed her fingers between the girl's thighs and penetrated her, almost lifting her off her feet. 'You like that, don't you, Frankie? Shall I frig you till you come, or shall I let Lisa do it?'

Leaving Frankie standing, she then took a cane from a large Chinese vase and paced over to Lee. She thrust it against his mouth, a red slit visible beneath the mask, saying, 'Kiss the rod.'

He obeyed, bowing formally to her. Lisa watched, appalled yet aroused. She still didn't believe this was happening. She stared at the sight before her, open mouthed. And then she reached out and touched Frankie's breasts, unable to control herself. She had never touched a woman before and never considered that she might want to. But she did, very much.

The girl's breasts were tiny, with little rosebud nipples. Still as a statue, Frankie could not restrain a stifled moan as Lisa pinched them.

To hear another female mewling in pleasure in response to her touch sent fiery darts through Lisa's loins. She experienced Frankie's arousal as if it were her own. She knew how she would feel and the moist heat increased between her legs.

Then she started as she heard the whistle and whack as the cane landed across Lee's posterior.

'Bend over, slave, and spread your legs,' Tanith commanded, and Lee leant forward, supporting himself on straight arms with palms pressed flat on the inlaid brass surface of the buhl table.

Tanith had obviously arranged him so that Lisa could see his raised buttocks, the amber avenue opened between them. A scarlet weal had formed on his right bottom cheek, and his cock was ramrod stiff.

His lean legs quivered slightly but he made no protest as the whippy cane bit into his flesh again and again. Tanith cunningly ensured that it caught him in a different place every time, till his flesh was criss-crossed with fiery lines.

Lisa was rooted to the spot, horrified yet amazed by the continued hardness of his member. She had imagined that pain would cause it to shrink, but it grew larger and more inflamed, jerking at each blow.

She could hear his rapid breathing which betrayed him as human, while the dead-white mask was that of a Pierrot doll, lifeless and inanimate. The cane rose and fell and he suddenly jerked, semen fountaining from his cock to fall to the table in glistening drops. He spasmed, fell to his knees, then placed his face close to the inlay and licked it clean of his secretions.

128

Tanith threw the cane away and he crawled over to lay his mouth on her instep. She accepted his homage, a curious little smile on her face.

She cocked an eyebrow at Lisa, saying, 'You don't want to beat Frankie? She'll be disappointed if you don't. See what ecstasy it has brought Lee.'

'I–I can't!' Lisa cried, scared of the unknown but knowing in her heart that she wanted to try it more than anything.

Tanith gave her a long, considering look, then took the whip, running its thong through her fingers thoughtfully.

'You're either very clever or deliciously naive, Lisa,' she said, then added lightly, 'I think you'll fit in here just fine. Come tomorrow. Now, goodbye.'

She stepped closer and kissed Lisa full on the mouth. The sensation was electric, soft and tender, and promised so much.

The clones watched through the slits in their masks, semi-nude and obedient.

That almost casual, dismissive kiss shook Lisa to the very foundation of her being. It bordered on a chaste kiss, the lips closed, yet it was much more thrilling than if Tanith had used her tongue.

Lisa pulled away with a gasp, more confused than ever. The heavily scented room, the peculiar dress of its occupants, that strange sense of fantasy, all played on her mind like a vivid dream, clinging round the edges of thought as she hurried off, finding her own way through the brooding, mysterious house. She breathed a sigh of relief, tinged with regret, as she let herself out of the front door and into the open space once more.

She rattled home at speed, in such a ferment of apprehension, confusion and lust that it was all she could do to reach her bedroom before quelling the fire sizzling within her by a rapid, vigorous and private manipulation of her own sexual parts.

* * *

129

Later, when she checked her answerphone, she found two messages. The first said simply, 'Hi, it's David. I'm back. Can we meet? What are you doing tomorrow night?'

This was followed by another. 'Lisa. Mike here. There's something I want to discuss with you. It's about your property. I'll be free this evening. How about you? Ring me.'

Chapter Six

*L*isa stood in the shower stall in a state of indecision. She needed advice. Not Mike's – in fact, she hadn't returned his call. Not even David's, though this was a more attractive proposition. It was too early for Martin and Phil to be in the shop so she couldn't speak to them.

The problem was Hawkhurst Abbey and its inmates. Should she or should she not accept the job? She was part scared, part intrigued; extremely shoked but absolutely fascinated and more sexually aroused than she had ever been in her life. Who would have guessed that the sleepy Deverels housed such unusual people, to say nothing of Daphne Nightingale and Arnaldo?

The jets were just right, and as she stood under their spray, she pretended she was in a tropical rain forest during a deluge, the exotic scent rising from the gel lathering her body adding to this illusion.

I want to run away, she thought, the water trickling down her breasts and hanging in fat droplets on her puckered nipples before falling to join their fellows making merry in her navel. Their crafty little fingers wormed through her soaking pubic hair and dipped into the fragrant passage between her thighs.

I'm tired of everyone hassling me, she decided, her

face raised as if to warm rain. There's Paul and his family, and this property which I know is falling apart. I love the old place but it will cost a fortune to renovate. Is that what Mike wants to talk about? He's been here, and anyone with half an eye can see that the roof is a disgrace, the tiles loose and the copings crumbling. If I try to sell it like this I'll get a fraction of its true value.

Anyway, I don't want to sell up, she decided. It's my refuge, my home. Somewhere to come back to when I've finished adventuring up the Amazon.

Like now. Here I am back in my own shower, and the bell is ringing. Who the hell can it be so early? She killed the jets, grabbed a towel and wound it round herself.

Valerie stood on the doormat.

'Oh, sorry,' she began, and Lisa knew she was not in the least repentant. 'Were you in the bath?'

'In Brazil, actually,' Lisa replied, aware of that vague air of disapproval which Valerie always exuded when they were together. 'It's all right. Come in.'

Valerie did so, frowning as she said, 'Brazil? Whatever are you talking about? You do come out with the strangest things sometimes.'

Lisa could not be bothered to explain. Valerie would fail to understand, anyway, having forgotten how to play long ago.

She closed the door and asked, 'What can I do for you?'

'Oh, nothing, dear. I was just passing and thought I'd pop in,' Valerie lied, glancing round the room critically. 'My word, you have surrounded yourself with odds and ends, haven't you?' she exclaimed. 'I suppose you've not had a good clear out since your father died. I'm sure I can dispose of things for you. The Woodlanders' charity shop –'

'I like it this way,' Lisa cut in brusquely, and swept a pile of books from a chair. 'Take a seat. Would you like a cup of tea?'

'I won't stop, dear, thank you,' Valerie said, then

plonked herself down, crossed her legs in her beige, chainstore slacks and continued. 'Paul and I had a long talk over the weekend. He went to see the vicar and you are both to go along next Saturday evening.'

'Really?' Lisa shouted from the kitchen, making herself a brew and then walking back, mug in hand.

'Yes, really, and I do think it's high time we looked for your wedding gown. You're leaving it awfully late.'

'I was hoping to find a lovely old second-hand one. Faded ivory silk, perhaps, with antique lace,' Lisa commented, knowing this would be like a red rag to a bull.

Valerie's face turned pink and her eyes bulged. 'You can't do that!' she cried. 'It wouldn't do at all. What would people think?'

'Frankly, I don't give a toss what they think!' Lisa retorted, while inside she thought, I'm sick of this – her, Paul and the whole shebang.

'Now, Lisa, be sensible,' Valerie persisted, with an obvious effort at keeping calm. 'Natasha and I are going to Bristol on Wednesday. Come with us and we'll visit the bride shop. As your matron of honour, she'll want a nice frock, too. I thought sky-blue, as it's a summer wedding. But this all depends on what we select for you. I do wish you'd hurry up. There are the four older bridesmaids to consider, to say nothing of the two tinies.'

No one had asked Lisa if she wanted Paul's plain sister to take on the job of the bride's chief helper. She liked Natasha and was sorry for her as she had always walked in Paul's shadow as far as their mother was concerned. She had married an unexciting, ineffectual man who was also involved in the family business.

Lisa had not been consulted about the other attendants either, selected from among Valerie's friends and acquaintances. Not that there was anyone she would have wanted, apart from Martin, and he was taboo. She had no close friends and hadn't kept in touch with the

133

one or two women students she'd been close to at university.

Now was the time to voice her resentment and mention the doubts besetting her concerning the whole affair, which was moving inexorably ahead with the relentless force of a juggernaut. Yet she felt it only fair to talk it over with Paul again.

'Can't make Wednesday, I'm afraid,' she said resolutely, picking up a dry towel and rubbing her hair.

The one covering her body fell open, and Valerie goggled at her all-over tan. Lisa adjusted it, discomfited by her prurient interest.

'Why not Wednesday?' Valerie said, recovering her aplomb.

'The flea market.'

Valerie gave an exasperated snort. 'That nonsense! Really, Lisa, you can't possibly put that before your wedding.'

Lisa looked at her through a mane of tangled locks and announced, 'I can. I do. It's my livelihood.'

Valerie leapt to her feet, demanding, 'Don't you want to marry Paul?'

'That's between him and me, don't you think?' Lisa said coldly.

'I can't understand you. It's the chance of a lifetime. You'll never find another man like him!' Valerie declared loudly.

'I haven't said I don't want him. You're reading that into it. All I've said so far is that I can't come shopping on Wednesday.'

The more heated Valerie became, the colder the freezing calm settled over Lisa. Valerie seemed to fill the room in her lightweight trouser suit that was a touch too tight over the hips. It would be new, of course, as would the blouse worn beneath, and the neat, small-heeled shoes.

'He isn't very happy lately,' she said accusingly, her eyes hard under the fringe of mascara-coated lashes. 'I don't know what's going on, but it's high time you came to your senses. Only weeks to the wedding, and you're behaving as if it wasn't important!'

'Of course it is! Vitally important. My whole life could be ruined,' Lisa snapped back. 'And his, if we make the wrong decision. Have you considered that? Leave it to us, Valerie. We're adults, and capable of sorting it out for ourselves.'

Valerie stalked to the door, every inch of her solid body conveying outraged indignation. 'All right, but don't say I didn't warn you,' she returned angrily.

It was on the tip of Lisa's tongue to ask if Mike had mentioned his phone call, but something in the back of her mind advised caution. Things were already bad enough between herself and her prospective mother-in-law.

Poor old Paul, she thought. The woman is a positive dragon. Fancy having her as one's dam.

'Don't worry about it,' she advised, opening the door and leaning against it as Valerie brushed past her. 'I expect I'll be seeing Paul sometime today.'

'Try not to upset him any more. He's a very busy man with a lot on his plate,' was Valerie's final comment as she swept down the stairs.

Lisa wandered back into the lounge. The visit had been disturbing but somehow it had proved a clearing house for her disordered emotions. She needed the job with Tanith and Fletcher. Whether or not she went on with the wedding plans, it was essential that she retained a measure of independence. Paul would huff and puff, and his mother would cause untold trouble, but if she succeeded in carrying this off she would have a regular income of her own.

On her way to Hawkhurst Abbey, she called in on Daphne, wondering if she would be welcome without phoning first. Arnaldo opened the front door and ushered her inside. He was in his shirtsleeves and a pair of skin-tight blue jeans, and looked impossibly handsome.

135

Lisa's spine tingled and her belly clenched, and she had to admit to herself that the reason for her visit had been to see him as much as the wish to consult Daphne.

'I've been washing the car,' he explained, smiling widely. 'Madame is in the garden, attending her flowers. I'll inform her you are here.'

He vanished down a passage and Lisa waited. She let the tranquillity of the house sink into her, finding it difficult to understand the antipathy Valerie felt towards things old and craftsman made and rare.

Arnaldo returned, watching her closely with dark, luminous eyes as he said, 'Madame asks if you will join her outside, Miss Sherwin.'

Neither of them moved, their gaze locked, then suddenly he had both hands under her skirt, caressing the satin-smooth flesh of her thighs. His full, pleasure-hungry lips found hers, which parted at once, his long tongue moving slowly and sinuously in the wet cave of her mouth.

She dragged away from him long enough to gasp, 'We can't! Not here. Someone might see us.'

He gave a throaty laugh and eased her backwards until she could feel the brown dado against her spine. He had been working and his body was hot, sweat making great arcs at his armpits and across his back. He smelled of sun and aftershave, and the crisp odour of linen and denim.

Lisa's hand strayed to his crotch, her fingers tracing the outline of his upright bough through the jeans. He caressed the insides of her thighs, her skirt falling back, its loose cotton weave giving him easy access to her secrets.

He bent his head and nudged at her breasts. She felt the damp warmth of his breath as his mouth fastened on one nipple through her white shirt. He sucked it, the friction between his lips and the fabric causing a delicious, tight coil in her womb. Her teat grew hard and tense, her breasts swelling in response.

136

He moved to the other peaked crest, leaving a round, moist patch through which her nipple showed, dark with passion. Keeping one hand on her thigh, he used the other to open the tiny buttons that fastened the front of her garment, baring both breasts to his sight and touch.

Her skin glowed darkly in contrast to the snowy fabric. He mouthed and sucked at the crimped areolae, moving from one to the other as he nipped and bit.

Lisa whimpered, her hand rubbing the shaft still trapped in the jeans. It was alert and ready.

Her breasts were on fire and their ache echoed in the bud swelling at the top of her cleft. Arnaldo cupped her buttocks, stroking the taut cheeks, then moved to her damp fleece and fingered it through the gusset of her panties. He worked the lycra strip to one side and pressed a fingertip into her, gently teasing her secret place. Her feet slid apart a little further on the mosaic tiled floor.

She reached for his buttons and released his stiff organ, her palm closing round it while she rejoiced in the feel of its velvety skin and the bulging glans, slippery with juice.

'It's so big,' she whispered into his mouth. 'I want to feel it in me.'

'Not yet ... not quite,' he breathed, kissing her neck. The touch of his lips raised the fine down all over her limbs. 'I want to make you burst with delight first, then I shall enter you.'

Shivers passed through Lisa and she could not restrain little sobs of pleasure as Arnaldo moved his fingers inside her. But she wanted his touch on her clitoris, which throbbed with unsatisfied desire.

She grabbed his hand and lifted it towards the seat of pleasure crowning the plump petals of her labia. Grinding herself against him, she cried jerkily, 'Touch me! Touch me there!'

137

His fingers moved over the tense head of her ultra-sensitive nubbin, and he said hoarsely, 'Like this?'

'Make it wet,' she urged.

He parted the dewy curls of maidenhair that bordered her lower lips, dabbled in her juices and returned to her clitoris. She jumped as his finger found it, then relaxed as he began that smooth massage that would bring her to climax. It was coming, but delayed by the strangeness of her surroundings and Arnaldo's prick pulsating in her hand.

She was impatient, fearful and worried in case something would interrupt that giddy climb to the heights. She released Arnaldo's cock and lifted her hands to her breasts, touching the prominent nipples. Allowing instinct to take over, she pinched the nubs of flesh, rolled them between her fingers and stroked and rubbed them until a thrill of desperate pleasure shot along her nerves and communicated with her clitoris.

Now she had reached the point of no return. Now, no matter what, nothing could stop her. She was on that roller coaster climbing ever higher to the ultimate peak of sensation. Gasping and shuddering, she gyrated her pubis against Arnaldo's hand, his finger palpating her thrumming bud.

With an anguished cry she reached her zenith, orgasm exploding in a thousand shimmering stars. She felt herself falling, disoriented and fragmented; almost destroyed by the fierce joy of it.

Then Arnaldo bent his knees and pushed slowly up, steering himself into her convulsing depths. He clasped her bottom, lifting her so that his penis sank ever deeper. She fastened her legs round his waist and hung on, riding him strenuously and wringing every remaining vestige of pleasure from it.

Arnaldo was strong and balanced her easily, speared on his cock, but her lunging hips proved too much for his control and he thrust wildly, then discharged upward into her spasming body.

Lisa slowly lowered her legs, his staff slipping from her, softer but still semi-erect. She was exhausted and replete, and buried her head against his chest, listening to his heart and his rapid breathing. He held her tenderly, and kissed her brow.

Applause rippled through the hall.

'Well done! I adore to see beautiful people in the act of love. There's nothing more glorious; a hymn of praise to the Creator,' Daphne cried, clapping her hands as she stepped from the gloom of the stairwell with a trug over one arm containing a pair of scissors and a cluster of roses.

Arnaldo turned his head, and Lisa looked across at her from the cradle of his arms. 'Mrs Nightingale –' she began, flushed with sexual heat and embarrassment.

'Daphne ... please,' she replied, her eyes twinkling in her superbly preserved face. 'I'm glad to see that Arnaldo pleases you. He pleases me, too. A delightful addition to anyone's household. I'm glad you called by. I wanted to see you before Wednesday. There's an important sale in a private house near Salisbury that I feel we'd do well to attend. It's not till Friday, but we should view the day before at the latest.'

'I don't think I can afford it,' Lisa said, coming down to earth with a vengeance.

'Let me worry about that,' Daphne replied, so casual in her full skirt and vest top that it seemed she was in no way disconcerted by the scene she had just witnessed.

Arnaldo tucked his serpent away and buttoned his fly. Lisa reorganised her knickers, pulled down her skirt and fastened her shirt. Daphne turned to him and said, 'Bring some iced lemonade into the garden, if you please.'

The garden was an enchanted spot. A very ancient and slanting mulberry tree spread its branches over a quarter of the lawn, and in a niche in the back wall stood a statue of Venus Aphrodite. The goddess's hand, which should have been screening her breasts from lecherous eyes, had long since fallen, leaving her arm truncated. Lichen grew over her plump mound like yellow pubic hair.

Flowers bloomed in borders and stone urns, and all manner of other things, too; leaden cherubs, cisterns, broken marble columns, classical seats and other spoils.

'I buy them in the auction rooms if they're going for a reasonable price,' Daphne explained. 'People like such objects to beautify their gardens.'

'Some do,' Lisa said gloomily. 'But not Valerie Garston. She's obsessed with newness that masquerades as antique.'

'Ghastly,' Daphne agreed, dead-heading a standard rose bush. 'And who is she?'

'Paul's mother.'

'Ah, I see. Your fiancé who has no manners in bed.'

'That's him. I wanted to talk to you ... I'm still unsure. I went to Hawkhurst Abbey about a job, and met Tanith Marlow again.'

'The red-headed siren. And?' Daphne glanced at her from the purple shadow of her wide-brimmed straw hat.

'Well, she has two weird servants, and her behaviour towards them was most unusual. She whipped them and they loved it. The one called Lee actually ejaculated under the rod.'

Arnaldo came out between a colonnade that supported a balcony. He was carrying a tray with glasses and a jug which he set down on a round, cast-iron table near a garden bench. He bowed and withdrew.

'This is not so strange, my dear,' Daphne said when they were seated and she had filled two glasses with the pale gold liquid, ice tinkling. 'There are many different ways in which sexual fulfilment can be achieved. You remember Mr Robillard buying the crops and canes you had for sale?'

140

'Of course. The way he flourished that whip gave me cold chills,' Lisa replied with a shudder.

Daphne laughed across at her, the sunlight dappling her face through the overhanging vines. 'There you are, then,' she said. 'If it thrilled you, a novice, think what it would do to those who seek the kiss of the lash to augment their pleasure. I told you Walter was my master. Perhaps Robillard will become yours.'

'I can't imagine it. I don't want to be whipped!' Lisa cried, and wondered why she found it necessary to be so emphatic. 'Tanith was dressed in an old-fashioned evening suit, and her servants ... well, I've never seen anything like them. They were wearing identical black catsuits and masks. White masks, like Pierrots; a man and a woman, but so eerie.'

'They play games, my dear. Everyone plays games, don't they? And they all wear masks of some sort or another, but we don't realise, thinking we see the real face,' Daphne assured her, lifting the jug again. 'Have some more lemonade. Arnaldo makes it himself from fresh fruit. He's almost as skilled in the kitchen as he is in the bedroom.'

Lisa placed her hand over the top of her glass. 'No, thank you. What do you mean about games?'

'Masks, my dear. Disguises. Your Mrs Garston, for example. Is she all that she seems? Is your fiancé? Who can you trust to show the real person within, eh? Do you show yours?'

This was a most disturbing conversation and Lisa felt herself floundering in a morass of uncertainty. 'That's true,' she conceded at last. 'We all have a side of ourselves that we don't display in public.'

'That's right, and Tanith was merely being a touch more honest, allowing you to see her in one of her guises. Much more honest, I suspect, than Mrs Garston.'

'There were other things, too. Their clothes were covered in zips which gave easy access to their privates. Lee's nipples were pierced and so was his belly button,

141

and he had a ring through his penis, while the girl, Frankie, had shaved off her pubes and had little rings down there.'

Daphne shrugged, saying, 'This is nothing new. It is said that Queen Victoria's consort had one. In fact, one of the penis piercing procedures is called the Prince Albert. Piercing of the nipples and genitals is supposed to heighten sexual sensation. Chains can be attached to them, and weights ... all manner of toys to aid the excitement or add to the feelings of total submission to another's will. They are ornamental as well. Your ears are pierced, aren't they?'

'Yes, but that's different,' Lisa flared up at her, then she remembered the rings in Martin's ears and eyebrow. Did he wear a cock ring?

'Not so very different,' Daphne said, rising and holding out her hand. 'And now, my dear, I want you to look at some photographs. Maybe they will help you understand the private world where pain and pleasure intermingle. Perhaps they will aid you to decide whether or not you wish to become entangled with Tanith Marlow and Fletcher Robillard.'

The shutters were part closed in the drawing room, the light filtering through. It was like walking under water; green, translucent and mysterious. There were several large leather bound albums lying on an occasional table.

Daphne sat down on an exquisitely fashioned walnut daybed and patted the space beside her, then opened one of the books. A dusty, musty smell rose from it. The setting and clothes suggested that the black and white photos were about 50 years old. The first ones Daphne showed Lisa were of a young girl, wearing an expression of utter boredom and indifference.

'That's me,' she explained with a faint, wistful smile, and touched the print affectionately. 'It was taken shortly after our wedding day.'

Posed against a sumptuously draped bed, the young

Daphne was the epitome of every man's libidinous dream, with her sulky mouth and contemptuous, heavy-lidded eyes staring insolently into the camera.

Gawky, almost awkward, she wore a skimpy camisole, the straps slipping off her narrow shoulders. Her breasts were as round as apples, with pointed tips. The lace hem of the short undergarment barely reached the tops of her splayed legs, her thighs exposed and a tempting triangle of silky hair at their fork. Black stockings covered her to the knees, upheld by ruched garters, and one of her hands cupped a breast while the other was at her crotch, a finger plunged inside to the first knuckle.

Lisa made no comment, heated by the lewd, suggestive nature of the picture, and passed swiftly to the next.

In this Daphne had one foot hitched on a stool, bending over as she fastened a high-heeled shoe. She was glancing provocatively over one shoulder as if to catch the voyeur staring up her short skirt. The pouting purse between her legs was on view, the full inner lips pushing through the outer ones.

In the next she rested on a heap of embroidered cushions on the bed, skirts rolled up to the waist to show her flat belly and fleecy thatch framed by the stretched elastic of suspenders. These were fastened to silk stockings that covered her lovely, wide-open legs.

The camera had been positioned between them, giving a foreshortened, detailed picture of her labial lips and large, well-developed clitoris. The light glistened on the silvery trail of wetness that highlighted every personal feature.

Daphne turned the page, and Lisa gasped, for this was a close-up of the model's genitalia. An open-crotch shot, where she sat with her pubis thrust forward, an absorbed, dreamy expression on her face. Her eyes were hooded and her tongue tip peeped from between her parted lips. Her fingers clasped her sex, opening the lips like ripe petals so that she might rub the prominent pistil in the heart of the flower.

'Your husband wanted you to pose like this?' Lisa whispered. 'They were for his private collection, I suppose.'

Daphne picked up a further album, saying, 'He helped to take the photos himself, but no, they weren't entirely for his amusement. He often showed them to his intimate friends. And that was not all. Look at these.'

Lisa saw Daphne in the pose of the stone nymph that stood in the garden, and a large, bearded man clasped her, his penis rammed into her womanhood. There was another with her bending over and gripping her ankles, the man behind her with his knees between hers to spread her thighs and allow him access. The bulbous end of his fully extended penis pushed into her fundament.

'He allowed this? He didn't mind you posing with another man?' Lisa cried, the split peach of her own sex giving forth juice.

'My dear child, that *is* Walter,' Daphne said, smiling.

'Oh, I see ... I didn't know,' Lisa murmured, thinking, That great, burly, overweight individual shafting the fragile-looking Daphne's rectum? She could not help asking, 'Did he hurt you?'

'You mean when he sodomised me? Oh, no, not once I'd been taught how and got used to it. Have you never –'

'No. Not ever,' Lisa cut in, blushing furiously.

'But you've thought about it? Wondered how it would feel?'

'Perhaps,' Lisa admitted, eyes down.

'I'll speak with Arnaldo. Maybe he'll initiate you, when you're ready to try. It gives a whole new dimension to fornication,' Daphne went on, her eyes gleaming with amusement.

She turned over the pages and said, 'These are stills,

but Walter experimented with the movie camera, too. Remind me to let you see some reels I've had transferred to video tape. He planned to make a full-length porno-graphic film, but never got around to it.'

Lisa stared at the pages spread open on the table, and her pulse began to race as it had when she watched Lee being chastised. Now she saw strange pictures indeed, of women chained to cross-pieces or bent over stools, naked and helpless. Some had gags thrust between their lips while others were wearing blindfolds. Dark stripes marked their flesh on thighs and buttocks. Walter, clad in black leather, held a whip.

Then there were men, also in bondage, their erect cock constricted by harnesses, with large, bare-breasted, fierce-looking women in basques and thigh-high, spike-heeled boots wielding paddles or crops. They used these to belay their victims, whose expressions were akin to ecstasy, not agony.

'We had a dungeon for these activities in our New York house,' Daphne said, matter of factly. 'Only those of a similar persuasion knew about it, of course. Out-wardly, Walter was a pillar of society; a sidesman at church and a magistrate. I suspect Robillard has a dungeon, too. No doubt you'll find out, if you work for him.'

'Work for him? Oh, Daphne, should I?' Lisa was frightened. She felt disgusted by the pictures, yet was aware of a sneaking feeling of arousal that made her skin crawl and her inner self spasm.

'I think you should at least talk with him. You need the money, don't you? It would be better to do whatever he and Tanith require than condemn yourself to a marriage that you know, deep in your heart, is not right for you.'

Hawkhurst Abbey was silent under the afternoon sun, rooted firmly in the soil as if it had been for a handful of centuries. Lisa left Mavis at the front steps and walked up to the door. It was open.

She waited for a moment, then taking a grip on her wilting courage, tugged on the brass bell-pull, startled by a clanging deep in the bowels of the house. It echoed and faded. No one came.

'Damn! Where are they?' Lisa asked herself wordlessly.

She entered the vestibule, then the Great Hall, shouting, 'Hello! Is anyone there? It's me . . . Lisa!'

Nothing. Only the portentous tick tock of a monumentally large and ornate longcase clock broke the tomblike stillness.

Lisa paced up to it, doing her homework as she muttered, 'Let's see . . . the case is walnut and floral marquetry. It has a brass dial with a rolling moon. Date? Possibly George III?'

'That's not good enough. You should be able to recognise the period and the maker to within a year. Look for the name of the manufacturer. It should be on the face,' she heard David Maccabene saying, somewhere in her head. 'OK. Hazard a guess at the value.'

'Twelve thousand pounds?' she ventured, thinking of her outdated copy of *Miller's Antiques Price Guide* which she had picked up when the West Deverel public library was selling off books.

'You'd be lucky!' he taunted. 'Might have been that ten years ago, but now you wouldn't see much change out of twice the amount.'

Lisa suddenly missed David with a need as sharp as pain. I'll phone him when I get home, she promised herself, but meanwhile there was the mystery of why the abbey now resembled the *Marie Celeste*.

Shafts of sunlight, grainy with dust and circling gnats, struck through the high, arched windows. Lisa glanced down a gloomy passage, wondering if it was true that the place had a dungeon. Though itching with curiosity, she wasn't brave enough to explore gangrenous basements and spidery cellars. Instead she approached the foot of the main staircase that looked as if it needed to be scaled rather than mounted.

'Hello!' she called up it hopefully, but there was no reply.

Gripping the carved banister rail with one hand, she went slowly up, ready to stop should someone put in an appearance. She rather wished they would. The house seemed to be listening and watching. The landing showed too many doors, and too many branching passages, and further stairs disappearing up and up. Everywhere she looked there was a valuable painting or ornament or item of furniture.

There was no doubt about it: Tanith and Fletcher certainly knew their trade.

Then Lisa heard the faint sound of music, dreamlike and distant – dance music, but not rock or hip-hop or even ballroom, though nearer to that than the rest. Somewhere a tango orchestra was playing. She followed the sound.

Her feet picked up the rhythm. She had always loved South American music, bastard child of Spain and the Dark Continent, born of conquest and slavery. Scenes from ballets filled her mind – the tango sequences from *The Golden Age* composed by Shostakovich, and another from William Walton's *Facade*. For years she had longed to learn to dance the tango.

The sound led her into a corridor that ended in a cul-de-sac. It was coming from inside a room to one side of a curving bay, where the window glass was comprised of leaded diamond panes. Lisa knocked on the door, then turned the lion-headed handle. It opened easily.

The music was louder, though Lisa could not see the source. It seemed to be all around her but she did not have time to wonder, for she was instantly captivated by the room itself.

It was as splendid as the rest of the building but had

147

an intimate, feminine atmosphere. There was no bed; simply a scroll-backed couch set near the window, a fireplace in a marble surround, several little gilt chairs and a mahogany dressing table with a swing mirror. Its top was covered by a lacy duchesse set on which lay a silver-backed hairbrush, a cut-glass powder bowl complete with swansdown puff, alabaster jars of cosmetics, bottles of perfume, a scent spray and a box containing several sticks of theatrical greasepaint. It was like stepping back in time, each item valuable and eminently collectable.

The walls were lined with fitted wardrobes, and Lisa realised that this was a dressing room, such as ladies or gentlemen would have had adjoining their bedchambers in halcyon days of yore. She touched the mirrored, ornate door of one and it swung open invitingly.

Her fingers encountered velvets and lace, chiffon and furs, beaded gowns, metal-brocaded muslins, cloaks and wraps. Cloche hats sat on shelves above, and shoes were laid in racks below. The clothing wafted perfume, like that of dried roses, mothballs and the faint aroma of a hundred gala occasions.

Lisa knew about period costume. She had made a special study of it at university and been roped in as wardrobe mistress for several college productions. She also knew the value of genuine pieces, and these were the real McCoy. The contents of this wardrobe alone was worth a fortune on the open market.

A cursory investigation of the others proved them to contain articles from later or earlier periods, and she found men's gear as well as women's. By her reckoning, the whole collection probably spanned a hundred years, and she had hardly skimmed the surface.

Her particular interest lay in women's fashions of the 1920s, the era when the tango was at its height of popularity. Rudolph Valentino had brought breathless female cinema audiences to the point of orgasm when he danced it in *The Four Horsemen of the Apocalypse*, she remembered reading. There was a large framed photograph of him on the dressing table.

He's not the modern girl's idea of a turn-on, she thought. A right greaseball with those slanting, heavily made-up eyes, thin, mean mouth and that side parting in his shiny, oiled black hair. He looks every inch the gigolo. Strange to think that he had been the dream lover of millions of women, and several committed suicide when peritonitis cut him off in his prime.

The clothes were hugely tempting, the music luring her into a sensual reverie. Surely no one would mind if she tried something on? She was spoilt for choice. What should it be? A flowing, slinky gown or something short, racy and symbolic of the New Woman, the flapper, the liberated good-time girl?

Fingers trembling with eagerness, she stripped off her skirt, shirt, bra and panties. Naked, she approached the first wardrobe again and rubbed herself against the silks, her skin responding to the sensuous feel of the luxurious fabrics.

Half buried in a silken, aromatic forest, she pinched her nipples into ripeness and then touched her most secret region. Her curling pubic hair was hot and moist, and she played with the brown plumes before alighting on her passionate bud. A few quick flicks awoke the little tyrant, but Lisa needed to dress first, her excitement mounting at the idea of attiring herself in these evocative garments.

She slipped into the voluptuous embrace of eau-de-Nil satin camiknickers edged with ecru lace, enjoying the feel of its languid sensuousness. This all-in-one reminded her of the 'body', but was much more glamorous and seductive, with wide knickers closed beneath the crotch by minute mother-of-pearl buttons.

Posing before the mirror, she was enticed by the sight of her nipples rising against a fabric so fine that the dark shadow of her pubic triangle showed through it. When she caressed herself there, she could feel the cushiony pelt and was a little concerned because her juices were already wetting the gusset.

Supposing she stained so rare an undergarment? But control was disappearing and restless desire spiralling through her, encouraging her juices to flow. The pulsing need for satisfaction obscured other considerations.

She unearthed flesh-coloured pure silk stockings from a drawer, carefully turned them inside out and pulled them on to just above the knee where she fastened them with red satin garters.

It looked more wanton than suspenders. Tarty, somehow, and she remembered the words of a rag-time rhythm song: 'I'm going to rouge my knees and roll my stockings down. And all that jazz.'

Maybe she'd do just that, later. There was bound to be rouge among the cosmetics. While searching for this, she opened a drawer and her breath caught in her throat.

There, resting in a cocoon of tissue paper, lay the replica of a penis, complete to the last detail. It was carved from ebony, and embellished with silver art deco designs. Lisa felt her knees weaken and the wetness between her thighs increase.

A dildo. A mock phallus made for solitary pleasure, or to share with an experimentally inclined partner. So, it was true that there was nothing new under the sun? She had often wondered about vibrators and dildos, tempted to buy one but too embarrassed to set foot in a sex shop. Mail order had been an alternative, but somehow she had never got round to it.

There was nothing to stop her trying this strange and arousing object now. She lifted it out and fondled its massive erectness. It was twelve inches in length and so thick her finger and thumb did not meet round it. Larger and longer than any human penis she had ever seen, its coldness began to thaw in her hand as she ran it up and down.

150

Would such a huge and solid object penetrate her vagina? Would she, in fact, be able to take it?

She lifted it to her lips, laving it in her saliva and sucking it into her mouth. So hard, foreign and strange, lacking the innate warmth and resilience of a man's cock. Yet, unlike that unpredictable piece of equipment, it would be entirely under her control, a thing to use for her own utterly selfish, unshared pleasure.

But first she wanted to try on the clothes, and in a way wanted to make herself wait for the ultimate joy of plunging the dildo into her heartland. Reluctantly, yet shivering with anticipation of joys to come, she laid it on the dressing table.

She rummaged in the wardrobe and pulled out several shoes, each one a delight. Some were too small for her, but she found a pair made of gold glacé kid with high, spool-shaped heels, cut-away sides and straps that crossed the instep and circled the ankle.

With these on her feet she could feel the role of flapper taking over. The mirror flung back her image: a shameless hussy, admiring herself in her revealing single garment, legs spread in glittering evening shoes, an expanse of thigh displayed between the knicker hem and the stocking tops.

Her hair was too modern. By rights, it should have been a severe bob with side points that curved like scimitars against her cheekbones and a dead-straight bang. There must be wigs somewhere among this fabulous collection, she thought, but for the time being she coiled her hair into a loose knot, fastened it with pins and added a black velvet bandeau with an osprey plume, worn across her forehead.

She sighed, leant towards the mirror and applied make-up. Heavy blue eyelids, thick mascara and rouged cheeks. Now she was a doll with Cupid's-bow lips. A flashy, defiant doll or maybe even a gangster's moll. It fitted her mood exactly.

She had already chosen the dress – a jade-green tunic

shimmering with fringes and beads, which she slipped over her head. It was unshaped, the waist very low and the skirt descending to a little below her knees. It left her arms bare, and had a deep square-cut décolletage. A long string of cultured pearls and a wide bangle on her upper arm and Lisa was ready to dance the tango with any handsome man-about-town who presented himself.

The music played on and she danced by herself in front of the mirror, but she needed a man's arms round her to guide her through intricate patterns with his nimble footwork. She wanted him to control and master her. David's face floated on her inner vision and her loins yearned. Arnaldo was a wonderful lover, but she liked David's humour and warmth, and his rascally dealings which she could never be sure were legitimate. Their encounter had been all too brief.

She stopped dancing and, still watching her alien reflection, lifted her fringed skirt and slid a hand inside the wide, loose leg of her camiknickers. Then she started to stroke her delicate inlet. Possessed by the urgent desire to watch herself masturbate – she briefly wondered what on earth had come over her – she sat down on a chair in front of the mirror. With trembling fingers, she slowly undid the buttons at the crotch. The material parted and she pushed it up and away, staring at her dark wedge and the furrow that divided it.

She stretched her legs apart, braced on the high heels, and her lower lips opened, soft and dark pink, gleaming temptingly. She fluttered a finger over her clitoris, light as a butterfly's wing, and there was a tightening in her throat and spasms in her belly. Easing down so that her pubis was pushed forward and higher, she explored her hidden self; the tight hole of her anus, the crease between that led so smoothly to her vulva. But always her fingers returned to her bud, tender fingers caressing that sensitive spot wherein lay the answer to pleasure.

All the time her eyes kept returning to the black dildo, patiently waiting to service her. With her heart pounding like a drum, she reached for it, moistened the tip with her tongue and held it at its base. Then she introduced it to her cleft.

First, she rubbed the slippery head over her clitoris which jumped in response. The feeling was spectacular. Next her labia were caressed by the shining black thing. Then, with her vulva exposed, she let the dildo start its explorative journey into her eager aperture.

So big, so cold; nothing like a man's shaft but better in some ways. She was able to angle it and rub her swollen clitoris with her fingers at the same time. She pushed harder, and harder still. The mirror showed it was disappearing inside her, inch by slow inch. She could feel it burrowing in, her velvety walls clamping round it and wetting it, making its passage sweet and painless.

Two areas of sensation: her clit and the monstrous phallus substitute that was filling her completely. She gave it a shove and squealed as it butted against her cervix. Keeping it there, she lubricated her clit head and stroked it rapidly, deaf and blind to all except satisfaction. The feeling was rising, flooding her entire being from toes to cortex, and as she rubbed her anguished bud, so she began to move up and down on the smooth ebony surface of her wooden lover.

To her amazement the dildo sought out and found exciting areas within her that she had no idea she possessed. Her clitoris had taken charge now, a swollen nub of intense feeling, taking her beyond the threshold of endurance. She spasmed into orgasm, consumed with such violent, annihilating pleasure that she screamed.

Her vagina convulsed round the dildo, wave upon wave of sensation pouring through her. She fell back in the chair, her eyes closed, keeping one finger on her throbbing bud and allowing the mock penis to remain in place until the final contraction had faded.

She opened her eyes and the room swung back into

perspective. Slowly, she slid the dildo from her valley. Its darkness glistened with her silver essences and she wiped it carefully before replacing it in the drawer.

Though the music continued, she no longer felt like dancing. Her body quivered, the spasms receding, and she knew that this was a once in a lifetime experience, equivalent to losing one's virginity. From now on she would want to repeat it, using a dildo when she was lonely, manless or just needing a change from her own fingers. She had been granted a glimpse of heaven and would never look back.

After taking off her borrowed plumage and dressing in her own clothes, she put everything away, closed the wardrobes and left the room, shutting the door quietly behind her. On reaching the hall, she found a piece of paper and scribbled a note for Fletcher Robillard, asking him to phone her.

It was still sunny outside and she was surprised to find how little time had really passed. She put Mavis in gear and drove away from Hawkhurst Abbey.

'The girl's a natural,' said Fletcher, his penis still buried to the hilt in the scabbard of Tanith's luscious arse.

He rocked to and fro, losing himself in ecstasy, the turbulence of his release surging through him and into her. Tanith gasped, her hand between her thighs, and worked herself to orgasm, her hips driving back against his belly.

They clung together for an instant, a beast with two humps, then he withdrew, dried his penis on a monogrammed handkerchief and slipped it inside his trousers.

Tanith tossed back her fiery locks and pulled down her skirt, saying, 'I told you she'd be good, didn't I? And doesn't she look great in costume?'

The dressing room reflected through the trick mirror was deserted, but they had watched Lisa from the apartment next door.

Both had dressed for the occasion. Tanith's gown was a magnificent, sophisticated jet-black creation. Long, low-necked, sleeveless and sequinned, it had a draped skirt with the sides pared away, leaving her bare at the hips.

Fletcher wore a faultlessly tailored dinner jacket, seventy years out of date. He had recovered his equilibrium almost at once after ejaculating, and now held out a hand to Tanith, saying, 'The music, my dear. It's time we went to the ballroom. Tango calls, as strong as sex, almost as strong as life itself – and I must answer.'

Chapter Seven

'*I*'m so sorry I missed you, Lisa ... if I may call you that,' Fletcher's deep, cultured voice murmured seductively down the phone.

'It was rather inconvenient,' she replied, her body responding instantly. Yet she was determined not to let him off the hook, thinking, Let's start as we mean to go on. I'll not have him walking all over me.

'A misunderstanding. I'm racked with remorse. Come to dinner, and we'll get down to business.'

Lisa was still under the spell of that dressing room filled with intriguing relics of the past, and had only just arrived at her flat when he rang. She had already reached a decision during the drive home, and now said,

'I'd like to do that. I must confess that I did take a look round and was impressed by the wonderful collection of clothes I found in an upstairs room. I suppose you know that you could sell them for a huge profit? So many party-goers want to get hold of old-time gear these days.'

'I know,' Fletcher said. 'You'd like to specialise in this area? I can arrange it.'

'Thank you,' she replied, flustered by torrid memories of the afternoon just passed.

'When would you like to come to dinner? Tonight?'

'I'm afraid I can't,' she said, thinking, I must see Paul and clear the air.

'Tomorrow?' Fletcher persisted.

'It's the market.'

'Not in the evening,' he reminded her. 'Shall we say seven-thirty for eight?'

'That will be fine.'

'Would you like me to pick you up?'

Panic seized her. In Mavis she could come and go as she liked, the van providing an escape route, and she had the uneasy feeling she might want to escape, fast.

'No, thank you. I'll drive.'

'I shall look forward to seeing you. So will Tanith. Goodbye, Lisa.'

'Goodbye . . .'

As she put down the receiver, she wondered what it was about Fletcher that affected her so much, even via the phone. She had only met him once, but been haunted by his hard gaze and enigmatic smile, the feel of his cool hand taking hers and the way his cock had grown erect when he pressed close to her as they struck a bargain over the whip. There was an aura of mystery about him, and the unspoken promise of journeys to the limits of bodily experience.

Her clothes felt hot and restrictive and she undressed to her knickers and fastened a brightly coloured sarong around her, then walked barefoot to the roof garden. She sat by the pool and tipped in a few ants' eggs for the carp. In so doing she met the baleful glare of Alfie, who was at his usual observation post, balanced on the stone rim.

His paws were tucked neatly under him as he patiently waited for a moment's carelessness on her part. If, by any chance, she neglected to keep the wire netting firmly closed above those delectable fishy snacks swimming idly among the lily pads, then he would hook one out, even at the risk of wetting his beautiful tobacco and gold fur.

'No chance, Alfie,' she said firmly. 'I've a good mind to report you to Martin.'

Without the slightest quiver of a whisker, Alfie fixed her with unblinking yellow eyes.

Lisa was not looking forward to the evening. She had to ring Paul and then get the boxes of goods together for the sale. The thought of going on a reconnaissance with Daphne lifted her spirits, though she was not happy about letting her pay. With any luck, she would sell something at the market, though not enough, she suspected, to finance the proposed venture to the select environments of Salisbury.

Closing her eyes, she allowed the peace of this sanctuary to soothe her, but was soon disturbed by the doorbell. Making sure that Alfie's cunning plan was well and truly thwarted, she returned indoors.

It came as no shock to find that her visitor was David.

'How nice to see you,' she said simply, though her heart seemed to have lodged in her throat. 'Did you have a profitable trip?'

'Not bad,' he conceded, habitually cagey like all dealers, then adding, 'Have you ditched your fiancé yet?'

'No,' she replied.

He walked inside and it was as if he had never been away. Lisa wanted to throw herself into his arms and then drag him into the bedroom, but restrained the rash impulse.

He looked good enough to eat. Wearing casual clothes that were from top designers – jeans by Versace and a Levi's trucker jacket – he was taller than she remembered.

'Your hair is different,' she said. It was shorter on the top, but with sideburns, and had fullness at the back.

'You like it?' he asked, the light playing over his green eyes and across the firm line of his mouth.

'Yes.'

Of course I like it, she wanted to say. I like everything about you, perfidious lover though I know you to be. Without thinking, she asked, 'How is Lady Fiona?'

He grinned, charmingly unrepentent. 'OK, last time I saw her. She didn't come to France.'

'Did she not?' she said, awash with relief but thinking, Do I believe him, and does it matter either way?

He placed a hand on her shoulder, looking down at her in a slow, considering manner as he said, '"He travels fastest who travels alone." I went there strictly on business. I want you to come to the barn and see what I brought back. I have a feeling you're going to approve.'

'Is my opinion important?'

'It is,' he said, and dropped his hand, glancing round the room. 'I like your things. Did you buy them?'

'Inherited from my father,' she answered, her shoulder feeling cold without the weight and warmth of his palm.

'He's a man of taste,' he said.

'He was. He's dead.'

'I'm sorry. Recently?'

'Last year.'

'So you're alone? No mother? No siblings?'

'No.'

'Only Paul . . . the fiancé?'

'That's right.'

She was on the defensive, unwilling to let him know anything further about her. Just for a while, when they had linked their bodies on the divan in his studio room, she had dreamed that this meant something to him. Then, with hardly a word, he had abandoned her, going about his business.

Hurt by this, she had resolutely attempted to cut him out of her heart. Unsuccessfully, of course, and here he was wheedling his way back in again, so easy and natural she could almost believe he cared.

159

He nodded, and said, 'I felt from the start that you needed friends.'

There was no answer to that and she watched him as he examined a painted bronze and ivory figure poised on an alabaster base, his eyes alight with interest and appreciation.

'This is lovely,' he said. 'Such a pretty girl. Deco, of course. Look at that beaded bodice and headdress, swirly skirt and barred shoes. Pity it's not signed. If it were, it would be worth a lot, despite the fact that she's mislaid a left hand while dancing through seventy years.'

Heat swamped Lisa, rising from her inner depths to her face as she remembered her shameful behaviour while wearing a costume not dissimilar to the figurine's.

'I wouldn't want to part with her,' she said, then turned towards the kitchen, asking, 'Would you like a beer?'

'I'd rather make love to you,' he answered frankly, and there was a thickening of the bulge at the front of his jeans.

'Make love or have a quick fuck?' she asked with newly acquired cynicism.

His eyes darkened and his mouth was hard. 'I don't think of you in those terms,' he said in clipped tones. 'Fucking is for people like Fiona. I hoped that we had more going for us.'

'After two meetings? Come off it, Mr Maccabene!' she cried, determined not to lose herself in him.

'Three, if you count the day we met at the auction.'

'When you ran up the bidding and forced me to fork out more than I'd intended,' she snarled, for this still rankled.

'Old habits die hard,' he demurred, then stroked the side of her face, grinning wickedly. 'And I can't promise I won't do it again, if we're both after the same lot. All's fair in love and war.'

'And auction sales?'

'Absolutely.'

Oh, damn and blast, she mourned, as his arm moved round her, pulling her against the hardness and heat of his body. How can I resist him when every drop of my blood is boiling like lava? I don't want to resist him. I want him to make mind-blowing love to me.

Why beat about the bush? she suddenly thought, and quickly said, 'Shall we go to bed?'

He nodded towards the door. 'In there?'

'Yes.'

'Should I carry you over the threshold like a virgin bride?' he asked, smiling.

'I don't think that would be necessary or appropriate,' she returned, but was delighted when he suddenly swooped and lifted her in his arms, something the prosaic Paul had never thought of attempting.

He smelled of CK One, his breath fresh as his mouth closed over hers. She remembered that mouth, and her own opened in response, sucking at his lower lip, caressing his upper, then easing her tongue forward between his teeth. His own fleshy organ of speech and taste was ready to tangle with hers in a wet, slippery dance of desire.

She admired his strength and skill as he pushed the door open with his shoulder and, still kissing her, strode into the bedroom and laid her down on the patchwork quilt.

'Macho man,' she teased, as he released her.

'I shall suffer for it tomorrow,' he said, laughing.

She slid her arms up round his neck, her fingers playing with the thick hair growing at the nape, and he knelt above her, thighs each side of her hips, gazing down into her eyes with an unfathomable look.

All laughter was banished from his face as he braced himself on straight arms, then said, 'I've never been to bed with you. Let's do it properly.'

He left her and took off his jacket, then pulled his shirt out from the waistband of his jeans and removed

161

that, too. His body was broad and well muscled; the skin a warm olive, his chest furred. Lisa, intent on admiring him, left her sarong in situ. For some reason she could not define, she was shy about revealing any more of herself to him. He had entered her domain and that was enough for the moment.

This was her den, her sacred place for sleep and contemplation. It was for love-making, too, but there had only been Paul. No other man had shared her bed. Paul was hardly appreciative, and had never commented on the way she had decorated the room, choosing the best pieces from her collection with which to grace it. The curtains were chintz and the walls were papered in peach and covered with framed prints of nude women by Victorian artists – very feminine and sensual and romantic.

David looked across at her and kicked off his sneakers, then lowered his jeans. He wore nothing beneath and she wondered if this was customary or if he had come prepared to bed her. She was almost as nervous as the first time, but now he was naked and they were on her territory.

Sitting on the bed, she allowed her eyes to feast on him. He was tall, straight, muscular and fit, not through any faddy exercise programme but occasioned by sheer hard work. This had given him a lean waist, flat belly and handsomely proportioned legs. He was a self-sufficient, masculine person, though lacking the aggression towards women that Paul possessed.

Lisa's eyes kept returning to the inky spread of fur from which his penis jutted.

He was completely uninhibited, facing her with his hands on his hips, legs slighty spread, so that she could look at every part of him. There was nothing hurried about the way he finally moved towards her and climbed on the bed beside her. She felt that he was savouring every moment, deliberately taking his time. And she admired his cleverness, for the leisurely pace of his wooing fanned her flame ever higher and made her impatient.

Her hands reached out for him as she rolled on her side so that she might coil her fingers in his chest hair, tweak the brown coins of his nipples, advance across his steel-hard belly and finally weave among the thick pelt that protected his genitals.

David kissed the rise of her breasts above the exotically printed Madras cotton that banded them, leaving a trail of fire everywhere he touched. His cock moved, nosing against her fingers, and Lisa opened them to allow the passage of that large, turgid part into the curve of her palm. He sighed, his mouth advancing to her throat and then her cheek, and finally his expert tongue flickered lightly over her lips before diving in deeper.

She lay, dying on his mouth, clasping his cock and almost seeing it with her fingertips as she read each feature of this highly individual organ. The skin was soft to feel but taut, the foreskin straining back from the swelling plum of the glans. She went down to his scrotum, enjoying the spongy feel of his balls and proud that he entrusted her with these symbols of masculinity. But it was his rod that drew her like a magnet; the power-packed, steely hardness of it, the bulging head and the crystal drop beading the slit.

'Not too much,' he growled against her lips. 'I'll come in a minute and I don't want this to be over yet. We've got a lot of catching up to do.'

Removing himself from her greedy grasp, he unravelled the knot that secured her sarong. It fell apart, while she lay on her back and let him take over. The fabric spread out around her, and her tanned body was exposed, except for the fraction of cotton hiding her Mount of Venus.

Her knickers were damp from her earlier arousal and a hot wave of desire made her honeydew flow faster as she remembered the ebony and silver dildo that had

163

filled her secret nook to capacity. That monstrous thing, that priceless toy, the like of which she had never known. So many things had happened to her lately, opening her to endless possibilities, and they were forcing her to admit the existence of an untamed, sensual, brazen side of her that had been suppressed until now.

She let it take a hold of her, a siren smile on her lips as she watched David watching her. He had that intense, lusting look of the male admiring his female's body with its alluring promise of sexual satisfaction.

His eyes went over her full breasts with their dimpled areolae and tight tips, her golden skin, shapely shoulders and slender legs, and his cock twitched. Lisa waited, her heart beating in measured thumps, and when at last his fingers encountered the broad halos of her nipples, she arched her spine to meet them. She gasped as he seized them, rubbing briskly with the balls of his thumbs, and her legs parted involuntarily, her panties edged with brown wisps of hair glinting with dew.

David leant over her, and she felt the warmth of his breath on her teats before the touch of his tongue. Then everything was blanked except the acute bliss of him sucking and nibbling at them, the right one fully extended before he passed on to the left.

She kept her hands away from his manhood, though the upright bough was enough to tempt a nun to break her vows. He was right. This must last and last, even though the blood pounded in her quivering clitoris, making her want to scream out for release.

She was obsessed with the shameless desire to show her secrets to David and hooked her thumbs in the elastic at the top of her briefs. In a split second she was completely nude. She raised her knee, held it away with one hand, and opened the other leg wide, presenting him with an unobscured view of her delta. The ripe, swollen lips were clearly visible through the fleece, the pearl between standing up stiffly.

Continuing to fondle her nipples with one hand, David slid down and pressed his lips to the silky skin of her inner thigh. His hair brushed the acme of her desire. 'Lick me,' she whimpered.

He moved his head and flicked his tongue over her pert-tipped bud while sensation poured through her. She could smell his expensive perfume and the seaweed-scented aroma of her passion. David did not stop, settling down to a steady rhythm – a soft lapping then a brisker tonguing – and his fingers on her nipples made it seem like she had three pleasure points, all intricately linked.

She wailed, a long, ululating cry that rose higher and higher in time to the superb movement of his tongue moving over her clitoris. Her body shook, racked with pleasure, and she squirmed in ecstasy as her crisis came upon her. It rose slowly, an awesome bubble of intensity that erupted in her depths as she ground her pubis against his mouth, his tongue and his nibbling teeth.

In the throes of her bliss, she cried out in a way she had never done before. 'Fuck me, David. Fuck me now, for God's sake!'

He eased back, though bringing his two thumbs down to take the place of his mouth, one at each side of her vibrating, gem-hard bud. Then he knelt upright between her knees and she reached for his cock, guiding it into her eager portal.

He grasped her thighs and gradually penetrated her, staring into her eyes the whole time, then glancing downward to watch his penis disappear, inch by inch, till the root butted against her clit, his pubic hair brushing hers.

She reached out her arms, wanting to embrace him and draw him down to cover her, but he held back, saying, 'No, Lisa. I want to see what I'm doing to you.'

He seized her by the heels and hitched her legs high, her ankles resting on his shoulders. Then he moved slowly in and out of her, while her inner muscles contracted and relaxed, matching his strokes. She was unbearably aroused watching his stalwart member pulling out to the tip, its brown length shining with her own libation. It paused there for a heartbeat, no more, then slid in again, disappearing from sight as their bodies joined.

David's face was tense, his lips drawn back over his white teeth, and he rested his hands on her breasts, fingering the excited nipples. His hips moved, driving his penis in short, to and fro bursts as he observed its progress in and out of her.

Her breasts bounced as his thrusts became faster, and she rocked her body against his, wanting him to lose control and come violently within her. Just for that fraction of time he was hers entirely; this strong, capable man who needed no one. But during the madness of the climactic moment, he needed *her*.

She felt him come in a great spurt, his penis pulsing and jerking like a separate entity fastened to his loins. He gasped and shuddered, then slumped, still joined to her but resting on top of her body, his face buried in the curls tangled around her throat.

Lisa lay supine with her eyes closed, relishing the feel of him and the smell of his hair and their mingled love juices. Unlike Paul, he managed not to squash her. The two men were so different that it was almost as if they came from separate planets. David quickly recovered from his exertions, easing off his weight but cuddling her close in the circle of his arms.

'Mmmm, that was really something,' he said, and she did not doubt his sincerity.

She sighed, satiated, at rest and ready to doze, when she was disturbed by the shrilling of the phone. 'Damn,' she muttered, stirring.

'Let the answerphone pick it up,' David advised sleepily, his hand trailing across her breast and down her ribcage.

'Better not,' she said, and sat up, reaching for the instrument on the bedside table. 'Lisa Sherwin here,' she informed whoever it was, though jerkily, for David was beginning his magic again by petting her nipples.

'It's Paul,' came the brisk reply, and she felt instantly guilty. 'Mother told me she'd been to see you.'

'Yes?' Lisa answered, hoping she sounded cooperative but finding it hard with an expert lover's finger sliding into her sensitive channel.

'She's worried, Lisa. Said you refused to go shopping for the wedding.'

'I explained that I couldn't go tomorrow. I'll be running my stall at the Corn Exchange,' she replied, wriggling her hips in appreciation of David's attention, which had now shifted upward to her bud.

'We need to talk. Now. Without further delay,' Paul said, in that crisp, no-nonsense way which usually reduced his workforce to shreds.

'All right. When?' All Lisa wanted to do was get off the phone and on to David.

'Tonight. I'll come round.'

'Wouldn't it be better if we met in a pub?' she suggested, not wanting him there and unhappy at the thought of being bullied and cajoled into something she did not want.

'No. Expect me at eight,' Paul stated, and hung up.

'The boyfriend?' David asked, and lay flat on his back, pulling her up and arranging her so that she was astride him, her wet cleft settled somewhere in the region of his navel.

'Yes,' she whispered miserably. 'I must see him.'

'And end it?'

She could feel his cock rising again, pushing against the crease of her buttocks, and she opened herself wider, willing for him to possess every part of her – even that forbidden place where she was still undefiled.

'I think so, but it's bloody difficult,' she replied, and her hands came to rest flat on his chest, fingers tickling his nipples.

'Sit on it,' he whispered, regarding her through half-closed lids. 'I want to feel you riding me.'

Lisa raised her bottom a little, and his perpendicular spear pushed against her vulva, needing no assistance to guide it in. It penetrated her vitals and Lisa sat back on it, taking some of her weight on her knees, rising up a little, then dropping down, enjoying the sensation of an impalement which was entirely under her control.

David clasped her haunches, aiding that rise and fall, while she sat with her spine straight and her head thrown back. Her fingers opened her sex lips and found her clitoris. Still swollen from its recent climax, it responded quickly and, as she adopted the regular up and down movement, she felt David's penis growing harder still.

'That's it,' he gasped. 'Work me till I come.'

Frenzy seized her and she rode him furiously, imagining the blood pumping through the veins coursing the length of his cock and its fiery head bumping against her cervix. She wanted to topple him over the edge, the bed becoming a battleground as each strove to attain gratification.

As she rubbed her clitoris, her fingertips touched his belly hair, then the smooth cock every time she rose away from it before plunging back. All that mattered to her now was the shattering pleasure orgasm could bring.

Had Paul or Valerie walked in at that moment, she would not have been able to stop hurtling towards her goal.

She came before David did, falling forward. He yelped as his semen gushed upward, seeming to ricochet through her entire body to her brain. They lay panting for a few seconds, then she slid to the mattress, exhausted. She was dimly aware of him taking her hand and holding it in his, and the warmth of his lips kissing it.

They showered together, playing like dolphins under the spray, then towelled each other dry and dressed, before sitting in the kitchen and drinking coffee.

'Can you cope?' he asked, regarding her seriously across the table.

'I don't know,' she replied honestly.

'Would you like me to stay and help you fuck Paul off?' he asked, a smile playing across his face.

'No. He might get punchy,' she said, half seriously.

'Don't you think I can handle him?'

'I'm sure you can, but there's no need to get involved.'

'Can I see you when he's gone?' David's face was serious again.

Lisa shook her head, wet hair coiling into tight ringlets that framed her face. 'I don't think that's sensible. It might be late.'

'Are you going to sleep with him?' David sounded angry.

'I don't intend to, but he's damned persistent.'

'I think I'd better stay.'

'No. I'll ring you after the market.'

'Can I see you tomorrow night?'

'I'm having dinner with Tanith and Fletcher.'

In the red glow of sunset his face took on a demonic slant, green eyes glittering ominously, and there was an edge to his voice that made her heart beat faster as he said, 'Why are you fraternising with the enemy, Lisa?'

'Because the enemy have offered me a job,' was her crisp reply.

He rose, saying, 'I see. Well, best of luck. You'll need it if you get into cahoots with those two.'

'That remains to be seen, doesn't it?' She wanted to ask more, but something told her not to.

169

She walked with him to the door where he gathered her into his arms, almost lifting her off her feet. 'Are you going to the sale at the Rathbone place?'

'Near Salisbury? Yes, Daphne has asked me to go along, though I've a feeling it'll be out of my league.'

He kissed her, a full, deep, satisfying kiss that carried a hint of possessiveness, then said, 'I'll see you there.'

'David,' she said, looking at him quizzically.

'Yes?'

'Don't push up the bidding, will you?'

He brushed a finger across one of her nipples and smiled mockingly, as he said, 'I might.'

'So that's it, is it? You don't want to marry me?' Paul said, seated on the couch, a glass of lager in his hand. He shook his head slowly, then added, 'I can't believe that, Lisa.'

'Believe it,' she advised, sounding confident but reduced to jelly inside. 'No blame to you. We're just not suited, that's all.'

His blue eyes slitted, and the anger he had so far controlled started to surface. 'You've got another bloke, haven't you? You're shagging someone else!'

It was hard to lie convincingly when, despite soaking in a hot bath, she kept catching whiffs of David about her person, but she tried, averring loudly, 'You're wrong, Paul.' Then she turned defence into attack. 'Good God! You men! Can't conceive that a woman would want to be free of them without immediately assuming she has another lined up to take their place.'

'It's usually the case,' he muttered, and drained his glass.

'Not with me.'

'You can't manage alone.' Paul was sticking to this stubbornly.

'I can,' she said, wishing she was as convinced as she sounded.

He eyed the room – the cracks in the walls, the patch

170

of damp like a map of Africa on the ceiling – then stated emphatically, 'This place is falling apart. I was going to have it repaired before we sold it.'

'There you go again!' she stormed, jumping to her feet and feeling stronger when she looked down on him. 'Organising me. I've told you I don't want to sell.'

'You might have to, if you finish with me,' he threatened darkly. 'The town planning people might condemn the building as unsafe.'

A bolt of fear shot through her. She had been dreading this.

'They wouldn't . . . They couldn't. Could they?' she faltered.

Paul stood up, his burly shoulders between her and escape. He stared down at her, saying heavily, 'They'd be within their rights if it was proved to be structurally unsound. The frontage may be unstable. A part of it might collapse on passers-by. You'd probably be liable for compensation . . .'

'All right. Shut up about it! I get the picture,' Lisa shouted angrily.

She took to a worried pacing, up and down over the threadbare carpet, her full skirt undulating around her legs. She had chosen something sensible for this meeting, not wishing to encourage Paul in the smallest degree. But the evening was too close to cover her arms or swaddle her body in a sweater, and her breasts rose and fell with her agitated breathing, the nipples like cones against the thin black T-shirt.

To her dismay, she saw that certain look in his eyes which denoted that his loins were responding, and though she tried to brush past him, he grabbed her arm and yanked her up against him. His breath was tainted with lager.

'Look here, Lisa. We can work it out, can't we? I'll put the wedding on hold, if you feel it's too much of a rush. I can't say fairer than that. Mother'll blow her stack, but I can handle her.'

'Your mother will want to kill me,' Lisa predicted gloomily. 'She can't stand me as it is.'

'That's not true,' he declared, and slid a hand round her bottom, pressing her against the swelling in his jeans.

Lisa wanted to bring up her knee and jab him in the balls, but she was looking at the room – the noticeable cracks, the damp patch – and an abyss of despair opened before her. She couldn't afford to offend him or part on bad terms.

'Could you do with another beer?' she asked instead, forcing a smile.

'Do I ever say no?' he said, grinning as he gave her buttock a final squeeze before releasing her.

Lisa scuttled into the kitchen and opened the refrigerator, buying time to collect her thoughts. To her horror, she heard Paul come in behind her. His hands landed at the back of her waist, pulling her into the heat of his crotch.

'Don't worry about the lager,' he said huskily, and lifted her skirt.

Lisa froze, half bent over, a can of lager burning icily into her palm. Her skirt was up round her waist and she could feel the solid mass of Paul's bare cock grinding against the strip of lycra that covered the avenue between her bottom cheeks.

'Stop it,' she enunciated clearly, though anger threatened to swamp her.

He chuckled and pushed her knickers aside, feeling for her vulva and working his cock head around it. 'Oh, come on, Lisa,' he urged, his thickened, slurry voice indicating that he had been to the pub before visiting her. 'You said you wanted us to try it in different ways. Bend over a bit more, darling . . . I'll give you a taste of different . . . Shove my old man right up you.'

'I said get off me!' Lisa hissed.

She swung round and hit him in the belly with the

172

beer can. He grunted, a look of utter astonishment on his face.

'You bitch!' he spluttered.

'Have you got the message?' she cried, a wild-eyed termagant ready to defend herself against all comers.

'Lisa . . .' he muttered, retreating towards the door. 'You'll regret this.'

'Maybe I will, but it's my decision. Now get out!'

I've blown it, she thought, driving towards Dunscombe for the dinner engagement. Yet her overriding emotion was one of relief.

She had unplugged the phone and gone to bed after Paul had left in high dudgeon last night, and had slept fitfully, dreaming of bossy officials who looked like Valerie demanding that she move out of her old house and into a new one in Kingsmead.

The flea market had been busy, but she was running low on stock and her takings were down.

'Never mind,' Daphne had reassured her. 'Think of the sale on Friday. I can't wait to see what's about. That's the fun of dealing. You can't predict how it will turn out.'

Fun if you're doing it as a hobby, Lisa thought as she approached Hawkhurst Abbey, but not if you're living on a shoestring and it's your only source of income.

It was still light – that hot-washed light of a summer evening. The sky was unreal, streaked with all manner of shades associated with fire, and the sun an orange ball on the horizon, with funereal purple night clouds gathering to act as pall-bearers.

She came to the house, black and solid, with its fantastic towers and barley-sugar twist chimney pots outlined against the sky. The light was reflected in the great bay windows, shining like blood.

Lee opened the door and led her inside.

The tango music was there again. Did they ever play anything else? she wondered. It became louder as she followed Lee through a succession of doors, eventually finding herself in a ballroom.

Ornate gilded pillars disappeared into the darkness. They were designed to resemble palm trees with life-sized figures of naked slave girls chained to their trunks. The walls were crimson and the drapes black, the sombre hues repeated in huge mirrors under the sub-dued glow of deco ceiling lamps.

There were plaster statues – women with huge breasts, short skirts, beefy legs and high-heeled shoes and men with outsized cocks and swollen testicles – and paintings, copies of Franz von Stuck, with his slyly smiling Pan, fighting fauns and beautiful, fatal Sphinx with her terrible kiss.

A couple were gliding on a shining sea of parquet flooring. It was Tanith and Fletcher, so absorbed in the dance that they did not acknowledge Lisa's presence.

The music was coming from the petal-shaped horn of an old-fashioned, clockwork gramophone. Frankie stood by, ready to crank the handle when the record finished. Two other couples watched from gilt chairs at little round tables, sipping cocktails and smoking Turkish cigarettes, the women using slim, elegant holders. All were dressed in the fashions of the jazz age.

Lisa flushed with embarrassment as she realised that far from stumbling on a neglected collection during her last visit, the garments in the wardrobes were put to regular use. Now her eyes were drawn to the lithe Valentino lookalike who was watching the dancers closely, stopping them now and again and demonstrat-ing a step, his arms round Tanith while Fletcher nodded and observed.

It *was* Fletcher, of course, but as Lisa had never seen him. He had been transformed into a swarthy gangster, a member of the Cosa Nostra, perhaps, trafficking in illegal drugs, boot-legging, gambling and prostitution. A wide-brimmed black felt hat was angled over his eyes, a white silk scarf was wrapped around his neck, and a dark suit clinched his supple waist and lean hips.

He caught Tanith as the teacher spun her to him, her tangerine silk dress swirling high, disclosing black stockings upheld by orange garters, an expanse of pale-skinned thigh and the bright, foxy wedge at her fork.

She halted gracefully, her feet correctly positioned in the Louis-heeled black shoes with ribbons criss-crossing the ankles. Her back was naked to the waist and Fletcher spread his bare hand over it. Leaning backward slightly, he supported her on his thigh, her legs dragging behind her as he took her weight, then assumed a rocking motion, guided by the feel of the music. Her left arm was wound round his neck while her right hand was engulfed in his, held tightly against his chest.

She lifted one leg to clamp round his hip, grinding her red-furred pubis against him. He stared down into her face, then pressed upward with his thigh, rubbing her between the legs. Not allowing her to find completion, he moved his feet in a pattern round her, leading her through the complicated steps as they slid across the floor.

The dance was supremely sexy: the man in command, the woman following, thighs touching, hands touching, her breasts pressed to his chest, her face against his cheek.

Lisa could feel a pulse throbbing in her core in time to the beat and, as she moved, the silk between her legs dragged on her lower lips. It was a soft, arousing friction. At that moment, Valentino approached her and bowed, speaking in an accent that was pure Home Counties.

'Would you like to dance? Normally, I wouldn't ask like this. I'd merely stare at you from my table and jerk my head. You would smile and nod or look away, depending on whether you fancied me or not.'

'I thought you might have been Argentinian,' Lisa

said bluntly, giving him her hand. She ached to get into the rhythm of the tango.

'I am,' he said, smiling widely. 'My name's Eduardo. My parents come from Buenos Aires but I was born and raised in England. They own a restaurant in Richmond.'

'And you teach the tango?'

'I do. I learned it from my father. He's a maestro, recognised world-wide. That's what I do . . . teach tango. Mr Robillard wishes me to teach you.'

He was a sexy-looking young man, and Lisa had already discovered the benefit of having a Latin lover. The hand holding hers was warm and smooth. He wore an evening suit, every hair was in place, and he wafted a pungent, musky perfume.

The record ended and Tanith and Fletcher ran towards them. He leant over and kissed Lisa on the cheek, a gesture of familiarity which she found surprising and not entirely pleasant. It was as if he had already taken charge of her. I'm not working for him yet, she reminded herself.

'You will learn the tango, darling,' he said, and his grey eyes bored into hers. 'It is essential to our partnership.'

'I'd like to. I've always wanted to learn. I know a little about ballroom dancing. We did it at school,' she told him, and immediately despised herself for prattling. Fletcher definitely raised her blood pressure.

'You'll be fine at it,' he answered, with his sardonic smile. 'But first you must dress suitably. It makes a world of difference if one is wearing the right clothes . . . creating the right atmosphere. I know you'll look wonderful, for I have already seen you.'

'When?' Lisa demanded, her cheeks hot with panic.

'The other day, when you found all those lovely things in the dressing room.'

'You saw me? H-how?' Lisa stammered, wishing the earth would open and swallow her whole.

'Never mind how,' he replied, his arm snaking round

her waist and his sinewy hand sliding lower to caress the line between her buttocks.

'I want to watch you again, doing everything you did that afternoon.'

Chapter Eight

Cocktails! What a wonderful invention, Lisa thought, giggling helplessly to herself.

She had read somewhere that they had been dreamed up late in the First World War (something to do with servant shortage) and adopted by the post-war Bright Young Things to help pass that tedious lull between early evening and dinner. They had christened it 'the cocktail hour'.

Lee, acting as barman and using an original, green enamelled shaker, served a variety of different drinks with quirky names, each glass ornamented with a cherry on a stick, or maybe an olive. Even before going into dinner, Lisa was feeling slightly intoxicated.

Chandeliers hung from the rafters of the hall. Their light broke in rainbow shards on lead-crystal glass and danced on polished Georgian silver and gilt-rimmed Royal Doulton the length and breadth of the refectory table. There Fletcher's guests sat surrounded by the panoply of war and his extremely desirable collection of antiquities.

Fletcher occupied a thronelike chair at the head of the board, with Lisa on one side and a platinum blonde called Carol on the other. Like the rest, she wore period costume; blue silk lounging pyjamas with a coiled silver snake embroidered over the left breast. The tunic was unbuttoned almost to the waist, displaying full orbs that jiggled whenever she moved, but Fletcher was not looking at her. His attention riveted on Lisa.

Tanith faced him, with Eduardo fawning on her, as well as a fat, balding man named Andrew, who was arguing with the Argentinian and claiming to be an expert tangoist, with trophies to prove it.

Another woman, known as Babs, heavily made up and with her hair cut in a severe bob, flaunted her angular body in gold lamé with fringes. Her escort, Jamie, several years her junior, had sleekly greased hair, marcasite and amethyst cufflinks and a black barathea evening suit with satin lapels. His handsome features were marred by a petulant expression.

Lisa felt completely out of her depth and was grateful for the cocktails.

She had no way of knowing if these were their real names or sobriquets adopted for the evening, as with their clothes. The scene had taken on the brittle quality of a Noel Coward comedy.

Lee and Frankie served the meal, their faces masked and their catsuits unzipped over nipples and private parts, available for touching. Course followed course, each superbly presented on the finest porcelain and accompanied by the correct wine – a Burgundy as red as blood, a Sauterne as pale as citronella and the sweet, tingling fizz of champagne.

The dessert was a triumph – a wickedly decadent concoction of peaches in brandy sauce, served with whipped cream and chopped almonds. More Bollinger followed, withdrawn from Regency wine coolers and poured, frothing, into cut-glass flutes.

Though shy at first, Lisa's confidence rose as she became aware of admiring eyes. Flushed with alcohol and filled with a bubbling sense of achievement, she allowed herself to recognise that she was beautiful.

She had elected to wear a black silk jersey dress, the tight skirt finishing just below the ankles, revealing stilt-heeled satin shoes. She had bought them in a fit of extravagance for the end-of-college ball where, alas, no Prince Charming had been forthcoming, despite the halter top that clung seductively to her breasts.

Tonight, after having spent some time deliberating on the vexed question of underwear versus exposure, she had decided to be daring, and was naked under the sensual fabric that brushed her thighs, stroked her bottom and caressed her mound. Her breasts swelled and her nipples were permanently erect due to the constant chafing as the jersey slid over them.

Her hair was swept up and secured on the crown by a velvet scrunchie, from which tumbled a profusion of ringlets, with a few wispy strands falling on each side of her face and at her nape. Rooting through her junk jewellery, she had come up with a jet necklace and matching earrings.

'I remembered that you were lovely,' Fletcher said, staring at her with those unimaginably cold eyes, 'but I didn't realise just how stunning. Congratulations, Lisa. Do you think you'll enjoy working with me?'

'I guess so,' she managed to say, astonished as he had not yet made a proposal or offered terms or done any of the things she understood employers usually did.

'I'll get a contract drawn up. When would you like to start? How about Monday?' he asked and, without taking his eyes off her, slipped a hand into the aperture over Frankie's depilated mound and touched the gold labial rings.

She stood by his chair without giving any indication that she welcomed or disliked this invasion, as impassive as a figure made of wax.

'Monday it is,' Lisa said, unable to look away because she was fascinated by the way Fletcher's long, strong finger toyed with Frankie's sexual parts and tugged at the rings to elongate the pink wings.

'She's so smooth there. Would you like to be shaved and pierced?' he enquired suddenly, his eyes razor keen.

'I've never considered it,' Lisa replied, keeping her voice down, though he had made no effort to do so.

'Haven't you?' he said, raising a sceptical brow. 'Not yielded to the temptation to peep in magazines that feature the art of body piercing? Not wondered how it would be to have a stud through your tongue? Or your clitoris? This is one of the rarest, and generally the province of the most dedicated piercing enthusiast. Wearing jewellery in the clitoral hood constantly stimulates it. You could have orgasms all the time, even walking along the street.'

'I don't think that's for me,' Lisa averred, though her gem tingled as he spoke of it.

He shrugged, and remarked, 'You might surprise even yourself, starting with depilation. Maybe I will arrange it, but your pussy is wonderful as it is . . . such a thick bush. Soon, I shall brush my fingers through it.'

His voice thrilled her to the core, a purely visceral feeling, and her juices flowed, wetting that very hair he spoke of so lovingly, and spreading to the inside tops of her thighs. He was so handsome with his aquiline nose, dark eyebrows, cleft chin and that sensual, kissable mouth. She wondered how many women had experienced his lips on theirs, and on their nipples and deltas, brought to ecstasy by his mouth and tongue.

Lisa guessed they would have been legion – young, not so young, rich and poor alike – but all would have to possess some quality or quirk that titillated his jaded appetite.

The others watched him frigging Frankie while engaged in their own pursuit of pleasure. Tanith sipped her demi-tasse of aromatic Turkish coffee, apparently unmoved when Eduardo inveigled his fingers into the top of her dress, teasing her nipples into sharp points.

One of Andrew's podgy hands had disappeared into the region of his lap, his far-away expression indicating that he was masturbating. Babs had opened Jamie's fly and withdrawn his long, curving penis, subjecting it to fellatio. Carol inserted her hand into the waistband of her pyjama trousers and started to rub her mound.

The atmosphere in the hall was charged – potent, sexual, almost narcotic in its intensity. Lisa's body pulsed in response. Shivers of excitement made her nipples rise even more, begging for caresses. She wanted to feel Fletcher touching her cleft, in the same way he was fondling Frankie's.

Every inch of her skin prickled with desire, her legs sensitive to the movement of her black hold-up stockings rasping against them as she crossed her knees. This brought pressure to bear on the rosebud emerging from the flushed labial folds.

Glancing up, she could see Frankie's nub protruding like a tiny fat thumb from the sharply defined slit formed by her swollen wet lips. Her body trembled, but she kept her straight-backed pose, looking neither right nor left nor even down, though she must have longed to watch what Fletcher was doing to her.

His finger flicked her clit head, but he looked at Lisa, spearing her with those steel-hard eyes, and said, 'How does it make you feel, seeing her about to come?'

'Hot ... aching ... needing orgasm myself,' Lisa brought out disjointedly.

'Tell me what's happening between your legs,' he insisted, speeding up his massage of Frankie's red bud, the lips forming a slippery groove around his finger as if wanting to suck it in.

His voice was husky, his words like a flaming arrow searing into the centre of Lisa's being. She could see that Frankie's control was slipping. A rivulet of sweat trickled down her throat from under the white mask, and her breathing quickened. She could not restrain her hip movements, her pelvis lifting to meet that devastatingly pleasurable stroking.

Lisa wriggled in sympathy, squeezing her thighs

together in an attempt to please the shameless little organ that dominated her sex.

'My clitoris is throbbing,' she panted, and reached down to drag a fold of her skirt into her cleft in order to rub it.

'No, Lisa,' he commanded, while a stifled moan escaped from Frankie. 'You are not to seek satisfaction until I say you can. Talk about your frustration. Make me feel it, too.'

Lisa froze, hand poised above her pubis, the ache transformed into a dragging pain. She had never spoken in this way before, but now it seemed like the most natural thing in the world. 'I'm wet,' she confessed, her face as pink as her hidden lips. 'My vagina's opening like a hungry mouth. But it's my bud that screams for mercy. I long to be rubbed there . . . a hard and slippery wet rub.'

Fletcher smiled, the sardonic lift of his chiselled lips both thrilling and terrifying, giving her an adrenalin rush.

'You want me to do it?' he asked, in a sibilant whisper. 'Or would you care for Tanith to use her skills on you? She will, if I give the word. Perhaps you'd appreciate being made to suffer for your pleasure? Confess your deepest, darkest, most perverted fantasy, and I'll gratify it.'

Daphne's photographs flashed across her inner eye: the humiliated girl who had yet succeeded in despising the voyeur, and those who had been bound by their master, welcoming the kiss of the lash and the restriction of the chains.

Suddenly she came back down to earth. 'There's nothing I want,' she declared, and attempted a laugh that rang hollow. 'I'm boringly normal.'

'Not from what I've seen of you,' he said, and paused in his work on Frankie's nubbin, withdrawing his hand and wiping his fingers fastidiously on the damask napiery.

A strangled sob broke from her lips and her hips pumped the air, tears of disappointment glistening like diamonds at the eye slits of her mask. He gave her a dismissive slap on the bottom and she knelt to kiss his foot before rising to walk away.

Down the table, Lisa could see Tanith sitting upright in her chair, smoking a cigarette. Eduardo had disappeared beneath the cloth, and she guessed that if she were to take a peek she would see him on his knees with his face buried between Tanith's thighs. Andrew was already doing so, bent at an awkward angle for a better view, his hand busy with the short, thick cock poking out of his trousers.

Babs had just brought Jamie off, her make-up smeared with his emission. Her tongue came out, licking in droplets with the slit-eyed enjoyment of a cat supping cream. Carol was beyond recall, her trousers pushed down her thighs as she massaged her avenue with such force that the glasses clinked.

Behind them, Lee and Frankie stood against the panelling, two thin, masked slaves awaiting to obey their master's will with the stoicism of zombies.

Fletcher rose and clapped his hands. At once everyone stopped what they were doing and looked at him. 'Tonight we have a novice in our midst,' he announced, a tall, distinguished figure, faultlessly attired and perfectly at home in that stately setting. 'You shall help me instruct her how to give rein her instincts and shuck off her repressions. Let us retire and contemplate the accomplishment of this pleasant duty.'

Lisa lay on silk, covered in silk, embraced by silk. Her eyelids felt weighted and she could not be bothered to lift them. Perfume filtered into her nostrils – the alluring scents of lilies, roses and jasmine mingled with herbs and musk in a sensual brew. And there was an undercurrent, too – the spicy, salty fragrance of women.

Voices murmured above and around her. 'She's awake,' someone said. It sounded like Tanith.

'What's happening? Where am I?' Lisa groaned, opening her eyes and struggling to sit up.

'This is my bedroom. You passed out, darling. Too much bubbly,' Tanith replied lightly, seated beside her on a wide divan spread with oriental quilts and heaped with bolster-shaped cushions. It had scarlet silk tenting looped above it.

'I'm thirsty,' Lisa croaked, feeling a fool. How embarrassing to get drunk on her first dinner party at Hawkhurst Abbey.

A glass of iced orange juice appeared by magic, served on a silver salver by Frankie.

Lisa sipped gratefully and marshalled her wandering wits. She looked round the room. More Eastern ornamentation – a vamp's lair, with crimson and gold walls, leopardskin throw-overs, arabesques, a latticed screen and damascened pots. A hooker stood on a round brass table. Two black marble statues of odalisques wearing turbans and nothing else, their big-nippled breasts jutting out aggressively, guarded the horseshoe-shaped Moorish doorway.

'Where's Fletcher?' Lisa asked, vaguely remembering collapsing, and then his arms about her as she was carried upstairs.

'Not far away,' Tanith said with a slow smile. 'Don't worry about him. We girls wanted you to ourselves. Who needs men? Have you ever been made love to by a woman?'

'No!' Lisa answered, shocked and struck by the expression on Tanith's face – a look charged with carnal desire.

Tanith slid closer to her and started to caress her bare arms. Her soft touch sent shivers down Lisa's spine.

'Have you ever wanted to experiment?' Tanith asked.

'Yes,' Lisa suddenly admitted, as much to herself as to her audience.

'I think we should demonstrate,' Tanith said, glancing at Babs and Carol, who lounged at the foot of the divan. Frankie stood a little apart, waiting for Tanith's instructions.

'It'll be a pleasure,' Babs replied, her fingertips gliding sensuously into the opening of Carol's pyjama jacket.

She was bigger than her, tall and striking, the gold lamé accentuating her small breasts. Carol leant into her, eyes half closed as the thin fingers stroked her nipples, till Babs relented, opened the jacket wide and closed her mouth over a taut, pink teat, sucking strongly. Mewing noises issued from Carol's arched throat.

'You see?' Tanith breathed into Lisa's ear. 'Carol's getting pleasure from Babs, possibly more than she would from a man. Women know how to please other women ... when to be gentle, when to be rough. It's like making love to oneself.'

She reached down and took one of Lisa's feet into her palm, caressing the toes through the fragile stocking. Her fingers passed lightly over the arch and round her ankle, then ascended to her calf, her knee and progressed up her thigh. Her breasts pressed against Lisa's, firm and full, the nipples brushing her own, which rose in response.

Tanith's delicate fingers worked round the top of Lisa's stocking and reached higher to feather across her mound. Lisa sighed and relaxed her legs, already hotly aroused by the scenes in the Great Hall during that unconventional meal.

Babs and Carol had shifted position, standing up and facing each other as they began the slow, graceful removal of each other's clothing, moving as if to music heard by no one except themselves.

Babs eased off Carol's jacket, running her hands appreciatively over the full, shapely breasts, and lingering on the darkly flushed halos. Meanwhile, Carol slipped the shoulder straps down across Babs's narrow shoulders. The molten gold fabric slithered to her waist then, impelled by its own weight, fell to form a shimmering puddle at her feet. Now Babs wore nothing but a pair of coffee-hued chiffon French knickers with wide legs and lace appliqué.

Her fingers at Carol's waist, she opened the side buttons, and the satin trousers joined the dress on the Aubusson carpet, along with Babs's knickers. Their bodies could hardly have been more different; the athletic flanks, flat bottom and little breasts of Babs and the generous bosom, rounded buttocks, wide hips and curved thighs of Carol.

As Lisa watched this fascinating display, transfixed, she was aware of Tanith's hand reaching its goal. Fingertips brushed lightly over her mons. Lisa parted her legs to receive this caress as Tanith's artful digits slipped neatly between the dark folds of her sex.

'No panties, Lisa,' she whispered, her breath scented with cinnamon. 'I guessed you weren't wearing any. Neither am I. Feel me.'

Despite the ferment of desire churning within her, Lisa was thrown into panic by the voice of conscience that insisted this was not normal. One should not fornicate with a member of one's own sex. It was forbidden. And this made it ten times more attractive.

Beneath Tanith's touch, Lisa's clitoris was aching, and as she began a circular movement of the sensitive sliver of flesh, all hesitation was banished. She opened willingly under Tanith's careful exploration, allowing her access to the lubricious entrance to her womanhood.

Tanith's mouth sought hers, a tentative meeting of lips; soft, enquiring, with not the lightest suggestion of force. Lisa met her tongue tip with her own. She tasted of spices and warm wine, and a hint of Abdulla tobacco. It was bewitching and delightful, so different to the men Lisa had kissed. Here there was no hint of the desire for conquest which even the most considerate of males can never quite banish.

'Touch me,' Tanith whispered against her mouth, and pulled up her tangerine dress.

Eyes closed, still lost in Tanith's kiss, Lisa moved her hand down, the tips of her fingers encountering soft skin and then the crisp feel of the red curls that flamed between Tanith's legs. It felt flat and familiar, like touching herself, and because she knew precisely how to pleasure her own clitoris she was able to locate and fondle Tanith's.

Needing to be naked, they took off their gowns and lay back on the bed, lips and hands discovering each other in perfect harmony. Lisa was excited by Tanith's moans of pleasure, no longer caring who caressed her just as long as the stimulation of her bud continued till she erupted. Performing the same loving act on Tanith, it seemed there was no division – hands and clits united in a joyous dance of passionate release.

Carol lay on the floor, with Babs kneeling over her, her backside to her partner's face as she lowered her sex to her eager tongue. As she received this benediction, so she bestowed it on Carol, leaning down to lap at the juice between her splayed thighs.

Tanith called out to Frankie. 'Come over here. Attend to Lisa's breasts.'

Frankie crouched beside them, fingers arousing Lisa's nipples, adding to the tumultuous sensations in her loins. Lisa increased her slippery friction on Tanith's nubbin, each quick-drawn breath and moan issued from her lover's lips adding to her confidence.

She could feel the coil tightening in her womb and the waves rising higher. The sensations became ever more intense, reaching a crescendo and rushing up from her toes to shatter in her brain.

And as she climaxed, she knew that Tanith was there too.

'Dirty slut!' Fletcher hissed, appearing from behind the bed curtains.

He leaped on Lisa, dragging her up with his hand in her hair, nails lacerating her scalp. She struggled, fought and scratched, attempting to draw back her knee and jab him in the balls. He was too strong for her, grabbing her by the back of the neck and jerking her forward with such force that she lost balance and fell face down at his feet.

'Dirty slut!' he repeated, shaking her. 'What are you? Say it!'

'Get lost!' she snarled. 'What the hell are you playing at?'

'Say it!' he repeated, his foot in the small of her back.

'No!' Lisa shouted.

'Very well,' he grated, his voice quiet now but all the more menacing. 'You must be taught a sharp lesson.' He swung round to the waiting, watching women, saying, 'Bring her. No clothes. Just her stockings and shoes,' then he disappeared as quickly as he had come.

'What's going on?' Lisa spluttered, struggling to stand.

'Do as you're told,' Tanith advised. 'The master has spoken.'

'He's not my bloody master,' Lisa muttered, but straightened her stockings and stepped into her black satin shoes.

Tanith gave her a serious, searching glance and went to the tall-boy. She returned with clothing over one arm, laid the things on the bed and started to dress. Soon she was wearing a pair of bronze satin camiknickers with the top drooping down over her breasts.

She looked more seductive, raunchy and powerful than when completely naked, with her legs covered in bronze stockings upheld by garters, her feet thrust into bronze shoes with high heels and her hands and arms encased in tight, bronze leather elbow-length gloves.

She took a riding crop from a cabinet drawer and made a few practice swipes.

'That sounds healthy. Someone's butt is going to sting

189

tonight,' Babs said, parading in front of the mirror in black calfskin breeches that ended in riding boots, and a metal-studded leather jacket. She adjusted the peaked leather cap set at an angle over her short hair.

Carol had changed into a French maid's outfit, complete with short, full skirt, tight bodice, frilled apron and cap. Court shoes bunched her calf muscles and black fishnet stockings emphasised the whiteness of her thighs and the brown fur of her wedge, framed between suspenders.

'Come on,' Tanith said, and they frog marched Lisa across the bedroom and into the passage.

At the end was an elevator surrounded by a cast-iron cage, elaborately scrolled in swirls of acanthus leaves and trailing vines. Tanith pressed a button and the gate slid back, giving access to a polished mahogany interior. It was the kind of lift once found in top-class hotels. The doors closed noiselessly and it began a steady, humming descent.

Dungeons, Lisa thought, perspiration breaking out at her armpits and under her breasts. Daphne was correct in her assumption. He really does have a dungeon!

'This is ridiculous,' she said indignantly. 'Fletcher has no right to do this.'

'On the contrary. He has every right,' Tanith answered smoothly. 'You came here of your own free will. No one will stop you leaving, if that's what you really want to do. Is it?'

'Yes! No ... I don't know,' Lisa cried, longing to go but wanting to stay just to see what was going to happen next.

Her blood was running fast, her pulse pounding. This was possibly the most exhilarating evening she had ever spent in her entire life.

'He's bloody high handed,' she complained. 'Acts as if he's God Almighty.'

'He is, around here,' Tanith replied, smiling as she

braced the crop between her gloved hands. 'His family have owned the abbey since time immemorial. They came over with William the Conqueror. Don't you recognise that Norman nose? They were never backward in coming forward when it came to *droit de seigneur*.'

Babs butted in eagerly. 'I'd have loved to be a lord in the days when it was the alleged right of a feudal baron to take the virginity of a vassal's bride.'

Tanith grinned at her, saying, 'You've a twisted streak.'

'I know. Isn't it great to be bi? We get the best of all possible worlds,' Babs answered smugly.

'The old days wouldn't have been so great. Fine if you were a man, I suppose, but what about girl power? They'd have burned you at the stake,' Tanith reminded her.

'So Fletcher really is well connected? It's not just a pose?' Lisa said, as the lift bumped to a gentle halt.

'He is. Of far better blood than that silly bitch, Lady Fiona,' Tanith replied, on a bitter note.

It was cold down there, a damp cold that penetrated the very marrow. Lisa shivered, goose-pimples stippling her flesh. She was taken along a stone-flagged passage, surrounded on all sides by granite walls with a low ceiling overhead.

They reached a heavily studded door. Tanith pushed it open and Lisa found herself in a long room with a vaulted roof, also constructed of grey stone. The air was warm, and she caught a glimpse of radiators. Whatever the purpose of this awesome place, Fletcher had ordained that its occupants should not die of pneumonia.

What was its purpose? It did not take a genius to supply the answer. A torture chamber? Almost, judging by the iron rings fixed to the walls and the rows of implements hanging there, such as manacles, whips, chains, blindfolds and gags. If she had not already seen

Daphne's photographs and realised their purpose, Lisa would have been even more apprehensive.

Games, she thought, looking at the people around her. They are indulging in adult games for amusement and sexual gratification. She saw Andrew, his portly body naked and stretched over a bench, wrists and ankles tethered. His cock was erect, sticking out from his underbelly, and he quivered, but whether in fear or anticipation it was impossible to ascertain.

Tanith approached him, standing where he could see her. He shook even more, his watery eyes goggling at her. 'Mercy, mistress!' he cried.

'Mercy? You expect me to show you mercy? A miserable slug like you? I saw you wanking at the dinner table. It was disgusting. What are you?' she cried, supremely disdainful as she stood there with her legs spread in the high heels, swishing the crop.

'I'm disgusting,' he moaned, his penis jumping. 'A foul, horrible slug.'

'And what should I do with you?' she hissed, the crop stirring the air in front of his face.

'Punish me, mistress.'

'How must I punish you?'

'Beat me, mistress.'

'Quite right,' she agreed, and moved round to his wobbling, pale-skinned bottom.

The sound of the crop meeting flesh echoed through the vault. Andrew grunted. Tanith whipped him again. He squirmed. Again the crop sought out its target, his pasty skin wearing red roses now. 'I can't come!' he gasped. 'I need – I need –'

'Take him!' Tanith ordered, staring down at her victim with supreme hauteur and distaste.

Jamie stepped forward, his erect member boldly outlined against the black of his trousers, erect and rigid as a lance. He spat on his hand, transferred the saliva to his cock and then parted the division of Andrew's rump. Bending his knees slightly, he plunged his phallus into the anus presented to him. Despite its size, it slid effortlessly up that well-trodden avenue.

Lisa tried not to watch, but was unable to keep her eyes away from the sight of that elegant young man working his cock into the fundament of the gross creature tied to the bench. Andrew groaned, and his face expressed pleasure not pain as he spurted, the white discharge shooting from him to spatter the stone flags. Jamie pumped faster as he reached the supreme moment, then he paused, breathing hard before withdrawing his weapon, slippery with his own tribute.

Inspired by this, Babs set about Carol, snatching up a tawse, ordering her to lift her skirt, and then applying it mercilessly.

Fletcher caressed Tanith's breasts as he looked at Lisa and said, 'Is she ready to dance?'

'Yes, master,' Tanith whispered, pressing her body to his.

'And you will dance with Eduardo.'

'Yes, master.'

Music echoed through the dungeon from hidden speakers. Tango again, but a different refrain. Lisa stood waiting, spine straight, head up, though horribly aware of her nudity and the vulnerability of her pudenda. She knew that her appearance was provocative – the stockings that gripped her upper thighs and the high-heeled shoes. She felt herself to be under lecherous scrutiny, in much the same way that Daphne had been, all those years ago, in the New York peep show.

Fletcher closed in on her and she did not flinch. He wore his mafia suit, tip-tilted hat, white opera scarf and white spats over his dancing pumps. She felt his fingers on her belly, tracing along the sharp line that edged the triangle of her pubic bush. He pulled at the curls.

'I told you I'd touch you soon,' he reminded, in that deep voice that went right to her G-spot. 'Now you'll dance with me, and learn the true meaning of tango.'

His eyes never leaving hers, burning into them with

hynotic ice-fire, he snapped his fingers at Tanith. At once Lisa felt hands at the back of her head, then sudden darkness as a scarf was bound round her eyes and tied securely.

'Why?' she whispered, groping for and finding his arm.

'You will concentrate on the music and me. Nothing else.'

With sight gone, her other senses came into their own; every nuance of the music, the smell of Fletcher, the taste of him on her tongue and the feel of his hands, guiding her across the floor. He stopped, held her firmly, and waited for the beat.

He clasped her left hand with his right and pressed her body against his chest with his other arm, his thigh brushing hers in a sliding movement as she stepped back and away from him.

The darkness disorientated her. She was forced to rely on Fletcher, accepting his mastery and moving as if she was an extension of him. He was the master indeed – of herself, as well as the tango.

Dip, slide, rock – her knees slightly bent, his feet weaving intricate patterns between hers, and her senses reeling under the impact of his closeness, his control and his perfect timing.

'I want you,' she whispered, and felt his penis leap in response, pressed momentarily against her pubis.

She lifted her leg high, bringing her cleft closer to that desired shaft, and the sweet, strong smell of her honey-dew reached her nostrils. He did not pause, and she was forced to take her leg down.

'You do?' he murmured, catching her as she stumbled, losing the rhythm.

'I do . . . only you,' she repeated.

'And David Maccabene?'

'You know about him?'

'Naturally. I keep tabs on my rivals.'

194

Blind behind the scarf, and weak with desire, she said, 'It's you I want.'

The music stopped and he halted abruptly, clutching her to him for a second. Then he let her go, yanking the blindfold from her eyes. His glittered as he stared down into her face.

'If you want me, you must accept everything I offer. Will you do that?'

'Yes,' she answered recklessly, unable to think further than having him slide his cock into her needy channel.

'Even this?' he asked, and spun her round.

With her back pressed to his chest, her buttocks hot against the hardness behind his fly, she faced the strange structure that stood in the shadows. Two beams were fastened to a base on the floor, about four feet apart. They sloped inward, coming together much higher up to form a rigid triangle. A thick, iron ring was set in the apex, and others at the lower corners and in various positions along the sides.

'What is it?' she whispered, rotating her backside, still filled with that insane, irrational urge to mate with this man.

'Let me show you.'

Before she realised his intention she found herself standing in front of the thing.

'Hold out your arms,' he said, his breath whispering over that erogenous zone where her shoulders joined her spine.

She did as he told her, but said, 'Is this a sick joke?'

'No joke, Lisa,' he answered, and metal cuffs snapped shut round her wrists. They were linked by a short chain. 'Now raise your arms high.'

'No, I won't!' she shouted.

'Rebellious,' he sighed, more in sorrow than anger.

In seconds she was tethered to the iron ring, the pull on her muscles making her yell. Someone adjusted it for her height, but even so, the position was uncomfortable with her face poking between the uprights and her arms

195

chained above her head. The worst thing about it was that she could not see who took off her shoes, parted her legs and stretched them open, chaining them so she could not move.

This can't be happening, she thought. I'm dreaming, surely? I'll wake up to find I'm alone in my cosy bed, so excited by this nightmare that I'll have to slip a hand between my legs and finger myself to orgasm.

It was no dream. She felt the ache in her biceps, and cool air wafting between her lower lips and private orifices that were completely exposed by the acute angle of her legs.

'Let me go, you bastard!' she raged, tugging fruitlessly at her bonds, yet aware of a secret tightness in her loins and juice seeping from her vulva.

'You'll learn to enjoy it,' Fletcher promised, and kissed her forehead, then slipped a hand down to her open sex, caressing the full outer lips and then the inner ones. He paused when he encountered her clitoris poking out like a miniature penis, adding, 'Ah, it seems you are already enjoying it.'

The chamber fell silent, as if holding its breath in anticipation. Fletcher had vanished from Lisa's limited field of vision. She knew a second of blind panic as she wondered if they had abandoned her there.

This was an awful thought. Not only would she miss tomorrow's viewing and let Daphne down, but she desperately needed to relieve the fullness of her bladder. There was no chance of crossing her legs in this position.

She screamed and clawed at the wood as white-hot pain took her off guard, scalding through her. Shock forced a dribble of water from her, but she had the presence of mind to clench her muscles and hang on. Her buttocks went numb for an instant and then throbbed into agonised life.

Fingers poked between the posts, examining her exposed parts. 'She's wet,' Tanith said. 'Very nearly peed herself, I think.'

196

Lisa felt her body responding, almost as if it no longer belonged to her. The ache in her bladder increased, along with the pain in her rump and the hot, yearning sensation in her sex.

Tanith palpated Lisa's clitoris, and her tongue followed the path of her fingers, licking the eager organ. Ripples of delight mingled with the waves of pain that flooded from the fiery stripe.

While she was permitting herself to be lulled into pleasure, the second blow fell. Lisa yelped and jerked against her bonds, the animal urge to empty the body proving too much. Her water gushed out, soaking her stockings and wetting the floor between her legs. Burning shame seared her, worse than the welts laid on her rump by Fletcher's whip.

'That's it,' Tanith murmured soothingly. 'Let it all go, darling. Free yourself . . . and enjoy.'

As she stroked Lisa's cleft, the sensation was joined by that of a hard object pressing against her part-opened vulva. Not a phallus. This thing was smooth, but not human. At once she pictured the handle of the whip. Fletcher was teasing her with it, pressing its solidity into her vagina. It was warmed by his grip.

He dragged it over the slippery labia and tapped the head of her clitoris, then poked it against the tight mouth of her virgin anus, before returning it to the easier access of her vagina. She could not resist working her hips back. She was desperate to be filled, every delicate membrane of her loins reacting to the heat of her crimson weals.

For a moment he granted her this pleasure, then took the handle away. Lisa waited with bated breath, flesh cringing, sex anticipating. The air whistled as the lash fell. Lisa shrieked again, her bottom glowing in a different spot. He never laid the stripes in the same place.

But now Lisa knew she would be rewarded, straining

forward to meet Tanith's touch. Slow fingers tickled her clitoris, then a tongue that tantalised the little bud before subjecting it to the steady licking it craved.

Glancing down, she saw her breasts, the nipples swollen to twice their normal size, and fingers with crimson-laquered nails creeping across to pluck at the needy teats. Lisa cried out, hovering on the brink of orgasm but not quite able to topple over and be consumed in its cleansing fire.

The lash landed unerringly and she almost welcomed its painful caress. Her buttocks quivered, the heat roaring through them to connect with her nub, her aching open cunt and her spasming womb.

The fingers on her nipples, the tongue on her clitoris and the stinging stripes reddening her bottom combined in a mighty orgasmic wave that rushed over her in a triumphant flood. Her whole body tightened, her vagina contracting and needing to be filled.

She gave vent to a high keening sound like a woman wailing for her demon lover. 'Fletcher ... Fletcher! Come to me. I want you ... only you.'

'Am I your master?' he asked, his hands on her haunches, smoothing in a cool, soothing lotion that eased the pain.

'Yes. Yes,' she moaned, consumed with longing.

'For ever?'

'Throughout eternity,' she vowed, totally divorced from reality.

'I shall expect obedience,' he said, working into the amber cleft of her buttocks, finding the entrance to her rectum and easing his little finger in to the first joint.

'I promise you,' she whispered.

She lay against the wood, almost embracing it now. She felt someone behind her, the brush of trousered legs against her thighs, and then the heat of a cock sliding between her lips and finding the wet gateway to her temple. She tensed, breathed deeply, then went stiff. Whoever it was smelled different. It wasn't Fletcher.

'Who are you?' she demanded, tugging ineffectively at her bonds and craning her neck in a futile attempt to see her assailant's face.

'Eduardo. Your tango instructor,' he replied, his hips driving his penis deep inside her.

'Fletcher!' she screamed. 'I thought it would be you!'

'Not this time,' he answered calmly, and now she saw him, standing on the other side of the triangle.

Tanith was on her knees between his thighs, his penis in her mouth as she moved her head up and down. His hands were buried in her hair, holding her to his pleasure while she brought him to crisis point.

Tears coursed down Lisa's cheeks, but her void was filled at last and she was wantonly glad of it. She could feel Eduardo's rising excitement and smell the exotic scent of Kouros, her own ambrosia, and his male odour. He pressed against the contours of her sore back, careful of her, yet impaling her with fierce little jabs.

Enduring, even taking a perverted pleasure in her humiliation, she gripped the struts with her bound hands, never taking her eyes from Fletcher's face as he pumped his seed into Tanith's throat.

Chapter Nine

'What a turn-out,' commented Bob Danvers, one of David's confederates, as they stood in the salon that had become an auction room.

'The Rathbone collection has stirred up a lot of interest. Did you have a shufty yesterday?' David replied, casting an astute eye over the crowd. He was on nodding acquaintance with many of them, mostly dealers, though there were a few private buyers.

'Yes, picked out one or two items, but didn't reckon on everything rocketing like it has. Nothing's gone for less than a hundred quid,' Bob moaned, a sallow, hatchet-faced man whom David had known for years.

He owned a shop in Bath, but most of his profits came from his reclamation yard. This had boomed under the demand for genuine late Victorian or Edwardian bathroom fittings, fireplaces, staircases and panelling. In an age of technology and the breakdown of family values, those who could afford it were harking back to an era when life was more secure.

'This isn't your scene, is it?' David said, for many of the lots that had already gone under the hammer were Regency, Georgian, Queen Anne and even older.

They were in keeping with this gracious room, with

its blue and white walls, Wedgewood friezes and modillion cornices. Its ceiling bloomed with paintings of mythological subjects where naked-bosomed goddesses sported amidst Arcadian groves, wisps of pale chiffon concealing their pudenda with a kind of mock modesty.

David considered it a crying shame that the Rathbone heir had a cocaine habit which had landed him deep in debt, necessitating the sale of items owned by his family for centuries. The house would be the next to go. It was already in the estate agents' hands. It would be bought by an Arab sheik, a religious cult, or an American millionaire seeking his roots, unless The National Trust came to the rescue.

'I'm more interested in the garden tools and ornaments, and kitchenware,' Bob admitted, thumbs hooked in the pockets of his canary-yellow waistcoat. 'But you never know, there could be pickings.'

'Not much left for us by the time Robillard has finished,' David growled, his green eyes flashing. 'He hasn't even bothered to be here in person, simply phoning in his bids. He's obviously marked out the territory, though I didn't see him yesterday.'

'Perhaps he got in with Lord Howard, and has already taken a gander,' Bob suggested, eyeing a rocking-horse which was now placed near the auctioneer's rostrum, its spotted sides and flowing mane and tail eliciting a buzz from the audience. 'That would cheer up my shop window,' he added. 'Especially round Christmas. But I expect we're talking upward of a thousand notes.'

'No doubt,' David agreed, then went on, 'Robillard probably does know Howard. The nobs tend to hang together, and he's one of them.'

He wondered why he had not talked Fiona into a private viewing. I'm slipping, he thought angrily, his eyes narrowed to emerald slits as he stared across the room to where Lisa was standing next to Daphne

Nightingale. *She's* to blame, he fumed. Bringing to the surface emotions I'd much rather not feel.

He had not intended this to happen, imagining they would have a casual affair and call it a day. But even when he was busy haggling with the owners of a couple of elegant, though rundown, chateaux in the Loire Valley, his thoughts had kept straying back to her.

He would catch himself wondering, would Lisa like that? And what would she think of these Napoleonic drapes, this glassware, that pair of oval giltwood mirrors decorated with carved, chubby-bummed Cupids?

Is it a sign of advancing years? he speculated, alarmed. Surely I'm not wanting to settle down? Perish the thought!

Then, of course, he had fucked her again – in her bed, in that tastefully furnished flat. Fatal. You shouldn't have done it, Dave, old boy, he lectured himself. It was just too cosy and domesticated. I could get to like it.

Bullshit. You're a free spirit, his old self asserted. And you shagged Fiona last night just to prove you're a horny, devil-may-care philanderer.

'Excuse me,' he said to Bob. 'Bit of business . . . catch you later.'

Bob did not answer, his attention pinpointed on the auctioneer starting the bidding for the horse.

Dave weaved agilely through the crowd to Lisa. She did not look at him, apparently absorbed in the glossy, expensively produced catalogue. It was Daphne who greeted him, seated in a Windsor chair, marked Lot 200.

'Hello, Mr Maccabene,' she said, smiling up at him and taking his extended hand in her beringed fingers.

'Mrs Nightingale,' he answered, obeying the instinct for gallantry that forced him to bow. She was that kind of lady.

'I hope you're not after the things I want,' she said, her coral lips twitching. She was flirting with him and he responded, admiring her spirit.

'I'll try not to foil you,' he replied, and glanced at

Lisa. 'How are you?' he said. 'You look tired, and there are blue smudges round your eyes. The Italians think this sexy ... denoting a night of passion. Had any passionate nights lately, Lisa?'

Her colour heightened as she returned, crossly, 'I think that's my business, not yours.'

He grinned, thinking, So she did go to Hawkhurst Abbey, and she looks as if she's been thoroughly fucked. But his smile concealed a hard knot of something that very much resembled pain and anger – and jealousy.

He tried to analyse this feeling. Normally he never experienced that humiliating, time-wasting, destructive emotion, working on the theory that one has no right to prevent another person from doing what they want.

All very well to theorise when it didn't really affect one, but this was different. The thought of Fletcher, or even Tanith, exploring Lisa's secret parts and, worse still, bringing to her that state of bliss which culminated in orgasm, made a red mist float before his eyes. He clenched his fists, needing to hit out.

'What particularly interests you, Mr Maccabene?' Daphne enquired, her softly modulated voice steadying him.

'There's a terracotta bust of a lady, signed "Lefevre",' he answered. 'And an easel dressing-table mirror, with a vacant cartouche, and embossed with four panels of angels' heads. The catalogue attributes it to Reynolds, but I think it's no earlier that nineteen hundred and one.'

'Small objects, then. No furniture?' Daphne went on, and accepted a cup of tea which Arnaldo had succeeded in obtaining from the canteen set up for the public during this two-day event.

'Ah, well ... yes ... furniture, of course. I'd like to get that crushed pink velvet and carved mahogany Bergeré suit. It's in mint condition. Had loose covers, I suspect, or was unused in a drawing room. Then there's a William and Mary walnut bureau-on-stand. I know a man who's looking for one and could pass it on at a profit right away.'

'It's very fine, I agree.' Daphne nodded. 'In fact, the whole sale is filled with most desirable pieces.'

'How true,' David replied politely, while all the time he was conscious of his penis beginning to stir under his stone-washed jeans as Lisa's perfume drifted towards him, evocative and enticing.

He wanted to hold her. No, to be honest, he wanted to take her somewhere private and plunge that eager male part of his into her tight, wet sheath. The memory of it embracing him like a warm glove made his erection grow bigger.

This is absurd, he thought wildly. I can't stand in the middle of an auction sale with a monumental hard-on.

'Can I buy you a coffee?' he said, moving closer to Lisa though it increased the turmoil below his belt.

'All right,' she replied hesitantly. 'I shan't be long, Daphne.'

'Take as long as you like, my dear,' she said, consulting her catalogue. 'Lots 150 to 155 won't be brought out yet.'

With his hand tucked under Lisa's elbow, he led her into the corridor. The main hall was a triumph of trompe l'oeil, the painted drapes and curtain swags lifelike and three dimensional, but David was not in the mood to admire it.

Instead of following the sound of voices and clattering teacups and the smell of homemade scones and cucumber sandwiches, he rushed Lisa up the back stairs, once used by servants. He was not familiar with this particular house but the layout in most mansions was much the same. The back stairs led to the bedrooms used by the masters, or maybe he could find a convenient linen cupboard or a dressing room – anywhere solitary that would suit his purpose.

He tried several doors. They were locked, but his perseverance was rewarded. He discovered a powder closet, where once dandies had sat, swathed in linen capes to protect their magnificent attire, while valets puffed a white cloud over their curled perukes to give the desired, snowy effect.

David dragged Lisa inside and locked the door. His lust was almost uncontrollable, his heart pounding heavily in his chest and the Levis chafing his penis and nearly precipitating climax.

She stared at him as he backed her against the wall, and protested loudly, 'We can't! Not here.'

'Why not? Kiss me, Lisa.'

Her mouth was honey-sweet and he calmed down, knowing by the way her tongue met his that the outcome was assured. They would not leave the powder closet till their mutual hunger had been assuaged. But this was, perforce, a quick snack, a mere aperitif before the feast which would surely follow later.

She sighed against his mouth, reached up her arms and linked them round his neck. They stood there for a moment, and he did no more than kiss her deeply. Her breasts pressed against his T-shirt. He could feel the points of her nipples through the cloth, and his serpent pulsed, demanding to be freed from its prison.

He had quickly staked out the closet, and now caught her under the backside and lifted her, the round globes warm and fleshy in his hands. He sat her on a small table standing by the wall, and heard her exclaim, but whether in pain or pleasure he could not tell, and it was not important in that tense and magical moment.

He placed a hand on each of her knees and parted them, then stood between and reached up under her skirt. It was like entering a silken paradise, her bare skin velvety to his touch. His fingers found the triangle of her panties, pushing the elastic aside and smoothing the curling fur beneath.

She reached down and gripped the bottom of her white cotton vest, pulling it up and over breasts cradled in a lacy brassiere. She slid the straps down and lifted one from its underwired cup, then the other, till both stood out like round, golden fruit, ready for plucking.

Mesmerised by these gifts crowned by dark areolae, David bent his head in homage, taking one into his mouth and tasting the nutty, perfumed teat which swelled under his tongue. She moaned and pressed her breast further in, her fingers rolling the other nipple till it increased in size to match its fellow.

He felt her thighs spreading apart, and moved his middle finger over the hairless centre of her cleft, the edge of her panties cutting across the back of his hand.

'You're so wet,' he muttered, leaving her breast as he felt her flesh part easily to admit his finger, her muscles clenching round it.

He fumbled with his fly zip with his free hand, got it open and released his cock. At once Lisa's hand descended on it, a shudder racing through him as he felt her fingers working up its length and circling the shining purple head.

'No,' she whispered. 'Don't put it in yet. Make me come first.'

She pushed her skirt higher, baring her belly and sex to him as she leant back on her elbows. Her panties were reduced to a vertical line pressed into her groin, the beauty of her dark wedge contrasting with the tanned skin. Between lay her treasure, the pink folds gleaming with juice and the delicious, pearly nub rising proudly from its cowl.

David hovered over it, delaying the sacred moment. He breathed in her scent, that powerful essence produced only when a woman is sexually excited. It excited him, too, proving that she wanted him and was as eager as he for the joining of their flesh.

She lay quiet as he gently manipulated her labial wings and stroked the wet avenue between. He recognised that pre-orgasmic hush, when she would be waiting as he drew her to the edge, his fingers smoothly lifting her towards the peak. He loved the feel of her, the smell of her, the way she shivered as his thumb-pad passed like a breath of ecstasy over her clitoris.

'You feel wonderful there,' he whispered, and she gave a short, sharp cry as she achieved her goal and convulsed under his touch, making his cock jump and his chest ache with passion. As the tension released, he enclosed her warm, swollen sex in his hand.

'Do it now, David. Fuck me,' she begged, squirming forward on the table top, lifting her thighs and hooking them round his waist, opening her loins to receive him.

Holding his cock, he guided the heavy bar between her legs and into the moist mouth that waited to engulf it. He gave a long-drawn groan as he thrust into her, and the expression of rapture on her face was so profound that he wanted to cry.

He had given her the greatest possible pleasure and now it was his turn. Passion mastered him, his balls hardened and his cock surged, plunging into and with-drawing from Lisa's marvellous wet notch. He pounded into her again and again, his hips meeting her inner thighs with a slapping sound. He heard her moan and felt her heels drumming against the small of his back, then he threw up his head, gasping and panting as the desperate frenzy of orgasm brought a roaring to his ears and tears to his eyes.

He staggered to his feet, leaning against the wall as his pulse slowed, then tucked his penis into his jeans and zipped up. As Lisa slipped down from the table, she half turned, her skirt hitched high in order to adjust her knickers.

He put out a hand and stopped her. 'What's that?' he said sharply, seeing long, reddish-blue bruises marring the sunbrowned skin.

She shrugged, not meeting his eyes, and pulled away from him, saying, 'It's nothing.'

'Nothing?' David would have none of that. He seized her and held her firmly under one arm while he pushed up her skirt and peeled down her panties.

Half a dozen stripes scored her bottom, unmistakably the marks left by a whip.

'Did Robillard do this to you?' he demanded sternly.

'I don't wish to discuss it,' she said firmly, though her face was almost as red as her weals.

'They weren't there last time I saw your arse, and you went to his house last night. Two and two make three, my dear, and I'm nobody's fool,' he stated loudly, anger fermenting inside him, along with another disturbing thought. 'Did you enjoy it when he whipped you?' he asked, on the rising tide of rage.

Lisa had smoothed down her clothing, looking remarkably cool and composed. 'David, please,' she began. 'No more questions. I'm going to work for him and Tanith, starting Monday.'

'I see. So we shall be in opposite camps. Charming!' he rapped out. 'And what does your fiancé have to say about all this? Perhaps he gets off on his girlfriend being whipped, then shagged. Is that it?'

'I'm no longer engaged to Paul,' she replied, her violet-blue eyes guarded.

The relief that poured through David shook him rigid. 'You're not? Given him the boot?' he said, managing to keep his voice calm.

'Something like that. It was after we'd been together the other night. I realised that I couldn't go on. He was too dictatorial. I need my freedom. That's one reason why I've taken the job at Hawkhurst Abbey.'

'Nothing to do with Robillard's quirks?' he asked nastily. 'You're not thinking of becoming one of his slaves, are you? Oh, yes ... word gets about in the trade.'

'And if I am?' She stood her ground, chin lifted mulishly.

'You'd be a fool,' he snapped, then covered his hurt by shrugging and adding lightly, 'But each to his own. I'm off now, Lisa. Back to the sale. I don't want to miss the William and Mary bureau.'

As it turned out, he need not have bothered, because he was pipped at the post by Fletcher, who outbid him by phone.

While he was still licking his wounds, Fiona descended on him, crying, 'Ah, there you are, darling! Where have you been hiding?'

'I've been around,' he answered, as she spread herself over Lot 300, a Biedermeier mahogany sofa with shell and acanthus mouldings which he mentally valued at £5,000.

'I wanted your advice,' she said pouting, her little breasts outlined under a fragile blouse and her long, perfect legs displayed to full advantage by a skirt in natural shantung. 'I've bought a silver cake basket which they said was William IV, but I may have given too much for it.'

'I expect you've done all right,' he said, wondering where Lisa had gone.

They had parted with a worrying kind of distance between them and he was eager to find her and put it right. No matter what she had done with Fletcher or intended to do in the future, David still wanted her.

'Will you have a look at it, and the other things? Come home with me, David. Nigel's away. I haven't really seen you much since you came back from France.'

'What about last night?' he murmured, leaning over the back of the sofa and inhaling the seductive perfume of Shalimar that clung to her hair and skin. Despite his feelings towards Lisa, he never could resist Fiona.

'Last night, darling, was out of this world,' she sighed, reaching up to caress the underside of his jaw. 'We'd better make hay while the sun shines. Nigel is talking about returning for a while. I think he's fallen out with his boyfriend. You've seen him, haven't you? Ray Follet. He has his own show on Channel Four. Clever drag artist, but so temperamental. Leads Nigel one hell of a dance.'

They stayed together for the remainder of the afternoon,

209

and David had no chance to speak to Lisa again. Though he saw her from a distance, he was too occupied with the lots he wanted.

The sale eventually drew to a close. 'They've made a packet for Lord Howard,' David commented as one of his sidekicks loaded up the van.

'Dear Howard, he's a sweetie but a prize prick,' Fiona commented, walking out with the cake basket and a pair of goblets engraved 1797. 'We'll drink champagne from these tonight, David,' she promised. 'To celebrate you being back in circulation.'

'And what about that?' he asked, nodding to the object which brought up the rear, borne carefully by one of the auctioneer's assistants.

'Isn't it gorgeous?' she cooed. 'A Tiffany glass and bronze lily lamp. 'It'll look lovely in my bedroom.'

'Wrong period,' David grunted.

'Bollocks,' she exclaimed, tweaking his backside as he leant over to shift a piece of furniture to a safer place in the van. 'I like it, and that's good enough for me.'

She climbed in beside him, part closed the rear doors, then pulled him down on a heap of dustsheets. 'David,' she murmured, her hands going to his fly. 'We've got time for a quickie, haven't we? I need you ... right now.'

'I must get back,' he temporised, as she unzipped his jeans and took his swelling penis in her hand and scratched over it with her silver-varnished nails.

Then she paused and said, 'I smell woman on your cock. Where have you been putting it, David?'

'I didn't have time to take a shower after I left you in the early hours. Had to get down here,' he said, hoping she would believe him.

'Really? You're a bad liar. It doesn't smell like me,' she remarked dubiously, but went closer and licked him.

She was amoral, indiscreet, selfish, greedy and irresistible, and he could feel the heat creeping from his lower back to his loins, his cock responding to her touch

210

as if it had a life of its own. He relaxed, knowing that his henchman had gone back to the barn to wait for him. There was plenty of time to service Fiona, keeping her sweet and on his side.

Why should he allow the thought of Lisa to stop him? Those marks on her buttocks. What had gone on at the Abbey last night?

Fletcher Robillard was his *bête noire*, and now his influence had spread to Lisa. David was disappointed in her. At least he knew where he was with Fiona; expecting disloyalty, prepared for unfaithfulness, enjoying her with his body, not his soul. Not even thinking about the possibility of a marriage of true minds.

He yielded to his basic instincts, lay back and wallowed in the feel of Fiona's tongue as she drew the length of his manhood into her mouth, sucking at it as if it was a luscious fruit. At the point of no return, the rushing beginning in his balls, he gripped her hair.

The rear door suddenly swung open. Lisa was framed there, her expression one of disbelief, horror and disgust. She froze momentarily and then left, slamming it behind her.

'Oh, shit,' groaned David, as he came into Fiona's mouth.

Mike was tired of listening to Valerie going on about Lisa. He wondered why she was being so vitriolic, saying at one point, 'I should have thought you'd be pleased the wedding's off. You never liked her, did you?'

'No, but I'm sorry for poor Paul,' she explained. 'He doesn't deserve this shabby treatment. Besides, what am I going to tell people? And we'll have to cancel the caterers, the cake, the band, the marquee. It's too bad of her.' Then she added an afterthought. 'I've bought a new outfit and a new hat. I was looking forward to wearing them. Now that silly cow has gone and spoilt everything.'

They were in bed, and she had started off on another tirade as soon as she woke. Mike appreciated her fire and vehemence and was aroused by the way her breasts bounced under the nylon night dress, almost inspired to roll her on to her back and stick his morning erection in her.

Almost, but not quite. He had other things in mind, and they involved Joyce Murray, the planning committee – and Lisa. It would be wise to conserve his energy.

Like a general mapping out a campaign, so he planned his as he stood in the bathroom shaving, his member in retrograde mode. He could hear Valerie on the phone, complaining about Lisa to someone – probably Natasha. At least it kept her off his back, having another person to moan to. And all this fuss about cancellations would keep her so busy that she would not notice his absence.

What he intended to do over the next few days would necessitate a number of lies – pressure of business was a good one, and the excuse of rehearsals never failed. Valerie liked to boast that her husband was a leading light in the Deverel Thespian Society. The faithful Maggie would cover for him, of course, should Valerie became suspicious, but here he had to juggle carefully, too, lest Maggie became jealous of Joyce.

The stress of such intrigue was enough to give a normal man a heart attack, but Mike throve on it. He hummed one of the songs he had to learn for his part in *Aladdin* as he patted aftershave into his cheeks.

Towelling off, he watched Valerie in the bathroom mirror. She looked blowzy in the critical light of morning. Stepping under the shower, he gave himself a lukewarm blast. That was better. Life was beginning to make sense.

When he reached his office he phoned Joyce, then Lisa.

* * *

212

The sound of the phone penetrated Lisa's dream, becoming a part of it – some weird scenario in which she was racing to catch a train, losing her baggage and responsible for someone else's children – and losing those, too.

'Hello,' she muttered groggily, the receiver clamped to her ear.

'Lisa? It's Mike,' came his determinedly jolly voice down the line. 'As you didn't ring me back I thought I'd give you another bell. Sorry to hear about you and Paul. Disappointed that I shan't be leading you up the aisle and giving you away.'

'What? Oh, yes ... Mike,' she replied, the dream rushing back into her subconscious, leaving little fragments of unease behind.

'Can I come and see you?'

'Er, I don't know,' she said, still confused. 'What do you want, Mike?'

'It would be a pity to lose touch. I promised to look over the building, didn't I?'

'I don't remember asking you ...'

'I think I'd better do it, anyway, just to be on the safe side. I could pop round at lunchtime. All right?'

'I suppose so.'

When he had hung up, she lay in bed and cursed herself. What a dope to say yes so meekly. People pleasing, Martin called it, and had advised her to give herself breathing space when a friend rang up asking a favour or, as in Mike's case, railroading her into doing something she was not sure about.

'All you've got to do is say, ever so reasonably, "Can you give me a moment to think about it? I'll ring you back,"' Martin had suggested. 'It works a treat, and allows you time to make up your own mind. Or try writing "NO" on a notice and sticking it on the phone.'

Mike had caught her on the hop, and she had forgotten Martin's sensible advice.

Damn and damn again! she thought when, at noon on

213

the dot, Mike rang the doorbell. By that time she had showered, dressed and gathered her wits. She wore a sarong and little else, intending to have a lazy day in the sun after the hectic ones just passed.

There was a lot to think about: Fletcher's weird establishment, Paul and the broken engagement, and last but not least, David, with his passionate possession of her at the sale and his later betrayal with Fiona. An emotion-tipped bullet had gone straight to her heart when she saw them on the floor of the van.

Men! she snarled to herself as she went to open the door to Mike. I've had it up to here with them.

Mike was looking crisp in a summer-weight, grey striped suit. Off the peg but expensive, none the less. He was usually well turned out but, like his wife, lacked class. Lisa wanted this interview over as soon as possible. He was invading her space and she resented it.

'Shall we go out for a spot of lunch?' he began, taking over immediately.

'No, thank you. I've already eaten,' she said.

'It's a scorcher today,' he announced, occupying a seat uninvited. 'Got anything to drink?'

'Beer, orange juice, tea, coffee ... water,' she replied edgily.

'Beer will do fine.'

'I thought it might.'

Irony was lost on him and he sat, smiling and assessing the living room. Lisa went to fetch the beer, then placed it on a low table by the couch.

'You've got a bad case of damp,' Mike began, peering up at the ceiling. 'Tiles missing, I shouldn't wonder. Mind if I take a look in the roof?'

Lisa shrugged, trying to put into practice Martin's advice, but unable to form her lips round the magic "no" word. She wondered, briefly, whether to get Martin up from the showroom, then decided against it. Mike might embarrass him with some tactless homophobic remark.

Now Mike went into the hallway and, standing on a chair, reached up and pushed back the trap-door leading to the loft. Grabbing the first rung of the folding ladder that gave easy access to this large space, he hauled it down, then mounted, disappearing from view. Lisa stood at the bottom of the steps, very worried.

He took some time, and she fretted. Had he found dry rot or deathwatch beetle? Was her house about to fall down?

When he finally reappeared, his prognostication was almost as dire. 'You need a new roof,' he announced, brushing the dust from his trousers. 'And there's a sizable crack running down . . . goes the whole depth of the outer wall. Subsidence. Very serious. Next, I'll inspect the parapet.'

This was no better, and he came back through the front window, saying, 'As I thought. It needs re-leading, and the pointing done and the stonework patched up or replaced, to make it safe.'

'How much?' she asked, feeling herself sweating.

He pulled a wry face. 'I'd have to do a proper estimate.'

'Can't you give me a rough idea?'

'The roof could be thirty thou. It's big and I can't tell what snags we might come up against. Lead doesn't come cheap, neither does Bath stone, and that's what you'd have to have or the heritage people would make you do it all over again. Then there's extra labour charges. I can't say for sure, Lisa, but you might be having to find fifty or sixty grand, possibly more.'

'What!'

'Sorry, but it's better that you know,' he went on, and placed an arm round her shoulders. 'Of course, all work will have to be carried out under the eagle eye of the authorities. It's a listed building. You could try to sell it, but I doubt you'd get much as it stands. No mortgage company would look at it.'

'What am I going to do?' Lisa wailed.

'If you'd have married Paul, I know he was prepared to have the work done,' Mike put in, reaching for his beer.

'But I'm not,' she told him, plumping down on the sofa, her sarong falling open over her knees.

'Well, perhaps I could help you,' Mike said slowly, and the couch creaked as he sat beside her, a little too close for her liking. She could smell the beer on his breath. It reminded her of Paul.

He was looking at her in a kindly, helpful way that made her want to trust him. Perhaps he wasn't so bad, after all, she thought, still reeling under the blow and needing a mature man to advise her.

If only Father was alive, she mourned, saying, 'I don't see how.'

'I'd be prepared to do all the repairs, and you could pay me back if and when,' he said softly, and slid an arm along the back of the sofa, enclosing her to the point of paranoia.

She did not want to risk offending him, yet sat forward, skirt wrapped tightly round her legs. In a dreadful, disbelieving yet having to believe way, she guessed what was coming.

Slowly she became aware that he was watching her and gave him a sudden swift sidelong glance. The look she saw on his face made the straightforward lust of other men seem innocent. Lecherous old goat! she thought, wanting to say it, but not quite daring.

'The price?' she said suddenly, body rigid.

'Price? I don't understand,' he began, giving her an oily smile.

Lisa went to rise, but he placed a hand on her bare arm. She did not pull away, but simply stared at him with blistering scorn.

'There's always a price. As a businessman you're well aware of this. So name it. Tell me what it will cost me in self-respect.'

He gulped, and his sweaty fingers stroked up her arm

216

to her naked shoulder. His muscular legs were apart and she could see the swell of his penis between them. The sight of it filled her with loathing.

'Lisa, you've got it all wrong,' he said gently. 'I've always admired you. Don't forget that I supported your venture into antiques. I'd hate to see you suffer, and want to look after you.'

She faced him like an animal at bay, snarling, 'And in return?'

He sighed and continued his upward stroking, his eyes on her breasts, barely covered by a fold of her sarong. 'I hoped that you'd come out with me some-times. Have dinner, perhaps . . . share a bottle of wine . . . and then, well, we'd let nature take its course.'

'You'd want to have sex with me, is that it?'

He looked pained, but now his hand was sneaking along her shoulders and down her spine, making her flesh crawl.

'Such a crude thing to say, Lisa. I was hoping for a more romantic attachment.'

'Oh, yes? With no sex?' she said sarcastically.

By now his hard-won control of his engorged prick was slipping. He turned towards her, his loose lips wet with saliva, as he stammered, 'I didn't say that. I want you, and I'll give you everything if you sleep with me. Let's start now, and I'll write you a cheque straight away.'

His hand clamped on one of her breasts, forcing the cotton down to the nipple. He moaned, and a small wet patch appeared beside the front closure of his trousers. Lisa slapped him, full forced and open palmed, across the face.

As he flinched, hand flying to his cheek, she jumped up, covered her breast and said icily, 'I think it's time you left, Mike. Unless you want me to make a phone call to Valerie.'

He got to his feet, his trousers still distended by the

unsatisfied mass behind them. His face was red and his eyes furious.

'All right. I'm going, but don't think you've heard the last of this. Maybe you'll change your mind when you start getting letters from the council.'

'Get lost,' she said, and turned her back on him, the sarong held about her like a royal robe.

But when he had gone, she forgot how to be brave, and sat on the couch, sobbing quietly. My home, she wept, my dear old home. What am I going to do?

She desperately needed a friend to talk to and, after mopping her face with a tissue, went downstairs. She pushed open the side door of the shop, but it was deserted – closed for lunch, presumably. Martin should have locked this, she thought. Anyone could break in, and his stock's valuable. Alfie's all very well, but certainly no Alsation. Where was he, anyway? He appeared to have vanished.

Maybe there's an intruder here already, the chilling thought struck, and she crept inside, starting when she heard a movement coming from the storeroom at the back. There *was* someone. Lisa was frightened but determined, silent on her bare feet. She peered round the door, and shrank back, astounded by the trail of scattered clothing, and the vision of Martin and Phil lying on a rug, naked in each other's arms.

She did not intend to stay, but could not move though riven with guilt at being a witness to such intimacy between lovers. There was something intensely beautiful and arousing in the sight of two strong men caressing each other so tenderly.

Phil worshipped at the shrine of Martin's cock, his fingers playing with the tight tips of his partner's nipples, standing out darkly against his suntanned chest, while his mouth closed over the bulging glans raised in supplication to his lips. Martin was as lovely as Adonis, and Phil so well muscled and hairy. His upright cock was short and sturdy, his balls hanging between his legs like ripe fruit, heavy with seed.

Lisa's clitoris spasmed and she opened her sarong and fingered it through the thin silk of her bikini bottom. Juice flowed from her, wetting her fingertip, and she rubbed herself without conscious thought. Phil rolled Martin over on to his stomach and lowered himself on top, slowing gyrating his hips. Both men's cocks were fully erect, and as Phil knelt back so that Martin could rise to his knees, Lisa could see those engorged organs springing from forests of pubic hair.

Phil anointed his hands from a pot of aromatic oil, then worked all the way down Martin's spine till he reached between his buttocks. Lisa heard Martin sigh and saw him spread his thighs a little, easing the way for Phil to spear his tight entrance. Martin pressed back against him till his organ was fully implanted and they rocked together for a while. Then Phil reached round under Martin's belly and took his penis in hand.

Lisa kneaded her mound in rising excitement as Martin shook and bucked and released a stream of semen. Thrusting hard into him, Phil, too, reached his zenith, then they rolled down together, clasped close and rested quietly.

Unable to reach her own completion under these strange circumstances, Lisa slipped away as silently as a wraith. She would have to find someone else to listen to her tale of woe.

Chapter Ten

Mike was never one to let the grass grow under his feet. After leaving Lisa, he phoned Joyce at home, aware that her husband was away for the weekend on a fishing trip.

'Mike,' she said, lowering her voice. 'Why are you ringing me here? I thought we said –'

'Meet me,' he ordered, having found that a direct, mannish, even bullying approach was the best way with her.

'Where?'

'I'll pick you up. We can drive somewhere private.'

'And if we're seen together?'

'It's Saturday. I told Val I had work at the office, which I did, but now I've finished. If anyone asks, we're meeting on Thespian business.'

'All right,' she whispered breathily, and he could tell by the quiver in her voice that she was excited. 'But don't come to the house. I'll be on the corner in ten minutes.'

They drove into the countryside, and he pulled into a leafy lane, killed the engine, slipped an arm round her and said, 'There's a field over there. I fancy a roll in the hay.'

'Oh, Mike,' she gasped, the colour rising into her face as she gazed owlishly at him through her glasses. 'It's a bit public.'

'Makes it all the more thrilling,' he said, grinning at her and stroking her pale stockinged knee. 'Don't you like doing it spontaneously, in unexpected places?'

For answer, she moaned and opened her legs a trifle, allowing him access to her thighs, her stocking welts and the delicate silk of her wide-legged panties.

He liked the way she always opted for French knickers, if she wore any at all, an advantage if their clandestine meetings were of short duration. Now she rested her hand on the bulge that had never quite disappeared since he was with Lisa, his penis throbbing with baulked desire.

It was a peaceful summer afternoon, smelling of meadow grass and wild flowers. He helped her mount the stile and, as she raised her leg, caught a tantalising glimpse of thigh and her sharply indented cleft pressed against the silken gusset. He always kept a blanket in the boot of the car for just such a contingency and, after they had walked to a shady spot beneath a tree, he spread it out on the ground.

His heart was thumping, heat pouring through him from exertion and the thought of how he was going to pay Lisa back for refusing him. He planned to have her grovelling at his feet, begging him to take her, her face uplifted to his crotch while he ordered her to pleasure his penis.

'This is nice,' Joyce said, lying back on the blanket and gazing up at the spreading canopy of rustling leaves.

He leant over and took off her glasses, placing them carefully in her handbag. He felt like a boy again, remembering teenage romps with girls in similar outdoor settings. Deep inside he hungered for the innocence of youth. Then, the merest touching of fingertips had given him wet dreams for weeks, and the brushing of lips in a chaste kiss was a million times more exciting than the open-mouthed conflict of tongues.

Where does it all go, the days of wine and roses? he thought, with unusual introspection. Now I'm an over-weight, middle-aged man who has to get his jollies with a wife he doesn't much care for, and a succession of women who are equally disillusioned. If only Lisa had been cooperative I might have regained my youth, or kidded myself I had.

He unbuttoned Joyce's bodice, and found that her breasts were modestly covered by a white cotton bras-siere. With a skill acquired through long practice, he unhooked it at the back and eased it from her breasts. He took them in his hands and cupped and squeezed them, his fingers flicking over the nipples till they reared up, rosy with desire.

'You're a lovely woman, Joyce,' he said, as if he meant it: compliments always got her going. 'Raymond is a bloody lucky chap.'

'Don't you think I'm a wee bit mature to be playing principal boy?' she asked, squinting up at him short-sightedly, her breasts quivering under his attentions.

'Never!' he vowed. 'With legs like that! You'll knock 'em cold.'

'D'you really think so?' she asked, smirking and holding one shapely limb out straight so that he might admire it.

'I could eat you,' he growled, and rucked up her skirt, using his hands roughly. 'I'm *going* to eat you, starting with your pussy.'

She squealed in mock fright, but opened her thighs wider as he lifted aside the loose knicker leg and ran his fingers through her brown plumaged nest. 'Fie, sir ... whatever are you about?' she cried, falling into the role she had played in *Les Liaisons Dangereuses*, her greatest triumph to date.

Mike entered into the spirit of it. He, too, had fancied himself as a French aristocrat and libertine. 'Madame la

222

Marquise,' he declaimed. 'My adored, wicked, wonderful lady . . .' He lowered his face to her mound, smelling her through the silk, then poking his nose inside, his mouth following the trail of his fingers.

He sucked at her labia and parted her with his tongue, licking the inner lips and fastening on her bud. She came quickly, thrusting up against his teeth. He freed his penis and rubbed the snout over her slippery valley, then rammed it into the humidity of her vagina.

He was aware of the sun burning down on his bare backside, the smell of crushed grass and wild flowers, the buzzing of insects . . . then everything, including Lisa, vanished from his mind. Every coherent thought was wiped out in the driving urge to relieve his balls of their load. He lost control, feeling the muscles of his belly tensing, his cock jerking as he spun off into space, powered by orgasm.

As he took Joyce home, Mike sowed the seeds of what he fondly hoped was Lisa's destruction, saying, 'Miss Sherwin's property is a definite hazard to the public. I've done a survey and it's way below par.'

'This must be reported to the planning committee,' she said, snuggling against his arm, warm and pliable and receptive.

'When can you get them to write to her?' he asked, taking the back road to the well-heeled district where she lived. 'It's urgent. I wouldn't like to be responsible if there was an accident.'

'Get out a written report, and I'll show it to them first thing Monday morning,' she promised.

'Spoken with all the authority of the Marquise de Merteuil,' he said, smiling confidently as he watched the road.

'Your servant, Vicomte,' she simpered back at him, her hand burrowing between his thighs like a small greedy rodent.

* * *

'A dishonourable man, this Mr Garston,' opined Daphne, pottering among her plants in the conservatory of Cranshaw House. 'I know his type. He pretends to be oh so respectable, yet has a mind like a sewer. Walter was rather like that, though one could forgive him, for he was never mean spirited.'

Lisa sat glumly in a cane basket-chair, arms folded round her hunched-up knees. 'He's right, though, about the building. Father never had any money to spend on it and neither have I. I don't know what to do for the best. Even if I work my rocks off for Fletcher, I'll never earn enough to take on the huge repair bills, and I doubt the bank will give me a loan without collateral.'

Daphne considered her over the spines of a tall cactus. 'Have you thought about getting what you can for it and moving to a terraced cottage?' she asked.

'Of course. I've looked at it every which way. I'd come out with hardly anything, and don't think I'd get a mortgage,' Lisa said, chewing the side of her thumbnail. 'And it would mean my tenants would lose their shop. I'd hate to do that to them. They're only just about making a go of it.'

'The gay couple you've told me about?' Daphne asked, settling herself in the chair opposite Lisa.

'Yes. They're so kind to me, and love each other very much. It would be terrible if anything dire happened that might split them up.'

'You're not happy about working for Fletcher? From what you've said about the dinner party, I should imagine you'd like to keep your independence, simply enjoying his mastery when you feel like it.'

'That's right.'

'But you like David Maccabene? So do I, incidentally. He's sound as a pound under all that blarney.'

'Yes, I like him, but there's always Lady Fiona lurking about.'

'You could change your mind and marry Paul,'

Daphne suggested, signalling to Arnaldo that they were ready for refreshments.

Lisa shuddered, saying, 'No thanks! He'd never let me forget that I turned him down. Neither would his mother. And even if I talked myself into doing it, I simply couldn't stand having Mike leching after me all the time. Can you imagine the speech he'd make at the wedding? Full of innuendoes and smutty, sexist remarks.'

'You're proud, Lisa, and I admire that,' Daphne said, smiling over the coffee pot at her, while Arnaldo placed cups, cream jug and sugar bowl within reach. 'But not too proud, I hope, to listen to my proposition?'

'I can't tell till you've put it to me,' Lisa answered, curiosity aroused.

Was Daphne about to invite her to enter a partnership? She had been adamant about adding Lisa's modest purchases at the sale to her own bill. Though she had protested that everything was way beyond her, there had been a few lots towards the end which contained the kind of bric-a-brac suitable for her stall.

The conservatory was one of the most pleasing corners of this amazingly warm and lovely house. Daphne used it as a breakfast room, liking to look out and watch the birds, and it was there she cherished her most tender and exotic blooms, fanatically keen on orchids.

Now she lifted her cup to her lips, took a sip, then observed Lisa's reaction as she said, 'I want to make you my heir.'

Lisa nearly dropped hers in astonishment, coffee slopping into the saucer. 'Your heir?' she repeated, stupefied.

'That's right,' Daphne said, nodding. 'For some time I've been thinking of retiring abroad. I own a villa near Florence and the climate suits me. I'm getting slightly arthritic ... creaky knees, that's all, but it interferes with my enjoyment of gardening. However, I was undecided, till I met you. I don't want to sell this house. It has too many fond memories. But I'm prepared to give it to you as part of your inheritance, with the proviso that I can stay here when I visit England, which won't be often. It rains too much.'

'The climate is changing,' Lisa stuttered, unable to think of anything sensible to say.

'Perhaps,' Daphne replied with a twinkle. 'But be that as it may, I'm ready to carry out my plan. What do you think?'

'You hardly know me,' Lisa began, completely overwhelmed. 'How can you trust it to me, almost a stranger?'

'I follow my intuition,' Daphne explained, and glanced at Arnaldo who, as usual, stood in the background. 'Isn't this so, Arnaldo? Didn't I tell you about Lisa after I'd met her for the first time?'

'You did, madame,' he agreed, subjecting Lisa to his dazzling smile.

'You're beautiful, talented and have guts, just like me when I was your age. I wouldn't see any man put you down. I have no children to whom I might leave my worldly wealth, and can't think of anyone more worthy than you.'

'I can't possibly accept such a generous offer,' Lisa brought out, still reeling under this bombshell.

'I'll be mortally offended if you don't,' Daphne answered crisply. Then her voice softened and she clasped Lisa's hand. 'There are no strings attached. I've instructed my lawyer and he's waiting for my final word. There will a few papers to sign, and then it's over to you. I've already packed personal things, or rather Arnaldo has. Many of my possessions are already in the Villa Norfini. Walter adored Tuscany and intended to die there, but fate decreed otherwise.'

'You've arranged all this in the short time we've known each other?' Lisa was still almost speechless with surprise.

226

'Let's say I was prepared before, but now I'm ready to go.'

'When?'

'As soon as you agree and I've finalised matters and booked a flight. We'll visit Messrs Godsiffe, Laughton and Beamish on Monday and get it all signed and sealed. Do you agree?'

'I'm stunned!' Lisa exclaimed. 'I don't know what to say.'

'Just say yes, and you can move in here as soon as I depart, then get the work done on your property and let your flat. I'll leave you the van and the car. We have others at the villa, haven't we, Arnaldo?'

'Yes, madame.'

'I have a few good friends there. Florentine society has always been a trifle *outré*, and they dearly love an oddity. The more eccentric one is the better. You must promise to visit me. This year, without fail,' Daphne insisted, and suddenly clapped her hands, adding, 'Come to the wedding.'

'Wedding?' This is getting more and more bizarre, Lisa thought.

'We're getting married, aren't we, Arnaldo?'

'Yes, madame,' he replied, stepping closer and looking down at Daphne with a look of tender devotion that warmed Lisa's heart.

'He's been with me for years, and we became even closer when Walter died. Such a dear friend and wonderful lover. We may as well make it legal, and I've left him the villa and a substantial income in my will, which won't affect your investments.'

'You've thought of everything,' Lisa breathed, clasping her hands to her breasts, daring to let hope take root within her. But she knew she would not really believe it until they had seen the solicitor.

'You accept?' Daphne said, leaning forward eagerly.

'Well, yes ... if that's what you really want. I'm

flabbergasted ... and, oh, Daphne, I'm going to miss you so much.' Lisa could hardly speak, choked by tears.

'We'll phone each other all the time,' Daphne promised, handing her a lace-edged, scented handkerchief, her own eyes wet. 'I expect regular reports on how you're causing mayhem among the men around here, all too cocky by far. You'll dominate them before you're done, have them jumping through hoops, and Cranshaw House will be your headquarters, the centre of operations.'

Lisa steadied, feeling laughter tugging at the corners of her mouth as she visualised it. Daphne was handing her not only property and money – but power.

'Don't worry. I'll report in,' she promised.

'There's only one other thing I'm going to ask of you,' Daphne said, while Arnaldo slipped a hand beneath her hair and started to massage her neck. She closed her eyes and almost purred under the blissful relaxation of tension at the top of her spine.

'Name it,' Lisa urged rashly, watching the interplay between them and seeing how Daphne shed years in his presence.

'I own several paintings,' Daphne began, moving her head from side to side under Arnaldo's skilful ministrations. 'There's one in particular, the most valuable of all. I want you to find a buyer for it. You're not to have it put up for auction by Sotheby's. You must sell it yourself. The insurance covers six figures.'

'Good grief! What is it? A Van Gogh?' Lisa cried, her fledgling dealer's instincts at full stretch.

'It's a chalk drawing by Dante Gabriel Rossetti.'

'Of the Pre-Raphaelite Brotherhood?'

'Absolutely,' Daphne said, and placed a hand over Arnaldo's, gently disengaging herself. 'Will you fetch it, please?'

A Rossetti! Lisa tingled with excitement, her brain filled with images of reproductions she had seen of this Victorian artist's work, once considered outlandish, even immoral, until finally accepted by the establishment. The popularity of his pictures had taken a nose-dive during the first half of the century only to rise again in the 60s and never look back.

How on earth had a Rossetti drawing come into Daphne's possession?

Arnaldo returned, bearing a medium-sized picture in a plain wooden frame. He set it up in the conservatory and Lisa stared at it in awe.

As far as she could tell it was typical of the Pre-Raphaelites: the attention to detail, the romantic medieval gown, the wealth of red-gold hair, the slightly thick throat and pouting lips of the model, her drooping eyelids and languid, sensual air, as of a woman exhausted after a visit from a virile lover.

'She's gorgeous!' Lisa cried, standing back so that she might view it more clearly.

'Isn't she?' Daphne replied, a catch of laughter in her voice as she came to stand by Lisa, an arm placed lightly round her waist.

'But who is she, and how did you get her?'

'That, my dear, is a sketch of Walter's great-aunt. I expect the artist intended to use it as the basis for an oil painting. Her name was Matilda, and this house belonged to her in later life, but she met Rossetti when she was young and he a middle-aged man. An interesting person ... addicted to laudanum. His wife, Lizzie Siddal, died of an overdose. He was always on the lookout for red-headed models; seemed quite obsessed with them.'

Lisa peered closely at the picture, wishing she knew more about art. 'How can you be sure of all this?'

'It's signed.'

'I can see that, but there must be something else,' Lisa said, having noted the scribble in one corner.

'Oh, there is. Matilda's diary, and a letter from Rossetti telling her that he had had it framed and wanted to deliver it himself. He indicated that he expected something more than money in payment. In fact, the story goes that she was his mistress.'

Daphne walked through the French doors into the drawing room and across to the escritoire, returning with a little book bound in faded red leather and tied with pink ribbon. A crumpled envelope was tucked inside.

'I see,' Lisa said slowly as she examined these fragile proofs of the work's identity: the diary with its elegant copper-plate writing, the letter purporting to be from the artist, signed, like the picture, DGR. Then she added the rider, 'So this would be its provenance?'

'Exactly. Proof positive of authenticity,' Daphne said. 'I would like you to have the experience of handling something as important as this.'

'Very well,' Lisa agreed. She could do nothing less. It was a modest request compared to the enormously generous and life-saving gift she had just been given.

'And . . . Lisa . . .' Daphne moved closer to her, took Arnaldo's hand and placed it on Lisa's breast, saying, 'I was so aroused when I saw you in the throes of passion with him. Will you do it again for me . . . now?'

He cupped Lisa's breast, the thumb stroking her nipple. She melted inside, becoming soft, warm and slippery wet. 'Certainly, Daphne,' she murmured.

Lee opened the door of Hawkhurst Abbey when Lisa rang the bell. At least, she supposed it was him. The build and black outfit were the same, but his mask was missing, showing a gaunt face with ash-blond hair clipped close to his skull.

'Hello,' she said. 'Is Mr Robillard or Miss Marlow in?'

'They are,' he answered, and she recognised the voice as Lee's. 'I'll tell them you're here.'

The hall, though huge, seemed suddenly claustrophobic. It was her first visit since that memorable evening when she had been initiated into the cult of the whip. Fletcher's lash had taken her virginity all over again –

ravishing her unschooled flesh in a consummation of pain, shame and unalloyed ecstasy. He had laid his brand upon her and she would never be entirely free of him. In the same way that a woman always remembers the man who robbed her of her maidenhead, so she would remember Fletcher's phallus extension – his whip.

Lee appeared like a shadow, and she went with him to the back of the house where, in a large storeroom, Fletcher and Tanith were supervising the arrival of their recent purchases.

'Ah, you've come at just the right time,' Fletcher said, pacing between bays in which were stored a multitude of treasures.

His assistants were using sack-trucks to wheel in large objects from a van parked in the yard outside. They offloaded them in an open area of this stone-flagged room, which might once have been the servants' hall. Some of the things were obviously items of furniture, wrapped in dustsheets, but there were packing cases, too.

'From the Rathbone sale?' Lisa asked.

Fletcher lifted one peaked eyebrow and smiled briefly. 'The same,' he said. 'Were you there?'

'I was, but I didn't see you.'

'I do most of my buying by phone. Don't need the hands-on approach any more.'

'I found it extremely interesting,' she replied, shifting over to stand out of the way of the panting, sweating, heaving helpers.

That's the understatement of the year, she reflected, thinking of the sexual adventure in the powder closet, though this had been ruined by the later memory of Fiona bending over David, his cock between her lips.

'I hope you don't lose your enthusiasm for the trade,' Fletcher remarked, and she was hugely embarrassed, her cheeks turning as red as the stripes that had not yet faded from her bottom.

The last time she had seen him was in the small hours of Thursday morning when those who had taken part in the scene in the dungeon were preparing to leave. She had been permitted to dress and remove her urine-soaked stockings. Lee had served coffee in the library, and the guests recuperated for a while before driving off into the dawn. Babs had strutted around in her leather gear, but Andrew had resumed his evening suit, controlled and bland, no longer the naughty boy suffering Tanith's chastisement. Tango music had been playing, while Jamie and Eduardo practised dance steps with Carol, quashing Andrew's offer to show them how.

'Lee will drive you home,' Fletcher had said, still appealingly sinister in his gangster attire.

'I can manage,' Lisa remembered protesting.

'Do as you are told,' he had answered in that cold, detached voice with the underlying hint of steel.

'My van . . .'

'He is insured to drive anything. Leave it to me.'

And now it all seemed a foggy, alcohol-induced dream, Fletcher businesslike in off-white chinos and sweatshirt, overseeing the delivery of his precious merchandise. Could this really be the man who had lashed her and ordered her to address him as master?

Tanith, too, had shed her dominatrix image, wearing practical, skin-tight jeans and crop top, her flaming Titian hair tied back from her face with a silk scarf. These were much more the sort of people Lisa had hoped for as colleagues, and she was tempted to mention her stroke of good luck and ask their advice regarding the Rossetti, even though Daphne had warned her to beware. Also, if she no longer intended joining their workforce, it was only fair that she informed them right away.

'There's something I should tell you,' she began. 'I can't start work on Monday. I'm going out with Mrs Nightingale.'

This would do for the time being, she decided. Better

232

not burn her boats until she had seen Messrs Godsiffe, Laughton and Beamish.

Fletcher's smile was warm and encompassing. He looped an arm casually round her shoulders, saying softly, 'As you wish, my dear. I gather that she's most experienced. You can learn a lot from her.'

There seemed to be a hidden meaning buried somewhere in his remark, and she shot him a sharp glance. Daphne had said he was devious. But Lisa was bemused in his presence, forgetting to be careful. That warm, lubricious feeling of arousal was stirring again between her legs, even though Arnaldo had thoroughly satisfied her.

Every nerve tingled as she rejoiced in the weight and strength of Fletcher's arm, and the brush of his hip against hers as he walked her over to the packing cases. She could see a slight rise beginning at his fly. If it became any larger it would ruin the cut of his trousers.

The assistants had gone. Only Tanith remained now, and she was absorbed in admiring the William and Mary bureau that David had wanted. Fletcher prised open the lid of a crate and removed a layer of straw.

'Look,' he said, his voice charged with pent-up enthusiasm.

He lifted out a ten-inch high pottery figure of a Chinese courtesan. She was wearing an orange jacket and brown striped dress, and the glaze was vivid.

'How much do you think this is worth?' he asked, turning the piece around in hands that had become as gentle as a woman's.

'I've no idea. I don't know anything about oriental antiques,' she admitted.

'She's from the Tang Dynasty,' he said, and put the statue to one side. 'I paid three thousand pounds for her, but my American contacts will give double to own her, to say nothing of this.' He dipped into the treasure trove again with the alacrity of a magician about to produce a rabbit from a top hat.

But no lop-eared bunny this, and Lisa gave a startled gasp as he placed it on the top of a tea-chest.

It was eastern, not Chinese. A group, not a single figure, and not only was it superbly sculpted, but also extremely pornographic. Lisa was unable to stop her hand flying to the apex of her thighs, pressing her skirt tight against her delta, tormented by the burning itch for sex that suddenly swept over her, exacerbated by the sight of the statuette.

'It's deco,' Fletcher said, observing her with his flinty eyes. 'Seems to have been inspired by Nijinsky dancing in *Scheherazade*. It's made of gilded bronze, exquisitely detailed. The clothes are cold-painted in metallic green, and studded with semi-precious stones.'

'It must have cost a bomb,' Lisa murmured, controlling herself and running a tentative finger over the smooth surface.

He gave a wry smile. 'It did,' he said. 'The price of such rare articles has risen astronomically in the last twenty years. And I shan't be selling this one. It came from old Lord Rathbone's private collection and wasn't on view to the general public – too decadent and erotic.'

Lisa was consumed with envy, an ignominious desire to possess the piece gripping her gut. Just to look at it made her feel incredibly randy.

A half-naked slave girl with chains banding her wrists was on hands and knees on the onyx base. Her breasts dangled, having escaped from the gem-encrusted bodice, her posterior in full view, each orifice, fold and nook carved in perfect detail. Her thighs were splayed, her head thrown back, and her expression was one of extreme bliss.

Below her lay another voluptuous female, her face between the kneeling woman's legs, her tongue reaching out to lap at the swollen nether lips, one hand playing with the slave's nipple, the other inserted into her own pleasure centre.

A sensuously graceful, divinely handsome man in a

234

gold turban and heavily embroidered bolero knelt behind the slave girl. His baggy pants were pushed down, his hands holding a large penis ripe for rutting which he was about to plunge into her anus. The group were frozen in time, yet so strong and forceful that it seemed they might spring into action at any moment.

Lisa and Fletcher breathed in unison as they studied the stimulating threesome. The realism was such that one expected to hear moans of passion, see the man's brilliantly detailed cock begin its journey into the slave's darkest and most secret recess, and witness the other woman's frantic movements as she brought herself to ecstasy.

'That's yummy,' Tanith murmured, joining Fletcher and Lisa in their worship at this shrine dedicated to sex. 'I think we should try it, don't you? We'll have to draw straws as to who is the slave.'

Fletcher's hand shot out, fastening like an iron talon on her upper arm as he rasped, 'I decide.'

'I'm sorry, master,' she returned meekly.

He let her go abruptly and turned his back, saying over his shoulder, 'Stay to dinner, Lisa.'

She was given no choice, and did not want one, still gazing at the erotic group, her head swimming with images in which she was the slave, Fletcher the caliph and Tanith the woman giving her oral stimulation.

'We need to change our clothes,' Tanith said in her ear, smelling divine; a heady mixture of scented hair and exotic perfume. 'The first of many changes, I shouldn't wonder. He's on a high. Nothing fires him up more than getting his hands on something others would give their eye teeth for. It makes him feel powerful, omnipotent . . . acts like a drug.'

They took the elevator to the dressing room where Lisa had discovered one of the abbey's many secrets. Fletcher had absented himself without a word, a habit to which she was becoming accustomed. But shortly after arriving at their destination, Lee tapped on the door and handed Tanith a note.

She read it, red lips curling in a pensive smile. 'As I suspected,' she said slowly. 'It's the mystic east for us tonight. How's your Kama Sutra?'

'I know it, of course.'

'You'll need to. Come on, let's see what we can find. It shouldn't be hard,' Tanith said, and started to root through the wardrobes. 'Fletcher was able to buy up some costumes from the Purple Epoch of Hollywood. Very Cecil B. De Mille and biblical epics. I'm going to wear one that belonged to Theda Bara, the first sex goddess.'

Like a little girl indulging in dressing up, so Lisa now entered a fantastic world of make-believe. Tanith was a superb guide, knowing which drawer contained yash-maks and paste jewellery, and where they might find diaphanous harem trousers.

'We should have a eunuch to help us,' Tanith explained, adding with a giggle, 'but none of the men around here have lost their balls ... not so as you'd notice. We women have more subtle ways of emasculat-ing them these days, haven't we?'

As she talked, she unearthed transparent scarves in brilliant colours, fringed and beaded jackets, tiny velvet waistcoats cunningly designed to show off the breasts, wide sashes and sequinned headdresses.

Lisa stripped, and so did Tanith, their bodies emerg-ing from their daytime clothes to be perfumed and oiled and moisturised, then draped in garments suitable for *The Arabian Night's Entertainments*.

Lisa blew out her cheeks. 'I look so different,' she said, standing in front of the cheval glass.

It gave her back her reflection, her eyes rendered enormous by a thin line of kohl drawn close to the blackened lashes. The lids were a glittering mauve. Ribbons and ropes of pearls had been threaded through her hair, and a little round hat, covered in shimmering spangles, placed on top, secured by jewelled bodkins. It had a gold tassel that spread over the crown and down one side.

Her costume verged on indecency: a short, tight bodice cut very low and thick with gold thread and beads and a pair of pink silk pantaloons, drawn in at the waist by a belt fastened with a diamanté clasp.

The shadow of her pubic wedge showed through the material, the shape of her cleft, thighs and buttocks clearly defined, even more arousing than if she had been entirely nude.

Tanith was radiant in floating robes of pale blue shot with silver threads, her full trousers riding low on her hips. She had glued a mock ruby in her navel. Her feet were bare, and anklets with silver bells tinkled with every step.

She caressed Lisa's nipples, the gold thread scratching them, and murmured, 'It doesn't matter which one of us he chooses to be on top, we'll give each other multiple orgasms tonight.'

The door to Fletcher's apartment was opened by Lee, who had a turban wound round his head. He was naked to the waist apart from a brass-studded collar, and the rings in his nipples caught the light, linked by a thin chain. His white cotton trousers fitted his lower legs tightly, but were draped round the hips, a fold falling open over his genitals.

Frankie wore an identical outfit, her breasts and backside bare and vulnerable and free to whosoever wanted to finger them and play with the rings piercing her private parts.

The room was lavishly decorated, Fletcher's den leading from his bedroom where he liked to study trade magazines and books devoted to art, music and antiques. Like Tanith's boudoir, it had been designed at the turn of the century when the fashion for the exotic prevailed.

The air was heavy with the smell of amber and sandalwood joss-sticks, bluish smoke curling snakelike from brass censors. Fletcher sat cross-legged on a divan heaped with brilliantly coloured cushions. He wore a gold tissue tunic and full red trousers caught in at the ankle where they met the tops of white leather boots with turned-up toes. His hair was hidden by a turban fastened with a flashing emerald brooch. It made his face seem even harder; more hawklike and imperious.

Lisa swallowed and resisted the temptation to fling herself face down on the Persian rug. He looked unnervingly powerful, and the ruthless force emanating from his every pore acted on her like a potent aphrodisiac.

Music stole through the evening, with drum beat and sitar forming strange harmonies; winding, intricate, with every note embroidered. Food was served on low tables: scented rice, meat in spicy sauces, the cool, fresh taste of natural yogurt, bowls of sliced melon sprinkled with ginger, and silver filigreed baskets of *rahat lokum*.

When Fletcher clapped his hands, the dishes were removed. He looked at Lisa, as darkly fascinating as a Persian prince in a fairy story, and said, 'You may take the role of the kneeling woman, but I think she was punished before her lord allowed her pleasure. Are you prepared for this?'

Lisa bent her head in assent, willing to agree to almost anything if she might experience the joy of union with this masterful man. He had teased her, tormented her, but denied her his phallus, and she burned to have him penetrate her.

He slowly got to his feet and towered over her, then snapped his fingers at Lee. At once the servant seized Lisa's wrists and held them in front of her. And, as on the former occasion, she saw her wrists banded by metal bracelets, heard the sinister click as they shut and felt the restriction of the shackles.

Fletcher nodded in approval, and undid the ball buttons of her brief bodice. Her breasts rose from it, and

238

he stroked her nipples while her whole body stiffened and a moan rose from her throat. Frankie unbuckled the jewelled belt and the pink harem pants whispered past Lisa's thighs and settled round her ankles. She kicked them away, glancing at the figurine that took pride of place on the table. Now she very much resembled the kneeling slave.

'You have been disobedient, and must be humbled,' Fletcher said abrasively.

Lisa knew that to enter into the spirit of this she must appear to protest. Indeed, she was almost sincere, dreading yet longing for the ordeal which she was sure lay ahead.

'I can't . . . I won't . . .' she stammered.

'You are stubborn, and need training,' he said with a sigh.

Tanith, stripped to her floaty robe, handed him a round object covered in white leather, with a long handle.

'What is it? What are you going to do to me?' Lisa cried, trembling in earnest now.

'You're too proud, girl. I must tame you,' he answered, flexing the paddle in his hands.

Lisa looked at it fearfully, thinking, Surely it won't be as painful as the whip?

'You can't be serious,' she whimpered.

'Oh, but I am,' he assured her, then smiled faintly. 'And, to test your submission, I shan't bind you. I command you to bend over and take your punishment freely, willingly and obediently.'

Part of Lisa longed to refuse, but she was also eager to know more about the dark half of her which was so acutely aroused, curious and eager, trembling on the brink of new discoveries.

Slowly, she bent from the waist, down and down till her hands rested on her ankles. She could feel her bottom cheeks opening wide, the small rosebud mouth of her anus exposed, and the furry mound beneath it, pinkish lips pouting in brazen invitation to be explored and possessed.

She saw those dashing white kid boots pass from sight, and then felt Fletcher's finger press against the tightness of her virgin hole. She smelt a sweet, oily fragrance and then the finger became slippery. Her anus opened and she cried out in surprise, pain and excitement as it began to worm into her tender fundament, preparing the way for something larger and more forceful. She wriggled her hips, fear and pain replaced by the urge to have him plunge his erect cock into her, penetrating her to the very heart.

The finger was withdrawn, and air took its place, the oil cooling on Lisa's perineum. Then she was almost knocked off her feet as the paddle came down with a loud swish, landing on her rump.

She recovered, righted herself, gripped her ankles and endured, her flesh smarting. The paddle fell again and again, spanking her bottom and the backs of her thighs. Though she managed to remain steady under the onslaught, tears ran down her cheeks and dripped to the rug.

'I think she's ready, master,' Tanith said.

Sobbing, every inch of her derrière seeming to have its own particular sting, Lisa took up her position, kneeling with her haunches in the air and her hands pressed to the floor. Tanith squirmed beneath her, mouth and fingers working at her nipples, across her belly and exploring the open chalice of her sex. Her fingertips strummed on the engorged bud that hung down from its retracted hood.

The pain of her flaming buttocks augmented the frantic waves of pleasure racking her as Tanith's lips and tongue brought her ever closer to the acme of sensation.

She felt warmth close to her backside, then the press of skin and coarse pubic hair. Then a huge, wet thing slid past her hungry vulva and prodded against the eyelet of her anus.

'Keep still, Lisa,' Fletcher whispered as he covered her, his lips at the back of her neck, his teeth gnawing the skin. 'Relax and let me have your arse.'

She groaned and braced to the assault as with small, sharp thrusts the mushroom-shaped head of his penis pressed in further. Her tight anal ring opened under its insistence, dilating as he destroyed the final frontier of innocence. The discomfort was immense, but so was the pleasure roaring up from her clitoris, swamping her with spasms so intense that the divide between the two sensations was blurred.

'You're so tight,' Fletcher muttered. 'Like a virgin there.'

She yelped as he drove his cock in with determined force. It felt as if she was splitting apart, her sphincter opening till the whole of his weapon was swallowed up in the narrowest, most intimate part of her body. He gripped her hips and straddled her, while Tanith drank at her flesh and, as he spent himself in her, Lisa reached such a raging climax that she almost danced on the impaling prong.

Chapter Eleven

*S*o, that's anal sex, is it? Lisa thought as she drove home. Well, Mavis, all I can say is I'm glad I don't regularly have to go through it. It's exciting, though, probably because it reeks of sin, and will, no doubt, get easier and even more pleasurable when I'm stretched in that department. But even so, I think I'd rather have his power-packed nine inches elsewhere, she told herself.

Parking up and bidding Mavis goodnight, she let herself into the flat, stood in front of the mirror and craned round to see what damage Fletcher had done. She gazed for a while at her blushing bottom, a sneaky ember of lust smouldering in her secret depths. He was certainly dynamic, like no one she had ever met.

She had a shower and went to bed, lying awake mulling over Daphne's extraordinary announcement. No more need to worry. She'd soon be solvent, and then some.

Gradually it began to dawn on her that this was actually going to happen. Grinning into the darkness, she curled up in a ball, tucked a hand between her legs and cradled her mound. Still buzzing with wonderful plans for the future, she fell asleep.

Messrs Godsiffe, Laughton and Beamish came up

trumps. At least, Mr Beamish did; a young man who was tiresomely bright and cheerful, with a willingness to serve that bordered on the unctuous. He obviously liked the idea of guiding Lisa through the pitfalls of property ownership and investments.

'I must tell Fletcher,' Lisa said, after Arnaldo had cracked open a bottle of Moët de Chandon back at Cranshaw House and filled three glasses. 'I shan't need to take him up on his offer of employment.'

'Do as you think best, my dear,' Daphne answered. 'I wish you health and happiness.'

'And I,' Arnaldo added, toasting her with his velvety, peat-brown eyes. 'But be careful. The wolves will be gathering as soon as they hear of your good fortune.'

'I'll offer Fletcher the chance to bid for the Rossetti,' Lisa went on, frothy bubbles tickling the back of her throat, somehow symbolic of her new way of life.

'And David Maccabene?' asked Daphne, eyeing her shrewdly.

'Maybe,' Lisa replied, for he was always there, a shadow on her mind. 'But I doubt that particular leopard will ever change his spots.'

'I think the one you really have to watch is Mr Garston,' Daphne said thoughtfully.

'I know. He's the worst kind of villain. Likes people to think he's such a fine guy, when really he's the hostile joker in the pack.'

Fletcher was as unemotional as ever when she tracked him down in the cool of the evening. He was in the den of Hawkhurst Abbey, and did not comment for a moment after she had told him her news.

He sat there, swishing the Courvoisier around in its finely blown brandy glass. 'I'm happy for you, of course, Lisa, but disappointed that you won't be working here,' he said.

'I want my own antique business,' she blurted out, having not yet grasped that her fortune would open doors and put her up there among those who were successful.

'You'll jack in the market?'

'For the time being. I'll be busy with something Mrs Nightingale has asked me to do. I'm to sell a drawing for her.'

His ears pricked up. He set the balloon goblet down on the sofa table and looked at her keenly. 'And what's so important about that?'

'It's by Dante Gabriel Rossetti,' Lisa said, bringing this out with an exhilarating sense of triumph that was almost sexual in its intensity.

His dark brows shot towards his hairline. 'A Rossetti? Here, in West Deverel?'

'That's right,' she averred earnestly, and moved closer along the divan, her body drawn to his like steel to a magnet.

'I want to see it,' he hissed, and his eyes were shards of ice piercing hers, yet they burned, too.

I'm in charge now, she thought, on a surge of confidence. I have something he wants most desperately. Let him wait. Let him sweat a little.

'Others must be given the opportunity,' she said coolly, crossing one leg over the other in her new designer jeans, giving him a flash of that seductive gap between the tops of her inside thighs. 'David Maccabene will be keen.'

Fletcher glowered at her. 'What does he know about fine art?' he demanded scathingly.

'I've no idea,' she answered, and leant into him so he could not miss the potent Frence perfume that breathed out from between her breasts.

Her own senses were spinning at such close proximity with a man she fancied like crazy. He was looking especially tasty in a long, paisley, dressing-gown style coat, opened over a pair of wide, loose trousers and a black knitted top with slashes down the front. She could

244

see his tanned chest through them and the glimpse of a nut-brown nipple. Her fingers tingled.

He smelled of summer heat, his wet hair and general air of well being suggesting that he had been using his swimming pool during the afternoon.

I can do the same, she thought, revelling in that feeling of rash extravagance which had borne her along on a whirlwind spending spree after she had seen Mr Beamish. It was better than winning the lottery. No more looking at price tags; she had simply picked out anything that took her eye. A pool was a definite possibility, if not for this summer then certainly for the next.

'I'll give a house-warming party,' she said, allowing her imagination to run riot. 'Will you come, and Tanith and the people I met here the other night?'

'If you'll let me organise it,' he answered meaningfully. 'Is there room for dancing?'

'Plenty. It's not as big as this place, of course, but we simply must dance the tango. Could we hire a proper orchestra? And everyone must wear masquerade costume. Let's decide on a theme.'

'How about silent movies?'

'Wonderful.'

Lisa's brain was in overdrive. Not only did she want to celebrate her ownership of the house, but was also looking forward to seeing Paul's face when he learned that she was now entirely independent. As for Mike? He was beneath contempt, but her plans included him and Valerie – and Fiona.

'I love being rich,' she chortled, losing that awe of Fletcher which had once rendered her tongue-tied.

'Doesn't everyone?' he questioned, with a twist of his sensual lips that made her sex pulse. 'And you deserve to have money, Lisa. You'll know how to spend it for maximum enjoyment. Use me, if you want advice.'

He's different, she thought, while it was still possible

to string coherent thought together. He has stopped patronising me.

One of his hands touched her breast, and he dipped a finger deftly down the deep 'V' of her T-shirt. She slumped among the cushions, hardly breathing as he explored along the low-cut edge of her Chantilly lace brassiere, her nipples growing erect under his caress. His face came closer, his breath scented with brandy, and he took her full lower lip between his teeth, nipping it gently, then sucking it, before including the upper one. Lisa was lost in a warm wash of pleasure as his tongue took possession of her mouth, exploring it thoroughly.

He succeeded in pushing down her bra and contacting her bare nipples, flicking over them till she shivered with delight. He thrust his tongue more deeply into her mouth, rolling the swollen rosy teats, then, impatient to view then, breaking the kiss and coaxing the T-shirt away from her body, dropping it over the side of the divan. The bra followed; her breasts rising, full and golden and the areolae brown, the crests dark and hard. He mouthed them for a moment, moving from one to the other, his fingers taking the place of his lips, keeping them both in a state of agonised want.

Then he held back, his grey eyes unusually warm and alive. 'Did the paddle mark you?' he asked, voice thick with excitement.

'My bottom glowed like a beacon,' she responded, reaching for the sexy bough she could see rising almost to his waist under the loose trousers. 'It's still red.'

'Let me see,' he demanded, and arched his pelvis against her seeking fingers, letting her explore the fullness of his male part.

Lisa clasped it, rubbing it through the silky black fabric. Her sex throbbed and her heart soared. This was the first time they had been really alone. There had always been a conclave of sycophantic followers. Now it was as if they were proper lovers, needing no audience to heat their blood and witness the consummation of their passion.

She stood up, kicked off her toe-post sandals and wriggled her jeans down, then presented her backside to him, bending from the waist. His cool palms smoothed the bruised skin, and his breath wafted over her spine. With eyes closed, she trembled under his caress, wanting to grab him, strip him, suck his penis, nestle his balls in her hands, and then have him plunge his spear into the supple warm sheath of her vagina – not the alien ring of her anus.

With something akin to dismay, she realised it would take very little to make her love this man.

He turned her, sat her down on the edge of the divan and seized the legs of her jeans, pulling them off. She watched him, feasting on his lustful, brooding expression, and then fell backward with her feet still resting on the carpet. With a hand on either thigh, she opened her legs and caressed the fluffy down of her mons, parted the pink petals of her labia and circled the throbbing bud that peeped from its fleshy nest.

She stroked over the erect nubbin lightly, and her womb spasmed. Her portal was wet, ready to receive Fletcher into her warm sanctuary. Peering beyond the concavity of her belly, the forest of hair and her own hands, she saw that he was looking down at her with a faint, cryptic smile. She closed her eyes, trembling with excitement.

She felt a touch other than her own on her clitoris. A finger flicked at the engorged, quivering crown. Lisa moaned and thrashed her head from side to side. The finger slid down and dabbled in the moisture pooling at her entrance, then spread it up her sex valley and massaged the seat of her arousal. Other fingers thrust deep inside her, plunging and withdrawing, imitating the movements of intercourse.

Her body bucked and threshed as she thrust her pubis higher to meet that heavenly invasion, the frisson on her clitoris never relaxing. But she wanted more than his fingers filling her. She wanted something big and forceful and pulsating with desire.

Urged on by this yearning, she heaved herself up on the cushions and reached for him. He stood between her legs and very slowly began to loosen the drawstring of his trousers, letting them slide down around his hips with dramatic results. His cock reared up in all its splendour and she grasped it, her hot palm enclosing the swollen glans while her fingers stretched down the rigid stem.

'It's huge,' she breathed.

'You've seen it before,' he answered, obviously pleased but amused.

'But never had it – not properly.'

He pulled her towards him and she felt the smoothness of the mighty helm nudging between her labia. Then he stopped, and she moaned in protest.

'Do you want me to do it to you?' he murmured, in that throaty accent which was like fire and wine to her.

'Oh, yes . . . yes. Do it . . . do it . . .'

'You're mine, aren't you? All mine. Everything you are, everything you own.'

'Yes,' she whispered, possessed by cock-struck madness.

'Have it, then,' he snarled, and thrust his penis into her.

Lisa screamed her pleasure as he penetrated her to the core, butting against her cervix and stretching the plush walls of her inner self. She embraced him with her thighs, yelling encouragement and urging him on as she felt his fingers pluck at her nipples and dive between their bodies to rub her clitoris.

He was fierce and violent, the swing of his loins driving her to a pitch of passion which tossed her headlong into an incandescent climax of such ferocity that she was sure she was dying. While the pleasure convulsed through her, she bucked to meet his thrusts, absorbing his power. He came with a roar that was pure animal. She felt his cock throb in her vagina, and her muscles clenched round it, holding him captive as he poured out his ecstatic libation.

He did not insult her by collapsing afterwards and using her as a mattress. Instead he hung over her, the sweat running over his brow to drip off his aquiline nose. Then he withdrew his partially erect weapon and smiled into her eyes.

'Satisfied?' he asked.

'Oh, yes,' she sighed, disentangling herself.

'Good,' he said. 'And now we'll go to the ballroom. Eduardo will be arriving shortly to give Tanith her dancing lesson. You'll join in.'

'But . . .' She could think of a dozen reasons why not, though none measured up to the appeal of tango.

'Hush,' he admonished. 'You want to be the star of your party, don't you? I'll make sure you are, but it'll mean work, work and more work. Tango can't be learned in five minutes. Your back will hurt, your feet will ache, you'll cry and I shall cane you, but it will be worth it when you take the floor in my arms and confound your enemies.'

It was time for Daphne to leave. A taxi arrived at Cranshaw House to take her to the airport. She looked pale but resolute and was supported by Arnaldo. He was handsome and dignified in a Milan tailored suit and Gucci shoes, every inch of him proclaiming wealth and position.

Lisa had already said her goodbyes, but there were last-minute kisses all round, and reminders and promises to phone. Then, after standing in the road and waving them off, she let herself back into the house. It belonged to her at last.

Now she could answer that annoying letter from the planning committee, tell them that she had everything in hand and, apart from their approval of the renovations, to keep their noses out of her business. Next she would have several builders give her estimates for the work, and decide who was the best person to tackle it. There was one firm she would ignore, and that was Everard Homes Ltd.

Arnaldo had interviewed applicants for the post of housekeeper, a necessary addition as Cranshaw House was too large for Lisa to manage alone. He had finally selected a woman who had once run her own hotel. Now she came from the direction of the kitchen, smartly dressed, a touch acerbic, the sort of no-nonsense person who could become a tower of strength.

'They've gone, then, Miss Sherwin,' she remarked.

'They have indeed, Mrs Harvey,' Lisa responded, feeling suddenly dejected and lonely.

Mrs Harvey smiled, saying, 'You'll miss them, no doubt, but we'll soon have everything in apple-pie order and running like clockwork.'

'Not too regulated, I hope,' Lisa warned, letting her know who was boss. 'I'm not used to it. I want to feel at ease in my own home ... like I was in the flat. I'm having a house-warming soon. We'll talk about it later. I'm going out now. Make sure the security system is on.'

'Yes, Miss Sherwin,' Mrs Harvey answered, respectfully.

Mavis had been put out to grass in the garage, and Lisa drove her new coupé to the town. The Bentley would be for occasional use only, and the van more often, once she got into the swing of things. There was so much to work out.

'A formal party. How grand,' Martin said, as they sat in the back room of the shop. Phil was brewing up, and Alfie stretched out languidly on the sunny window ledge.

'You're invited, and Phil. It's fancy dress,' she said, swinging her legs under the new skirt which had cost far more than she liked to recall. Once she had shopped exclusively at Oxfam.

Martin eyed her suspiciously. 'Oh, yes, and what's it in aid of? Your coming up in the world?'

'A house-warming,' she countered, but her eyes danced.

'Lisa Sherwin, I've known you for a long time,' he went on, wagging a finger at her. 'And I recognise when you're up to something. Come on. What is it? Who's going to be at the receiving end?'

'Well . . .' she temporised, accepting a mug of tea from Phil. 'Let's just say that I'm sending invitations to Paul, his mother and Mike Garston . . . not forgetting David and Lady Fiona.'

'Ah,' Martin said sagely. 'Getting our own back, are we?'

'Sort of. You haven't met Fletcher and his gang, have you? I'm sure you'll be in for a few surprises, and so will Paul and co.'

'You've got a witchy look about you,' Phil commented, grinning.

'*Moi?*' Lisa exclaimed, making her eyes big and innocent. 'I simply don't know what you mean.'

She still felt more at ease with Martin and Phil than anyone else, and had offered them the flat to move into once the building had been repaired. They had accepted. The lease on their cottage was crippling, and short term, too. The next time it was renewed the rent was bound to go up. The flat would suit them admirably, and Lisa did not want to let it to strangers, though she had warned them to keep an eye on Alfie with his appetite for goldfish.

'Well, of all the cheek!' Valerie cried, her face reddening with temper. 'Have you seen this, Mike?'

'What?' he said wearily, slumping on the couch before the large television screen in their lounge. There was a football match he wanted to see and now it looked as if she was going to talk all the way through it.

'Came by hand, pushed through the letterbox,' Valerie went on, holding out an envelope belligerently. 'It's from Lisa. That jumped-up little cow has the nerve to send us an invitation to a house-warming. She wouldn't be anywhere if she hadn't got in with that dotty old crone who used to ride around in that great car with a greasy dago as chauffeur.'

'We'll accept,' he said firmly, perusing the deckle-edged card with its gilt italic lettering. He could almost smell Lisa on it. 'I'd like to take a look at the place.'

'*You* would,' she rapped out nastily. 'Got no pride, that's your trouble. I wonder if Paul has had one? She wouldn't have the neck, would she? Bet she would – she's brassy enough for anything. I'll phone him.'

Mike sighed and reached for a beer. He was plunged in gloom lately, unable to shake off the depression even when with Joyce. If anything, this made it worse, for he could no longer pull strings and get Lisa into trouble. Word had soon spread through The Foresters as to what had transpired between her and Mrs Nightingale. The news had jerked the rug from under Mike's feet. There was no way he could manipulate Lisa now.

He could hear Valerie rabbiting on to Paul. Her voice grated on his nerves.

'She sent you one! She's no idea of right and wrong,' she shouted, as she always did down the phone. 'You're well shot. The things I've been hearing about her ... Well! Men and all sorts. Oh, so you're going? In that case, we'd better go, too. Who did you say will be there? Mr Robillard from Hawkhurst Abbey, and Lady Fiona? That makes a difference, I suppose. No, Paul, I'm not a snob. How can you say such a thing?'

'Lisa, is this some kind of game?' David said, finding her in the flat busily engaged in packing. He balanced the invitation card in the tips of his fingers.

'No game, David. Nothing more than people usually play. Like you and Fiona, for example,' she said, and he detected venom in her voice.

Could it be that she was jealous of her ladyship? Had she resented seeing him spurt into another woman's mouth? He had to admit it had not been one of his finest moments.

'I suppose congratulations are in order,' he ventured, trying again. It would have been possible to cut the atmosphere with a knife.

'Thank you,' Lisa said frigidly, without looking up from the books she was stacking in a box.

'Don't you want to hear what I have to say about my relationship with Fiona?' he persisted.

'No,' she said with ice-maiden finality.

'No chance of sex then?' he inquired impudently.

'Get stuffed, David,' she said.

'That's what I mean,' he continued.

'On your bike. I'm busy.'

'OK,' he said, and strolled towards the door. 'I'll come to the party. Can't speak for Fiona, but she never misses a bash. Fancies Fletcher Robillard rotten. See you there.'

'There's a drawing you may care to view,' she informed him, in the same way she might have recited a train timetable. 'A chalk drawing by Rossetti.'

'Not old DGR?'

'Yes.'

'It's got to be a fraud.'

'No, it isn't. Mrs Nightingale is the owner and she has asked me to sell it for her. Care to take a look? Fletcher wants it.'

'Does he, by God? Then I guess I can't refuse.'

She looked up, smiling sweetly and saying, 'I thought you'd feel that way. Goodbye, David ... till the party night.'

'Damn woman!' David growled as he let himself out. What annoyed him most was not Fletcher or Fiona, but the fact that as soon as he had set eyes on Lisa again,

253

his penis had reacted, leaping to attention as if it had not seen the inside of a love tunnel for weeks.

As self-appointed master of ceremonies, Fletcher had taken over the preparations. Mrs Harvey was dismissed for the weekend, and her place taken by Lee and Frankie. Caterers and florists had delivered during the day, and the sound equipment had been set up. He had decided against a live band on the grounds of discretion. This was to be no ordinary party.

Lisa was as nervous as a starlet on opening night. She was about to be launched and was eternally grateful to Fletcher and Tanith who, once she had explained the circumstances of her broken engagement, were only too willing to assist and not slow to see the advantages.

Though Fletcher had no ambition to join The Foresters, looking down his aristocratic nose at such plebian pursuits, he had found it was always useful to have town worthies in one's pocket for future reference. He had never been above blackmail, emotional or otherwise.

Satisfied that all was ready, the reception room transformed into a dimly lit, slightly sleazy nightclub, Lisa ran upstairs to her bedroom. This was the finest in the house, once used by Daphne, and the sanctum where she and Arnaldo had begun Lisa's rites of passage.

She was trembling with anticipation, strung out on a sexual rack. Who would she have that night? Fletcher – she wanted that. Or Eduardo, her teacher who tempered dance lessons with those of amour?

Often he had demonstrated the true meaning of tango, its dark sensuality rooted in deep passions. He had carried it to the ultimate conclusion, his manhood emerging from the tightness of his trousers, his lips and fingers readying his pupils' bodies to receive it and the rhythm of the music becoming one with the pounding beat of their blood.

As Lisa remembered each passion-filled hour, her

breasts became firmer, the nipples hard as pebbles. While she showered in the magnificent marble and Islamic-tiled bathroom, she allowed images to pile up, one on the other, stoking her fire. She relished the slippery feel of gel lathering her skin, and deliberately pulled at her nipples, teasing them into points, then walked her hand down over her navel, past her flat belly and into her luxuriant bush.

It was sweet torture to part her cleft, smell the oceanic fragrance meeting that of chestnut gel and toy with her hard nub. But she kept orgasm at bay. She wanted to wait, so it would be all the more piercing when it finally came, be she with Fletcher or Eduardo . . . or David.

Angry with him though she was, the sight of his swarthy, handsome face in the flat the other day had nearly been her undoing. She had found it nigh impossible to refrain from touching him, even though she had caught him flagrante delicto with Fiona. But tonight, who could foresee what might happen? It was all down to fate. She was becoming a believer in kismet and the laws of karma.

On a high pinnacle of excitement, she prepared herself with the greatest possible care, following photographs of the early Hollywood vamps in order to put on her make-up. Every feature was exaggerated; eyes, brows, cheekbone and lips. She painted her face as if it was a canvas, making it sultry and seductive. Her hair was a wild mop of curls, her body sinuous and near naked in an emerald-green sheath of tussore silk, fringed and spangled, the skirt slit thigh-high.

Black silk stockings with lacy welts, ruched garters, high-heeled green satin shoes, no knickers and a positive deluge of perfume, and she was ready. The final touch was a black velvet mask, topped with peacock feathers. It covered her nose and brow, her eyes glittering mysteriously through the silver-sequinned slits.

Her guests were arriving as she swept down the stairs. Her disguise was complete, hiding her everyday persona. It was not until she glided over to the Garstons and Paul and said, 'Welcome to Cranshaw House,' that they recognised her.

'Bloody hell, I didn't know you,' Paul spluttered, his concession to masquerade costume being his rugby shorts and jersey, stripy knee-socks and trainers.

How on earth did I ever go to bed with *that*? Lisa thought, as she gave him an alluring smile and said, 'What an original outfit. Well done, Paul.'

Her sarcasm coiled, snakelike, through the hall, but he was unaware.

'You've done well for yourself, haven't you?' Valerie remarked, and if looks could have killed, Lisa would have suffered an immediate cardiac arrest. 'Big house, but it could do with modernisation.'

'*Chacun à son goût*,' Lisa said, certain that Valerie would not understand her. 'I love your dress,' she added, insincerely. Which silent movie was she meant to be from? she wondered.

Valerie preened herself, half bold, half embarrassed, as she answered, 'It was made for a tarts and vicars party at the mayoress's last Christmas.'

'It suits you,' Lisa said, and this time she was sincere.

Valerie was instantly recognisable, even though she wore a kitten mask. She made an ideal tart in a strapless red satin wasp-waisted corset with long gilt suspenders clipped to the tops of fishnet stockings, sling-backed shoes, black panties and a pillbox hat with a spotted veil on her freshly bleached hair. Her opulent breasts almost spilled out, and the thin silk of her panties was stretched across her plump mound, a scarlet love-heart placed dead centre.

I'll bet she couldn't wait for another chance to wear that rig out, Lisa thought cynically. Strange how, deep down, the most respectable woman wants to dress up as a hooker – or rather the popular conception of how a hooker dresses.

Mike was completely out of character as a vicar, in a

black suit and dog collar. He leered at her through a gargoyle half-mask, and she stiffened her spine and introduced him to Tanith.

'This is Mike,' she said, giving a faintly malicious smile. 'I've told you about him.'

'Mike, how lovely to meet you at last,' Tanith gushed, permitting her breasts to almost slide from her loose-fitting, deeply divided bodice as she stepped towards him.

She shimmered and shone, a vision of exotic delight in a Parma violet, heavily beaded dress that ended just below her knees, the hem dipping in handkerchief points. Her mask was fixed to a stick so that she could hold it to her face when she wanted. It emerged from a gold tissue frill, shroud white, decorated with purple flowers. The eyeslits slanted at the outer corners, marked with sweeping, exaggerated lashes.

Martin sashayed across the hall on Phil's arm. 'Paul, you know Martin, don't you? He owns Charisma.'

Martin was totally transformed, and needed no mask to conceal his identity. He could have been a tall, elegantly lovely mannequin showing off a Poiret gown in a Paris showroom, all turquoise satin and feathers. Wearing a burgundy bobbed wig with a fringe and kiss-curls brushing his rouged cheeks, he epitomised the flapper – lean, flat chested and leggy.

Paul's eyes nearly popped out of his head. 'Martin? Is it really you?' he stammered.

'Too true, ducky,' Martin trilled, crimson lips curving archly. 'But you can call me Martina, just for tonight. You're coming to see my act, aren't you? I'm part of the cabaret.'

The reception room was already filling: not too many people, just a select few whom Fletcher could see might be useful at a later date. They circulated, admiring each other's costumes. There was a Charlie Chaplin and a Gloria Swanson, a troubadour, a jester and a musketeer. Several ladies, imagining their masks would give them anonymity, had appeared scantily clad, as Cleopatras, nautch-girls and Roman slaves.

A buffet had been laid out in a side room, a cold collation set among epergnes of flowers and silver figurines in risque poses.

The decor and the food and wine had all been calculated to stir the senses and loosen the control, cunningly stage managed by Fletcher. Lee and Frankie, two thin black shapes apart from their exposed genitals and deathlike masks, waited to serve dishes and fill glasses. Champagne corks popped like miniature artillery. Voices rose higher, laughter became raucous and inhibitions came tumbling down.

David and Fiona arrived late, and Lisa did a double take when she saw him. Her heart performed a somersault and landed somewhere in her groin.

He had scorned wearing a mask, devilishly handsome. He was a threat to any maiden's virtue in crimson velvet breeches that fitted from waist to knee without a wrinkle, so tight that they scooped hollows at his flanks and outlined the bulge at his crotch. It was even possible to discern the ridge of his foreskin.

His brown arms rippled with muscles, and his tanned, dark-haired chest was part hidden by a leather jerkin. A wide burgundy sash drew attention to his supple waist and the tautness of his arse. With a bandana round his head, gold hoops in his ears and black boots with turned-down tops, he could have trod the decks of any galleon flying the Jolly Roger and terrorising the Spanish Main.

'That's a most suitable choice of costume,' Lisa remarked pithily, amazed by her self-control, for her mouth was dry and her sex wet. 'I always thought you were a pirate.'

'I'm flattered,' he answered, his lips forming into a lupine smile under the pencil-thin line of false moustache. 'I fancy a go at the old swordplay. Don't you recognise Douglas Fairbanks, who swung from riggings and jumped in and out of ladies' bedroom windows on the silver screen?'

'You know about him? I'd never have taken you for a silent movie fan.'

'I'll have you know I passed much of my misspent youth in the company of my great-grandmother, who taught me to love music, antiques, the cinema and how to cheat at cards. She claimed to have slept with Doug,' he returned, his green eyes dancing.

'She sounds like some lady,' Lisa said, unsure whether to believe him.

'She still is. All of ninety-five and with an eye for the men. I asked her not long ago if she still has orgasms.'

'And?'

'She told me not to be a twit. What a question! Of course she does.'

'You've never invited *me* to meet any of your precious clan,' Fiona chipped in, pouting, her eyes flashing between the slits of her tiny jewelled mask.

'You've never asked, darling,' he drawled. 'I didn't think you'd be interested in the hoi polloi. You're always telling me I'm low caste.'

'Don't be so disagreeable,' she begged, rubbing herself against him.

Lisa wanted to slap her, that vain, spoiled creature with alley-cat morals. And, to cap it all, she was looking absolutely ravishing. Her gown must have cost a king's ransom, the damson-red bustier raising her breasts so high that the pointed red nipples poked over the lacy rim. The costume was loosely based on one which might have belonged to Marie Antoinette, via Hollywood and various high-class brothels.

Her wide skirt was supported on a hoop and seemed solid enough, but as she moved it swished open, slit in several places. A flash of leg was shown in court shoes, and a slender thigh, a bare expanse of bottom and the wispy fronds on her sex.

Lisa turned away from them as Martin stepped on to

the low stage at one end of the room. The lights dimmed and a single spot focused on him. Music blared and he went into his act, miming Berlin cabaret songs *à la* Marlene Dietrich.

He was sex incarnate – vulgar, insolent, raunchy, wildly provocative – and the audience adored him.

As he left the stage to thunderous applause, Lisa slipped over to congratulate him, but Paul was there first, sweating, drunk, clapping and shouting. 'Martin . . . Martina . . .'

'What is it?' Martin said in his gentle voice, eyes brilliant under the heavy blue liner.

'I don't know,' Paul spluttered. He did not even notice Lisa, who was watching from the shadows. 'I've had too much to drink, but even so . . .'

'Why don't you come somewhere quiet and talk to Phil and me?' Martin suggested, and glanced down to where Paul's penis bulged behind his shorts. 'Looks as if you're in a state. It can't be me that's inspiring such a tribute, can it?'

'You're lovely,' Paul gasped, out of his depth. 'I want to touch you. This is awful. You're a man. I want to touch you, but I'd like to wear that dress while I'm doing it. Give us a kiss.'

'But I thought you liked girls,' Martin replied, one strong, satin-gloved hand warding Paul off as he made to grab him. 'Are you sure you're an Arthur not a Martha?' He winked across at Lisa, lifting a peaked brow as if to say, I told you so.

She gave him the thumbs-up sign.

'Come on, Paul,' Phil said, taking charge, superb in his naval officer's tropical whites. 'Up to our room, and we'll see what we can do to sort you out.'

At midnight the masks came off. It was Lisa's turn to perform. The audience formed a circle, seated at small tables, drinks to hand. The opening chords of music stole out and Fletcher walked on to the floor.

He stared across to where Lisa sat and nodded

imperiously. She smiled and went to him. He seized her by the wrist and spun her into his arms. An audible sigh rose from the throat of every female present.

He was a panther, a savage, a sleek dominating animal. Valentino lived again in him. He wore Spanish costume: high-waisted trousers like a second skin, clinging as he moved, a cummerbund, a short, tight jacket, white shirt, red shoestring tie and a wide-brimmed hat tilted forward over his brow.

Inspired, almost possessed, he made her a part of himself, to rock with him, slide with him, step with him and *feel* with him. She would have followed him to hell and back in that sublime moment of complete unity, deeper even than when their bodies had been locked in sexual congress.

He held her firmly to him, his cock hard against the line of his fly, pressed a hand in the small of her back, then went lower. The thin material of her dress worked between the crease of her buttocks, the tip of his finger advancing towards her forbidden entrance.

'Dance,' he hissed, his smooth cheek resting on hers. 'Nothing matters but the dance. Remember how I whipped you when you made mistakes? I'll whip you again, later. I'll have you again, later. Now dance.'

Lisa was in a trance, the spirit of tango possessing her, an almost incarnate entity. They swayed and swirled together and performed intricate figure-of-eight patterns. They were one. They were superb. They posed as the music stopped; beautiful, elegant and redolent of carnal desire.

The audience went wild. Eduardo seized Valerie and hauled her to the floor, bending her to the tango. Fiona almost fell into Jamie's embrace, her limp arms up round his neck. Tanith, Carol and Babs seized Mike, performing a strange ritual dance with Andrew joining in.

Those who were usually so careful of West Deverel's

morals had lost the last of their inhibitions, dancing, kissing and slipping away to fornicate.

Lisa stood in an alcove a little apart, her eyes on her guests. It was shadowy there. The kaleidoscopic lights now flashing over the dancers left her corner in darkness. Her libido was at full peak. She was wet between the legs. Her hand wandered over her breasts, touching the aroused nipples. Success was a mighty passion rouser, and she felt very successful indeed. Fletcher had been pleased with her performance. He had not said as much, but had expressed it with every part of his body.

She relaxed, savouring the sensations that were rippling through her breasts and clitoris. The tussore slid up easily as she groped for her mound, finding her avenue and sinking a finger between the split peach of her sex. Then she became aware of another hand closing over hers and the pressure of someone, warm against her spine.

She breathed deeply, inhaling his smell, and Fletcher nuzzled her neck and feathered a finger over her nub, rubbing it gently. The air cooled her buttocks as he used his other hand to lift her skirt. The front of his thighs brushed the backs of hers as he eased into position, sliding his penis towards the entrance to her tender shrine.

Climax was almost on her, and she bore down on his cock, taking it deep inside her. He moved slowly and rhythmically, as if he still danced, gyrating his hips rather then using a straight, thrusting, in and out movement. His glans rubbed her cervix and his finger massaged her clitoris, while her own hands cupped her breasts and stimulated her nipples.

The music rose to a crescendo. So did she, aware of him pumping hard as she spilled over, shuddering and flushing as the intense, beautiful sensations of orgasm flowed through her. Fletcher supported her, still filled by his cock, and his arms folded round her like dark wings.

Chapter Twelve

'*B*ut I'm married!' Valerie protested, as Eduardo led her into one of the guest rooms.

Her objection sounded half-hearted, and Lisa smiled grimly from her hiding place behind the thick window drapes.

Tanith squeezed her arm. She was the instigator of this voyeurism, having whispered to her downstairs, 'Eduardo's doing his stuff. A good-looking stud like him ... Valerie must think it's Christmas. You want to see her get her comeuppance, don't you?'

Now they exchanged a grin in the dimness, and Lisa peeked through a gap in the curtains, seeing her once prospective mother-in-law, flushed and tipsy, in the arms of the dance instructor. He held her tightly, and her feeble struggles stopped as his mouth clamped down on hers. He advanced a hand up the side of her waspie, reached one breast and cupped it firmly.

Valerie wrenched herself free. 'No!' she cried, and slapped his face.

'Hypocrite!' Tanith hissed against Lisa's ear. 'She can't wait to have his cock in her.'

Eduardo's face darkened. He grabbed Valerie, pulled her towards the bed, sat down on it and put her across his knee. 'You're a naughty girl,' he admonished. 'And naughty girls have to be punished.'

'You beast,' she whimpered. 'You have no right to do this.'

Her arched position made her breasts rise over the strapless bodice, dangling down on the far side of his lap. Holding her effortlessly with his left hand, he reached round to tweak her big teats, stretching them, then letting them spring back.

Lisa felt the aching pleasure in her own nipples, touching them through the tussore. A dark skein of excitement wound through her as she saw Tanith engaged in the same pursuit. She, too, must be recalling dancing classes they had shared with Eduardo, she thought.

Tanith's hand delved into her crotch, beads flashing as she lifted the handkerchief hem and found her neatly trimmed mound and the treasure concealed within. Lisa was torn between watching her masturbate and seeing Valerie get her just desserts. Both visions were so warming that her own bud clamoured for relief, and she slipped a finger into her wet delta and rubbed herself.

'You need a lesson in manners, Mrs Garston,' Eduardo reproved, and wrenched down her black panties, exposing the pallid globes of her fleshy buttocks.

Valerie kicked and threshed to no avail, her struggles doing nothing but further expose her bottom crease and pouting, hair-fringed sex.

With a glance towards the window embrasure where his fellow conspirators hid, Eduardo brought his open hand down across her posterior.

She squealed and lashed out with her feet, losing a shoe in the process. He did not stop spanking her till her haunches were blotched with bright pink, palm-shaped marks and silvery love juice trailed over her intimate parts and inner thighs.

Eduardo straightened his legs so that she slid down

264

them and lay on the floor at his feet. Her costume was in disarray, her breasts spilling out and her panties round her ankles. Her mascara had run, ringing her tear-filled eyes, and she was in a highly emotional and excited state.

Legs apart in black Hessian boots, Eduardo slowly unbuttoned the front flap of the white buckskin breeches which were part of his hussar's uniform. His member jutted out, and Valerie gave a breathy sob. It was big and upward curving; a solid bough of flesh.

'Oh, my God,' she wailed, and clapped her hands over her eyes.

'Look at it!' Eduardo commanded.

'I can't ... I mustn't,' she cried, but was peering through her fingers.

'False modesty,' he sneered. 'It fascinates you. Have you ever seen one so large? I'll make it bigger. Watch.'

He held it in one hand, pulling the foreskin back and pushing it up again, his weapon rearing through the slit in his breeches.

'Oh, this is terrible,' she gasped, making no attempt not to look. 'How dare you expose yourself to me!'

'You want me to cover it? OK,' he said, and yanked her knickers from her ankle with the toe of his boot, then swooped it up and swathed his phallus in the scrap of black silk.

'You're perverted!' Valerie cried.

'And you love it,' he returned, making the satin tent waggle as he moved his penis. 'This will fire your fantasies when you frig yourself.'

'I don't!' she shouted, her face flaming.

'Liar. Think of me next time you do it. Come closer.'

He gripped her by the back of the neck and forced her to her knees between his thighs. Then he pressed her face to the silk-covered package at his crotch, her lips open over the tip of his penis showing above it.

'I'll scream for help,' she threatened, though her voice was muffled.

265

'Not with this in your mouth,' he said, and pushed his glans between her teeth, successfully gagging her.

Unable to resist, Valerie moved her head up and down. Lisa could hear soft, sucking sounds as Eduardo sat there, legs splayed, looking at his busily occupied captive.

He withdrew suddenly, and Valerie stared up into his face. 'What now?' she asked, eagerly. 'What other awful things are you going to make me do?'

For answer, he dragged her up and laid her on the bed, then opened her legs wide and knelt between them, saying, 'You have luscious private parts, Mrs Garston. Used to fucking, by the look of them.'

'Only with my husband,' she insisted, straining towards him.

He slid a finger into her, and wriggled it. Valerie gasped, her breasts shaking. 'Don't . . .' she whined.

'Don't what? Don't stop?'

'I can't bear it. It's not fair to make me . . .'

Very slowly he stroked her dark pink avenue and landed on the crimson bud swelling from its cowl. Her cries became faster and her breathing jerky as he rotated his thumb on her pleasure point. Her hips rose and her heels drummed on the quilt, and she gave a long yowl as she came.

'Do you want me to put my cock in you?' Eduardo asked, fingers plunging in and out of her.

'Yes, please,' she moaned.

He scowled and shook her. 'Say it properly,' he demanded. 'Say, "Fuck me, Eduardo."'

'I can't use that vulgar word.'

'Say it!' he shouted, and implemented his words by slapping her thighs.

'Fuck me, Eduardo,' she yelled.

He lifted her legs and hitched them round his waist, then drove his erection into her. Valerie shrieked, thrusting upward to meet it, and Lisa watched with thudding heart as her enemy lost all restraint, bucking, writhing, moaning and crying under this virile young man's assault.

When Eduardo gave a final lunge that brought him to completion, Lisa and Tanith stepped out from behind the curtain. Valerie's eyes widened in horror as she stared at them over his shoulder.

'What are you doing here?' she panted.

'Watching you, Valerie,' Lisa said, scornfully. 'Seeing the real you under all that pretentious garbage.'

'He made me do it,' Valerie bleated.

Lisa laughed. 'Oh, yes?' she said caustically. 'What a stroke of luck. You were forced to do the things you've always secretly dreamed about. Get a life, Valerie. Accept you're an ordinary human being, not some tin-pot idol, Mrs Norman Normal, backbone of the W.I.'

Eduardo shifted off Valerie, leaving her exposed, and she sat up shamefacedly, trying to tuck her breasts back into her corset top. 'Don't tell anybody, will you, Lisa?' she begged. 'Not Mike . . . and not anyone who belongs to The Woodlanders. I'd just die!'

'I won't grass you up, providing you're civil to me from now on. But if I find out you've been bad-mouthing me, then I promise you, everyone will know.'

With that, Lisa marched from the room with Tanith, hellbent on her next mission.

Fletcher had turned the cellar into a dungeon. It wasn't as grand as the vaults of Hawkhurst Abbey, but impressive enough with the stone walls draped in black and scarlet and fearsome-looking instruments suspended on rings. Lit by smoky candles in sconces, it was a place dedicated to the dark gods.

'Time for fun and games,' Tanith said, stalking over to the recumbent figure tethered to a bondage table.

She had changed her outfit, now wearing a black leather basque over which her rouged nipples protruded, a tiny cache-sexe, suspenders and thigh-length PVC boots with stilt heels. She carried a bull-whip, running the thongs lovingly between black gloved fingers.

The bound man was Mike. He stirred from his alcoholic haze, and stared around him blearily, muttering, 'What the hell . . .'

Lisa threw off the hooded cloak that shrouded her, displaying her body, also covered in leather – a blood-red catsuit unzipped to the waist. It turned her into a demon in the flickering light. She glanced briefly at Babs and Carol, the former in a laced bodice and minimal skirt, the latter in a bustier and tutu, with no panties, thick black stockings and ballet shoes.

'Good evening, Mike,' Lisa purred, running her eyes over his heavily fleshed naked body then tapping his limp cock lightly with the riding crop clenched in her fist. 'I hope you're enjoying the party.'

'I was,' he grunted, tugging at his manacled wrists and ankles. 'I must have passed out. OK. You've had a laugh, now unchain me.'

'I'm afraid we can't do that, Mike,' Lisa said thoughtfully, and flicked his penis, rolling it from side to side across his hairy underbelly. It started to grow. 'Not till I've seen you squirm. I've brought my friends along to help.'

'Well, I'll be damned!' Tanith exclaimed, leaning over Mike and touching his member with the tip of the whip. 'He must like this. He's hard as a flagpole, the dirty bugger.'

Mike's legs were wide open, his testicles supported by the bench, two ripe plums in a wrinkled sac. Babs reached out a hand and squeezed them.

'Girls, girls,' Mike murmured. 'Won't one of you sit on it for me?'

'We might,' Tanith said, and swished the whip, bringing it down across his right thigh, her skill such that it landed with extreme accuracy without touching any other part of him.

He yelped and pulled against his restraints, but his

cock remained erect, a crystal tear escaping from the slit.

Lisa caught it on the tip of one finger and smeared it over his lips, saying softly, 'Do you remember threatening me, Mike? What was it to be? My body in exchange for you keeping the council sweet?'

'That wasn't very nice,' Carol cooed, and straddled him, up on her knees so that the crown of his cock hovered beneath her sex.

Babs stood behind him, reached across and twisted his nipples. Mike gasped and struggled to meet Carol's tantalising avenue with the end of his upright phallus. She giggled and pushed back the net tutu, revealing the pink petals of her flower and holding them apart so that he could stare at that desired place while unable to touch it. She inserted a finger, wet it with juice and started to rub her clitoris.

'You think you're a one with the ladies, don't you?' Tanith said. 'I'll bet you've never met any like us.'

Carol moved away and Babs produced a pliable leather strap. Mike protested to no avail as she bound it round the base of his penis.

'There,' she remarked, admiring her handiwork. 'That'll slow you down; stop you coming till we say you can.' She turned to address her companions, adding, 'Who wants to have a go?'

'Let's hang him up first,' Tanith suggested, and at her signal, Lee and Andrew appeared from the shadows.

Mike fought but was hampered by his manacles. They overpowered him, dragged him over to the cross-piece and chained him to it. The sweat was running down his body, his expression one of anger and apprehension, yet his cock remained hard, poking from the thicket of belly hair, his balls dangling between his widespread thighs.

'That's better,' Tanith commented, pacing round him, her high heels clicking. 'Now we can get at him on all sides.' She brought the whip down across his back.

'You bloody bitch!' Mike hissed, between gritted teeth.

'That's not the way to speak to a lady,' she scolded, and whipped his legs. 'See what happens to bad slaves.'

She pointed to where Andrew lay across the couch, his quivering bare arse raised to Lee, who began to belabour it with a paddle. After half a dozen blows, he parted the round, flushed cheeks, dipped his fingers into the liquid oozing from Andrew's cock and applied some to his own erect member, then plunged it into the other's nether hole.

'You wouldn't?' Mike cried, fresh sweat breaking out in his armpits. 'Not a man . . . I've never been into that.'

'No? Maybe it's time you tried it. Paul's found his forte, so Mark and Phil report. Nowhere to hide. The masks are off,' Lisa said firmly, and laid about him with the riding crop.

She gave herself over to the demonic power that now possessed her. She was Kali, Durga, Medusa, taking her revenge on all the men who had ever hurt her – starting way back with the cheating Harry at university. Then Paul, who had not had the courage to face his own sexuality, denying hers. And Mike, the would-be father substitute who, far from protecting her, had sought to debase and betray her.

Here she could be truthful, all pretence banished. She whipped him harder, rejoicing to hear the whack of leather on flesh and his anguished cries as he strained at his bonds, his penis harder than ever and weeping with need.

'Let me have him,' Babs insisted, and put her hands on Mike's shoulders, levering herself up, one leg wrapped round his hips. She steered his turgid part into herself, riding up and down on it.

Tanith's whip landed on his back, making him jerk forward, driving himself deeper into Babs. He groaned, desperately seeking his release, but she climbed off him

270

and stood on the stone flags, with Carol between her thighs, licking her to completion.

'Bitches . . . bitches . . .' he moaned.

'Down you go,' Tanith said, and pulled a lever which lowered the contraption to the floor.

She stood over him, pulled her cache-sexe aside and then crouched above his belly and eased herself on to his shaft, taking it inch by inch into her slippery depths. He responded with frantic jerks, obviously hoping to come off but prevented. She deliberately denied him the rhythm he needed, her inner muscles gripping him like a steel trap that might snap his organ.

Lisa unzipped the catsuit till it parted all the way up her crease. She lowered herself over Mike's face, her hot, wet valley open as he reached out with his tongue and lapped at it. Babs was at the other end, tormenting his balls, while Carol pinched his nipples.

He wrenched his mouth away from Lisa's secret garden, pumping with his hips and desperately striving to spend himself in Tanith before she moved away.

'Damn you! Untie me, you slags, and I'll show you what a real man can do,' he shouted.

Their laughter rang through the cellar. 'A real man?' they scoffed, and removed their perfumed bodies from his, leaving him bereft of the rich wealth of their flesh.

'Yes. A real man. I could take you all on, one after the other,' he declared frantically, poised on the edge but refused completion.

'You're a bully, Mike,' Lisa said, her eyes glowing. 'Admit that you don't really like women and are afraid of them. Admit that you've enjoyed being overpowered by us.'

'That's crap,' he snarled savagely.

'We're going now,' she went on, caressing her nipples and teasing them into points to add to his distress. 'Think about what I've said, and don't ever bother me again.'

271

'You can't leave me like this!' he shouted, his cock hard and throbbing.

'Lee will see to you, when he's finished with Andrew,' Lisa said. She picked up her cloak and walked away, her arm linked with Tanith's.

'It is, of course, a fake,' David said, strolling into the kitchen after the guests had departed.

'What is?' Lisa asked, taking out the jar of instant coffee and spooning some into two cups.

She was wearing a green silk kimono embroidered with chrysanthemums. She was naked beneath, needing to be free of clothing. She was tired but exalted.

'The Rossetti,' he answered, sitting astride a stool at the table. 'I've taken a look and there's no way it's genuine. A clever fake, I'll grant you. Might even have been done by Harry Treffry Dunn – he was his helper, copyist and general dogsbody – but I don't think so, somehow.'

'You're such a know-it-all,' she said, exasperated, plonking the cup down in front of him. 'Why are you so convinced it's a fraud? What about the provenance?'

He shrugged his wide shoulders under the leather jerkin. His bandana had been pulled off, as had the false moustache. 'Experience coupled with a nose for it,' he said, with a smile.

His confidence needled her. 'You're always so goddam sure of yourself,' she grumbled. 'And who said you could look at the drawing? I don't remember giving you permission.'

'Thought I might as well, then the evening wouldn't have been entirely wasted.'

'You haven't enjoyed it?'

'Not having to watch you making an exhibition of yourself with Robillard.'

He looked angry enough to strike her, but Lisa made no move, out-staring him. 'What's it to you? Fiona was your partner, wasn't she?'

272

'We arrived together, yes, but she's now got the hots for Jamie. He's gone back to Newstead Manor with her.'

'Oh, so she's got a new lapdog, has she?'

His dark brows soared down in a threatening frown. 'I was never her lapdog. We had a business deal going.'

'And that included blow jobs, did it?' she said witheringly. 'She'll have met her match in Jamie. He's a selfish sod who'll rip her off and leave her flat.'

'That's *her* problem,' he said, and cocked an eyebrow at her, adding, 'You sound pleased.'

'I am. I've had a great time and sorted out a few people who were bugging me. It's wonderful to have power, isn't it?'

'Yes, but don't let it go to your head. You're a lovely, compassionate woman, Lisa, and I'd be sad to see that go.'

'What do you care?' she asked, looking across the table and testing him.

'More than you realise,' he answered, then stood up. 'I'm hungry. What say we fill a tray, pick up a bottle of wine and take it to bed?'

His audacity took her breath away. 'What makes you think I'm interested in you?' she said. 'You come in here, viewing my drawing uninvited, and then expect me to bed you?'

'Of course.'

His arms went round her unresisting body, hands delving into the kimono's opening. Fingers skated over her nipples while his lips nibbled her ears, neck, throat and the upper swell of her breasts. He held her between his strong thighs, and she could not avoid the hardness of his penis under the velvet breeches.

Later, she wondered why she had bothered to make a token protest, as they lay in her beautiful art nouveau bed and he spread ice-cream over her breasts and licked it off. Wondering no longer came into it when he pressed strawberries into her vagina, sucked them out and transferred them to her mouth, fragrant and succulent,

273

tasting of her juices and his, as well as the fruit's sun-warmed nectar.

There had been no hesitation or stopping to eat when they had reached her room. It had been a case of clothes off and bodies joined without delay. The first urgency assuaged, they had eaten and drunk the cool white wine, then experimented in a dozen different ways, culminating in him using her as a plate from which he slurped and lapped, satisfying two appetites at once.

The sky was smudged with pinkish dawn light, the birds beginning their hymn of praise to the rising sun, when at last they slept, after showering together and discovering new sensual ways to use soap and gel and jets of warm water.

Lisa lay curled in David's arms, her heart feather-light, but still holding something of herself in reserve. There was no way she was going to immerse herself in him just yet. Time would tell if he was a worthy long-term companion or not.

Guided by Mr Beamish, Lisa had called on the offices of Balfour, the autioneer, when it came to selling the Rossetti.

Obeying Daphne's instructions, she had refrained from contacting one of the major auction houses, merely hiring Balfour to conduct operations and being very circumspect when it came to informing prospective buyers. By the morning of the sale there were half a dozen genuinely interested parties, including Fletcher and David.

It was held in the reception room of Cranshaw House, the drawing propped on a carved ebony easel.

Lisa was acutely nervous, butterflies making merry in the pit of her stomach. She felt the responsibility keenly, but was determined to do her best for the friend who had given her so much. She recognised the people who had already been in to view, and was amused to see Fletcher and David greeting each other with the cool politeness of a pair of duellists before the cry, 'En garde!'

Silly creatures, she thought. Men, ruled by pride and idiotic rivalry. Do they ever grow up?

She had not heard from Paul since the party and Mike appeared to have melted away. She had seen Valerie once in the supermarket. Politeness itself, she had pumped Lisa about Eduardo, hinting that she was thinking of learning to tango. Lisa had given her his business card. The rest was up to him.

Mrs Harvey served coffee, and then Balfour stood behind a table to the right of the easel and cleared his throat.

'Ladies and gentlemen,' he began. 'This morning I have been instructed to take your bids for a most important and rare item ... a chalk drawing by Dante Gabriel Rossetti, alleged to be of a Miss Matilda Kirkpatrick. You have seen her diary and his letter to her, which will, of course, be included in the sale. There is a reserve, naturally, but I want to start the bidding at ten thousand pounds.'

Just to hear that figure mentioned made Lisa gulp, though she knew this was only the beginning and they would soon be talking telephone numbers. She was still not quite used to hearing large sums of money bandied about.

The sale proceeded briskly. There was an iron-faced American woman who was keen, the custodian of a museum, a private collector, and a gentleman seeking a wedding present for his daughter. But after a while, they dropped out.

The contest was now between Fletcher and David.

A tense silence held the room in thrall as the bidding rose. Lisa was confused by David's persistence. Judging by his disparaging remarks about the drawing, she was surprised that he wanted it. Then her pulse steadied as she concluded that he must have a buyer lined up. He

275

would keep his opinions as to its validity to himself, and make a killing.

He's as slippery as an eel, she decided, and her desire for him cooled a little. He was definitely not to be trusted. She would be a fool to throw in her lot with him.

Fletcher's face was strained, and she wanted him to have the Rossetti; that commanding, elegant man who had taught her to understand her darkest desires. Yet there was David who, despite her wariness, was undeniably an intelligent individual who made her laugh, shared her taste in music and took her to blissful heights with his love-making.

She was torn between the two, and it angered her. She wanted to belong to herself entirely, not be tossed about like a storm-racked vessel on a sea of emotion.

Balfour took out his handkerchief and wiped it over his red, sweating face as the bidding reached an all-time high. 'Well, sir,' he said, addressing David. 'Mr Robillard has topped your last bid. Will you go any further?'

David appeared to consider carefully, smoothing a hand over his jaw, glancing across at Fletcher, then saying, 'I'll up it by five thousand.'

A gasp rose from the onlookers. Lisa's heart was all over the place. He could never afford that, could he? Then she guessed that he probably could. David would take risks, it was true, but nine times out of ten he stood to gain.

'Mr Robillard?' Balfour said tremulously, looking at him.

The contestants' eyes met, and antipathy flared.

This is about me, as well as the drawing, Lisa realised with a shock she felt in her bones.

'Another five,' Fletcher said crisply.

'Mr Maccabene?' Balfour ventured.

The whole room held its breath, then David shook his head. 'I've finished,' he said.

'No more bids anywhere, then?' Balfour asked, his

eyes sweeping over the audience. 'Very well ... Going, going ... gone.' He struck the table with his gavel. 'Sold to Mr Robillard.'

The sudden relief of tension was almost tangible. Fletcher walked up to David and said magnanimously, 'Hard luck, old man.'

'Not at all,' David replied, his green eyes as cold as ice. 'I think you've bought a pup.'

Fletcher stared at him down his patrician nose. 'Nonsense,' he said dismissively.

'It's a fake,' David continued, nonchalantly perched on the edge of the table, and Lisa felt like screaming. Why couldn't he accept defeat gracefully and leave it alone?

'A fake! Never,' Fletcher insisted, approaching the easel and taking a closer look. 'It has all the hallmarks of Rossetti, and it's signed.'

'So it may be,' David answered, strolling up to stand by him. 'But it might as well have been by executed by Joe Bloggs. It certainly isn't the work of DGR. Superbly done, though. I almost fell for it.'

'It can't be a fake,' Fletcher insisted, his eyes blazing with anger. 'I would have known. I'm an expert on Victorian artists.'

David shrugged. 'Have it your way,' was his riposte. 'But I guarantee that if you cart it up to Sotheby's, they'll say the same.'

'Bullshit,' Fletcher grated, but his face was paler. 'If you really believe that, why did you go on bidding?'

David smiled, a mocking smile that held a trace of smugness. 'For the hell of it,' he told him. 'To see how far you'd go.'

'And if I'd dropped out?'

'Then I'd have found a punter to take it off my hands. Someone like you who thought he knew all there was to know about Rossetti,' David answered with infuriating calm.

'Damn you,' Fletcher snarled. 'I'll prove you're wrong.'

'That's up to you,' David retorted, then turned to Lisa, extending his hand and saying, 'Ready for lunch? Or do you have to call Mrs Nightingale with the news?'

'Lisa has already promised to come out with me,' Fletcher said, stepping in.

She stood there, the drawing room slowly emptying, apart from Balfour and Mr Beamish who had their heads together discussing the financial ramifications of the deal. She looked from Fletcher to David, weighing one handsome face and sexy body against the other.

Just for the moment she was heartily weary of both of them, huffing and puffing and trying to be top dog. She backed towards the door, saying, 'I'm sorry, but I have business to sort out. I'll speak to you later.'

With that, she fled the room, leaving them staring after her.

'That's splendid,' Daphne said from Florence, sounding as if she was no further away than the next street. 'So they took the bait, did they?'

'Falling over themselves, but David is sure it's a fake. He bid against Fletcher for sheer devilment,' Lisa answered, seated on her bed and resting the receiver against her cheek.

Daphne chuckled. 'Excellent. I said you'd have them in a spin, didn't I? They both want you. That's what this is really about. What are you going to do? Who is your *numero uno*?'

'I don't know,' Lisa confessed.

'Ah, this means you haven't yet met your soulmate,' Daphne said wisely. 'Leave it in abeyance. Come to Italy.'

'When?'

'Now.'

'I couldn't, not at such short notice.'

'Why?'

278

'I've got too much to see to here,' Lisa said, thrown into panic.

'Then come to the wedding in September.'

'All right,' she said. 'I'll see about flights.'

'Let me know the time of landing and Arnaldo will pick you up. I'll speak to you before then, anyway. Oh, and Lisa?'

'Yes?'

'David was right.'

'What?'

'It *is* a fake. It was done by a highly skilled artist friend of Walter's. For a joke, more than anything else. And we constructed the diary and letter between us . . . old paper, ancient ink . . . it wasn't difficult.'

'But why? You're rich. You don't need the money,' Lisa cried, feeling as if the floor was shifting under her feet.

'I like to trick those who think they know everything. Fletcher can afford it. He'll sell it, anyway, probably for double the figure. This is our secret, Lisa. Don't tell anyone.'

It would have been better if Daphne had kept silent. The knowledge of fraud weighed heavily on Lisa's conscience, but over the weeks the scene at the sale gradually lost its edge. Fletcher sold the drawing to an Australian tycoon with more money than sense, and thus scored a point over David, who had never missed an opportunity to mock him about his mistake.

It took some time for the reality of Lisa's wealth to sink in, and when it finally did, she was able to put that "NO" sticker on her phone and mean it. No one could bug her any more. She heard through the grapevine that Paul was engaged to the daughter of a Forester and a Woodlander.

'I pity the poor cow,' she said to Martin.

He pulled a face, and replied, 'Yes, indeed. I suppose he's still trying to stay in the closet, but he'll have to come out one day, and then the shit will hit the fan.'

Eduardo told her that he was having trouble with Valerie. She had become obsessed with him, no longer a stuck-up prig but a tormented, passionate woman who had learned to love the hard way. Though she had found Paul his new fiancé, she was too absorbed in Eduardo to pay much heed to the wedding arrangements, content to leave them to the parents of the bride.

Lisa was negotiating to buy the property next to Charisma. Martin, Phil and herself were cooking up the idea of opening an antique showroom, incorporating it with the gift shop. With the Mercedes van and a healthy cheque book, she could sally forth to the auction sales undaunted, though often plagued by David, who could not resist bidding against her and then dropping her in it.

She was still sharing her bed with him and, when she fancied something different, spending time with Fletcher at Hawkhurst Abbey. But both of them were becoming a little tedious, expecting a commitment.

Lisa was not yet ready to give one. She had too much to do, riding high on an upsurge of confidence. She was learning fast, and was a competent dealer now. She sometimes made errors, but less frequently, her knowledge of bygones growing daily.

September was approaching, and she announced that she was off to attend Daphne's wedding.

'But, Lisa,' David complained when they were in bed one evening. 'Why are you doing this? Can't I come with you?'

'No, you can't. I'm going to see Arnaldo make an honest woman of her. I shan't be away long,' she soothed, twining her legs with his, her breasts brushing his nipples while her hand worked up and down his shaft.

'I've got contacts in Florence,' he said slyly, rubbing his chin against the top of her spine in a way that gave her goose-bumps. 'I could show you the ropes. Italian dealers strike a hard bargain. You need someone experienced with you.'

'I'll cope. Besides, Daphne will be there, and she's almost as ruthless as you when it comes to haggling. Maybe I'll phone and you can come on over. We'll see. I make no promises,' she said, and climbed aboard him.

'This is foolish,' Fletcher said as he guided her through a set of tango steps later that night. 'You're only just beginning to get the hang of it. I need you here. If you insist on this rash course of action, I shall be forced to cane you.'

'You must do what you think best, master,' Lisa said, a frisson of excitement speeding along her nerves into her loins. 'But there's no way I'm going to miss a trip to Florence.'

'You're a stubborn female,' he growled, and slapped a hand across her silk-covered bottom.

She sighed and raised her leg in the dance routine, resting it round his thigh. Her fringed tangerine skirt flowed back, displaying her black stockings, and she gyrated her hips, bringing pressure to bear on her sex. The dim, ornate ballroom, the heady music and rustle of silk against her skin made her super-sensitive to the sexual ripples in the air.

'Have a great time and don't worry about a thing,' instructed Martin, as he and Phil carried her bags into the departure lounge.

'I intend to,' Lisa said, feeling extraordinarily carefree. 'I've always wanted to visit Italy. Daphne has promised to take me to the Teatro De Verona to see opera as it should be performed, in a Roman amphitheatre, under the stars.'

'Will you be OK?' Martin asked, fussing over her like a mother hen. 'Don't worry about the house. We'll look after it, and Mrs Harvey will be there. I've got the phone number and we'll give you a bell. Next door should be selling any minute now. I'll see to everything, with the help of that dishy Mr Beamish. I think he fancies me.'

'You're nothing but a slapper,' Phil chided him, clearly confident that it was all hot air. 'When you come back, we'll meet you, Lisa. Unless you want anyone else, of course. David or Fletcher?'

'Who knows?' she said with a smile. 'But thanks, I'll probably rely on you to do it. Off you go now and open Charisma.'

She flung her arms around them and kissed them warmly, a little choke of loneliness in her throat. If she would have liked anyone along at all, it would have been them. She watched them leave, then picked up her shoulder bag resolutely as a disembodied, crackly voice announced that passengers for Florence could now embark.

A tubelike corridor, and she was on the plane. She was nervous, having only flown once before when she went on a package holiday to Spain with a couple of girlfriends. Her father had scrimped and saved so that she might go. A rattly old airbus, a cramped hotel, sea, sunburn and awful youths who got drunk and behaved badly, making Lisa ashamed that they were her fellow countrymen.

This was all behind her and it felt right to be occupying a prime position, wearing an expensive casual outfit. She was slimmer and tanned a deep golden bronze by the long, hot summer. She knew she breathed out class. This elusive quality had always been there, but Daphne had given her the chance to bring it to the fore.

The jet engines throbbed and her body responded. This was adventure, life expanding before her, and she intended to enjoy it to the full. First-class accommodation, something she had never dreamed she would be able to afford, meant the luxury of a roomy seat, stewards to wait on her and the possibility of stimulating travelling companions. And she knew Arnaldo would be there to greet her when the plane touched down on Italian soil.

She glanced round at the other passengers and caught the eye of the man in the aisle across the way. He smiled and her lips lifted in response. He was dark and handsome, wearing a somewhat bizarre, up-to-the-minute outfit by a Japanese designer. The snakeskin-patterned trousers were exceedingly tight, rather like leggings.

Lisa deliberately dropped her magazine. She bent to pick it up, her breasts swinging forward under the low neck of her brief top. His eyes were on her cleavage. He retrieved her paper and handed it to her, saying, 'Are you going to Rome?'

'No. Florence,' she replied, admiring his agile, long-limbed figure, and the interesting fullness between his thighs.

'So am I,' he said, with a wide smile. 'I buy and sell antiques.'

'Well, there's a coincidence. That's my trade, too,' she answered, her blood warming as she thought of the pleasant hours ahead. Would it be possible to become intimately acquainted with him on the journey? She slanted him a glance, adding, 'Do you, by any chance, dance the tango?'

'Funny you should ask,' he said eagerly, leaving his seat and taking the one next to her, wafting maleness and classy body-spray. 'I do, as a matter of fact.'

'Ah, that's interesting,' she murmured, remembering the fringed and spangled dress in her suitcase. It was hers now – Fletcher had given it to her as a parting gift.

She put him and David on hold, and concentrated on this sexy stranger, crossing her slender bare legs under her short skirt and observing the way in which his eyes feasted on them, then glanced beyond her knees to the shadowed area above.

Smiling inwardly, Lisa accepted his homage, anticipating a trip which might prove more rewarding than she had thought possible: an ideal way to celebrate her coming to maturity.

BLACK LACE NEW BOOKS

Published in May

SAVAGE SURRENDER
Deanna Ashford
£5.99

In the kingdom of Harn, a marriage is arranged between the beautiful
Rianna and Lord Sarin, ruler of the rival kingdom of Percheron, who is
noted for his voracious sexual appetite. On her way to Percheron,
Rianna meets a young nobleman who has been captured by Sarin's
brutal guards. Their desire for each other is instant but can Rianna find
a way to save her young lover without causing unrest between the
kingdoms?

ISBN 0 352 33253 0

THE SEVEN-YEAR LIST
Zoe le Verdier
£5.99

Julia – an ambitious young photographer – is invited to a college
reunion just before she is due to be married. She cannot resist a final
fling but finds herself playing a dangerous erotic game with a man
who still harbours desires for her. She tries to escape a circle of betrayal
and lust but her old flame will not let her go. Not until he has
completed the final goal on his seven-year list.

ISBN 0 352 33254 9

MASQUE OF PASSION
Tesni Morgan
£5.99

Lisa is a spirited fine-arts graduate who is due to marry her wealthy fiancé in a matter of weeks. As the day draws closer, she's having second thoughts, though, especially as her husband-to-be is dismissive of both her growing antiques business and her sexual needs. The rural English village where Lisa lives is home to some intriguing bohemian characters, including the gorgeous David Maccabene. When David introduces Lisa to kinky ways of loving, her life is set to change in more ways than she can imagine.

ISBN 0 352 33259 X

CIRCO EROTICA
Mercedes Kelly
£5.99

Flora is a beautiful lion-tamer in a Mexican circus. She inhabits a curious and colourful world of trapeze artists, snake charmers and hypnotists. But when her father dies, owing a large sum of money to the dastardly Lorenzo, the circus owner, Flora's routine is set to change. Lorenzo and his perverse female accomplice, Salome, share a powerful sexual hunger and a taste for bizarre adult fun. They lure Flora into their games of decadence. Can she escape? Will she even want to?

ISBN 0 352 33257 3

COOKING UP A STORM
Emma Holly
£7.99

Abby owns a restaurant in Cape Cod but business is not booming. Then, suddenly, someone new comes into her life: a handsome chef with a recipe for success. He puts together an aphrodisiac menu that the patrons won't be able to resist. But can this playboy-chef really save the day when Abby's body means more to him than her heart? He's charming the pants off her and she's behaving like a wild woman. Can Abby tear herself away from her object of desire long enough to see what's going on?

ISBN 0 352 33258 1

BLACK LACE BOOKLIST

All books are priced £4.99 unless another price is given.

Black Lace books with a contemporary setting

ODALISQUE	Fleur Reynolds ISBN 0 352 32887 8	☐
VIRTUOSO	Katrina Vincenzi ISBN 0 352 32907 6	☐
THE SILKEN CAGE	Sophie Danson ISBN 0 352 32928 9	☐
RIVER OF SECRETS	Saskia Hope & Georgia Angelis ISBN 0 352 32925 4	☐
SUMMER OF ENLIGHTENMENT	Cheryl Mildenhall ISBN 0 352 32937 8	☐
MOON OF DESIRE	Sophie Danson ISBN 0 352 32911 4	☐
A BOUQUET OF BLACK ORCHIDS	Roxanne Carr ISBN 0 352 32939 4	☐
THE TUTOR	Portia Da Costa ISBN 0 352 32946 7	☐
THE HOUSE IN NEW ORLEANS	Fleur Reynolds ISBN 0 352 32951 3	☐
WICKED WORK	Pamela Kyle ISBN 0 352 32958 0	☐
DREAM LOVER	Katrina Vincenzi ISBN 0 352 32956 4	☐
UNFINISHED BUSINESS	Sarah Hope-Walker ISBN 0 352 32983 1	☐
THE DEVIL INSIDE	Portia Da Costa ISBN 0 352 32993 9	☐
HEALING PASSION	Sylvie Ouellette ISBN 0 352 32998 X	☐
THE STALLION	Georgina Brown ISBN 0 352 33005 8	☐

- - - - - - ✂ - - - - - - - - - - - - - - - -

Please send me the books I have ticked above.

Name ....

Address ....

....

....

.... Post Code ....

Send to: **Cash Sales, Black Lace Books, 332 Ladbroke Grove, London W10 5AH, UK.**

US customers: for prices and details of how to order books for delivery by mail, call 1-800-805-1083.

Please enclose a cheque or postal order, made payable to **Virgin Publishing Ltd**, to the value of the books you have ordered plus postage and packing costs as follows:

UK and BFPO – £1.00 for the first book, 50p for each subsequent book.

Overseas (including Republic of Ireland) – £2.00 for the first book, £1.00 each subsequent book.

If you would prefer to pay by VISA or ACCESS/ MASTERCARD, please write your card number and expiry date here:

....

Please allow up to 28 days for delivery.

Signature ....

- - - - - - ✂ - - - - - - - - - - - - - - - -

BLACK
l a c e

WE NEED YOUR HELP . . .
to plan the future of women's erotic fiction –

– and no stamp required!

Yours are the only opinions that matter.

Black Lace is the first series of books devoted to erotic fiction by women for women.

We intend to keep providing the best-written, sexiest books you can buy. And we'd appreciate your help and valued opinion of the books so far. Tell us what you want to read.

THE BLACK LACE QUESTIONNAIRE

SECTION ONE: ABOUT YOU

1.1 Sex (*we presume you are female, but so as not to discriminate*)
     Are you?
     Male   ☐
     Female   ☐

1.2 Age
     under 21   ☐   21–30   ☐
     31–40   ☐   41–50   ☐
     51–60   ☐   over 60   ☐

1.3 At what age did you leave full-time education?
     still in education ☐   16 or younger ☐
     17–19   ☐   20 or older   ☐

1.4 Occupation _____

1.5 Annual household income _____

1.6 We are perfectly happy for you to remain anonymous;
     but if you would like to receive information on other
     publications available, please insert your name and
     address

     _____

     _____

     _____

     _____

SECTION TWO: ABOUT BUYING BLACK LACE BOOKS

2.1 Where did you get this copy of *Masque of Passion*?
     Bought at chain book shop   ☐
     Bought at independent book shop   ☐
     Bought at supermarket   ☐
     Bought at book exchange or used book shop   ☐
     I borrowed it/found it   ☐
     My partner bought it   ☐

2.2 How did you find out about Black Lace books?
     I saw them in a shop   ☐
     I saw them advertised in a magazine   ☐
     I read about them in _____
     Other _____

2.3 Please tick the following statements you agree with:
     I would be less embarrassed about buying Black
     Lace books if the cover pictures were less explicit   ☐
     I think that in general the pictures on Black
     Lace books are about right   ☐
     I think Black Lace cover pictures should be as
     explicit as possible   ☐

2.4 Would you read a Black Lace book in a public place – on
     a train for instance?
     Yes   ☐   No   ☐

SECTION THREE: ABOUT THIS BLACK LACE BOOK

3.1 Do you think the sex content in this book is:
   Too much   ☐   About right   ☐
   Not enough   ☐

3.2 Do you think the writing style in this book is:
   Too unreal/escapist   ☐   About right   ☐
   Too down to earth   ☐

3.3 Do you think the story in this book is:
   Too complicated   ☐   About right   ☐
   Too boring/simple ☐

3.4 Do you think the cover of this book is:
   Too explicit   ☐   About right   ☐
   Not explicit enough   ☐

Here's a space for any other comments:

SECTION FOUR: ABOUT OTHER BLACK LACE BOOKS

4.1 How many Black Lace books have you read?   ☐

4.2 If more than one, which one did you prefer?

4.3 Why?

SECTION FIVE: ABOUT YOUR IDEAL EROTIC NOVEL

We want to publish the books you want to read – so this is your chance to tell us exactly what your ideal erotic novel would be like.

5.1   Using a scale of 1 to 5 (1 = no interest at all, 5 = your ideal), please rate the following possible settings for an erotic novel:

Medieval/barbarian/sword 'n' sorcery ☐
Renaissance/Elizabethan/Restoration ☐
Victorian/Edwardian ☐
1920s & 1930s – the Jazz Age ☐
Present day ☐
Future/Science Fiction ☐

5.2   Using the same scale of 1 to 5, please rate the following themes you may find in an erotic novel:

Submissive male/dominant female ☐
Submissive female/dominant male ☐
Lesbianism ☐
Bondage/fetishism ☐
Romantic love ☐
Experimental sex e.g. anal/watersports/sex toys ☐
Gay male sex ☐
Group sex ☐

5.3   Using the same scale of 1 to 5, please rate the following styles in which an erotic novel could be written:

Realistic, down to earth, set in real life ☐
Escapist fantasy, but just about believable ☐
Completely unreal, impressionistic, dreamlike ☐

5.4   Would you prefer your ideal erotic novel to be written from the viewpoint of the main male characters or the main female characters?

Male ☐   Female ☐
Both ☐

5.5 What would your ideal Black Lace heroine be like? Tick as many as you like:

Dominant ☐   Glamorous ☐
Extroverted ☐   Contemporary ☐
Independent ☐   Bisexual ☐
Adventurous ☐   Naïve ☐
Intellectual ☐   Introverted ☐
Professional ☐   Kinky ☐
Submissive ☐   Anything else? ☐
Ordinary ☐   _____

5.6 What would your ideal male lead character be like? Again, tick as many as you like:

Rugged ☐
Athletic ☐   Caring ☐
Sophisticated ☐   Cruel ☐
Retiring ☐   Debonair ☐
Outdoor-type ☐   Naïve ☐
Executive-type ☐   Intellectual ☐
Ordinary ☐   Professional ☐
Kinky ☐   Romantic ☐
Hunky ☐
Sexually dominant ☐   Anything else? ☐
Sexually submissive ☐   _____

5.7 Is there one particular setting or subject matter that your ideal erotic novel would contain?

_____

SECTION SIX: LAST WORDS

6.1 What do you like best about Black Lace books?

_____

6.2 What do you most dislike about Black Lace books?

_____

6.3 In what way, if any, would you like to change Black Lace covers?

_____

6.4   Here's a space for any other comments:

_____

_____

_____

_____

Thank you for completing this questionnaire. Now tear it out of the book – carefully! – put it in an envelope and send it to:

Black Lace
FREEPOST
London
W10 5BR

No stamp is required if you are resident in the U.K.